Rachel
HOWZELL
HALL

TRAIL of ECHOES
A DETECTIVE ELOUISE NORTON NOVEL

TITAN BOOKS

TRAIL OF ECHOES
Print edition ISBN: 9781783296613
E-book edition ISBN: 9781783296620

Published by Titan Books
A division of Titan Publishing Group Ltd
144 Southwark Street, London SE1 0UP

First edition: May 2016
1 2 3 4 5 6 7 8 9 10

A CIP catalogue record for this title is available from the British Library.

Printed and bound in Great Britain by CPI Group Ltd.

Did you enjoy this book? We love to hear from our readers.
Please email us at readerfeedback@titanemail.com or write to us at
Reader Feedback at the above address.

To receive advance information, news, competitions, and exclusive
offers online, please sign up for the Titan newsletter on our website:

TITANBOOKS.COM

For my mother, Jacqueline, who kept us from being lost

WEDNESDAY, MARCH 19

1

AT TWELVE THIRTY ON A RAINY WEDNESDAY AFTERNOON, I WAS BREAKING ONE OF my cardinal rules as a homicide detective: Never eat lunch with civilians. But on that Wednesday in March, I sat at a Formica-topped table in Johnny's Pastrami with no ordinary citizen.

Assistant District Attorney Sam Seward had eyes the color of mint leaves, hands that could palm Jupiter, and a mind agile enough to grasp the story arc of *Game of Thrones*.

I had a crush on Sam.

He liked me, too, even though I associated "bracelets" with "handcuffs" and smelled of gun oil more than lavender. And so when he had asked if I wanted to grab a pastrami with him, I had immediately chirped, "Sure. Why not?" I *wanted* to have Normal People Lunch with ketchup that squirted from bottles and conversations about March Madness instead of murders, bodies, and blood. More than that, I *wanted* to have Normal People Lunch with *Sam*.

And now he smiled at me like the secret goof he was. And I futzed with the belt of my cowl-necked sweater like the nervous virgin I hadn't been in twenty years.

Outside, clouds the color of Tahitian black pearls and drizzle softened the crimson glare of car brake lights. Inside, the diner smelled of meat and onions, and George Harrison crooned from hidden speakers about the way she moves.

"Elouise Norton," Sam said, shaking his head. "I cannot believe it."

I nibbled a sliver of pastrami. "Why not? I do violence all day."

"Which is why I can't believe you'd watch a show on your downtime that's all decapitations and grit for an hour and three minutes."

I gasped. "*You* made me watch it."

He smoothed his slate-blue tie. "Couldn't talk to you about the Darson case forever."

Sam was prosecuting Max Crase, the man who had murdered high school cheerleader Monique Darson, her sister Macie, and my sister Victoria. Now recovering from a brain tumor, Max Crase had pled insanity. And well . . . "insane" was just one word I'd use to describe him.

"Nor do I want to talk about the Darson case now." I smiled at Sam, then pointed at his face. "You have mustard . . ."

He squinted at me. "Get it off, then."

My heart pounded—I loved challenges.

I waited a moment . . . then leaned forward.

He moved aside sandwich baskets and almost-full glasses of Diet Coke, then leaned forward but only a little. "Closer," he demanded.

I waited . . . then obeyed.

His butterscotch-colored cheeks flushed.

With his face an inch away from mine, I parted my lips.

And the bell tower tolled: the ringtone for Lieutenant Zak Rodriguez.

Sam crooked his neck, going for the kiss.

But the bell tower tolled again—louder and crankier this time.

"Sounds official," Sam whispered.

Going cold, I sank into my seat. "It's my boss." I reached for

Sam's hand as my other hand grabbed the phone from my purse.

"Where you at?" Lieutenant Rodriguez asked.

"Having pastrami and soda pop."

"With Taggert?"

Sam kissed my hand before he let go.

"Nope."

"Pepe and Luke?"

I pushed my bangs off my flushed forehead. "Nuh uh."

Lieutenant Rodriguez sighed. "Please say you're not with your ex."

"Don't worry. I'm not."

"Hate to break it up, but you're on deck. Some joggers found a body up in Bonner Park."

My ankle holster, stuffed now with my lunch gun, pinched my skin—death had a way of yanking you from Wonderland. "Really? This early in the day?"

"And whoever left it there is one cold son of a bitch."

"Aren't they all?"

"He put it in one of those large duffel bags, the kind soldiers carry. And he left it there on the trail. In this weather."

Outside our window, the wind had picked up, making palm fronds frantic and street signs swing. Back in the calm mustiness of Johnny's, someone had dropped a quarter into the tabletop jukebox and had pressed E6: Olivia Newton-John asking if I've ever been mellow.

"Yeah," Lieutenant Rodriguez was saying, "and where he left it? Up on that trail? It ain't the typical boneyard. Anyway, I'll call Taggert and we'll meet you over there. Maybe you shoulda had one of your salads today. Edamame and shit instead of all that meat."

Martha Bonner Park. Hills, trees, valleys—a beautiful jewel in the city's crown. I jogged, hiked, and fed ducks there whenever I wasn't watching divers pull guns and bodies out of its murky-green fake lake.

"Gotta go?" Sam asked, eyes on his iPhone.

"Yep."

"Same here. I'm helping to plan Congresswoman Fortier's jazz funeral."

"Saturday, right?"

He nodded. "A second line down Crenshaw. A horse, a brass band, all of it."

I dug in my purse for the car keys. "How many permits did you all have to pull for a New Orleans homegoing in the middle of Los Angeles?"

He rubbed his face. "You have no idea. And I hear all of NOLA is coming to usher her into the great beyond." He emerged from behind his hands with a smile. "But I'm glad we had a moment to ourselves."

I blushed. "Me too."

Even though this was our first date, nothing else needed to be said or explained. *I gotta go.* No apology, no weird hostility. He, too, had to keep LA from exploding.

Oh, how I liked Sam.

Hand in hand, we walked to the parking lot, stopping at the light-blue Crown Vic that would stink of mildew until August.

"So you owe me." Towering over me, Sam rested his hands on my waist.

I tensed, aware of my bulky ballistics vest, hoping that he didn't think that was all . . . me. "Owe you? For what?"

"For ending our lunch so soon."

I shivered—not because of the forty-degree weather. "Bullshit. We were basically done."

"I wanted pie."

I straightened the collar of his black wool overcoat. "Fine. You'll get your pie."

Then, my freakin' iPhone *caw-cawed* from my pocket: the

ringtone for Colin Taggert, my partner of nine months.

Sam dropped his hands and backed away from me. "If your case is a dunker, come over tonight and watch something other than a basketball game. You could bring pie."

"Maybe."

"You'll call me?"

"Yes."

And the eagle *caw-cawed* again: America was calling.

I plucked the phone from my pocket. "I'm on my way," I told Colin, slipping behind the Ford's steering wheel. In the rearview mirror, I watched Sam climb into his black Bimmer.

"The body in the—" Colin sneezed, then sneezed again. "The body in the park. Prepare yourself: it's a girl."

Just when you're trying to be mellow.

2

I HAD ONLY WANTED TO HAVE NORMAL PEOPLE LUNCH WITH A HANDSOME MAN—
the first lunch of its kind since divorcing Greg Norton.

"But then you've always been a bit of a diva," Lena Meadows said. She and my other sorority sister, Syeeda McKay, had crammed their heads together to fit in the iPad's shot.

I had found a parking space close to the park's fake lake. The millions of raindrops pebbling the Ford's windows softened the glares of the blue and red lights from patrol cars and fire engines. "Lunch was really . . . Sam's so . . . so effin' . . ."

"Say it!" Syeeda shouted. "Hot. He's so effin' hot."

Lena moved her face closer to the iPad's camera. "So have we broken our three-month dry spell?"

I gave them an exaggerated frown. "No, we have not."

Lena shouted, "Boo!"

"Pastrami is supposed to be the gateway meat," Syeeda screamed.

I threw my head back and laughed, long and hard.

"It's cuz she's dressed like an Amish settler," Lena said. "A big-ass *sweater,* Lou?"

"It's raining, Lena," I said. "I could catch cold."

"But the ex is out of the picture, right?" Syeeda asked.

I lifted an eyebrow. "Sam's or mine?"

"Both."

14

"Yes, for me. As for Mr. Seward, he told me that they only talk about the dog. She has custody, not that she even likes the dog. Or Sam."

"He's not ambitious enough?" Syeeda asked.

"He likes being a DA for now. But Rishma wanted to be the mayor's wife yesterday."

Syeeda smiled. "You're seeing him tonight, yes?"

"Maybe. He wants . . . pie. Hope you don't mind me missing DVR Wednesday."

"Only want to see you laughing in the purple rain," Syeeda said.

"Then I'll come home really, *really* late," I said, skin flushed.

A minute later, I stood near the Japanese bridge in Martha Bonner Park, my heeled boots sinking in mud thick with candy wrappers and cigarette butts, surrounded by cops, firefighters, and paramedics.

"Where you at?" I growled into my Motorola radio.

"Don't move," Colin said. "The White Knight's comin' to get you."

I slipped my messenger bag across my chest. "Doesn't look like a Wednesday, does it?"

No kids swinging from monkey bars or retirees walking the trails. No personal trainers leading small classes of round housewives on a patch of grass. The ducks on the lake had remained, but no preschoolers threw crumbs of stale bread.

"Cuz it's raining," Colin pointed out. "You Angelenos don't do rain."

A handful of civilians had gathered behind a barrier made of rope, canary-yellow crime-scene tape, and six thousand of LA's bravest.

Just three miles from my division, and located in Baldwin Hills, Martha Bonner Park was home to gray foxes, raccoons, skunks, possums, and forty-one species of birds. And they weren't stupid enough to scamper around in this weather. Just us smarter creatures. The 380 acres of land boasted playgrounds, picnic areas, seven miles of hiking trails, and the man-made fishing lake. The park also sat in the middle of the highest concentration of black wealth in the nation. The homes on the park's perimeter cost thousands of dollars less than their equivalents in Brentwood and Santa Monica— here, you got more house, more land, and maybe even an orange tree. Ah, segregation.

"Lou! Up this way." Colin Taggert strode toward me. His blond hair lay flat on his head, and his Nikes and the hems of his nylon track pants were caked in red mud. His tanned skin looked pea-green, as though he had been bobbing on a dinghy for three hours.

He pointed at my trench coat, sweater, and heeled combat boots (if Doc Marten and Salvatore Ferragamo had a baby . . .). "You *almost* got those right," he said, pointing to the boots.

"I'm in a good mood," I said. "Wanna take a chance?"

He blew his nose into a bouquet of tissue. "I was supposed to go boardin' up in Mammoth tomorrow."

"A warm cabin sounds really good right now."

"I invited you," he said. "We could've grilled some steaks. Snuggled in front of the fireplace. Guzzled cases of beer."

I cocked an eyebrow. "Why? So you could give me your cold?"

"Oh, I'd give you *something*—" He sneezed, then shoved his nose into the tissue.

I grinned. "If this is you seducing me . . ."

He started back to the trail still wiping his nose.

"Ooh, baby," I said, following him. "The way you sneeze, and all that snot. Ooh, Colin, you give me fever. I'm getting hot from just being around you."

Without looking back, he threw me the bird.

We traveled a well-developed gravel road lined with parked earthmovers and green park services pickup trucks. We veered right and onto a red-dirt trail that ran between large overgrowths of coastal sage, eucalyptus, and cypress trees.

I stopped at the large trail marker. "Where we going?"

Colin pointed to trail 5, northwest of the red "You Are Here" dot. "A mile and a half up."

Dread knotted in my stomach. "Who'd dump a body that far from the parking lot?"

A police helicopter roared across a sky now the color of tarnished silverware. The rain had stopped, but fog rolled in from the Pacific Ocean four miles away. Up ahead, through the brush, forensic lights burned like supernovas. Clumps of patrol cops dotted the trail, and a few uniforms gave Colin and me a "what's up" and a "good luck."

"Before I drove over," Colin said, glancing back at me, "a man stopped by lookin' for you. Tall, black, older. Didn't leave his name."

That visitor had been Victor Starr, the man who had contributed sperm toward my existence and then abandoned the results eight years later. Back in December, he had spent the night wrestling with angels or some crap like that because, after being MIA for almost thirty years, he had showed up on my front porch, expecting hugs, tears, and a heartfelt chat over cups of International Foods coffee.

Yeah. That didn't happen. I had better shit to do that day, and the next day and the next day and today and tomorrow.

"Second time this week he's dropped in," Colin said. "Some dude you meet outside AARP headquarters?"

"Ha," I said.

"So who is he?"

A nerve near my left eye twitched. "Victor Starr."

Colin looked back at me again, eyebrows high this time.

"Yeah," I said. "Really."

He chuckled. "He's just like you: he doesn't know when to give up. You're Little Lockjaw and he's Daddy Lockjaw. So sweet—I think I'm gonna cry."

"And I think I'm gonna vomit," I said. "Anyway: you said 'girl.' Do you mean that in its colloquial, sexist usage? Or do you mean 'girl' as in '*girl*'?"

"As in 'girl.' Teenager, if you really wanna get technical. Could be the one who went missing last week."

"Yeah, *that* narrows it down." *Not.*

Just last week, over in Inglewood, a teen girl had been abducted from her driveway; and in Gardena, another teen had been kidnapped by her stepfather. And then there was Trina Porter, the fourteen-year-old stolen earlier this month from a bookstore near my old neighborhood. We had no clue where Trina was or if she was even alive. So again: *which girl?*

Guess I'd find out soon.

3

WE CAME TO A CLEARING OF LOW GRASS AND MUD WHERE TWELVE CIVILIANS stood around as two patrol cops interviewed each person one at a time. Detective Luke Gomez, plump and short-legged, was snapping pictures of the group.

"Think the monster's still hanging around?" Colin asked.

"Now that we're here with our questions and suspicions and nosiness?" I shook my head.

Detective Peter "Pepe" Kim, Luke's partner, was talking to a light-skinned, middle-aged black man dressed in a khaki-shorts park ranger's uniform. The ranger resembled Smokey Robinson with his café au lait complexion, short curly hair more gray than brown, and fine nose butched-up with a mustache. He was muscular for an older guy, and, like me, he wasn't dressed for this weather.

Colin sneezed.

I frowned. "Thought you were going home."

"L.T. caught me at the door. How was lunch with Seward?"

"Fine."

"I was picturing you going out with some muscle-head. The opposite of your ex."

"I did—Lena fixed me up with the Dodger, remember?"

He laughed, then nodded. "Oh yeah. Angry Pitcher."

I sighed. "Dude needed a Zoloft and a bubble—" My step

faltered, and I covered my nose with my hand. "Oh *shit*."

Colin reached into his pants pocket and pulled out a little tub of Noxzema. "Since I can't smell a thing." He offered me the jar.

The pastrami in my gut soured as I swiped cream beneath my nostrils.

Colin made a sad face. "And you're wearing such a nice sweater, too."

We reached the tarp and the victim now hidden beneath a yellow plastic sheet—and guarded by one big man in a wet trench coat.

"Good lunch?" Lieutenant Rodriguez asked, his gray eyes squinting at my muddy boots.

"The best lunch I've had in a very long time." I pulled latex gloves from my bag and plucked a flashlight from my coat pocket. I stepped beneath the tarp, then lifted the plastic to find a large, unzipped, green canvas duffel bag. The earth beneath the bag looked different, wet and moist but not from rain. A few maggots wriggled in that strange-colored earth, and some flies buzzed around me. But not a lot of flies. Not *enough* flies.

Jane Doe's left leg and foot—size 6 maybe, pink nail polish—were sticking out from the bag and had settled on the dirt. Bare calf . . . Bare thigh . . .

I ducked from beneath the tarp. "Wow."

"Yeah," Lieutenant Rodriguez said.

As I took out my binder, I glanced back at Smokey Robinson the Park Ranger—he was still speaking with Pepe, but now he was also gazing at me.

What did he see? Did he *find her?*

The man winked at me.

My scalp crawled, and something inside of me shuddered.

"The first responder," Lieutenant Rodriguez was saying,

"tried to protect any evidence from contamination, but in this weather . . ." He looked up to the wet, gray sky, then pointed his flashlight beam down to the mishmash of shoe prints and trash left in the mud. "And we won't get any good shoe prints since thousands of people run this trail every year."

"Maybe that's why he chose this spot," I said. "It's private but still a little busy."

"Evidence destroyed by the constant flow of traffic?"

"Yep. Where's Zucca?"

"On his way."

"You tell him to bring a plant guy and a bug guy?"

My boss nodded.

"The responding officer?" I asked.

"He's interviewing witnesses," Colin said, wiping his nose. "So now?"

"So *now* we grab everybody we can and we walk." I glanced at my partner. "But you—"

"I'm cool," Colin said, wanting to blow his nose again but not daring to.

"You have a *cold* at a *scene*."

"I won't sneeze no more," Colin promised, wide-eyed and panicky.

I turned to Lieutenant Rodriguez with pleading eyes.

"Taggert, don't touch nothing," the big man ordered. "You gotta sneeze or cough or breathe heavy, do it *away* from the scene." He regarded me. *Satisfied?*

My scowl said, *Not at all.* I pointed at Colin. "Don't fuck this up. Not this one."

He blanched. "I won't. I promise. I'm good. Okay?"

Even if you solved them, child cases—abuse, assault, neglect, murder—snatched pieces of your soul. Some cops, some pediatricians, and some social workers filled those holes with booze and blow. And for those of us totally

21

hollowed out? The barrel of a gun.

So today, if I had to lose parts of myself because some monster committed an act of horrific violence, I refused to have that monster freed from life in prison or the stainless steel table all because Colin's mucus had tainted Monster DNA.

"If I see one drop of snot from you, I *will* kick you to the curb," I warned my partner.

Colin rolled his eyes. "I'm not stupid, Mom. I heard you, all right?"

I glanced back at the park ranger—he knew these trails, the life of the park, peak visiting hours, which areas were more populated and at what times.

And that wink he gave me . . .

Who the hell winked thirty yards away from a dead girl?

4

NEVER THOUGHT I'D BE WALKING THROUGH HIGH GRASS AND CLOMPING THROUGH mud on a March day boasting forty-degree weather and threatening clouds. But there I was, one woman in a long east-west line of uniforms, detectives, any free hand with a badge, slowly walking together, arm's length apart, flashlights bright, jaws clamped tight, hoping to find something and expecting to find the worst—nothing at all.

Each man and woman, positioned from the trail to the hillside, had their eyes on the ground. Searching. For a girl's shoe, a monster's footprint, a gun, a bloody *something* that would tell us who she was or who the monster was. Behind us, a bearded videographer recorded the search, and ahead of us a tall black man carried a metal detector. No clicks or chirps emitted from his contraption: No bullets or bullet casings. No calls out. No whistles blown.

It was the cleanest city park in the history of city parks.

We strip-searched down to the large clearing that separated Bonner Park from those million-dollar homes. Then, we returned to the blue tarp, empty-handed and drenched from rain now falling from battleship-colored clouds.

"Well?" Colin asked me.

"He got here," I said. "And then he left the girl, which means he left something behind. They always leave something behind."

"Zucca and his crew are almost done taking pictures of the girl for now," Lieutenant Rodriguez said. "Nothing obvious so far."

"And the coroner?" I asked.

"En route."

I sighed. "The monster gets luckier every time we're en route."

I wandered toward the tarp, stopping now and then to peer at the hillside and then down at strange whorls left in the mud there . . . and there, just five steps away from the tarp. I stooped near those whorls, and, since I had no evidence tents with me, I left one of my business cards by each whorl to mark the spot. Then, radio to my mouth, I called Arturo Zucca, my favorite forensics tech, and told him of my discovery. "Could be nothing. Could be everything."

"I'll send Bruce and Leslie over to take pictures and imprints," Zucca said. "And I'll have 'em take pics of the personnel's shoes, too. Could be ours."

It was almost three o'clock, and wetter and colder than it had been all year in this drought-stricken state. Two hours in and we'd only collected a Bazooka gum wrapper, two burned matches, a smashed plastic water bottle, and an orange peel. The duffel bag, Jane Doe, and now these whorls in the mud were my only hopes.

I noted the current temperature—forty-three degrees—then sketched the scene in my damp notebook. Weather-water snuck past the barrier of my cowl-necked sweater and pebbled between my shoulder blades. Those drops became rivulets, trickling down my spine to soak my ballistics vest, sports bra, and, for the most ambitious trickles, the waistband of my wool slacks.

Colin, shivering with fever, sneezed.

"You okay?" I asked, looking up from my sketch.

"Shouldn't you be used to cold, wet weather, being from the Springs? All that snow and ice and Pike's Peak and whatnot?"

His eyes looked like he was underwater. "I'm not going home, so don't ask."

"Just don't get snot on my scene," I said. "But if you really start looking like crap, I get to send you home. Deal?"

"Uh huh," Colin said.

"Lou!" Zucca was calling from beneath the tarp.

I dropped my mask back over my nose and mouth and returned to the tarp.

"How old do you think she is?" Zucca asked.

I clicked on my flashlight and stared at Jane Doe's half-mast eyes, at the black T-shirt—Abercrombie & Fitch—and at the corn-kernel-shaped birthmark on her right hip. "Thirteen, fourteen," I said, swiping at the few buzzing blowflies.

"Where are the bugs?" Colin asked.

"These aren't enough for you?" Zucca snarked. "Good question, though. Anyway, look what I found." He opened the duffel bag wider.

Green leaves and shiny black berries the size of cherries were scattered around the girl.

"A clue," I said, a prick of hope in my chest. "Hooray."

"What kind of plant is that?" Colin asked.

"According to my plant lady," Zucca said, "it doesn't grow in this park. She has an idea, but she's not saying until she's sure."

"Her unofficial answer?" I asked.

"Bad-shit berries," Zucca quipped.

I frowned. "So the monster did her somewhere else then."

"Yep."

Colin and I wandered back to the trail to gaze at that east-facing hillside. The dirt, mud, and plants looked flatter, recently disturbed. Chunks of that hillside had collapsed because of the rain, and now gnarled brown roots from sage and other plants were exposed. I pointed to the high grass. "What if he dumped her up there, on the higher slope, in thicker brush. Then, when it started to rain . . ." My finger traced the route in the air, dropping down to the tarp. "She slid down over there."

"But how did she get *up* there?" Colin wondered. "I'm no geometry wiz, and I sucked at physics and the metric system, but that incline seems steep, close to vertical."

I shrugged. *The monster expects me to fail.* So many obstacles—from the outdoor setting to the crappy weather. He knew that his tracks were literally covered by rain and mud. *Except for those whorls.* He had left those behind.

Moments later, a crime tech wearing a Tyvek suit stuck into the mud little yellow flags that led from the tarp, over to Bruce and Leslie huddling over those suspicious whorls left in the mud, and, finally, up the slope.

"When we talk to witnesses," I said to Colin, "we'll ask if they saw a man hoisting a duffel bag. And let's also get pictures of their shoe bottoms."

I gazed at the homes peppering the other side of the bluff—the residents there enjoyed views of the basin, the Santa Monica Mountains, and the Hollywood sign, each nearly invisible in the drizzle. Century City sat to the west, and downtown skyscrapers sat to the east. Down below, cars on La Brea Avenue sat bumper-to-bumper because of the rain and the mysterious curiosity on the hillside involving a police helicopter.

I could also see the Jungle, that dense collection of low-to-no-income apartments that, once upon a time, had been my home. One day, I planned to tell my daughter Natalie about growing up in that ghetto, about gun battles in the alleys that made Auntie Tori, Nana, and me lunge beneath our beds. I planned to drive her past that concertina wire and those iron fences. "See?" I'd say with pride. "That's where Mommy grew up."

But I didn't have a daughter named Natalie. I was a month away from my thirty-eighth birthday, and Natalie was as real as Snow White, and the man that I thought I had loved, was pretty sure that I had loved, but what *is* love really? was now selling our dream house as part of our divorce settlement.

My stomach cramped—bad memories, too much pastrami.

A low growl rumbled from above—far-off thunder. The northwestern sky over Pacific Palisades flashed with white light.

"Storm's almost here," Colin said.

"He left her with the best view of the city," I whispered. "A place where she'd certainly be found. Why?" I swallowed hard, uneasy now. "I'll handle the autopsy."

"Bless you," Colin said, then sneezed.

Pepe joined us, notebook in hand. His shellacked black hair *still* hadn't moved. "How ya feelin', Taggert?" He didn't wait for Colin's response before turning to me. "So Mr. Park Ranger says he didn't see anyone on the trail except for a few joggers."

"You take pics of his boots?" I asked.

Pepe reddened. "Did not."

I sighed. "Anything else?"

He cleared his throat, then said, "The ranger also said that gang-bangers have been hanging around. Smoking, gettin' high—"

Colin sneezed.

"Dude," I said to him, "go home. *Please?* Weather's only gonna get worse."

He shook his head. "But what about witnesses—?"

The sky opened up then, sending wanton raindrops that fell without hesitation or modesty. Standing on the highest natural point in the LA basin was the last place I wanted to be during a storm.

"*Go*," I shouted at Colin over the roar of rain now pounding the tarp. "We'll finish up here and wait for the medical examiner to arrive and take possession of the girl. Since I don't want you dead, I'm ordering you to go home, get some rest, watch TV, then come back in tomorrow. You'll help catch him. I promise. Cross my heart."

After a sneeze and a wave, Colin trundled back down the trail.

We *would* catch this monster.

I knew that like I knew light could not exist without dark.

"So," Pepe said. A lock of hair finally surrendered and draped across his forehead. "These women said they saw a man."

5

OTHER THAN THE BUZZ FROM THE CHOPPERS, THE CLEARING SOUTH OF THE CRIME scene was especially quiet for a homicide. No wailing from a distraught mother or shouting from an angry uncle, *This ain't right! This ain't right!* No calls to Jesus. No grumblings about the cops not caring and not doing shit.

The two women who "saw a man" shivered in their wet sweat suits and faux Pucci head scarves. They huddled together beneath a tired pink umbrella that threatened to collapse from this phenomenon called rain. They peered at my head—Lieutenant Rodriguez had yanked off some guy's LAPD baseball cap and had given it to me to wear.

The thick, dark-skinned woman with the eyebrow stud was Heather Artest.

The other woman was also thick and mixed with some type of Asian. And because she had watched too many episodes of *Law & Order,* she would only tell me that her name was Cynthia. "Why do you need my last name? I don't wanna give my last name."

"Give me a last initial, then," I said.

"Q."

"Great. So who saw what?"

"We was walking right over there." Heather pointed to

the trail south of the tarp that ran beneath a canopy of eucalyptus trees.

"And we smelled something dead," Cynthia said. "But I'm in the forest, so I'm like, 'whatever, it stank in the forest.'"

"So we kept walking," Heather continued. "And the more we walked, the worse that smell got."

Cynthia nodded. "That's when our girl Vanessa said—"

"Who's Vanessa?" I interrupted.

"She was walking with us," Heather said. "She saw the bag first."

Cynthia took hold of the umbrella. "She's the one who said, 'That looks like a person's leg comin' out that bag.' Then, she took some pictures with her phone."

I narrowed my eyes. "And where is Vanessa?"

"She freaked out," Cynthia said. "When we found the park ranger, he had one of the other rangers take her down to the community center. She may still be down there."

"So what happened next?" I asked.

"We kept walking," Heather continued, "and we got close enough to see—" She covered her mouth with a shaky hand.

"The black girl from the Jungle," Cynthia said. "Is it her? Is it Trina?"

"We don't know much yet," I admitted. "May I ask the obvious question?"

"Why were we walking in the rain?" Heather asked.

"Diabetes and New Year's resolution," Cynthia explained.

"And it's *rain*, not lava," Heather said, rolling her eyes.

"She's from Seattle," Cynthia announced.

I nodded. "May I see the bottoms of your tennis shoes?"

Cynthia lifted her left foot.

No whorls.

Still, I took a picture with my camera phone.

Heather lifted her foot.

Lines, squares, no whorls.

I snapped another picture.

"Why you takin' picture of our shoes?" Cynthia asked.

"We ain't done nothing," Heather complained.

"Don't worry," I said. "Just procedure. You were close to the body and I just wanna make sure that any shoe prints we find aren't yours."

"Why it seem like a lotta black girls gettin' kidnapped this year?" Heather asked.

"Don't know," I said.

Even though Poor, Black, and Female was my Everyday, this case worried me. One thing, however, did *not* worry me. I knew for sure that Jane Doe was not my sister. Because Victoria had been found. Finally.

"What about the guy you saw?" I asked the couple. "Tell me about him."

"He was coming from that direction." Cynthia pointed toward the tarp.

"Was he carrying anything?" I asked.

"His hands were in his pockets," Heather said.

"Can you describe him?"

"He was tall," Cynthia said.

"No, he wasn't," Heather countered with a frustrated head shake. "He was, like, five eleven."

"That's tall."

"To Mini-Me."

"Anyway, he was black."

"*Girl,* you need glasses," Heather said. "You couldn't even tell *what* he was cuz he was wearing a baseball cap and this big jacket with a turned-up collar. Black jacket, blue cap."

"No," Cynthia said, "it was a black jacket, and a *black* cap."

"No, the cap was wet from the rain so it just *looked* black."

Cynthia shrugged. "You probably right."

Then the women looked at me.

"Did the cap have a team name on it?" I asked. "Any kind of marking?"

"Umm . . . ," Cynthia said.

Heather shrugged. "Can we go now?"

I blinked. "That's all you can tell me?"

"We gave you specifics," Heather snapped.

"Right. A not-too-tall, tall man of indeterminate ethnicity wearing a black jacket and a dark baseball cap." They had described every man in Los Angeles County—but not the park ranger in khaki. "What time did you start walking the trail?"

"A little after eleven," Heather recalled, "and I know it was a little after eleven cuz my mom had just texted me, telling me that she had picked up my son from kindergarten."

"And so you're walking," I said, "and you got *where* when you first spotted the bag?"

The two women led me to the slight bend in the trail, right before the canopy of trees.

"And you kept walking?" I asked.

They nodded.

"Let's walk now."

And we walked.

"When did you see the guy in the cap?" I asked.

"Right . . . about . . . now." Cynthia stopped in her step.

We had walked eleven paces—and had a clear view of the blue tarp and the trail. There were no trees above to create shadow.

"His shoes were really muddy," Cynthia said.

"So what?" Heather said with a frown. "It's raining. They supposed to be muddy."

"Was he walking fast or slow?" I asked.

"Kinda hurrying but not running," Cynthia said. "He had

32

his head down and his chin was kinda tucked into his collar cuz of the rain."

Or because he didn't want them to see his face.

"And what time was that when you saw him?" I asked.

"A minute or two after I got the text from my mom," Heather said.

"Did he say anything to you?" I asked. "Speak to you at all?"

Heather shook her head. "He ain't said a word."

"Where did he go once he passed you? Did he stay on the dirt trail or did he take that gravel service road?"

The women shrugged.

"Who called 911?"

"I tried to, but my call kept dropping," Cynthia said.

"So we ran to that road and waved down the park service truck," Heather added.

"And we told that park ranger what we saw," Cynthia said.

"And then *he* called 911," Heather finished.

"Your girl Vanessa," I said. "Can you describe her for me? I need to talk to her, too."

Heather pulled out a phone from her sweat-pants pocket and found a picture of Vanessa: round face, caramel complexion, nose ring, black and pink dreads.

"And her phone number?" I asked.

"Why you need her number?" Cynthia asked.

I sighed and stopped myself from rolling my eyes. "Cuz she may have pictures of this guy. I can keep calling *you* to reach her, or I can call her directly. Ladies' choice."

Cynthia groaned, then sucked her teeth.

Heather rattled off a number.

I thanked them both, then gave each my business card. "And if you see Vanessa before I reach her, please tell her to call me ASAP."

As Luke took Heather's and Cynthia's official witness statements, I headed down to the base of the trail. My feet felt thick and numb in my fancy combat boots, and I'm sure the burning on my chest was a rash caused by my wet sweater. But I couldn't stop.

I needed to find Vanessa. And I needed to find the man in the baseball cap.

6

VANESSA WITH THE CAMERA WOULDN'T ANSWER HER PHONE NO MATTER HOW many times I called. When I wasn't calling Vanessa, Victor Starr texted.

I only need 10 minuites.

Hello you are there?

I'm am not a bad man.

I ignored his messages, but texted Sam—*sorry, no pie tonight.*

By the time I reached the bottom of the trail, the rain had changed directions. Didn't matter to the crowd now gathered near the trail's start.

Angelenos retreated indoors when it rained—we melted, Wicked Witch of the West–style, if more than six raindrops touched our skin. On this day, though, we possessed the physiology of gremlins—the crowd grew every five minutes, all, "What's this about a dead body?"

At least sixty people now stood behind yellow tape guarded by three female patrol cops. Wearing track pants and jogging shorts, the gawkers had already been at the park taking a prestorm jog. But then they had stumbled upon *the* dinnertime story to tell, and they now hoisted their cell phones high above or before them.

Reporters that knew me shouted questions in my

direction, questions that our public information officer would soon answer.

Is it Trina Porter?

Have you notified the family?

Is it gang-related? A drug deal gone bad?

I scanned the crowd in search of Vanessa but didn't see a black chick with pink dreads. Nor did I spot a not-tall, tall man wearing a dark baseball cap.

Amber Andersen, a field reporter from Channel Five News, was interviewing a portly black man who wore a clingy, suck-you-thin exercise suit. The man kept pointing at the hill and turning away from the camera, and Amber kept turning him back.

What is he telling her? What did he see?

I pulled the radio from my bag and called Pepe. "There's a guy down here talking to a reporter. Have a word with him, why don't you?" I gave him the guy's description. "He's pointing up the hill as though he was there. Ask him if he saw anyone carrying a big bag. And please remember to get pics of his shoes."

A brown, one-story building sat fifty yards to my left—the park's community center. Maybe Smokey Robinson the Ranger had returned to his office. Maybe Vanessa still needed quiet after coming upon a body in a bag and was now sipping cool water from a tiny paper cup.

The downpour intensified as I quickstepped toward the community center. The muck made my boots burp. I took one step too quick, and my legs flew from beneath me. I landed on my ass, and my hands sank into gooey, wet earth thick with dying insects. My anal-retentive gene activated, and before I even thought of standing, I swiped my muddy palms on my pants and trench coat, *get it off get it off.*

A man's hand—tanned, strong—reached down from

behind me. "At least all of you is covered in mud now."

Nerves jangled, I said, "Ha, yeah." I looked over my shoulder to see his face.

"Hi, there." He smiled to show off perfect white teeth. His. Not purchased. He had olive-colored skin—Black Irish, Spanish, or French—a day's-growth beard, cocker spaniel–brown eyes, and thick brows that a vain man would have waxed. He was muscular but not meat-head muscular like the Angry Pitcher. He was *thisclose* to being average-looking for Los Angeles, but attractive enough that I wouldn't vote him off the island.

On the other hand, he would've voted me off immediately—I looked as though I'd pulled an all-nighter at the local pig and crawfish farm.

"Other than the baseball cap," he said, "you're not really dressed for recreation. Kick-ass boots, though."

I accepted his hand to stand and winced as pain sparked up and down my left arm. "I try to slip in the mud at least once a month. Keeps me humble. Close to the ground. Like Wilbur from *Charlotte's Web*."

He retrieved my bag, which had landed in grass, then pointed at my badge hanging on a lanyard around my neck. "You're a detective."

"That's what it says, yeah. Thanks for helping me out." I took my bag from him, then limped toward the community center.

Kind Stranger walked beside me. "I saw you storming down that trail. You okay? You're holding your arm."

I cocked an eyebrow.

He smiled. "I'm a doctor. Hence my concern."

I stopped in my step. "It hurts when I do this." Then, I waved my arm as though I was flagging down the last bus out of Compton.

His forehead wrinkled with concern. "Then, don't do that. *Smaller* circles."

37

"You go up that trail today?" I asked, resuming my journey to the community center.

"Too iffy, with all the mud. On my days off, like today, I jog around the lake. But I saw all the squad cars and ambulances, so I rushed up to see if I could help."

"The proverbial doctor in the house?"

"Doctor and former EMT." He blushed, then added, "I did the same after Katrina. And 9/11 and . . . Haiti. Just dropped everything and . . . Not by myself. Doctors Without Borders." He shrugged and offered me a shy grin.

My face warmed. "We have it under control. Thank you again for rescuing me."

"So is it true?" he asked. "What you guys found?"

I gave him a slow smile. "*Found?*"

He gave me the same smile. "Lemme guess: no comment on an ongoing investigation."

I pulled at the center's door. *Locked.* I knocked, wincing as my left wrist sparked again.

He frowned. "You should probably get that checked out. Just my humble, professional, Emory School of Medicine–trained opinion."

"You're right," I said. "I will." A lie. Was I bleeding? Lame? Dead? Cops didn't do doctors. At least, not in *that* way.

"Do you know who they found up there?" he asked. "Yes, I'm asking anyway."

"Don't know who she is. But at least she's been found." I peered past the center's iron-grated windows. No Vanessa. No Smokey Robinson the Ranger.

"This park seemed so safe," he said, shaking his head. "And it's always crowded. Somebody must've seen what happened."

I held out my healthy right hand and we shook. "Thank you for offering free medical advice that will go unheeded until it's too late."

"Anytime. So if I have anything to add to your investigation—?"

"You know something?"

He smiled, then said, "How would I reach you, Detective . . . ?"

"Norton. And you're . . . ?"

"Zach. Is there a law against making shit up just to see a pretty detective again?"

I tapped the puddle beneath my boot. "False reporting. A misdemeanor. Look, I really—"

"What if I wanted to ask the pretty detective out for coffee and conversation? You do like coffee and conversation, right?"

My left arm tingled, and I glanced back at the crumbling hill where my team huddled over a dead girl. Getting picked up a half mile away seemed like laughing at a funeral. Yes, life continued, but damn, could Jane Doe get a moment? And could Vanessa freakin' call me?

"Thank you for the offer," I said, "but I really don't have—"

"Detective Norton!" Amber Andersen had snuck beneath the yellow tape and was now standing a few feet away. "Detective, could I have a moment?"

I frowned, then said to Zach, "Thanks, again."

"How do I get in touch with you?" he asked. "Seriously: in the clinics, I hear all kinds of random neighborhood gossip."

I reached into my pocket for a business card. "If you hear anything."

He studied the card as I tromped back to the trail.

"Good luck," he shouted.

I gave him a thumbs-up—I'd need all the luck in the world.

7

AT ALMOST SIX O'CLOCK, MY TEAM AND I HAD WORKED THE SCENE FOR FIVE HOURS, and our mood matched the weather: cold, wet, and bitter. The rain had stopped, but another storm front still charged toward us.

"What the hell's taking so long?" Pepe groused as he lit his third cigarette in twenty minutes. He stood with Luke and me at the lip of the bluff, waiting for deputy medical examiner Dr. Spencer Brooks to finish with the girl.

We scowled at Brooks's team.

They scowled back at us.

Zucca and his crew had drawn the shortest stick—they had to wait until after Brooks moved Jane Doe to gather any evidence hidden beneath her.

My feet and wrist hurt, and my body ached from wearing a miniholster stuffed with a G42, a ballistics vest beneath a muddy sweater, and a drenched trench coat.

Brooks didn't care about my aching feet or Pepe's chain-smoking. He had a job to do, and as an old friend of mine at the coroner's office said: it's the best of jobs, it's the worst of jobs, and it's the most important job.

Important job or not, a storm was still barreling upon us, and each inch of rain hampered our ability to see the toes of our shoes. A bank of halogen lamps bathed the trail and hillside with pure light and kept the darkness at bay. Those yellow evidence flags noting the girl's descent onto the trail barely stood upright in the mud and grass.

"We need to get her out of here," I muttered, still glaring at Brooks's team.

"I tried scowling. Doesn't work." Luke opened a packet of *saladitos,* then offered me one. "The doc ain't comin' out, not now, not ever."

I popped a salted apricot in my mouth, then checked my phone—nothing from Vanessa.

"I wonder who she is," Pepe said. "And why the hell is she here?"

"I wanna see that duffel bag." I reached again into Luke's packet of *saladitos.* "Maybe there's a name or a tag or a company . . ."

"Think it's a random drop?" Luke asked.

I readjusted the baseball cap, bristling from the combined stink of my wet hair and the sweat from the cap's original owner. "Doubt it."

Truly random crimes were rare. John Wayne Gacy, for instance, had hired many of his victims to work for his construction company. And some of Wayne Williams's kills had been prostitutes he'd known.

"This monster knows her," I said. "And I need to find him before L.T. makes me push her to the back burner. Anyway. Pepe, what's up with the guy in the suck-you-thin suit?"

"A bullshitter. He nearly pissed his pants when I badged him. He was nowhere near this trail. Just wanted his fifteen minutes. And the park ranger—name's Jimmy Boulard—he's coming in to give an official—"

"Lou!" Brooks was calling.

Dread settled on my heart like a raven on a bare tree limb.

"Here we go," Pepe said, killing his cigarette between his fingers.

Brooks swiped at his cinnamon-colored nose with the sleeve of his Tyvek suit. His eyes had disappeared behind the fogged lenses of his wire-rimmed glasses.

"Well?" I asked.

"She's cold but not stiff," Brooks said. "Dead maybe forty-eight hours. The cold weather and the low number of bugs makes it hard to tell right now." He gazed at the girl who was decomposing even as we stood over her. He pointed at her darkened left side. "See that?" Then, he pointed to the tops of her thighs, which were darker than her side. "And there? And that?" The right side of her face was mottled. "Differing lividity."

"Which means what to us?" Luke asked.

"When she died," Brooks said, "the blood pooled in different patterns. If she had died on her back and had been left in that position—"

"The blood would've settled in her back," I said. "She was moved."

"A couple of times," Brooks said.

Didn't want to hear that. Processing one crime scene was difficult enough, but another scene that you didn't even *know* about?

A crack of thunder boomed.

Pepe and Luke glanced at the sky.

My breathing had already quickened. *Where did she die? If not here, where?*

Brooks aimed his flashlight beam at the girl's left hand, assaulted now by blowflies. "Flies are here now when they weren't just an hour ago."

And more flies, in just that moment, found the girl. The tarp now buzzed.

Brooks pointed to abrasions on her arms and cuts on her leg. "Don't know yet who or what made those."

"He didn't bury her," Luke said. "How come?"

"No time," I said. "Digging a grave is hard work. And in this case, the shrubs and leaves worked just as well."

"Until the rain came," Brooks added.

Another crack of thunder.

My scalp crawled as I counted. *One . . . two . . . three . . . four . . .* And the sky flashed.

"As far as getting latent prints off of her . . ." Brooks shook his head. "Maybe we'll have a better chance in a controlled environment."

"And the probability that we'll find the monster's prints on her body?" I asked.

He gave a one-shouldered shrug, then clicked off his flashlight. "We should get going before we're caught in a landslide. Before any evidence she has left on her washes away, making your job all that more difficult."

Usually, we spent three days at a crime scene. This park was the worst crime scene possible. Clues were now washing away and dissolving because of rain and wind, while the rest of it was being buried in mud or had been stolen by animals. Bits of evidence, from Jane Doe, from the monster, were being lost every second, and there was nothing I could do about it.

Had it been only six hours since eating pastrami with Sam? Six hours since we lingered at that table, George Harrison and Olivia Newton-John serenading us?

Another crack of thunder . . . *One . . . two . . . three . . .* A flash of lightning.

I turned to Pepe. "Pull all the missing persons reports from the last month. She's a kid—somebody's missing her."

"What about the paperwork?" Luke asked with a cocked eyebrow.

Colin usually handled the bulk of incident reports and warrant requests. He was the Mark Spitz of Paperwork. But since he was now collapsed in bed with a temperature of 133, someone else had to do the job . . . and Luke could barely spell "homicide."

I groaned. "I'll handle the reports while I'm waiting for the autopsy to—"

Boom!

Thunder.

One . . . two . . .

A light whiter and far more dangerous than the halogens filled the sky.

As a three-person team maneuvered the girl into a protective bag, Brooks came to stand beside me. "I know this took longer than what you wanted, but I needed to take my time."

"You think it's Trina?"

He let out a long breath, then shrugged. "I'll be working on her. Whoever she is."

"Good cuz this could turn—"

"Political? Don't most homicides turn political?"

"But we have an especially shitty record right now serving and protecting young black females. And speaking on behalf of young black females, I'm sick to hell of it and when are the fucking cops gonna do something about it?"

"How many missing kids this year?" he asked.

"Stranger, family, suspicious, or unknown missing?"

Brooks said, "Surprise me."

"Right now," I said, "there are about 450 kids missing in LA County."

"And murders?"

"About forty. Only six females, but four of those six were black."

"Doesn't sound too bad in a city of 9.9 million people."

"Six is too many."

"But how many of those missing children will be found alive?" he asked. "And how many girls get home safely after school each day and live happily ever after?"

Optimism. For cutters like Brooks and murder police like me, optimism was a condition as rare as hens' teeth. *Happy endings?* What were those? If I was standing anywhere near you, that meant shit had just gone left, your life had changed forever, and there'd be no happy ending.

8

HAPPY ENDINGS. THAT MYTH STAYED WITH ME AS I FOUGHT MY WAY THROUGH "LA
in the Rain" traffic. Accidents—cars against cars, cars against
bikes, cars wrapped around light poles—peppered every third
mile, and so it took an hour to reach Syeeda's Miracle Mile
neighborhood. Since the divorce, I had squatted here, walking
distance from the Farmers' Market, the Grove outdoor mall,
and CBS Studios. I finally pulled into the driveway next to
Lena's Range Rover and climbed out of my SUV. Rain fell
like liquid silk on my face.

Lena snored in the armchair as Syeeda, on the couch,
played *Mass Effect* on the Xbox. Crust from brie-filled
sourdough bread sat beside wineglasses stained from
Cabernet Sauvignon.

"Looks like you and your herd of goats just crawled from
beneath a bridge," Syeeda said, pausing the game. "Either
you and Sam hit it in the backseat of the Porsche, or . . ."

I clomped over to the love seat and collapsed into the deep
cushions. "I feel like sunshine." I reached for the wine bottle,
then took a long pull. I plucked *Midnight Rendezvous,* my
latest bad romance, from between two sofa cushions. On the
book's cover, a woman with long blond tresses rode a dark-
haired centaur wielding his giant . . . wand.

"I can't believe you like that shit," Syeeda said.

I found a page, then read, "Daemon sought to quench their loving lusts on that eve, nay that dark, dark night. It was clear that she was just a virgin, a perfect goddess to carry his centaur seed." I whooped and kicked my feet in the air. "Centaur seed! C'mon, that's awesome."

Lena groaned, then turned over in the chair. "Must you cackle so loudly as I lay here, passed out?" Mascara and eyeliner ringed her eyes, but the diamonds in her ears gleamed as bright as Venus.

"So, what did I miss?" I asked, shoving the book back between the cushions.

Syeeda turned her attention back to the game. "Fitz or Jake? Huck be crazy. Melly be schemin'. And Olivia wore this bad-ass coat I want to buy, like, yesterday. And . . ." She paused the game again, and this time, she placed the controller on the cushion beside her.

"Uh oh," I said. "Gimme a minute." In one last pull, I finished the wine. "Tell me."

"Who gave him my address?" Syeeda asked, eyebrow cocked.

I frowned. "He showed up *here*?"

"Yep," Lena said. "He didn't believe us when we told him you weren't here."

My face burned. "I'm sorry, Sy. Maybe Mom gave him . . . or Greg . . . Shit."

Syeeda stared at me, then said, "You need to figure this Victor Starr thing out."

I sighed, then stood. "I will. As that great philosopher Dan Quayle once said, 'The future will be a better tomorrow.' Tonight, though, I need to take a long, hot shower. Fall into bed and close my eyes for three hours. And then wake up and see a man about a dead body."

THURSDAY, MARCH 20

9

A PILE OF SIXTY MISSING CHILDREN REPORTS SAT ON THE WOBBLY DESK NEAR Brooks's file cabinets located in the bowels of the Los Angeles County Coroner's office. At almost seven in the morning, I plopped into the raggedy chair and plucked a report from the pile.

Quida Chisholm, born February 7, 2003 . . . I, the mother, returned from work on March 16 to find Quida missing . . . eighth grade home school . . . Quida was the same race as my Jane Doe. Probably around the same age, too. But Quida was shorter, had darker hair, and was about fifteen pounds heavier.

Quida's report went into the no pile.

The next five reports involved three boys and two Hispanic girls.

No, five times.

A yes pile did not exist yet, but there were six reports in maybe.

I stood from the workstation and stretched until every bone in my body clicked. The asteroid-colored rash on my chest still burned, but a soft LAPD T-shirt and hydrocortisone cream had contained the blaze. I grabbed the reports and lumbered down the hallway to the autopsy suites. Someone had microwaved oatmeal for breakfast—the scent of warm brown sugar wafted along the corridors, only to be lost in the clinical stink of formaldehyde and death. The blisters on my feet still made me wince, but the Nikes' memory foam treated them better than yesterday's fancy boots. Little acts of kindness.

I ducked into the dimly lit antechamber. On the other side of the double doors, Brooks was scrubbing his hands in the stainless steel sink. Two of the exam tables hosted bodies covered in white sheets, with one of those patients so obese that parts of it slopped off the table. Brooks's assistant, Big Reuben, a giant in cornrows, was removing a soup ladle from one of the cabinet drawers. No rush. Just another day at LACCO.

This early in the morning, I thought that I would've been sleeping off too many glasses of red wine. Waking up next to Sam Seward in his bed. My hand drifting down his happy trail to claim his early-morning gift to me. Thought I'd be foggy-headed, deliciously sore, bursting with a story to tell Lena and Syeeda. Giggling, gasping, and shrieking. Being a Girl.

I *was* foggy-headed—no restful sleep.

And I *was* sore, though not deliciously, from tromping in mud, falling in mud, and bending over to examine mud.

I certainly had a story to tell—but not the one I wanted to share over Moscow mules and jalapeño poppers.

My cell phone vibrated in my bag.

A text from Sam.

Had a great time. Had hoped to still be talking about GOT. But death happens. What if we had dinner @ home tonight?

My fingers hovered over the phone's keyboard as stainless steel appliances of death clinked around me and called me to work. I typed my response: *I cram to understand you, Sam.*

A few seconds passed before he texted back. *What's confusing?*

52

You still hanging around.

I'm like a cat. Feed me once . . .

Shame on you, I typed.

Feed me twice . . .

Magic?

U not skeered, is you?

I chuckled. *Hell yeah, I'm skeered.*

A pause, then: *Don't be.*

The saw's high-pitched whir pulled me out of Sweet Valley High and back into the autopsy antechamber. Sober now, I tapped SETTINGS on my phone and assigned the "*Star Wars* Theme Music" ringtone to Sam's number. Then, I saw that two voice-mail messages had been left as I'd arrived at the coroner's office. The first message had been my ex, Greg. Something-something . . . condo selling . . . real estate . . . something.

I deleted the message, then listened to the message from my mother.

Georgia Starr's voice, bourbon and pecans, drifted through the speaker. "You're still avoiding him. And so he keeps calling *me* to make *you* talk to him. I remind him that although he left you when you were eight, you continued to grow, and today you are an adult."

"What the *hell,* Mom?" I muttered.

Why hadn't she blocked Victor Starr's calls? Why did she keep talking to him? I'd told her a zillion times: you don't have to pick up the phone.

"So I don't know what to say," she continued. "And honestly, I don't even know why I'm calling you. Because I understand. This is *your* relationship, not mine. But whatever you do, do it. And soon. *Please.* I love you, okay? Call me later."

Your relationship.

A "relationship" meant that the involvement was two-way, mutual, *existing.*

I had a relationship with Greg. Antagonistic. Nostalgic.

I had a relationship with Sam. Fledgling. Tentative. Exciting.

What I had with Victor Starr was neither tentative nor antagonistic. Since our so-called reunion in December, he kept trying to see me. I had not returned his phone calls. And when he returned to knock on the front door of the condo, I hadn't answered. In the last twenty-four hours, he had invaded the station and Syeeda's front porch.

All because *he* wanted to talk to me.

So? We all *wanted* something.

And he didn't deserve to get what he wanted. At least not from me.

He had written me three letters and had mailed them to the station. *Sorry . . . please . . . let me explain . . .* I'm guessing here since I never opened those letters and chose instead to shove them into the mail room's shred bin. No more stupid Jedi mind tricks with Victor Starr. I wanted no apology. I wanted no explanation. I wanted nothing from him—except to be left alone. And up until last December, he had been very good at doing that, leaving me alone.

A Jedi, he was.

10

GOD BLESS THE DEAD. NOT ALL OF THEM ARE MOURNED.

Almost five thousand unclaimed bodies were listed on the Los Angeles County Coroner's books. More than 750 would be cremated and their remains stored in small black boxes. They would remain at the county's crematorium for two years, waiting for family members to step forward and claim them. Alas, not enough families did.

"Ready?" Brooks asked me.

Now covered in a smock and a face mask, I stood across from the medical examiner. Jane Doe lay between us. "I'm ready." A small lie: what regular person could properly prepare herself for bone cracking and blood scooping? I wasn't a regular person—this was my way of life—and yet that "about to faint" feeling stayed with me.

I should've been accustomed to the scalpel's glint and the saw's whir, Brooks's muffled breathing, and Big Reuben's dead-eyed gaze. I should've especially been accustomed to the ordered chaos of a dead body. Most times, I cracked jokes (*a monster and a zombie walk into a mortuary*) and pried into county drama (who was caught *where* doing *what* to dead Mrs. Feingold?). Not this morning, though.

"Detective Norton," Brooks said.

I jerked out of my fugue—both Brooks and Big Reuben

were staring at me. "I was just . . ."

Brooks's eyes softened as he gazed at the girl. "It would be a wonderful thing if we could ID her today. Don't want to see her unclaimed." He sighed, then said, "Here we go."

He then pressed a foot pedal and the overhead microphone clicked. "Thursday, March twenty, seven fifteen A.M." He stared at the scale's blinking numbers. "She's . . . 45.3 kilograms."

One hundred pounds.

"And 154.9 centimeters."

Five feet, one inch.

Her face, legs, and abdomen had swollen with gasses. Her skin was mottled and black in some places, green and blistery in others.

Brooks peered into the girl's eyes. "Pupils are fully dilated. Eyes are hazel or green." He stepped on the pedal to turn off the mic. "Really, Lou: there should be a *lot* of bug activity right now. Blowflies and houseflies in every opening of her body and . . ." He sniffed, cocked his head, then sniffed again.

I chuckled. "You smell something?"

"Funny. Not sure." He clicked on the mic. "No bruising around the neck . . ."

A weird-colored fluid—black, emerald, crimson, peach—sluiced down the side canals of the exam table.

I swayed a bit, then squeezed shut my eyes. Once the wooziness passed, I glanced at the digital clock above the entryway. Almost seven thirty.

"Birthmark," Brooks said, "on her right hip, two and a half centimeters. And bruises on her hips and thighs." He counted five bruises on her left calf alone, then measured each. He clicked on the penlight clamped to his face mask, then bent closer to peer at something. "Two injection marks on her left thigh."

My eyes roamed her body, stopping at the weird coloring.

Differing lividity. Why had he moved her so much?

Brooks walked to the other side of the table. "One injection mark on her right thigh." He pressed the pedal, then grunted.

"Maybe she was diabetic," I offered.

He grunted again, then pressed the pedal, directing his attention to the girl's discolored feet. "Significant bruising on the top and bottom of the patient's left foot. The discoloration suggests a Lisfranc injury and occurred while the patient was alive. X-ray will confirm."

The girl's right hand was curled into a fist.

"Now examining the patient's closed right hand." He pried open her fingers.

She held a dull white object the size of a Jelly Belly and flecked with brown grit.

Brooks squinted at whatever it was. "The patient is holding a tooth in her right hand."

Before I could ask a follow-up question—whose tooth, her tooth, which tooth, why a tooth?—I blurted, "What color were her eyes?"

Brooks clicked off the mic and snapped, *"What?"*

"Her eyes."

"I'm looking at her feet right now, Detective."

"What color?"

"Green or hazel."

"Wait. Birthmark. I read that—"

"Are you gonna let me—?"

I stepped over to the counter and grabbed the maybe pile of missing persons reports. Holding my breath, I flipped through each document. *Not her . . . Not her . . . Her!*

The color photo was one of those glamour shots taken at the mall. This girl had green eyes, a wide nose, and cashew-colored skin. She wore lots of fuchsia eye shadow and coats of purple lipstick. If you wiped away the paint that had tramped her up to look twenty-seven years old, she'd be the girl now lying on Brooks's table.

"Thirteen-year-old Chanita Lords," I said. "Missing since Friday, March fourteen."

Brooks sighed, and his shoulders slumped with relief.

"At least now she has a name," I said, my gaze still on the photograph.

"Five days have passed since Friday," Brooks said, nodding. "He kept her alive for at least two of those days." He looked down at Chanita Lords. "At least that's what her body's telling me."

"Let's talk about the tooth," I said.

He opened Chanita's mouth, then shone light into the darkness. "Probably hers—there's an empty space where it would be. Can't tell when it was removed, though. More tests needed."

"Why pull it out?" I asked. "Why let her keep it?"

"Don't know."

"Strange."

"Let's do internal," he said.

"Before you do," I said, "can you tell me what killed her?"

He shook his head. "Not right now."

"And latent prints on her body?"

"Once they send over a tech, we'll look."

"Mind if I scoot, then?" I backed away from the table, not strong enough this morning to endure heart, kidneys, and guts in a scale. "I'd like to confirm with the family now that we know."

He waved me away. "I'll try to get all the tests pushed through as quickly as I can."

Dressed now in a respectable light-gray pantsuit and loafers, I trudged back out to the parking lot bustling with cars beneath stormy gray skies. As I neared the Crown Vic, I noticed a small white object sitting on its roof.

It had been carved out of marble. A woman—a goddess, maybe—held the head of a bearded man in one hand and a knife in the other.

Hunh. A tchotchke you'd buy in a souvenir store near the Colosseum in Athens.

I glanced around the parking lot: no one was looking in my direction. Not the trio of secretaries in panty hose and Easy Spirits and not the sheriff's deputy hoisting a travel mug and a lunch cooler. I squinted at the figurine for a moment more, plucked it from the roof, and shoved it into my coat pocket.

Not every day you found a goddess on the roof of your car.

I slid behind the steering wheel. "Now, where am I going?" I peered at Chanita Lords's missing person report again and found the girl's address. "Crap."

6873 Hillcrest Avenue, Los Angeles, CA 90008.

Today would be a long, long day.

11

A LITTLE AFTER NINE O'CLOCK, I PARKED IN FRONT OF THE WROUGHT-IRON SECURITY gate that "protected" Chanita Lords's apartment complex from the terror lurking on the streets. The gate sat wide open—terror would have no problem gaining entry. Barefoot toddlers wearing soggy diapers and clutching baby bottles filled with red punch zigzagged from apartment to apartment, rambling close to stairways and trash chutes.

Next door, the two palm trees that had flanked the entrance to my childhood home still stood, but wind, fire, and disease had lopped off the top of the right palm, and BPS in red spray paint and bullet holes of varying calibers had nearly destroyed the trunk of the left tree.

Dark clouds gathered in the sky above. Because, of course.

"Home sweet hell," I muttered, shouldering my bag.

Back in 1960s Los Angeles, the community of apartment buildings located between Hillcrest Avenue and La Brea Avenue earned the nickname the Jungle because of the surrounding lush green: palm and banana trees and hillsides covered in wildflowers and wild mustard. Many apartment units were larger than some single-family homes, and the units' swimming pools made having to use laundry rooms doable.

"My dad's old Ford Maverick used to wheeze up this hill," I told Colin over the Motorola. "Boys in the yellow apartment building over there, the one with the couch on the lawn? They used to throw bottles at Tori and her friend Golden because they wouldn't stop to talk. And we used to chase monarch butterflies in the park around the corner." I sighed. "Once upon a time, the Jungle used to be cool."

"So what happened?" Colin asked as he tried to park his Cavalier a few feet from my old apartment building.

"The Riots," I said as my fingers brushed against the marble figurine in my coat pocket. "Burn, baby, burn. Terrorists in Dickies. PCP. Guns . . ."

"And now look at you: the Man."

I frowned as he pulled the car in and pulled the car out again. "You park like a ninety-year-old. It's gonna be lunchtime by the time you—"

"It's a weird space."

"Yeah, it's one of those parallel spaces the size of a car."

Finally, Colin parked, then climbed out of the Cavalier. His gray wool suit looked a little baggy on him—sick-skinny. As he made his way to my car with his binder, he tightened his gray striped tie, then blew his nose into a tissue.

"I missed you," I said.

"Whatever, Lou."

"No, seriously. I had to do all the reports and shit. I hate that stuff and you do it so well. So yes: I missed you."

Colin eyed me, waiting for the jab. When the jab didn't come, he said, "Why are you being so nice . . . ?" He squinted, then grinned. "Hey, now!" He held up his hand, ready to high-five.

I cocked my head. "What?"

"You and Sam last night, right? Explains you being nice to me, the glowing skin . . ."

"Why can't I say something kind, first of all? And, second, why are you in my bed? Sam and I didn't hook up, not that it's any of your—"

61

Colin rolled his eyes. "Oh, c'mon, Lou. What the hell's your deal?"

I gaped at him. "Dude. We were at a crime scene for how many hours yesterday?"

He smirked. "That's when you need to get laid the *most*."

"Can we now focus on work, please?" I gazed at apartment buildings with swanky names that hadn't changed in twenty years. Baldwin Manor. Hillside Terrace. Ocean Breeze Homes. Crumpled-up paper, aluminum cans, and glass bottles littered patches of dirt where lush grass had grown back in the eighties. A few tenants and their homies loitered on the balconies of the apartment-ground units. Everyone had noticed Colin's and my cars, and breakfast joints had been snuffed out and the Game's "The City" had been turned down.

The sights, smells, and sounds of this place gave me a twisty stomach and damp palms. A small but not insignificant part of me wanted to hustle back to my car and race down the hill. But the larger part of me—the part that wore a badge and gun and owned a set of steel ovaries—refused to scamper.

I hadn't walked this small stretch of sidewalk since my tenth-grade year. That's when Mom and I moved to a different, less jacked-up neighborhood, Tori-less, Dad-less.

"Look." Colin pointed to a nearby telephone pole.

A yellow "Missing" flyer featuring Chanita Lords's photo had been stapled into the wood.

Colin yanked the paper from the pole, then handed it to me.

In this picture, the teen's hair hid beneath a dark-colored do-rag. She wore no makeup, but her eyebrows looked freshly waxed. Her French-tipped fingernails rested on her cheeks.

Pop-pop-pop-pop-pop.

Colin said, "Somebody's shootin'."

"I fell for that trick once," I answered, remembering a

certain storage facility and a certain crazy man named Christopher Chatman.

"We get warrants for her bedroom and phone?" Colin asked.

I nodded. "Luke should be sending them over any minute now."

"Good mornin', Officers."

The overly solicitous voice belonged to a young black man stretched out on the hood of a black Cutlass Supreme. He wore red corduroy house shoes, red Clippers basketball shorts, and a white wife beater as clean as a southern grandma's bathroom floor. Green and blue ink swirled on his arms and neck—BPS, RIP, illegible names, faces of crudely drawn females.

"Morning." I held up the yellow flyer. "You know her?"

"Maybe." He pulled a cigarillo and a lighter out of thin air, then lit up. "That's some shit right there. I heard some Mess-cans have a hand in that. They tryin' to take over up in here."

Colin cocked his head. "Why would Mexicans kidnap her?"

"C'mon, Officer," Dude said. "I know y'all got to pretend that shit ain't like it is. But *you* know and *I* know that they want us gone. They tryna chase us out like they did to all the niggas in Highland Park. And please: y'all ain't about to bust some Mess-can Eighteenth Street bangers. Nah. Y'all want us to go head to head, *mano* to *mano*." He puffed on the cigarillo, then added, "These Mess-cans keep on messin' with our girls, shit's gon' jump off fo' sure."

"What you smoking in there?" I asked. "You paranoid as fuck."

Dude was right about the race thing, though. The Latino gang, Eighteenth Street Westside, co-terrorized the Jungle to the Black P-Stones' displeasure. City officials tried to downplay the hostilities between the two gangs by claiming

63

that the violence wasn't racial but stemmed from desires for more territory and the always-expanding drug trade. Despite injunctions that prohibited members from hanging out in certain neighborhood "safety zones," both gangs started randomly killing children who lived outside those zones. Two weeks ago, a black gang member shot and killed a three-year-old Mexican boy. Two days later, a Mexican gang member shot and killed a ten-year-old black girl. Neither child nor their parents had been affiliated with gangs, but had still been targeted. If not for the color of their skin, then what?

In Dude's opinion, Chanita Lords represented yet another casualty in this unacknowledged race war.

In truth, white people were actually about to take over up in here just as they were taking over Highland Park. Developers planned to tear down the Jungle and replace it with a hospital campus, new shops for folks riding the still-in-construction metro train, and expensive apartments and condos that folks like Dude and Eighteenth Street thugs could never, ever afford.

"You bang?" Colin asked him now.

I clamped my lips together to keep from laughing.

Dude chuckled. "Sound like you just learned that word yesterday, Officer."

Colin blushed. "Just answer the question."

"Naw, I don't bang," he said, avoiding my glance.

I squinted at him. "So that BPS on your left bicep stands for . . . ?"

"Boston Public School," he said, grinning.

I rolled my eyes. "And the tat that says 'Nita' on your left wrist?"

He gaped at it, and his brows knitted as he tried to come up with an explanation.

"You think it's possible that Chanita's disappearance is related to something more . . . nasty and fucked up?" I asked.

Dude studied the cigarillo between two tobacco-stained fingers. "Like Jeffrey Dahmer and shit?" He curled his lip and shook his head. "First of all, ain't no white man without a badge gon' come up in here and snatch no girl." He nodded at Colin. "Y'all some crazy sons a bitches, but y'all ain't *that* crazy."

An LAPD helicopter now buzzed overhead, and we all glanced up at it.

"So nobody odd around that doesn't belong?" Colin asked.

"There's this Chester that lives in Nita's complex," Dude said. "Raul Moriaga. Now *he's* fucked up."

"So you and Chanita," I said, eyes on Dude's tattoo. "You were *dating*?"

"I ain't said that," Dude spat. "She was . . . a good friend, know what I mean?"

My skin crawled, and my mouth opened to reply, but then closed. Dude had to be older than sixteen. He had to be older than *eighteen*. I opened my binder. "What's your name?"

"Ontrel."

"Last name?"

He didn't reply.

I cocked an eyebrow. *Well?*

"Shaw."

"And how old are you, Mr. Shaw?" I asked.

"Just made twenty-two yesterday."

"Well, happy birthday," I said, scribbling his name and age onto the notepad. "I'm Detective Norton, and this is Detective Taggert." I narrowed my eyes. "Good friends?"

"Ain't like we was married or shit," Ontrel said, frowning. "We hung out, watched movies, et cetera et cetera. Ain't no thang—Nita was mature for her age."

"She was *thirteen*," Colin spat.

Ontrel gave an oblivious shrug. "Age ain't nothin' but a number."

"And according to the law," I said, "thirteen will get you four."

He snorted. "Like y'all give a fuck about black girls fucking."

"I give thirty fucks about black girls fucking," I said. "Especially minor girls. And since that is now the topic, I'll need your DNA."

Ontrel's smile dimmed, and he sat up straighter on the car's hood.

"So," I continued, "now that I have your full attention: what's been going on around here since Nita went missing?"

Ontrel sucked his teeth. "What you think? Regina pissed cuz y'all ain't found Nita yet. Pissed at me cuz I wasn't with Nita to protect her. Like I said, we wasn't no married people, so I don't know what the fuck Gee wanted *me* to do."

I could only blink at him as my mind grappled with the monstrous age gap. Twenty-two and thirteen and Chanita's mother *approved*? Had I become that bourgie since fleeing this place?

Ontrel chuckled, more annoyed than amused. "Gotta do what you gotta do to survive. I protect Nita from a lot of these fools up in here. Give her and her fam' money when they broke."

"Well, then," I said, "the parade will be next week. I'll be sure to bring your medal and key to the city."

"And she been gone for five days," Ontrel said, scowling, "and she ain't back *yet*. What you so worried about, Detective?" To Colin: "Why you standin' here *now,* Officer? Neither of y'all know shit about us up in here."

As a former resident, I knew plenty. But I didn't care to qualify to this statutory-rapist dope head. I wouldn't show him my physical scars left from getting jumped in the laundry room two hundred yards away from where we now stood. Nor would I relive for him those terrifying nights when helicopters like the one above us busted up my bedroom's darkness with their damn-bright searchlights because someone like *him* had been shot in the alley beneath my window.

Anger now stuck in my throat like a hastily swallowed jawbreaker. "Where were you when she first disappeared?"

Ontrel's scowl deepened. "Like I told that other cop: Social Security with my moms."

"Folks can vouch for you?" Colin asked.

"Yup."

Colin made a note in his binder. "We'll need you to come down to the station for a formal interview."

"Fuck that. I already had one of them."

Colin shook his head. "But that was with—"

"Thanks, Ontrel," I interrupted, then pointed at his slippers. "Them Jordans?"

Ontrel said, "Ha," without humor.

"What shoes do you normally wear?" I asked.

"Jordans. Black and red ones."

"When you come to the station," I said, "please bring three pairs of your favorite sneaks."

"What for?"

"Cuz I ain't got nothin' to do all day except explain shit to you."

Ontrel leaned back on the windshield with his arms crossed. "I ain't had nothing to do with Nita disappearing. Put *that* in your police report. I'm innocent."

Three teenage girls wearing puffy nylon jackets poured out the gates of the apartment complex next door. Their tropical-fruit-color-streaked hair matched their tropical-fruit-color tight jeans. *Mango, guava, and kiwi. See me! Pick me!* Someone *had* picked a girl their age who had come from this very place. Chanita Lords had probably been the brightest thing in the monster's life.

Ontrel hopped off the Cutlass (not "hopped," since that verb took energy, and Ontrel had smoked away his energy). No. He *melted* off the car. "Am I free to go, Detectives, or y'all gon' send some more cops to talk to me? Make me confess to some shit I ain't do? Or you gon' take me now?" He held out his tattooed wrists.

Colin's phone rang from his jacket pocket, and he wandered to his car to answer the call.

I nodded up at the helicopter. "We're here all the time. If I want you for something, I'll come back. Right now, though, we're just chatting. Shootin' the shit, neighborly like."

The three girls closed the distance between the apartment building and Ontrel and me. Teeth snapping gum. Thighs rubbing against each other. Acrylic fingernails scratching scalps. Smelling like sour apple Jolly Ranchers, Pink hair lotion, and cigarette smoke.

Of all the ghettos in the world, Chanita Lords had to come from this one.

"Ontrel, who you talking to?" the girl with the natural scowl asked.

"None of ya biz-ness," Ontrel said. "What y'all want?"

"Drive us to the liquor store," Braids ordered. "We need something to *drank*."

"She look too old for you, Trel." The chubby one who had been smoking a Parliament tossed the still-lit butt toward my loafer.

I jerked my shoe away. "What the—?"

The girls laughed.

Scowler said, "You see that bitch jump?"

"That *bitch* a police detective," Ontrel growled.

Their heads dropped.

"Who's the bitch now?" I asked.

Colin returned to stand beside me.

"You her partner?" Chubby One asked him.

"Yeah," he said.

"You cute for a white boy," she said.

"Thanks, I guess." To me, he said, "Got the paper."

Warrants. Yay.

"Why ain't y'all in school?" I asked the girls.

"Teacher in-service," Scowler said. Then, she gazed at Ontrel with fluttery eyes—somebody had a crush.

"You can ask my mom if you don't believe us," Chubby One said.

"I'll let y'all's PO's handle your attendance records," I said.

Scowler sucked her teeth. "Why we gotta have probation officers?"

I lifted an eyebrow. "You don't?"

Silence.

I pointed at Ontrel. "See you soon, yes?"

He gave a curt nod.

I strode to the entry gates.

Impervious to Kevlar, the hard glares from those three girls burned my back.

Of all the ghettos . . .

12

WITH WARRANTS TO SEARCH CHANITA'S BEDROOM AND CELL PHONE NOW in our possession, Colin and I marched through the courtyard toward the girl's apartment. In my binder, I also possessed a picture of Chanita on Brooks's table, and its sadness eked through the binder's leather and seeped into my tired soul.

"Sorry back there with Ontrel," Colin said. "Forgot that nobody knows she passed."

Despite the ibuprofen I had popped before leaving the house, a headache was forming beneath my right eyebrow. "Just remember: we're playing chess when we're working a case. Not checkers with its jumping all over the board and quickness and shit. Got it?"

Colin said something, but my thoughts had turned back to finding the goddess on my car. Who had left it there? Why—?

"You ignoring me?" Colin asked.

I blinked. "I'd *never* ignore you, Colin dear. Everything you say and do is of the utmost importance to me."

The magnolia trees thrived—large green leaves but no white blooms. The dwarf palms looked dry and diseased, brown fronds or no fronds. The buildings' green paint had peeled in places and faded to white in others. Wet towels and underwear hung out to dry on every balcony.

"We will *not* mention the tooth," I said. "Nor will we mention the duffel bag."

"What about the needle marks?" he asked. "Or the conversation just now with Mr. Boston Public Schools?"

"Nope. None of that."

Once we reached apartment 5, I took a deep breath, told myself that I didn't have a headache—what headache?—then knocked on the door.

Silence blanketed the complex. No televisions or stereos blasted from living rooms. No girls laughed on stairways. No women gossiped at the mailboxes. A ghost town.

The door opened, and the aromas of fried pork chops and simmering collard greens wafted out to greet us. An older black woman with sagging cheeks and flat, tired eyes stood there. She wore a royal blue housecoat dusted with flour, pink slippers, and a pink scarf that covered the curlers in her hair. "Yes?"

My stomach gurgled—I hadn't eaten real food since yesterday's pastrami with Sam. And even that didn't compare to the meal being cooked now. Colin and I both flashed our badges.

Before I could say, "Homicide Division," the old woman grinned and looked to the heavens. "Thank you, Jesus."

The mole on the left cheek. The upper canine tooth that touched her bottom lip. The same apartment she had occupied since I was five years old.

"Are you . . . Miss Alberta?" I asked.

The woman's eyes narrowed, and she cocked her head. "Yes, and you . . . look familiar."

I pointed to the apartments on the other side of the complex. "My family . . . We lived in apartment seven and—"

She gasped, and her eyes widened. "Your daddy drove the 105."

"That's right." My mouth lifted, fell, and then twisted. From surprise: she was *still* living here? Anger: two of my laundry-room bullies, Angelique and Dominique, were Miss Alberta's daughters. And worry: how was Chanita Lords related?

"Are you Chanita's mom?" Colin asked.

"No. That's Regina, my daughter. She's in the shower right now. I'm Nita's grandmother, Alberta Jackson."

Regina, a baby when I lived here, had been too young to join her siblings' reign of terror.

Alberta opened the door wider. "Come on in and sit. Y'all excuse my appearance." She slapped the front of her house-coat and little clouds of flour puffed around her.

Drawn curtains darkened the large living room. A big-screen television and a black leather couch took up most of the space. The latest issues of *Ebony* and *Essence* sat on the black lacquer coffee table alongside the large-as-an-atlas family Bible and television remote control. A box of yellow "Missing" flyers sat near the front door.

Alberta beamed at me. "Just look at you. All tall and beautiful. A police officer. The Lord is *good*. I know your momma must be so proud, after all that."

All that. Days after Victoria's disappearance, Alberta had brought over a dish of noodles, orange cheese, and probably tuna. I'm guessing, since Mom had dumped the casserole into the garbage disposal. "They smoke PCP over there," she had explained to me.

"Want something to drink?" Alberta asked.

"Yes, please," Colin said.

I said nothing, still wary of food and drink prepared in a kitchen of PCP smokers.

"Comin' right up." She trundled into the small, yellow-tiled kitchen, then shouted, "Reggie, detectives is here." To me, she said, "Maybe now we can get some answers, since you know us and know how things go around here." She touched her heart-spot. "And 'specially since all this happened to you and your family."

I gave a curt nod, then turned my attention to the framed photographs hanging on the walls. These pictures captured Chanita, Regina, and Alberta in different versions of Fabulous. But there were also shots of Malibu's foggy seaside, downtown Los Angeles nightscapes, and an older woman's gnarled hands. Pictures a collector would professionally mat and hang.

"Ain't much changed since y'all left," Alberta said. "Remember Michi, the little Japanese lady who'd trim the bushes up front like bonsai trees? She still in nine. And Miss Candy from up front? She dead, but Lamar and Quinton still livin' there. How's your momma doin'?"

"Good," I said.

"Still in LA?"

"Yes, not far from the Ladera Ralphs."

Alberta laughed. "She didn't like me much back then. But we all had our struggles. Tell her I say hi." She returned to us with two glasses of grape soda. "Nita took those pictures," she said, handing me a glass. "That girl got a good eye, don't she?"

"She certainly did." I bristled. *Shit. Just used past tense.* I peered at the shot of a homeless man and his mutt walking past a parked Bentley. Sorrow set in—these photographs, just like the autopsy picture, made my stomach ache.

"Wanna see her awards?" Another woman's voice.

She stood in the doorway separating the living room from the bedrooms. She looked close to vanishing in her red and black kimono. Her head had also shrunk, and the red scarf around her hair shadowed her expressionless, blemished face. She hadn't slept since forever—the bags beneath her eyes testified to snatches of sleep and crying when she wasn't sleeping.

I knew that look—Mom had worn the same expression for ten years.

And this woman had to be Chanita's mother.

I held out my hand. "Hi, Ms. Drummond. I'm Detective Norton—"

"She used to live over in apartment seven," Alberta shared. "You probably too young to remember. But the news story last June—remember they found them bones down in the plaza? That was Detective Norton's sister."

Regina sighed, then retreated down the hallway.

Colin and I excused ourselves from Alberta, taking the glasses of soda with us.

Photographs lined the hallway walls: stray dogs, homeless men, prideful gang-bangers . . .

Regina stood at a bedroom's doorway.

"We have news about your daughter," I said.

She nodded. "In here."

Chanita's fuchsia and white comforter and matching curtains reminded me of my own teenage bedroom. Instead of Michael Jackson and LL Cool J posters on the walls, though, Chanita had taped-up posters of Bruno Mars and Beyoncé. A white dresser held fruit-scented body sprays and lotions, fingernail polishes, rolls of film, and a small television set. Countless ribbons, trophies, and certificates crowded the mirror, a small bookcase, and a desk.

Regina sat at the foot of the bed, then met my eyes. "Tell me."

Dry-mouthed, I opened my binder to that picture of Chanita taken by Big Reuben. "Yesterday, we found a girl . . ." My throat closed as I held out the picture. "Is this your daughter? Is this Chanita?"

Regina didn't take the picture. Her eyes dipped once to the image there, then jumped back up to meet mine. "She dead?"

I said, "Yes."

Her nostrils flared. "Soon as the sun set and rose on

Saturday, I knew . . . And then the news yesterday, saying that y'all . . ." She shuddered and gasped and crumpled into a ball.

Out in the hallway, Alberta wept and called on Jesus.

Colin sat next to Regina on the bed. I perched in the chair at the desk.

And we sat like that until the billowing curtains lay flat against the window.

Alberta entered the room and handed her daughter a box of tissues.

Regina plucked several sheets from the box, then wiped her face. Then, she sobbed into her hands again.

Colin moved so that Alberta could sit next to her daughter and hold her.

"We need to ask a few questions," I said. "We need to know what happened that day, okay? I know this is hard, but it's very important."

Regina took several deep breaths, hiccupping as she exhaled. "Uh huh."

Alberta took her daughter's hand and kissed it.

Regina wiped her eyes with her sleeve. "On Friday, my mom went to get Nita from school. Nita gets out late cuz she had newspaper—she's one of the photographers."

"And where did she go to school?" Colin asked.

"Madison."

My pulse jumped—I was a Madison alum. But then so was almost every kid who lived in this area.

"And where were you?" Colin asked Regina.

The woman scratched her cheek, then cleared her throat. "I had an appointment."

We waited for the rest of the explanation.

Regina sat there, though, scratching her cheek, staring at the carpet.

"I waited in the car for twenty minutes," Alberta said,

ending the silence. "Then, I went to the classroom. Mr. Bishop—he's over the newspaper—he was getting ready to leave. He said that Nita didn't come to newspaper, which was odd cuz she went to school."

"So Mom called Nita's cell phone," Regina said, finding her voice again. "No answer. Mom called *me* and told me that Nita wasn't at school, that she didn't know *where* she was. I flipped the hell out cuz that didn't make no sense. I was like, *What you mean, she ain't there?*"

"I drove over to the mall," Alberta recalled, "and walked around Walmart cuz that's where she gets her pictures printed. But she wasn't there. She wasn't anywhere."

"When I got home," Regina continued, "I started looking around the streets. I asked *everybody*: 'Did y'all see Nita? Y'all talk to Nita today?' Nobody knew nothing."

"And I didn't believe that," Alberta said with an angry shake of her head. "Not for one second. Folks just don't up and . . ." She choked and clutched her neck. "After talking with some of her friends and with Mr. Bishop . . ." She shook her head and gazed at the carpet. "Nobody had seen her since lunchtime."

"Gone since lunch and nobody noticed?" Colin gawked at me. *What the hell?*

"When did you call the police?" I asked.

"Around eight thirty Friday night," Alberta whispered.

I did the math: 12:30 to 8:30. You could drive from Los Angeles to Las Vegas and back. In eight hours, you could fly from Los Angeles to Miami. Forty percent of children abducted were killed before we were even called. Within twenty-four hours, ninety percent of those abducted kids were dead. Chanita missing for eight hours? Too much time.

"The cops who took the report didn't seem worried," Regina said. "They thought she was probably off with some boy doing who knows what. I knew she wasn't cuz Nita not

76

that type. But this time I hoped that they was right. I hoped she had just run away, that she just wanted out of this place for a little bit. At that point, I didn't care. I just wanted her to come home." She sank into her mother's arms again and wept.

And we waited.

Regina wiped her wet eyes on her robe's sleeve, then smiled to herself. "Taking pictures was gonna get her outta here. Back when she was little, I used to give her those cheap little throwaway cameras and she'd run around, snapping everything, telling us to say 'cheese.' One day, I took one of the cameras to Walmart to be developed. And I was saying to myself, *Why am I throwing my money away? This girl probably took pictures of fingers and feet.*"

She closed her eyes as she remembered. "She took pictures of her dolls, of my mom, of me. But they were *good* pictures. *Really* good. I was like, *Wow, my baby took these?* I got 'em somewhere . . ." She started to stand, but sunk back to the bed.

"When was the last time *you* saw Chanita?" I asked.

"I dropped her off at school like I do every morning," Regina recalled. "She was wearing these new jeans she had begged me to buy. They was those low-cut ones. You know, the ones that show your panties whenever you bend over? I thought they was too sexy for a thirteen-year-old, but all the other girls was wearin' them, and she kept begging me and begging me to buy them, and so I gave in."

She grimaced and glared at the closet, the place that had provided sanctuary for those low-rise jeans. "I seen how the boys looked at her. They used to always say, *Ooh girl, you got some pretty eyes.* And . . . He probably saw her in them, and she was already curvy, more of a woman at thirteen than *I* was at thirteen. Them jeans called too much attention to her body."

"Whatever she wore," Colin whispered, "didn't give anyone the right to hurt her."

Regina squeezed the bridge of her nose. "I just wanna wake up from this."

"Tell me about the days before she disappeared," I said. "Was everything okay? Did you two hang out, argue . . . ?"

Regina chewed her bottom lip as her eyes turned hard. "I had been . . . *away,* and I was just gettin' back into everything, so . . ."

I pulled the chair closer to Regina. "Did Chanita have a phone?"

Regina nodded. "One of those cheap little LG phones."

"Did you have a family locater on it?" Colin asked, scribbling into his memo pad.

She frowned. "Huh? We can't afford that shit."

Colin and I looked at each other. Then I touched Regina's wrist. "We're asking—"

"I don't need some dumb electronic whatever *now,*" she spat. "Unless it's gon' bring her back to life or something."

"What about an e-mail account?" I asked.

"Chanita Lords at Gmail dot com," she said. "But she only used it for this online tutoring academy and for YouTube."

Thinking about those needle injection marks and the broken foot, I asked, "Was Chanita diabetic? Any recent injuries?"

"Nah," Regina said. "She was healthy." She turned to her mother.

Alberta nodded. "She was fit as a fiddle."

"Do you have any idea who would harm her?" Colin asked.

Regina's leg jiggled up and down. "I tried to keep Nita away from Ontrel Shaw's nasty ass. He live over in Hillside Manor. Anyway, I threatened her. Told her to stay away from him cuz he was too old for her. He ain't going nowhere even if you gave him a map and a bus pass. I told her that I was gonna take her camera, that I was gonna send her to Saint Louis to live with her other grandma. Nothing worked. It was the only thing she disobeyed me about."

Regina covered her mouth as her eyebrows crumpled. "I just didn't want her to get pregnant. I kept begging her to wait, to just hold off. She told me that she and Ontrel wasn't interested in having sex." She rolled her eyes. "Come on now. What grown man you know ain't interested in sex?"

I cocked an eyebrow. "Ain't no grown man I know."

"If she got pregnant," Regina said, "I was goin' straight to the police." She took a shaky deep breath and pushed it out. "One time, I found condoms in her backpack. If she wasn't havin' sex, why she got condoms then? Ontrel better hope y'all don't find none of his DNA on her."

"You shouldn't hope that, either," Colin said. Flushed, a vein pulsed in his neck.

"*Excuse* me?" Regina tilted her head.

I tossed my partner a glare, then said, "Let's—"

"You don't know a damned thing *about* me," Regina spat at Colin.

I held up a hand. "Let's get back to what's real, right now," I said, shooting one last glare at Colin. "Back to identifying anyone who could hurt Chanita."

Colin gave a "whatever" shrug, then turned away to look at pictures on Chanita's desk.

"Other than Ontrel," Regina said with a new edge in her voice, "people think Eighteenth Street had something to do with it. And then there's the Mexican dude down in apartment one. The cops asked him some questions when Nita first disappeared. His name's Raul Moriaga."

Ontrel Shaw had also mentioned Moriaga.

"You know if he's been in trouble before?" I asked, writing in my binder.

79

"He been to jail for molesting kids," Alberta said. "I'd catch him staring at Nita."

Colin and I exchanged looks.

"What about any men in Chanita's life that were around?" I asked.

Regina crossed her arms. "Like what *kind* of men?"

"Like boyfriends of yours?"

"What about them?" Regina spat.

"Were they around a lot, and were they around Chanita at all?"

She crossed her legs. "I don't know what you asking. They came over sometimes. They knew who she is."

"*They?*" Colin asked, pen paused on the pad. "How many—?"

"Your last relationship was when?" I interrupted.

Regina squinted at me. "I just broke up with somebody, and he moved out a month ago."

"He lived *here*?" Colin asked. "With your *daughter*?"

Regina scowled. "Why you got a problem with me? Why you talkin' to me like *I'm* the one who killed her?"

I touched Regina's clenched fist. "I'm gonna need the names of your last ex as well as any other ex-boyfriends who knew Chanita. We want to talk to everyone, because right now we don't know who could've done this."

She pulled her glare from Colin to gape at me. "I didn't . . ." Her eyes misted with tears as she tugged at the kimono's belt. "Didn't have to worry about Nita. Other than hanging around Ontrel, she stayed out of trouble. She was nerdy. That's why them girls that hang out around here kept jumpin' her. For being a nerd the first time, and then they jumped her again cuz ShaQuan—the one who lives in this complex—she wants to be with Ontrel. They broke her arm, and some other bones I ain't never heard of, over a thug."

"Is Nita's dad around?" Colin asked.

"He's away," Alberta said.

"Away *where*?" I asked.

Regina shrugged, then looked toward the window.

"You know how that can be," Alberta said to me. "They here. They not here. Ain't nobody's fault. It just . . . is."

Colin sighed. "Any male relatives—?"

"Why y'all keep blamin' the victim?" Alberta shouted.

"We need to know *everything*," I said. "Feelings be *damned*. If you want us to find out who killed her—"

"Everybody in jail, okay?" Regina snarled. "Satisfied? We hood rats. Is that what you wanna hear, Miss Detective Who Made It Out?"

Colin placed his hands on his hips. "Look—"

I gave him a slight headshake. *Let's not go there.*

Regina glared at me and pointed at Colin. "*He* needs to get the fuck outta my house. Matter of fact, you *also* can get the fuck—"

"Reggie," Alberta said. "They here to help."

Regina stood, hands on her hips. "Let's see how your white ass do out there without your ghetto tour guide."

Alberta shushed her daughter. "Relax, now. None of this is helping Nita." To Colin, she said, "She's just . . . just . . ."

Colin blinked at me—I nodded. *Relax.* He sighed, then flipped a page in his notepad.

"This newspaper teacher, Mr. Bishop," I said. "What's his relationship with Nita?"

"He's very involved," Alberta said. "He's also her counselor, and so he pays a lot of attention to her. I think she had a crush on him." She allowed herself to smile.

"Did that worry you?" I asked as I wrote 'MR. BISHOP' in my notes.

Regina shrugged. "That's normal, ain't it? I mean, he's

81

cute, smart, about somethin'. The only positive man in her life. I'd be worried if she *didn't* like him."

"Were they together a lot?" I asked.

"He drove her to stuff," Regina explained. "Photo contests, art exhibits . . . He believed in her more than anybody else did at that school. And he tried to get those girls suspended for all that they did to her." She hid her face behind her hands. "I miss her so much. It's like a giant piece of me is just gone. I'd do anything just to have her back with me and . . ." Regina gasped, then bent over to sob into her lap.

"It's okay, Reggie," Alberta said, patting her daughter's back. "Nita ain't in no more pain. She takin' pictures of the angels now."

"I need to search her room," I whispered, search warrant in my hand. "Just to see if there's anything that will tell us if she went to meet someone or—"

Regina stared at the court order. "Do I have to stay here?"

"No. I'll also need Nita's phone number to see who she called."

Alberta rambled off her granddaughter's phone number.

"It's Moriaga," Regina announced. "He shouldn't even be around here. Why y'all even let him out of jail? He's a predator." She shuffled to the door, but stopped in her step. "Y'all see us and only look at the outside. *They poor, so we don't need to do nothing.* Y'all thought she hung out and smoked weed and slept with bangers like Ontrel and that's all she was about. But we ain't all the same up in here."

Regina peered at me with granite eyes, determined to make me understand, to make me *remember.* "Chanita watched *Big Bang Theory* and took pictures and she was on the honor roll. Sometimes, she made me get up at the crack of dawn so we could see the sunrise. She was my Nita." She swallowed and crumpled the search warrant into a ball. "And she was better than what I would've ever been."

Colin and I found nothing strange in those drawers. No inappropriate pictures or diaries or love letters. Just lots of photos. Still, we shot pictures and then confiscated a yearbook, three birthday cards, and a notebook.

"Ready?" Colin held seven evidence bags filled with Chanita's things.

I glanced around the room one last time. *That.* I took a picture with my phone, then walked to the window. Above the bed's headboard hung a framed photograph: a vine of dusty-purple, star-shaped flowers. I lifted the frame from its hook.

"Why do you wanna take *that*?" Colin asked.

I stared at those flowers—yellow beaks, bent-back petals—until spots swirled before me. Finally, I shrugged.

I didn't know why I wanted that picture—I didn't believe in voodoo or premonitions. But this picture . . . There was something about this picture.

13

IT WAS ALMOST ELEVEN O'CLOCK BY THE TIME COLIN AND I REACHED OUR DESKS in the Detectives' Bureau of the Southwest Division Community Station.

Pepe stood at the copier, watching INFORMATION WANTED flyers with Chanita's picture whoosh into the tray. Luke, goofy grin in place, held court with formerly sexy secretary Ruthie, who loved cops and all things leopard print. Her thick hip butted against the arm of Luke's chair—and Luke didn't mind that hip or her obnoxious perfume.

Someone had appropriated a whiteboard and had gridded names of basketball teams in the NCAA Championship: Duke, UCLA, Kentucky, and on and on. The handcuffed suspects seated here and there talked smack with detectives— not about their arrests but about the teams that would make it to the Final Four.

The red voice-mail light on my phone blinked. Neither of the two messages had been left by Brooks or Zucca, but I could save fifty dollars on my family phone plan or make another donation to the Los Angeles Police Memorial Foundation. My iPhone chimed—an e-mail from Dr. Zach. *Good morning! Just wanted you to have my email and a picture. It really was great meeting you yesterday. Hope your wrist is better. You followed doctor's orders right?* He had attached a selfie, taken at a nurse's station.

My stomach gurgled and pulled my attention away from the e-mail—Alberta Jackson had gifted Colin and me with a plate of corn muffins. I had gobbled my six on the drive back to the station, and now, corn meal, butter, and PCP sat in my stomach like cement.

"I've never seen anybody eat corn muffins like that," Colin said, chuckling.

"I've never eaten muffins like that." I sniffed the vase of red-and-yellow-striped roses placed near my computer monitor. Yesterday, before our lunch date, Sam had sent me these roses, and this morning they still looked fresh and young. Simple beauty in my jacked-up world.

Colin took a long gulp from a near-empty DayQuil bottle, then shivered.

"Your poor liver." I reached into my coat pocket and pulled out the figurine.

He blew his nose, and it sounded like fluid between his ears was being vacuumed. "What's that?"

"No clue."

"Why do you have it?"

I placed the piece on top of my monitor. "Someone put it on my car this morning."

"Why?"

"Don't know. It was just . . . sitting there."

Colin grunted.

"Let's see." I took a picture of the figurine with my phone, then used Google image search. "Here she is."

Colin rolled over to my desk and stared at my monitor.

"Melpomene," I said. "The Muse of tragedy."

Colin chuckled and pointed to her feet. "Those boots look like yours."

I pointed at the head she clutched. "Mask of tragedy."

He pointed to the knife. "And a deadly weapon. She *is* you." He rolled back to his desk.

"Melpomene." I tore my eyes away from the Greek gods Web site and held up the list of Regina's ex-boyfriends. "I'll start on this."

"Have at it," he said. "What the hell's up with that family? No men, too many men, but not the right man. Nobody married? Nobody living . . . normal?"

"Tell me, Detective Cleaver, what is 'normal'?"

"C'mon, Lou." He rolled his eyes. "Okay, I'll play. What is 'normal'? Mom, dad, kids. Or mom, mom, kids. Dad, dad, kids. Everybody together for dinner. Church and parks and bikes and chores and shit. One parent tucks you in at night; the other makes you waffles in the morning. Or quinoa or flax or whatever the fuck you all eat out here for breakfast. That progressive enough for you?"

"Your father wasn't around much to make you waffles or take you bike riding."

"He's air force."

"He tuck you in at night? He go to church with you on Sundays?"

Colin twisted his lips.

I said nothing and let silence complete my argument.

He said, "Fine."

"We need to find out where Chanita was stolen on Friday," I said.

"ID a place that may have video? Which can be anywhere."

I nodded. "And . . ." I pulled the case file from my bag and found Chanita's missing person report. "Murder book—I started completing reports last night, and Gwen probably has a few things that can go in."

Colin rolled his chair over to my desk. "Is she working the other missing girl?"

"Let's see." I typed "Trina Porter" into our database. "Gwen Zapata listed as lead." I skimmed Trina's report. "Wow."

"What?"

"Trina lives on Santo Tomas. A few blocks west of Chanita."

"Connected?"

"Too early in the case for such dramatic statements."

He opened his binder, flipped pages, then jabbed the numbers on my phone. After three rings, the voice-mail lady announced that the mailbox for this number—Chanita's—was full.

"Probably Regina and Alberta calling her all night," Colin said.

My turn: I punched in a number I now knew by heart.

Ringing . . . ringing . . . The voice-mail man told me to leave a message.

"Hi, Vanessa," I said. "This is Detective Norton again. I really need to talk with you." I left my number, then ended the call.

Pepe came over and held up a flyer he'd created. "I'll get a few cadets to pass these out. Oh, I e-mailed you the shots Luke took of the crowds yesterday."

I peered at the flyer. "Only ten thousand dollars for a reward? That's stingy."

"Lot of missing girls," Pepe said with a shrug. "And they just upped the reward for the Porter girl to fifteen K."

I turned back to my computer. Along with the missing person report, the database also contained pictures of Trina Porter. She was a brown-skinned girl, pretty, long braids in one picture, and a short, slick bob in the second. Missing since Friday, March 7.

"Gone thirteen days," I said. "Taken on a Friday, just like Chanita."

"And she lives in the same area as Chanita," Colin told Pepe.

"Get the map," I said, my gaze still on Trina's picture. "The big, wipeable one."

According to the information we had, Trina had been last seen at the bookstore down in Leimert Park. She wore a pink hoodie, purple jeans, and purple Nikes.

Colin pinned the wall map that showed our policing area.

"Where was Chanita last seen?" Pepe asked.

"School," I said, "except she wasn't—"

Laughter interrupted our conversation. Luke and Ruth.

"He still work here?" Colin asked.

Pepe and I gave each other looks.

"He's finding himself right now," Pepe said.

I returned my attention to the map. At Nicolet and Hillcrest, I pushed in a blue pin. "Any other girls we want to include?"

Pepe sat at my desk and clicked around on the computer. "Maybe, but these two dates are a little older. Bethany Wilson, fourteen, missing since November seventeenth, lives on Parthenon."

I push-pinned Parthenon Street.

"Tawanna McFuller," Pepe continued, "thirteen, went missing on November twenty-fifth. Lives on Gelber Place."

"Same neighborhood?" Pepe asked.

I nodded.

"Connected?" Colin wondered.

I stared at the map, at the proximity of each blue pushpin to another. So close. Too close. In age. In race. In residence. Still, I said, "Too soon."

"So now what?" Colin asked.

I turned to him. "*Now,* we take a field trip."

14

THE FIELD TRIP WAS DOWN THE HALL, TO THE LEFT, AND INTO THE TINY CORNER cubicle of a baggy-eyed lady detective who had been working missing persons cases for too long. Gwen Zapata, pewter-skinned and hunched, had already been slumped and defeated when she transferred from Seventy-seventh to Southwest six years ago. And, now, she blinked at me from behind her desk. "You're fuckin' joking, right?"

I gaped at Colin, who stood in Gwen's cubicle entryway. Then, I looked back at Gwen. "Missing people *do* get found. Elizabeth Smart, those three women in Cleveland, and . . ." My words caught in my throat as I took in the walls of her little office—every space had been covered in rainbow-colored flyers. HAVE YOU SEEN HER?

Gwen snatched her blue LAPD stress ball from the desktop and squeezed as she swiveled in her chair. "Those girls you named? Exceptions to the rule. You know and I know that every hour that passes, the chances of finding any of these girls—"

"Especially brown-eyed girls with melanin issues?" I snarked.

She snorted, then waved to the flyers. "Black, white, plaid. The chances are slim to none. And I'd put my money on none every time. Speaking of which"—she turned her attention to

Colin—"are you the one collecting?" She opened a desk drawer and grabbed her wallet.

"Lou is," Colin said.

Gwen handed me a twenty-dollar bill. "Michigan State."

I pocketed the money. "So when Chanita's folks called—"

She raised a hand. "Hold on. If you've come over here to blame me—"

"Why would I do that? You do something or *not* do something?"

Gwen rolled her eyes. "They were holding out on me, okay? I did the best I could."

Detective Peet had thought the same of my mother—*she's holding out*—and so he hadn't searched for Tori as hard as he should have. "Girls do shit" had been his philosophy. And, now, I wanted to scream at Gwen, *Bullshit on you doing your best*. But I couldn't isolate her—we needed as many helping hands as possible.

"So no one knows *where* Chanita was taken?" I asked.

"A Mrs. Watson," Gwen said, "who lives on King, not far from the school, says she saw Chanita at the bus stop in front of Krispy Kreme. But we haven't been able to confirm that yet."

"You talk to anybody in Eighteenth Street?" Colin asked.

Gwen smirked. "Why would I talk to *them*?"

"Because they're one of the most violent gangs in the city," I said, my voice tight. "Because rumors abound that they did it."

"Says who?"

"Says everybody we've talked to."

She waved her hand. "Bah."

"Well," I said, "we'll talk to them since, you know, we wanna solve the case and all."

"I did question Ontrel Shaw," Gwen said. "He sometimes beats the girls he dates."

"Says who?" I asked.

"Rumors abound," Gwen cracked.

"He been arrested for a domestic?" I asked.

"Bunch of other misdemeanors but not that one," Gwen said. "Give him time, though."

"What about Trina?" Colin asked.

Gwen's ears reddened as she tossed the stress ball back onto her desk. "I don't appreciate you two comin' at me like I'm sitting here cuttin' coupons all fucking day."

"I see no coupons," I said. "So Trina—any similarity to Chanita?"

"Trina's just like Nita," Gwen said. "She ain't your typical missing girl. Neither kid did drugs. Neither were runaways, nor did they trick. They got good grades in school. Hell: they *went* to school. Trina's family, though. They're very different from Nita's."

"How?" I asked.

Gwen shrugged. "For starters, Regina got out on the Tuesday or Wednesday before—"

"Got out?" Colin said. "As in got out of *jail*?"

"You surprised?" Gwen asked. "The woman's got sticky fingers and a quick pen. Chanita was tired of her fuck-ups, and they fought, Chanita and Regina, up until that Friday morning when Regina gave in about those tight-ass jeans."

"And Trina's family?" I asked.

"Mom—Liz—is hardworking, some type of legal secretary. Husband was killed in Afghanistan last summer. Church folks. Nobody in jail. No men hanging around. Not a day goes by without six phone calls from her. At this point, I don't know what to tell that poor lady."

"But you *are* still looking," Colin said.

"No, I'm not looking." Gwen rolled her eyes, then met mine.

"I saw that Trina Porter also attended Madison," I said.

"Uh huh."

"What about Bethany and Tawanna?" Colin asked.

"View Park Prep over on Slauson," Gwen said. "And to answer your original question: do I think Trina's case is related to Chanita's?"

"Or to Tawanna's or Bethany's?" I added. "Cuz if so . . . you know what that means."

"You do your job," she said, turning away from us, "and let me do mine. Now if you'd both get the fuck outta my office . . .'"

"So, I guess we're done?" I asked.

"Yep," she said without a glance back at us.

As we stomped back to our own squad room, Colin tapped me on the shoulder. "Zapata's been doing this too long. It's kinda like when you can't smell skunk anymore. It's not that tomato juice works, but it's olfactory exhaustion."

"Maybe."

"You're gonna have to compartmentalize," he advised. "Distance yourself. Say that Tori's case—"

"Watching *Dr. Phil* and reading *National Geographic Kids* won't make you a yogi, Colin. Don't psychoanalyze me today."

"Just wanna help." He ambled over to the March Madness whiteboard.

"Noted. Thank you." I sank into my chair.

A postcard sat in my mail tray. It was of an oil painting of nine naked young women bathing in a lake. A man kneeled on the nearby shore, his hand dipped into the water. *Hylas and the Nymphs, 1896.*

No stamp. No return address. My name had been written in green-inked, block letters. There was a message:

QLRM GSV DROW IFNKFH. BLF ZIV DVOXLNV.

Weird shit. I always got weird shit. Santa got mail from preschoolers, and I got postcards. And when Colin returned to his desk, I held it up. "This was in my tray."

He rolled over to my desk and stared at the message.

QLRM GSV DROW IFNKFH. BLF ZIV DVOXLNV.

He shrugged. "Weird shit." When I didn't agree, he cocked his head. "No?"

"Oh, it's weird," I said. "I'm just curious, since it doesn't smell like pee or weed. So it's not from one of our regular nuts. The more I stare at the letters . . . It looks like a puzzle maybe."

He grunted. "Okay."

"The most frequently used letter in the English language is *E*."

"And you know that because . . . ?"

"I'm smart." I grabbed pens and a pad. "But the lonely *Q* that starts the message is not an *E*. Probably a *T* or an *M* most likely."

"Most likely," he mocked.

I ignored him. "The most frequently used three-letter word is 'the.' "

He pointed to *GSV*. "Right there."

"Let's solve it, shall we?" I copied the message onto the pad in black ink, then, in red pen, wrote *T* above the black *G*, an *H* above the black *S*, and *E* above the black *V*.

"My brain hurts," he complained, "and I'm bored."

"Shh."

"You do this a lot?"

I nodded. "Grew up doing puzzles. My mother likes those big books of crosswords, cryptograms . . ." I slipped letters in, crossed letters out until . . .

JOIN THE WILD RUMPUS. YOU ARE WELCOME.

I chuckled like Ralphie from *A Christmas Story* decoding his secret message from Little Orphan Annie. Except my postcard and secret message weren't an Ovaltine commercial.

"Is this a marketing piece?" Colin asked. "For one of your ex-hubby's video games?"

"A game with nymphs? Maybe. He told me that he's working on some . . . Wait. Wild rumpus. Maybe he's doing steam-punk meets Greek myth meets *Where the Wild Things Are*." I slipped the card and its translated message into my binder.

"I liked that story," Colin said. "But steam-punk makes me nervous."

"Women who can spell make you nervous."

Join the wild rumpus. You are welcome.

What was Greg selling now?

No time for fake puzzles, though, when I had a real puzzle to solve.

The intercom on my desk phone beeped. "Lou." It was Lieutenant Rodriguez.

"Yep?" I said.

"Get over here. *Now*."

15

I SAT IN THE CHAIR ON THE OTHER SIDE OF THE BIG MAN'S BATTERED OAK DESK, which was piled high with stacks of aging manila folders. Hunched over, my chest almost hit my knees, not because he had torn into me—we were still in the trailers before the feature had started—but because no heat from the sun snuck past the iron grating on his windows and because he kept his office at ten degrees. And I've never thrived in the cold.

"You're stepping on toes," Lieutenant Rodriguez said. He rearranged the collection of Dodgers bobbleheads shadowed by all the dead-people folders. "You're stepping on toes and you haven't even had the case for a whole two days yet."

"She's half-assing it," I complained, "and she's a tattle-tell in addition to being lazy."

"You can't compare Chanita's case to Trina's, okay? It's too soon for that." He twisted in his high-backed chair as his gray vampire eyes burned into mine. "Stay the hell away from Zapata. She'll bring you down with her 'Abandon hope all ye who enter' bullshit."

My stomach tightened as the Matt Kemp bobblehead on my boss's desk nodded in agreement. With the only light coming from a desk lamp, the toy's shadow played on the wall. And I thought of that episode of *Twilight Zone,* the one that—

Lieutenant Rodriguez snapped his fingers. "Hey. You listening?"

I gave him a practiced smile.

He waited for me to speak, but when I only continued to smile, he asked, "Worried?"

"Not yet, but I'm driving to the station to board the train."

"You've worked harder cases. The eighty-year-old Jane Doe in the alley. That murder-suicide right after Christmas. And then there's crazy-ass Christopher Chatman and crazy-bitch Sarah Oliver. She still hiding down in Venezuela?"

"Yeah." In addition to helping Chatman kill his wife and kids, Sarah Oliver had double-tapped her husband, Ben, in their Infiniti SUV, leaving his body and that car in a mall parking lot. Then, she'd scooped up their daughter from Ben's grandmother's house and boarded an early-morning flight to South America.

"That case was different," I now said to my boss. "None of those cases were—"

"Serial?" He leaned forward, elbows on his desk. "Max Crase did your sister Tori, Monique and Macie Darson, the college—"

"But this one just feels . . ."

"Nasty."

Ice crackled across my chest. "Girls."

"I know. And I understand. I got two at Chanita's age, remember?"

Someone knocked on the door.

Lieutenant Rodriguez pointed at me. "You got this. I'm counting on you." Then, he shouted, "Yeah?"

The door opened, and Colin's head popped in. "Dr. Brooks is on the line with results."

I rushed back out into the bright glare of fluorescent light, back to my metal desk with Colin and Lieutenant Rodriguez trailing behind me. I motioned for Luke and Pepe to join the huddle, then hit SPEAKER on my phone. "Hey, Doc. We're all here. What's up?" I grabbed a pen and a notepad and plopped into my chair.

"First," Brooks said, "the bad news: the rape-kit results came back. They were positive. The good news: he left semen."

I tapped the pad with my pen. "That's pretty bold, ain't it? Not using a condom?"

"I'll send it out for DNA," Brooks said, "which, you know, takes time. And I couldn't find any prints on her body."

"He'll leave semen but no fingerprints?" I said.

"The X-rays also showed a recently healed right arm," the ME reported.

"Chanita's mother told us that she had been jumped by school bullies," I offered.

"Would you like to know why there weren't a lot of bugs?" Brooks asked.

"Yes," we all said.

"Those needle marks in her thighs," Brooks said. "He injected her."

"With?" I asked.

"Bug repellant."

I gawked at the phone, then at my team. And we stared at each other in silence, confused by Brooks's words. "Huh?" I said. "Come again?"

"Bug repellent."

"Before or after he killed her?" Colin asked.

"After."

"Why?" I asked.

Brooks chuckled. "That's your job, Detective, not mine." He was turning pages. "Some other tox reports came back. No alcohol or recreational drugs in her system, *but* this is a bit strange. There were low concentrations, just traces, really, of atropine."

No one spoke—just looked at each other and shrugged.

"Umm," I said, "you're gonna have to tell us . . ."

"It's a toxin," Brooks explained, "but a nonirritant, which is why her internal organs weren't inflamed. And you don't need a lot of it to kill someone."

"Painless?" I asked.

"No. Bodily fluids dry up first—spit, tears, sweat. Then, after a few minutes, the body numbs. You close your eyes, and that's that."

I wrote the word carefully in my notes, as though misspelling "atropine" would cause my own numbness, dehydration, and death. "How is it given?"

"For Chanita, I can't tell right now," Brooks admitted. "But in the few cases I've worked before, the patient drank it as tea."

"Atropine," Lieutenant Rodriguez said, staring at the word on my pad.

"Yes, sir," Brooks said. "You may know the plant name."

"Which is?" I asked, pen poised.

"Deadly nightshade."

16

DEADLY NIGHTSHADE.

The violet-colored bloom flashed onto the large monitor in the conference room where we now gathered. A half-finished large pepperoni pizza and two cans of Coke sat in the middle of the table near the projector. On the room's north wall, Colin had pinned scenes from Bonner Park—with Chanita in the shot and then out of the shot, the trails, the bluffs, the bowl of green that separated the park from those hillside homes.

"Chanita took a picture of this flower," I said, tapping the laptop directional buttons. I reached into the expandable file and pulled out that picture. "This one looks different. In her picture, the petals are all open."

"Does that happen at a certain time of year?" Pepe asked.

I scrolled down the Web page. "Flowers appear in June, July, and September."

"She couldn't have just taken that picture, then," Colin said. "Too early in the year."

"So where was she last summer?" Pepe asked.

"We need to talk to her mom again," I said, adding this question to my notepad.

"And *why* did she take a picture of it?" Luke wondered.

"Guess we need to find that out, too." I scanned the article that accompanied the picture now on-screen. "*Atropa belladonna* plant. Absorbed through skin and ingested . . . very poisonous . . . difficulty swallowing . . . paralysis . . . death." I looked up from the laptop. "Shit."

Colin and Lieutenant Rodriguez both stared at the image of the deadly flower. Pepe wrote in his notepad as Luke studied Chanita's shot.

I wiped my greasy fingers on a napkin. "So what do we know about him?" I stepped to the whiteboard, grabbed a red marker, and wrote "MONSTER" at the top of the board.

"He's male," Luke offered.

"He's a sexual predator," Pepe added.

I wrote those two things, made an arrow, then scribbled an action item: "Check sex offenders near vic."

"Why would he leave semen behind?" Colin wondered. "Either he wants to get caught or he knows he'll be difficult to trace."

All of that went on the board.

"He has some knowledge about poisons," Pepe said.

"Cuz you just don't drive to Walgreens and buy atropine," I said, writing.

"He breaks shit," Colin said. "Her left foot, maybe."

I put a question mark by the word, then added, "Her tooth, possibly."

"*Her,*" Pepe added.

"How poetic," Luke snarked.

My face warmed, and I shot Luke a "you're an asshole" glare.

"He's strong," Pepe said, ignoring his partner. "He carried her to that spot."

"He knows the park," Lieutenant Rodriguez offered. "Not just the hours, but the terrain."

"He's possessive," I added.

The men gave me quizzical looks.

"He injected her with repellent to keep the bugs away,

interrupting the natural . . ." I narrowed my eyes. "Interrupting the natural order—he thinks he's God. Bugs, yes, but also her life, her tooth—*he* took all of that. None of it happened naturally. Her foot—*he* broke it to keep her from running. And, finally, he killed her—the ultimate act of a god."

"The Lord giveth," Luke said, nodding.

"And the Lord taketh away," Lieutenant Rodriguez completed.

We shuffled through the pictures Luke had taken of the crowds at Bonner Park. Every shade in the genetic pool was represented. More men than women. Older—who could jog and walk in a park at midday on a Wednesday? Each face presented the same levels of interest and fear. No one—no *man*—appeared to be too invested in what we had found on trail 5.

"I don't think I see him," I said, pushing away my stack of pictures. "And the witness statements are boring as hell. Everyone saw something and saw nothing."

"What about Chanita?" Colin asked. "What do we know about *her*?"

"A thirteen-year-old in a relationship with an older man," I said. "Ontrel or maybe even the monster. She has a special talent—photography. Poor, gifted, and black."

Lieutenant Rodriguez rubbed his face, then pulled down his cheeks.

I caught his eye, then cocked an eyebrow. *See? Just like I said: this won't be easy.*

Luke reached for another slice of pizza. "She got any *amigas*?"

"Probably." I wrote "Talk to friends" as another action item, then stared at Chanita's profile. Which of these things had attracted the monster? "Let's look at our suspects so far." Then, I made a list.

1. *Ontrel*
2. *the Mexican Dude in Apt 1*
3. *Mr. Bishop at school*
4. *Regina Drummond's boyfriends*
5. *18th Street*

"Knowing that she died from atropine poisoning," I said, "I'm close to crossing off the gang-bangers. But I won't. Not yet. And I'll run the pedos in the area, see who's good for this."

Colin would continue to handle the murder book and join me in interviewing the entire city of Los Angeles.

"I'll work with the Gang Unit on those *hijos de putas*," Luke said. "Somebody caught up in that sweep last week probably wanna make a deal by now."

"And handle Nita's phone, too." I turned to Pepe. "I don't know if we need to worry much about family finances, so comb through any tips that come in and talk to her friends." And to Lieutenant Rodriguez: "Maybe we can get press coverage on this. I'll ask—"

"Don't know if that's a good idea," he said, eyes narrowed.

I bristled. "She'll be fine."

"Lou . . ."

"Sy's fine," I said, "and we need the community involved."

Syeeda had also grown up in the Jungle—her dad worked with my dad, both driving city buses. And, like me, she and her brother and sister, Kenny and Eva, had made it out. She was now editor in chief of *OurTimes,* a *Times* supplement that addressed issues facing blacks living in the "urban" areas left ragged by the Rodney King–verdict riots and the Rampart-LAPD scandal. Published twice a week and having a circulation of 55,000, *OurTimes* usually provided nothing hard-hitting or controversial. Only articles on church renovations, police station open houses, and high school sports, all drowned in a pond of ads for fish markets and grocery stores. Sometimes, an article that fulfilled the paper's original mission found its way in, but not often. Because *OurTimes* didn't do investigative reporting, and it sure as hell didn't win any Pulitzers.

And Syeeda hated that.

This article about Chanita Lords, though, would serve a purpose for us both.

After the meeting ended, Lieutenant Rodriguez came to stand with me at the whiteboard. "Solving this will be a feather in my cap. And your promotion to Detective *Sergeant*."

I crossed my arms as something pinged behind my eyes.

He chuckled and shook his head. "I know—I've said that too many times."

I placed the marker in the tray without comment. Black women and LAPD promotions went together like chips and vomit.

"I'll give you whatever you need," he said. "I'll call in every favor I got." He shoved his hands in his pockets, then nodded at the board. "When you crack this, when you stop this son of the devil . . . They'll *have* to pay attention. You'll solve it and get another stripe."

I stared at the "monster" list, at all the men in Chanita's life.

"What are you thinking?" my boss asked.

A new headache crackled on one side of my face. "Even though I know there's no such thing as total closure, I just want them to have it. For her people not to know . . . I don't want that for them."

My family and friends had scattered Tori's ashes months ago, yet I still expected to see her alive. *Is that her head in the grocery store? Is that her perfume?* My eyes never rested as I scanned faces in the crowds. That face, of course, was never hers. And then, I'd remember: she can't be Tori.

Tori's gone.

And I'd move on . . . Until the next time. At a farmers' market, at the movie theater or the grocery store. Still scanning faces. Still expecting to find Tori alive this time. Still chasing hope like the French boy chasing that goddamned red balloon.

17

OURTIMES WAS LOCATED ON CRENSHAW BOULEVARD, A MILE FROM TRAIL 5 IN
Bonner Park. The building did not exude the confidence and
importance of downtown's historic *Times* building with its
murals, chevrons, and stainless steel. *OurTimes* lived in a
single-story brown structure with smoked-glass windows
and a modest sign tagged with BPS and crossed-out 40NHC.

Colin had remained at his desk—I needed to handle Syeeda
alone. And, now, I climbed out of the Crown Vic, the headache
still thriving despite Advil chased by Diet Coke. The woody
aroma of barbecue from the joint across the street rode atop
the drizzle from gathering storm clouds. The cold air helped
ease the headache, but the respite would be very temporary.

Because Mike Summit, *OurTimes*'s assistant editor in
chief, all fake spray-tan and preternatural black hair, met me
in the lobby.

"Speak of the devil," he said.

"That's *Detective* Devil," I corrected.

Mike and I had met many lives ago: I was a uniform, and
he worked Metro. He was a poseur even then. Too scared to
lift the city's skirt and gape at the ugly, the scary, the what-
the-fuckery that existed there. He didn't like me much,
although we hadn't hung out together long enough for him to
make a proper assessment. Ten minutes together, and I had

assessed him plenty: dull, stupid, and humorless on his best days. The waxed Vandyke beard, the silver wire-rimmed glasses, the snakeskin boots, the lisp . . . His affectations grew like eyelashes—one flitting away only to be replaced by a thicker, shinier one.

"I'm here to serve and protect," I announced. "And you do what again?"

Mike rolled his eyes. "You haven't changed, I see. This way."

We didn't speak again until we had reached a cold, dark cubicle next to a roaring copier. He pointed to the dank space. "Syeeda's on a conference call. You can hang here for now."

I placed my bag on the desk. "Something wrong, Mike Summit?"

His cheeks colored. "Other than the fact that you're a power-hungry, badged thug in jack boots? Other than the fact that you beat Eli Moss—?"

"Are we talking about the same asshole who tried to burn down my house with me in it?"

"Other than the fact that you beat him to a pulp and got away with it?" he continued. "Other than the fact that the missing-girls story is *my* story and that *I'm* the one who initially reported on it months ago?"

I glanced at the flickering light above me—the fluorescent tube was filled with fly and termite corpses. "Yeah. Other than that."

"Other than the fact that you are here right now because you're friends with Syeeda?"

I smiled. "Other than that, too."

"Narcissism, pure and simple," Mike lisped. "I'm not gonna pretend otherwise. You know, Syeeda treats you with kid gloves. I had my own ideas—in particular, the lack of interest of law enforcement in this case, but did she want to hear them? Hell no. She had already decided to be sympathetic to you and your crew, who just stand around and sip coffee all day and let girls go dead and missing for days and weeks and months at a time."

I shrugged. "You got me. Girls *are* dead when I'm standing anywhere near them."

"As far as I'm concerned," he continued, "this is *my* assignment. I won't say that this is reverse-discrimination, but I strongly suspect that it is."

"Get off the cross, Mike. People need the wood. And also? It's *nepotism,* not 'narcissism.' And your way with words is probably why Syeeda is handling this story. That and the fact that you came to the Jungle that one time when we found the blue-haired hooker in the alley? It was in the middle of the day on a Monday and you stayed in your car with the doors locked. Remember that?"

Mike grayed.

I plopped into the chair, then plucked my cell phone from my bag.

"Are there any suspects?" Mike asked.

"Can't say." I checked e-mail: a forwarded prayer from Mom, a bookstore coupon for 30 percent off all fiction, and a new friend request from Facebook. Colin had also texted me: *Ontrel just gave DNA. &u got something from Sam. Oowee!*

The telephone on the desk chirped.

I grabbed the handset before Mike could. "*OurTimes.* How may I direct your inquiry?"

Mike muttered something, then wandered down the corridor.

Syeeda laughed. "You don't have to be so formal on internal calls."

"Just being a bitch."

"You? No way."

"Mike was keeping me company."

"Where is he now?"

"Hopefully, playing in traffic."

"Oh, dear," she said. "Come over and try not to shoot anybody."

Syeeda's large office, fly-free and bright with light, inhabited some other corner of the universe. A framed photograph of Syeeda standing with Walter Cronkite hung on the wall alongside her degree from UC Santa Cruz. The journalist sat at her desk, mock-ups in neat stacks near her keyboard. Her brown eyes were bloodshot, and her butterscotch complexion was losing the Pimple Blitzkrieg. No sleep. Too many french fries. She wore her usual outfit of gray slacks and a white button-down shirt, but with a variation: a red cashmere sweater instead of a gray one. She had captured her long hair into a ponytail. "Save the Paper" mode.

"I'm guessing Mike whined to you about the story," she said.

"Of course. And if I do this with you, I want control."

Syeeda crossed her arms. "Umm . . ."

"We want the same thing, Sy. Tell the world, find the killer, get justice. But we need to handle it—"

"Your way?"

"And with much discretion. Mike Summit will *not* have a big role in this. He's nothing but a fame-chasing he-whore."

Syeeda stood from the desk and wandered to the window. "It's raining again. Traffic's gonna be crazy tonight, and if it rains on Saturday, when the city's rolling Fortier's coffin down Crenshaw . . ."

I glanced out the window—so much water that I couldn't see the funeral home across the street. News vans had parked there—pretaping segments before Fortier's jazz funeral. "We both have a connection with the people there," I said, "with that neighborhood. They'll talk to you before they talk to

Mike or to any other *Times* snot who grew up in Palisades or Brentwood." I grinned. "Although they'd jump Mike. That man needs a good mugging."

Syeeda readjusted her ponytail. "He does, but not while on assignment. That's all you or I need right now. *Innocent white man attacked by black youths. Story at eleven.*"

"I can't really tell you much," I said. "Friends or not, this is a delicate one."

She nodded. "I want to make her *real*."

"I know, but I can't promise you a lot."

"Okay, okay."

"First, though. Chanita lived in my old apartment complex."

"Small world."

"And the woman who lives in her apartment lived there when we were kids. *And* she's Chanita's grandmother."

Syeeda's jaw dropped. "Get the hell out."

"Crazy, right? And I had a crush on one of her sons."

She smirked. "Let me guess: he had nice eyes."

I smiled and nodded. "And he had a wavy shag and his name was Paul and last time I saw him was in the backseat of a black and white. We caught him hot-wiring an IROC."

Syeeda tucked her knees beneath her. "So your childhood crush is Chanita's uncle."

"And who says Los Angeles is a big city? It's practically Mayberry."

"Since we're Mayberry, then," she said, "is Chanita's case related to Trina Porter's case?"

"Off the record?"

Syeeda nodded.

"Maybe."

"And is she related to the other girls who disappeared back in November?"

"Maybe. Same age, same neighborhood."

Syeeda closed her eyes, then rested her forehead against the window. "This is bad, huh?"

"Bad times two."

She reached beneath her desk and pulled out a white mixing bowl. "Spencer wouldn't even talk to me about it. He kept saying, 'It's fucked up, Sy. It's fucked up.' "

I pointed at her. "Which is why I can't trust Mike with this."

She wrinkled her nose. "He complained to my boss about this already. He's accusing me of reverse racism. I may have to throw him a bone."

My chest tightened. "Fine. Finger and toe bones, then. Nothing else or I'm ghost."

"So what else can you tell me? That no one else knows? *On* the record." She placed the bowl on the floor behind her chair. Plop . . . plop . . . plop . . .

And as raindrops fell into the bowl, I told her that Chanita's left foot had been broken and that she had been sexually assaulted.

"Any suspects?" she asked, writing on the closest legal pad.

"No," I said, "but we *may* have a person of interest. And please use that phrase. Not 'suspect.' No arrests are being planned for now, all right?"

She nodded, still writing.

Syeeda was one of my best friends—but she was also a reporter.

I couldn't trust her, either.

18

PEPE MET ME IN THE GARAGE, CIGARETTE STUCK BETWEEN HIS LIPS, DARK EYES red and swollen. His hair had lost its hold, and a thick lock draped over his forehead. He stepped back as I opened the driver's-side door. Then he said, "I don't know what to do."

I placed a hand on his shoulder. "He'll come around."

Pepe shook his head. "I shouldn't have told him. We were fine as we were."

"You and Luke have been partners for six years. You went to Catholic school together. You're Cecilia's godfather."

He snorted, then leaned against the car. "He said that he didn't care what the new pope says. He doesn't want a *fag* taking care of his daughter when he's gone."

A flare shot in my gut. "He *said* that?"

"He caught himself before he said the f-word. Not that the word matters." He tossed the cigarette to the ground. "He's gonna tell everybody. I know it."

Hands on my hips, I glared at the concrete. "I'm gonna talk to him."

"Lou—"

"Yes. Cuz fuck Luke, okay? He can cheat on his wife throughout their entire marriage but now he gets to be Catholic and shit? Not on my team. You've always had his back, and if that means nothing to him, he can fuckin' . . .

go kick rocks on Jefferson's team."

"L.T.—"

"Knows," I said, meeting his eyes. "All Rodriguez cares about is that whiteboard and having every one of those little blank squares checked by the end of the year."

"And Colin?"

"Colin barely cares about who *he's* sleeping with." I sighed. "How do you say 'Go to hell' in Korean?"

"*Toejora.*"

"Next time Luke makes a crack," I said, "tell him that *I* said, '*Toejora.*'"

Pepe reached into his jacket for the box of Camels. "I . . ." He tapped out a cigarette but shoved it back into the box. "I . . ."

I nodded. "Yeah. I know."

Someone in the squad room smelled like wet dog.

That stink, and not the homeless man spewing obscenities en route to an interrogation room, made me open my bottom desk drawer, grab the near-empty can of Febreze, and spray the air. I sniffed again, then sprayed in the direction of Watson's desk behind me.

Better, but only a little.

I rubbed my eyes, then stared at the nearby coat rack and millions of neckties hanging there. I focused back on the names written on my notepad, where I had crossed out just one name: Stalin Dickerson, the man who'd just moved out of Regina Drummond's apartment last month. Stalin had been in jail on weapons charges when Chanita went missing. The other ex, Maurizio Horsley, had no jacket, and his last known address was off Degnan Boulevard—a hop over from Madison Middle School.

I dialed Horsley's phone number.

"Yes?" A woman.

I identified myself and asked to speak with Maurizio.

"Mo is in Phoenix," she said, sounding bored. "He's coming back tonight, I think."

I thanked her, ended the call, glanced at Sam's roses and then around the room: Pepe was on the phone; Luke was on the phone. And Colin stood at the copier.

Perfect. I opened my desk drawer and plucked a sea-salt caramel from the box Sam had sent—caramels so fancy they required refrigeration and boasted an expiration date a week after purchase. I closed my eyes as the salty-sweetness melted in my mouth and made my toes curl. I've never smoked cigarettes, but this must have been close to experiencing Newport pleasure.

After the caramel break, and a "whew," I pounded my fists on the desk, ready for work.

Who is Raul Moriaga?

According to Regina and Ontrel, he lived in apartment 1 and had allegedly watched Chanita Lords from afar. But who did the state of California say he was?

I logged onto the Web site of the California Attorney General and clicked on Megan's Law—Registered Sex Offenders. In the address search bar, I typed Chanita's address, then selected Within a One-Mile Radius. The map of 90008 filled the screen. Each blue square—and there were so many blue squares—represented a sex offender living in the area. Thumbprint-sized faces of men sat beside those blue squares.

So much perversion, so little time served.

I selected the square directly atop Chanita's address, the square belonging to a droopy-eyed Hispanic male with a light-brown goatee and a buzz cut. *Raul Guillermo Moriaga. 5 foot 6, 140 pounds.* I clicked Offenses. *Rape in concert by force. Rape of drugged victim. Oral copulation. Lewd or lascivious acts with children under 14 . . .*

Wow. Damn. Hell.

If Moriaga's predilections had broadened in scope—from oral copulation to kidnapping, rape to murder—then Chanita Lords would fit in the roster of victims.

"That homie in apartment one?" Colin asked, looking over my shoulder. He coughed and it sounded like a year's worth of tar bubbling in his lungs.

I elbowed him. "Dude, cover your mouth."

"Sorry." Colin used my mouse to click on offense summaries. "Raul's been busy. Think he could've kidnapped and killed Chanita, and maybe even Trina?"

"You sure want me to do a lot of thinking."

"Well, do you?"

"One sick thing leads to another sick thing, and, pretty soon, you're Jeffrey Dahmer." I clicked on the X to close Moriaga's mug shot, then blinked to force the con's face out of my visual cache. "And Ontrel Shaw's DNA?"

"On its way downtown." Colin returned to his desk, coughing into the crook of his elbow. "He came in with his mom. She vouched for him being with her at Social Security— she needs him to drive her places cuz she's blind in one eye. You see, Lou, Trel is a good boy who just fell in with the wrong crowd, who's scared of guns, really, and wants to be a psychologist when he grows up."

A symphony of strings and horns sounded from my cell phone. The *Star Wars* theme.

Hey! Sam texted. *Resisted texting until now. Still on for tonight?*

I nibbled my thumbnail and tasted sea salt and caramel again.

Another text. *U need to clear your head after a day of*

114

murder. I know this great technique. Let me show you!

My heart fluttered so hard that my butt lifted an inch from the chair. I tapped the phone's tiny keyboard. *Please show me. May have to show me more than once-slow learner. ;)See you @ 8.* I sent him Syeeda's address, then grabbed the box of fancy caramels from the drawer.

"You're smiling." Colin's voice pulled me out of Wonderland.

I squinted at him. "What?"

"You're smiling. Sexting Sam?" He rolled over in his chair and reached for a caramel.

I slapped his hand. "Nuh uh."

"You got three left," he complained.

"And you still have typhus."

"It's just a cough now," Colin said. "And you shared Greg's shit all the time."

"Cuz Greg shared *his* shit all the time."

Colin rolled back to his desk. "We heading back to talk with the Chester on your screen?"

I glanced at my desk clock—it was almost four thirty. "Yep. We have time."

Raining again, so we couldn't return to the park and look for any evidence now sloshing down the hillsides, being consumed by raccoons, or getting crushed by the metal treads of earthmovers charged with pushing fallen earth back onto the hillsides.

Just as I grabbed my bag to leave, Pepe escorted a tall, lanky woman with black and pink dreads into the squad room.

Vanessa!

The woman's bloodshot eyes darted from my shoulder holster and Glock to the handcuffed young brown men being escorted by stern-faced patrol cops.

Pepe nodded to the woman. "This is Vanessa Watkins."

115

Vanessa and I shook hands. "Thanks for coming in, Ms. Watkins," I said, smiling. "I've been very eager to talk with you."

We remained at my desk since all the interview rooms were now occupied.

"Here's a little refreshment, compliments of the house." Colin handed her a can of Sprite.

She said, "Sorry I haven't called. I've never . . ." She chewed on her bottom lip.

I offered an encouraging smile, then said, "Let's start from the beginning."

We took notes as Vanessa told a story similar to the one her friends had told. A late-morning hike on trail 5. Seeing the canvas bag on the trail. Smelling something awful. Glimpsing the leg poking out of the bag. And, finally, snapping pictures before losing it and being escorted down the hill.

"Did you bring the phone you used on Wednesday?" I asked.

Near tears, she pulled the pink Android from her jacket pocket. With a shaky hand, she handed me the device. "I ain't never seen a dead body before, not counting funerals. I almost threw up. I almost—" Then, all color left her face. She grabbed my wastebasket and shoved her head deep inside of it. All kinds of shit erupted from Vanessa's belly and splashed into the depths of the plastic container.

One of our handcuffed guests shouted, "Damn, that's nasty."

I had pushed my chair back and now gaped at the back of my up-chucking witness.

Pepe dashed to the break room and returned with a stack of paper towels.

And we waited until the poor woman had nothing left.

"You okay?" I asked.

Vanessa nodded. "I'm so sorry." She accepted paper towels from Pepe.

Colin, the only one with a stuffed nose, left the squad room with the trash can.

I opened Vanessa's soda can and held it out for her.

Vanessa guzzled the Sprite, then burped delicately behind her hand. "I'm so sorry."

"Happens all the time around here," Pepe said. "No worries."

I found the five pictures she'd taken on Wednesday, then e-mailed them to my in-box.

"It's like I can still smell the body," she whispered as I handed her back the phone.

Pepe placed a protective hand on her shoulder. "We're gonna need you to fill out a form, okay?" Then, he escorted the woman over to his desk to complete a formal witness statement.

Colin returned to the pen with my linerless wastebasket.

I was studying the shots Vanessa had taken.

Selfie on the trail . . . Vanessa, Heather, and Cynthia, biceps curled, posing at the park map . . . Far-off shot of the canvas bag . . . Closer shot of the bag and leg . . . A man walking toward her, head down . . .

"That him?" Colin asked, pointing at the man.

"He's wearing gloves," I said. "Look."

A thin band of skin flashed between the glove and the cuff of his jacket sleeve.

"Light-skinned," Colin said.

"Light-skinned 'what,' though? Black? Hispanic? Or darker white?"

The man's head was down. "Protecting his face from the elements?" Colin wondered.

"Maybe."

"Can we put him on a poster?"

117

I clicked on the picture to enlarge it. "What would we be asking people to look for?"

He was between six feet and six foot three, muscled but not too much. Even with my vast experience in patrolling a city of almost 3.8 million people who checked all kinds of boxes, I couldn't tell if this man was black, white, or Martian.

The only distinguished thing about him? He wore a dark baseball cap.

The New Orleans Saints.

19

THE SUN, BLOCKED BY STORM CLOUDS FOR A WEEK NOW, HAD COMPLETELY abandoned Los Angeles for a more exotic locale, like Fiji or the Antarctic. For the second time that day, Colin and I parked near the bullet-peppered telephone pole that had held Chanita's yellow "Missing" flyer. My shoulders tensed as I climbed out of my Porsche SUV. Didn't really wanna be here, especially at this time of day, especially in nasty weather like this. Monsters liked the dusk, and they thrived in the rain.

"What y'all want *now*?" Young, snide, female.

Those girls from the morning came to stand on the other side of Colin's Charger. They had changed out of their fruit-colored jeans and into tight camouflage pants and faux UGGs.

"You talk to adults like that all the time?" I asked Scowler.

"And adults who are also cops?" Colin added.

Even I had to roll my eyes. *Fuck da police, Taggert.*

Scowler placed a hand on her hip. "What y'all want now, *Mister* and *Lady* Officer?"

These girls reminded me of Miss Alberta's daughters and their friends. Back then, Dominique and Angelique had stuck out their legs to block the stairway leading up to my apartment. *What's the password,* they'd always demand. *We ain't gon' let you pass without the password.* Of course, I never knew the password. Stuck there, I cried as they laughed.

After several torturous minutes, they moved their legs from my path, and I rushed up the stairs with our laundry or the mail now wet with my tears. Mom and Tori complained that I let them bully me. "They just messin' with you," my sister always claimed. "They'll leave you alone if you quit acting like you're scared of them." So I ignored them. And ignoring them only made them angrier, and soon their juvenile taunts no longer thrilled them. One afternoon, they jumped me in the laundry room. Busted my lip, loosened a tooth, and left bruises on my back in the shape of shell-toed Adidas.

Little bitches.

"You guys know that Chanita Lords is dead?" I inquired now.

The chubby one zipped up her puffy nylon jacket, then said, "Uh huh. Ontrel told us after Regina told him."

Scowler sucked her teeth. "I ain't gon' let somebody steal *me*."

"Ontrel told us who you are," Scowler said. "And he said that you used to live here and that you knew Miss Alberta, like, a hundred years ago."

"And now you get to carry a gun and hang out with white people," Braids said.

"Yay, me," I said, smirking.

"You shoot anybody?" Chubby One asked.

"Ladies," Colin said, "let's—"

"That mean she shot somebody." Scowler turned to Colin. "We know *you* have."

Colin's face reddened.

"Aw," Chubby One said, "be nice. Leave him alone."

Then, all three girls laughed.

"So what do you think happened to Chanita?" I asked, nonplussed.

Annoyed, Scowler pushed out a breath. "That's a stupid question. Coulda been anybody who killed her."

"Tell me your name," Colin demanded. "I'm not diggin' your tone."

Braids snickered and stage-whispered to Chubby One. "Did he just say 'digging'?"

"You got something to say?" Colin asked.

Colin hadn't interacted much with girls who talked back, swerved their necks, whose stank attitudes wafted off of them like burning toast. He had only met the ones who could no longer talk back or suck their teeth.

"Names, girls," I said.

Scowler said, "My name's S-h-a capital Q-u-a-n."

"And you two?" Colin asked, pen on pad.

The two other girls looked to ShaQuan.

ShaQuan nodded.

Braids said, "Treasure."

Chubby One said, "Imunique."

My pen froze on the pad. "You're what?"

"Imunique." And she spelled it for me. "Ontrel and Lamar and them call you Lockjaw. Said you like a pit bull on a baby's head."

I shrugged. "A pit bull, huh? That's a new one. So, ShaQuan: what do you mean, anybody could've killed her?"

ShaQuan peered at me with small, hard eyes—the eyes of every bully in every neighborhood in every nation in the world. "Anybody. Coulda. *Killed*. Her."

"Nita didn't hang out with us," Treasure explained. "Her grandma was always drivin' her to the Valley and stuff for classes so we ain't seen her that much."

"She was always gettin' in cars with grown-ups like she was important or somethin'," ShaQuan added. "Why ain't nobody asked *them* nothing?"

"Who's 'them'?" Colin asked. "Who are the adults she hung out with?"

121

ShaQuan pulled gelled tufts of hair back beneath a barrette and into the pitiful up-top ponytail. "Y'all keep messin' with us cuz we black. And we got in *one stupid fight* with Nita and now everybody wanna blame us."

"What was the fight about?" I asked.

"She disrespected me," ShaQuan said. "She called me a loser on Facebook. So I'm, like, say that shit to my face."

"Everybody brave on the Internet," Treasure said.

"Did she say it to your face?" I asked, eyebrow cocked.

"She said it," ShaQuan said.

"And you beat her down, right?" Colin said, nodding.

ShaQuan sucked her teeth. "People think Nita was perfect, but she wasn't."

"How was she not perfect?" I asked.

Treasure picked at a zit with her fingernail. "Regina used to make her boost shit all the time. *And* Nita always talked about gettin' pregnant by a baller so he had to take care of her and the baby." She swerved her head. "That ain't somebody who all sweet and innocent."

"And she tried to trap Ontrel," ShaQuan spat. "She used to poke holes in his rubbers."

I smirked. "Really?"

ShaQuan dropped her eyes to the sidewalk. "Uh huh."

"When did you see her last?" Colin asked.

"Friday," Treasure said. "She got into an SUV."

"With who?" I asked.

The girl shrugged. "The windows was tinted."

"Did you see the license plate?" I asked.

"It started with a number," Treasure said.

I waited for more.

Treasure rolled her eyes. "Dang, what else you gotta know?"

"Well, for starters," Colin growled, "try getting the tone outta your voice."

"What tone?" Treasure asked in that same tone.

"You talk to your mom and dad like that?" he asked.

The girls looked at each other, then laughed.

The color returned to Colin's face, but his lips disappeared. "Would you three laugh if I took you down to the station for questioning?"

ShaQuan smiled. "Which station? Downtown or Seventy-seventh? I been to both."

The trio laughed some more.

Jaw clenched, Colin looked to me for help.

I winked at him. *Sorry, kid.* "So what kind of SUV did Nita get into?"

"It was like a Yukon or Tahoe or somethin' like that," Imunique said.

"Anybody around here drive a truck like that?" Colin asked.

"What we look like?" ShaQuan snapped. "The DMV?"

Stepping back, he ran his hand through his hair.

I could feel Colin's blood pressure rise. "Ontrel drive an SUV?" I asked the girls.

"Or do we need to grab him and ask him ourselves?" Colin asked.

"Ontrel drive a Bonneville," ShaQuan said with no extra flavor.

"Around what time did you see Chanita?" I asked.

"Like after school let out," Imunique said.

"You speak to her?" I asked.

They considered each other with worried eyes. Finally, ShaQuan offered, "We said hi."

"And?"

"We asked where she was going."

"And?"

ShaQuan opened her mouth, but changed her mind and shrugged.

"Was she alone when you talked to her?" I asked.

All three nodded. "And then the truck came," Imunique said, "and drove her away."

"Where were you when all this was happening?" I asked.

"King and MLK," Treasure said.

"By the Krispy Kreme?" Colin asked, writing in his pad.

"At that bus stop," Imunique added.

"Yup," the other two agreed.

Just as Gwen Zapata's witness had remembered.

"On Friday," I said, "did you tell the cops about the SUV?"

"No," ShaQuan said. "Ain't nobody asked us nothing about no SUV."

I sighed. "You think Ontrel could've—?"

"No," Treasure shouted, eyes wide. "He innocent. Cops always messin' with him. Y'all—" Tears filled her eyes, and she turned away from me.

"I think Mess-cans did it," Imunique said as she pulled her braids into a loose bun. "They be hatin' on us, tryin' to run us out of here, and so they took Nita and showed us that they ain't scared of us."

"Payback," Treasure added as she dried tears on her jacket's sleeve.

"Them cholos from Eighteenth Street roll up in here all the time," ShaQuan complained. "Visitin' they moms and sisters and fifty-million relatives all livin' up in one apartment. Always trying to start shit. They coulda took Nita and drove her to East LA or to Mexico or to hoochie-coochie-la-cucaracha-wherever-they-live."

"And then they drove her to Bonner Park?" Colin asked.

"Yup," the girls said together.

"They almost killed my cousin two weeks ago," Imunique claimed. "They shot him over on Parthenon. He still on life support."

"Does your cousin bang?" I asked.

"Yeah, he bang," Imunique said, her gaze hot with offense. "But that don't give them no right to be shootin' at people."

"That's what she get," ShaQuan muttered.

"You mean Nita?" I asked, pulse banging in my throat. "Why would you say that?"

"Cuz she wanted to be white," ShaQuan said, head cocked, hand on hip.

"She talked like you," Imunique said to me. "Like a white girl."

"She was all, *I'm better than y'all cuz I'm on the honor roll,*" Treasure added, her voice high to affect snootiness.

"And *that's* why we kicked her ass," Imunique said.

"Shut up," ShaQuan spat at her friend. "You talk too damn much."

Treasure shook her head. "And I don't believe she really dead."

I blinked at her, but Colin spoke first. "You're fuckin' kidding me."

Treasure gaped at him. "You don't *know.* Regina is sus."

"*Sus?*" Colin asked.

"Suspect," I told him.

"She do all kinds of crooked shit," Treasure continued. "She may be runnin' an insurance scam or somethin'. That bitch be gettin' *over.*"

Back in the day, Miss Alberta also got over—using food stamps that had somehow been *liberated* from neighbors' mailboxes. Receiving Social Security checks for Dominique, who was stupid but far from special needs. So the reality of Regina learning the fine art of scamming at her mother's knee? Certainly.

Treasure cocked her head. "Have y'all seen Nita's body?"

I said, "Yes. Of course we have."

Unblinking, Treasure said, "Y'all check for a pulse?"

Colin clapped. "Okay. This is ridiculous. We need your *guardians'* phone numbers."

"Why?" Treasure asked.

He explained to them about witness statements.

The girls rambled off their numbers.

I held up my hand. "Quick question—"

"We gotta go." ShaQuan set off east.

"We're not done," Colin said.

"We under arrest?" she asked.

"Of course not," I said.

"So, like I said, we gotta go."

I waved. "Where you headed, if I may ask?"

ShaQuan grinned at me. "Girl Scouts."

20

Through windows and patio doors, shadowy figures camped around glowing television screens. I didn't know if Texas or Arizona State was winning, but the sounds of crowds roaring, high-top sneakers squeaking, and sports announcers pontificating echoed throughout the apartment complex.

Colin strode beside me through the courtyard. His face still twitched with anger, and his lips had not returned to their original spot.

"You okay?" I asked.

"Who the fuck are raising them little twerps? Where I'm from, you talk to adults like that, you get popped in the mouth."

"Where *you're* from," I said, "people burn crosses to scare *my* people, all in the name of Jesus. Not all you people." I paused, then added, "Just sayin'."

The pungent aromas of marijuana and trash traveled on the wet night air. The lights in the courtyard had died, and now tiny orange lights flickered ahead like fireflies. The shadows had been smoking all kinds of shit, but now joints were being hastily rubbed out between fingers. Soon, someone would burn microwave popcorn to mask the smell.

"Interviewing child molesters makes my stomach hurt," Colin complained. "Hell, the *idea* of Raul Moriaga scrambles

127

my logic more than murder does. In a weird kinda way, murder makes sense. You hurt me—"

"I kill you," I said.

"You scare me."

"I kill you."

"You have something I want."

"I kill you."

We reached Raul Moriaga's apartment. A small handwritten sign had been taped next to the doorbell.

NO SMOKING! NO FUMAR!

Colin banged on the door.

The peephole darkened.

We both held up our badges.

The door opened, and a weasel manifested as a man poked his head from the darkness. He wore a wispy brown porn mustache and a scar that ran from his nose to his jaw. His slicked-back hair connected his head to his torso without benefit of a neck. A blue teardrop had been tattooed beneath his right eye. He opened the door wider, and the smell of french fries drifted toward us. "Yes?"

"I'm Homicide Detective Lou Norton, and this is my partner—"

"I don't know nothing 'bout that girl." Moriaga nodded toward the rear apartments.

"We just wanna talk, Raul," Colin said.

"I ain't had nothing to do with that girl."

"Heard you the first time, amigo," Colin said. "Can we come in?"

Moriaga narrowed his weasel eyes, opened the door wider, and motioned us into the dark. "It's kinda cold in here."

"Cold is just a state of mind." I placed my hands on my

hips so he could see that I was carrying—no one liked that kind of surprise.

His gaze dipped and he flinched. *Surprise!*

A large aquarium filled with fish dominated the eastern wall of the dark living room. The tank's blue and white fluorescent lights made shadows reach across the carpets. There was no television or stereo. Just the aquarium, a dark-colored sofa, a plaid armchair, and crumpled fast food bags on the carpet and counters.

"Can we get some more light on, Raul?" I asked.

"Umm . . . it's . . ." He sighed, then said, "Okay." He clicked on a floor lamp by the door, and then hustled across the living room to flick on the kitchen light-switch.

A magazine had been shoved hastily beneath the armchair's cushion—didn't want to know what he'd been reading. A beer can sat on the coffee table alongside paperback editions of *Into Thin Air* and *Great Expectations.*

Colin wandered to the aquarium. Orange, blue, scarlet, yellow—no one fish looked like the other. Some hid in the coral while others dashed over rocks.

"How big is this tank?" Colin asked.

"Sixty gallons, salt water." Moriaga stood beside Colin, and together they gazed at vibrant-colored fish dashing through castles and anemones. "I love lookin' at the different colors, you know? Before I was arrested, I used to work at a fish store."

He pointed to a moving spot of blue and yellow. "That's a royal angelfish right there. And that's a clown fish, and a harlequin tuskfish, and a betta. That's a royal gramma, a damsel. Stay still, girl. She's a regal tang. Over there's a coral beauty, a pajama cardinal fish, and a yellow-headed jawfish."

"Impressive," Colin said.

"Yeah," he said. "The last time I was in, my cousin took care of 'em for me. Not these right here. A different group. He owned the store I was workin' at. You don't want just anybody lookin' after your babies. Not only cuz they expensive, but they all got they own personalities, and you don't want 'em to die on you."

"Fish have personalities?" Colin asked.

Moriaga's reflection glimmered in the acrylic. "Hell, yeah, they do. That one right there?" He pointed at the brown spotted fish with a maimed fin now hiding behind a large gray rock. "That's Raquel. She shy. Hides in the rocks and only comes out when it's time to eat. She got a bad fin."

Having had my fill of fish stories, I headed to the couch. "We never named our fish. We just put 'em in a bowl and fed them fish food once a day."

"Don't mean to be rude, Detective," Moriaga said, "but that's kinda jacked up. Fish need they space. This tank ain't the ocean, but at least they can claim some territory. At least they got some space to swim around in."

My face numbed, and my lips barely moved as I muttered, "At least."

"I do everything for 'em," he continued. "I keep it dark in here cuz the sun makes algae that can kill 'em. And then the temperature—you gotta watch the temperature."

Colin sat in the armchair. "How long were you in?"

"Almost a fuckin' dime," Moriaga said. "All my fish died, but my cousin, man. He knew I was innocent. Everything was taken from me, so he's like, 'I'll get you some more fish when you're out.' So, these fish right here? They was like my welcome-home gift. They keep me calm." He touched the tank's glass before turning to us. "They my babies. They all I have."

"Let's chat," Colin said.

"Okay." Moriaga hustled over to the couch and sat a little too close to me. His eyes sparkled, and he smelled of peppermint. "Like I said, I didn't know the girl over in five. I seen her a few times, but I don't talk to nobody. I'm just tryin' to keep my chin up and my head down, you know? Get back on the straight and narrow."

I shifted my thigh away from his. "You ever talk to Chanita? You know, just a casual hi, neighbor to neighbor?"

"Like at the mailbox or whatever? I said hi a few times. Neighbor to neighbor."

"Ever see her in the laundry room?" Colin asked.

"One time, I offered to help her cuz she did a buncha folks' washin' around here to earn some cash and the laundry basket looked heavy."

"And she let you help?" I asked.

He shook his head. "She ain't wanna cause no problems."

"For you?"

"For her. She datin' a Blood. He kinda known for kickin' females' asses. So I let her be."

"You got any connections to Eighteenth Street?" I asked.

"Two cousins—they third cousins, though. I don't bang."

"So the mailbox and the laundry room," Colin said. "Those the only times you and Chanita talked?"

Moriaga tented his fingers. "Lemme think . . ." He closed his eyes, thought some, then opened his eyes. "Oh. There was this other time."

I squinted at him. "This *other* time?"

He held out his left hand and pointed to a scar on the web between his index finger and thumb. "I was changin' the water in the tank and a rock cut me. I ain't had no first-aid kit or nothing, so I ran over to five cuz I know females buy bandages and peroxide and shit. Nita was there alone. She saw my hand and hooked me up." His eyes fixed on the scar as he remembered. "That was nice. Somebody takin' care of me."

I watched him for a moment, then asked, "How long you been out, Raul?"

131

"Almost six months. I ain't goin' back again. Learned my lesson. No more hangin' out with the wrong crowd. My mom and pops ain't bust they asses for me to be in and out of the pen. And they legal. We ain't no wetbacks, crossin' no rivers and runnin' from *coyotes*. Pops was in the U.S. Navy."

"Why do people think you're involved in Chanita's death?" Colin asked.

He jiggled his legs. "Cuz they racist. Mexicans livin' in the Jungle get blamed for everything, man. We takin' black people's jobs. We takin' black people's apartments. Now, we stealin' they kids. I ain't *never* touched they kids. I ain't even *attracted* to black people." He paused and his Adam's apple bobbed. "No offense, Detective Norton."

I shrugged—my ability to be offended had died the moment I stepped into this ice cave.

"So your prison convictions?" Colin asked.

"I think they said Selena was thirteen or fourteen." Moriaga sat back on the couch, then shook his head. "But that shit got twisted. She smoked meth *and* crack—that shit make you look older than what you are, you know? And she told me she was nineteen. I was, like, whatever man, let's do this. To be honest, she looked like she twenty-three."

I didn't blink. "Uh huh."

"And Jazzy?" He shrugged. "I ain't even *touch* that girl, and I sure as hell ain't take her to my uncle's garage. She was at the fish store, and it was raining, and I asked her if she needed a ride, and she said yeah. I sure as hell ain't *kidnap* her. And Bri . . . I didn't even *know* that girl. And that one really ticks me off cuz it's already bad going to jail for something you did, but when you go for something you *ain't* did?"

Okay. So. Raul Moriaga was the Ex-Con Framed for Everything. To his credit, he had tried to be so normal, so affable—he liked fish and reading Charles Dickens. But, then, how many citizens walked their dogs, did their laundry, then preyed on the most vulnerable once the rest of us had been lulled by the monotony of Everyday? That is, until we were snapped out of our sleep by a rape, an assault, or a murder by *that guy? That guy seemed so normal.*

"Convicted offenders can't live near places where children congregate," I said. "There's a park down the block on Santo Tomas."

"The law says a quarter mile of any *school,*" Moriaga explained. "I ain't high-risk."

My heart jumped in my chest. *He* wasn't high-risk? If a man with thousands of convictions wasn't high risk, who the hell *was*?

"And this is LA," Moriaga said. "Where *ain't* there kids?"

Colin squeezed the bridge of his nose. "Were you around the day Chanita disappeared?"

Moriaga hopped off the couch and bounded over to the aquarium. He opened the canister of fish food that sat on the tank's top and drizzled flakes into the water. "I was in San Diego hangin' out with homies I ain't seen in a while."

"Where in San Diego?" Colin asked.

"At the sports arena. For this Control Machete reunion concert."

"And how long were you there?" I asked.

"The weekend."

"And then what did you do?"

"I came back here." Moriaga smiled. "I told y'all: I ain't about that life no more."

"That's wonderful to hear," I said. "But you're a registered sex offender, and we have your DNA on file. So let's cut the crap, all right, cuz the machine's gonna tell me the truth."

The ex-con shook his head. "I ain't done nothing like what you saying."

"Fine," I said, "but I still want the names of your homies in San Diego as well as the name of your PO."

Moriaga rattled off names and phone numbers.

I slipped my pen and pad back into my bag. "You working now, Raul?"

Moriaga laughed. "You know how hard it is for a felon to get a job? It's like the system's setting me up to fail." He smiled, then said, "Is the LAPD hiring? I can type, do shorthand, file. Got my AA when I was in. Went to counseling, too. They put me on some brake fluid."

"What kind?" I asked.

"Paxil *and* Eulexin. I got me a sexual addiction, and I let it get the better of me. I'm straight now. I ain't no diaper sniper, a'ight? Them girls just looked older than what they was."

I stood from the couch, now eager to return to fresh air and the outside's darkness. "Just know that if you're lying to us, we'll be back. If you leave this state anytime soon, if you leave this *country,* we're gonna have a problem. You've jumped bail a few times, and the marshals had to hunt you down at the border. If you put me through any bullshit like that, you'll be back in prison, and I'll see to it that you're in general population." Even in hellholes like Pelican Bay, child molesters were persona non grata.

"I ain't goin' nowhere," he said. "I ain't got nothing to run from."

"One more thing," I said. "Can you bring me all of your shoes?"

Moriaga cocked his head, then headed to his bedroom.

Colin followed him.

Both men returned. Moriaga carried three pairs of sneaks in his arms.

I took pictures of the bottoms: whorls, stripes, and chevrons.

On one pair, the Adidas, the tread was thick with red mud.

My heart thudded in my chest. "Mind if I borrow this pair? We'll process them as soon as possible and get them back to you." I pulled a large evidence baggie from my satchel and handed it to Colin.

Moriaga darkened as he stared at his confiscated kicks, but he said nothing.

A minute later, he walked us to the front door. "I ain't killed *nobody*, Detective Norton. I did my time, even for shit I ain't done." His eyes glistened with tears. "I just want a new start."

21

NO ONE ANSWERED AT CHANITA'S APARTMENT, WHICH MEANT WE COULDN'T ASK her family about the teen's whereabouts during the bloom time of deadly nightshade. And so Colin and I tromped back through the courtyard and past those security gates.

Hillcrest Avenue had been abandoned by fake Girl Scouts. North of us, a troop of fat gray storm clouds had wrapped the black Santa Monica Mountains. Trees rustled in the wind, and a few loose palm fronds fell onto the wet sidewalk.

"I wasn't expectin' that," Colin said as we approached our cars. "He was very polite, especially compared to the young ladies who greeted us. In total denial about his crimes, though. But, hell, no one in jail admits to 'doing it.'"

I cocked an eyebrow. "You obviously didn't read his jacket."

"I skimmed," Colin said, placing the bag with Moriaga's shoes into the Charger's trunk. "I've been sick, remember? Anyway, the guy's obsessed with his fish. He cares about something. Wonderful, right?"

I went rigid and not because of the cold. "Guessing by your reaction, you did even less than *skim* Moriaga's jacket. His fish. His babies. Pet therapy. Touching, huh?"

"Kinda." Colin pulled out his cell phone. "Other than the fact that they dictate the amount of light that comes into his apartment, it's not that weird."

My mouth twisted into a crooked smile. "Colin, Moriaga would drive around LA County, offering young girls a ride home. Some would say no. Some would say yes. The ones who said yes got in his car. But he didn't drive them home. No, he drove them to his uncle's garage in El Monte. That's where he *raped* them. After a few hours, he'd drive them back. Then, he'd buy a fish, name it, and add it to his sixty-gallon saltwater tank."

Colin paled.

"He has ten of them in that aquarium," I continued. "Graciella, Jasmine, Janelle, Bianca, Keisha, Leila, Brianna, Esmeralda, and Selena. Those are the names of the girls he *raped,* Colin. And the tenth girl? He closed her hand in a vise and chopped off three of her fingers and most of her palm. Because she was black—that's what he told her. Hence, the fish with the gimpy fin named Raquel. The last kid he took wasn't a girl, and there ain't no fish named after Hector. The boy told his sister about what Moriaga had done to him, and the rest is history."

Colin opened his mouth to respond, but he was too busy having a stroke.

"Not so touching now, is it?" I chuckled, pleased to see his perceptions bashed against the sharp rocks of reality. I glanced at my watch—almost six thirty. Enough time to stop by Mom's, rush home, shower, and throw pasta into a pot of boiling water. "So, I need to leave."

"Just like that?" he said, eyes glazed.

"You wanna stand around some more and talk about how sick that poor, polite man is?"

He pushed out a breath, ran a hand through his hair, and plucked his phone from his jacket pocket. "Don't you have a date tonight?"

"I do."

"I'll take Moriaga's shoes to the lab before I go home." With a slick smile on his face, he was now texting on his phone. "That girl I met in the aisle at Walgreens? Carly? Wants to be my naughty nurse tonight."

I pivoted on my heel. "Wonderful. Don't leave your cocktail unattended this time."

"Who thinks of shit like puttin' Visine in drinks?"

"Ladies who steal money from their date's wallets while he's busy crapping on the toilet cuz she put Visine in his rum and Coke."

"Happened to me *once*, Judge Judy. Geez. Shouldn't have told you." He tossed me a salute, then whistled to his car.

By the time I reached my mother's neighborhood, the rain had come. Puddles abounded, and drivers slowly navigated the slick streets as though the pools of water were made of liquid nitrogen and kittens.

Martin, Mom's boyfriend, was dragging a green trash can from the side of the house to the street. Even by the way he lined up that green can with the blue and black ones, I could tell that the large man in the wet tracksuit and sopping house shoes had retired from the U.S. Marines. A major, he'd seen action in Vietnam, Iran, Iraq, and Afghanistan. But he hadn't yet conquered Georgia Starr.

"Lou!" he boomed now. "How's it goin', girl?"

We hugged.

At seventy-two years old, Martin was still solid muscle. Tonight, he smelled of wet grass and beer. "I just stopped by to help your mom . . ." He waved a beefy hand at the trash bins.

Guess we were still pretending that he didn't live here most of the time, even though I had spotted his slippers—the very ones on his feet now—on the left side of her bed more than once.

He tapped my shoulder. "Thanks for that gift certificate. Nice resort."

"You get in some golfing?"

"Oh yeah." He ran his palm over his wet and wavy silver hair. "Not used to being pampered. I've been to Palm Springs before, but not *that* part of Palm Springs. Your mom loved it. Wants to go back."

I faked a sneer and pointed at him. "And you *will* take her back."

He stooped to snatch a wet newspaper from the sidewalk. "Stopping over for dinner?"

"Nope," I said, walking to the front door. "Just bringing the queen some entertainment." I held up a gift bag filled with puzzle books. "Is everything okay?"

He gave me a strange look, then rubbed his neck. "Oh, you know."

A very real sneer found its way to my face, and white-hot rage swept over me.

Victor Starr.

Since his return, that son of a bitch was upending everything, including this long-awaited, loving relationship Mom had found after denying herself happiness for so long.

The television in the living room was on and turned to the Arizona State–Texas game. Mom sat in the sunroom, pink-framed glasses perched on her nose, short gray hair wrapped in a silk scarf. A small lamp on a tiny table burned brightly and illuminated the tomato and basil plants, as well as the crossword puzzle she was now working.

"What's an eight-letter word for 'neighborhood'?" she asked without looking up.

I brushed dried tomato leaves from the other chair and sat. "Vicinity."

She narrowed her eyes, then shook her head. "Another word."

"Umm . . . Environs."

She wrote the word, then smiled at me. "Hello, dear daughter."

I held out the gift bag of books. "*Pour toi*."

She leaned over and kissed my cheek. "Just in time."

"You've run out?"

"Umhmm." She pointed to the curled-page puzzle books near the succulent garden.

"Guess where I was today?"

She opened a new book. "Standing in a dark alley, blood everywhere?"

"Close." I plopped into a chair. "Back in the Jungle, at our old apartment building. Miss Alberta's unit, to be exact."

Mom sucked her teeth. "She *still* there?"

"Yep. She says hi."

"One of the sons finally turn up dead?"

"No, but her granddaughter did. Nothing like you'd expect. In the gifted program at Madison. A talented photographer . . ."

"That's too bad." Mom leveled a gaze at me. "Maybe now Alberta knows how it feels. If she had a husband, maybe I'd go over and try and sleep with him."

"Whoa," I said, holding up a hand. "What the hell, Mom?"

Her eyes went hot. "That woman was always chasing after your father. I wouldn't be surprised if . . ." She shook her head, then stared out at the dark, wet yard.

"Hello?"

She sighed. "Will you call that man, please? You being stubborn is drawing this out, making it longer and more torturous than it has to be."

I stared at her coolly, not threatened, not at all.

"He calls me like we're still married." She closed the crossword book and tossed it on the footstool. "Twice a day, morning and evening."

"Does he *know* you're divorced?"

She frowned. "Are you seriously asking me that, Elouise?"

"I just don't remember you two going down to the divorce court and having it out over who's the rightful owner of our grocery-store set of encyclopedias."

Mom stood from her chair and stomped out of the sunroom. "Let me show you."

I followed her through the living room and hallway, past walls of framed pictures of Tori and me in childhood, of me in a cadet's uniform, of Mom and her sister Savannah.

We reached her bedroom, a mecca for Laura Ashley fanatics—blue and yellow flowers everywhere. The only nonfloral objects were the bed's headboard, the dresser, and the desk set.

Arms crossed, I leaned against the bureau and spotted Martin's reading glasses and *US Veterans* magazine on the nightstand.

Mom pulled out a desk drawer stuffed with folders and grabbed a thick accordion file. She removed the bungee cord, browsed through the papers, and then pulled out a section of yellowed newspaper, which she thrust at me. "I didn't need his permission to get divorced."

State of California District Court . . . in RE the marriage of: Victor Starr . . . Your spouse has filed a lawsuit against you for dissolution of your marriage . . . must serve your answer upon petitioner within thirty (30) days of the date you were served with this summons . . .

The date: March 26, 1990. I had just started high school.

"I remember . . ." The paper shook in my hands. "You wouldn't let me read the paper on my own. You'd hand me the comics or the Metro section."

"Because I didn't want you to read *that*," she said, pointing to the clip.

Serve by publication. Place a legal notice in the paper where your spouse had lived last. The notice ran once a week for four weeks. After that, your spouse (in this case, Victor Starr) was considered served.

"Did he see it?" I asked.

"I don't care," Mom said, her neck swerving just like ShaQuan's. "He saw it, he didn't see it, doesn't matter to me. Victor and I are legally divorced."

"Maybe if you showed—"

"Why? Why do *I* have to do everything? *He* gets to leave, and now *I* have to do something? *Again?*" Her nostrils flared as spit gathered at the corners of her mouth. "I don't care if his heart is broken and bleeding. He had a choice: his wife and family—or his *dick*. I don't need to tell you which he chose."

My face burned, and I handed her the newspaper.

He had left that Sunday morning for the newspaper and a bag of lima beans for my science project. More than twenty years had passed before he stood on my porch—and without the bag of beans. And now I wanted to ask Mom, "Who did he leave us for?" since she'd tossed sex into the kettle. But the thought of her answering made me light-headed. I wasn't ready for *that* truth—part of me still called nipples "nickels" and believed babies lived in heaven with storks wearing postal caps.

"Our last breakfast together," I said, "did you know . . . ?"

She clutched her neck and stared at the carpet. Then, she shrugged.

That day, Mom had stood at our picture window, tugging her earlobe, then perched on the couch to work on a big book of crossword puzzles.

"That night," I said, "you were supposed to make lasagna."

"But I couldn't—we had to plant your lima bean." She inhaled and slowly released it. "He's trying to destroy what I have, Lou." She shoved the file back into the drawer. "He's always been a jealous man who hated any attention I received. Insecure bastard. Needed me to kiss his ass every day, all day.

"I've told Martin over and over again: I don't love Victor. That part of me no longer exists. That *woman* no longer exists. But that *bastard* is trying to wreck it all."

And now, I felt so very tired. My injured wrist throbbed, and my knees ached because now I knew my job: serve as a distraction to Victor Starr. Be a rodeo clown for the bull.

"What the hell does he want?" I asked.

"To be in our lives again."

"As though nothing *happened*?" I asked. "And if we don't want him in our lives?"

Mom's lip curled. "He'll bully his way in. He's stubborn like that, Elouise, and he expects me to bend just like I would have bent thirty years ago." She tried to blink back tears, but one escaped and slid down her cheek. "I'm this close"—she held up trembling, pinched fingers—"this close to taking a gun and killing that man. I swear I'll do it, and you'll end up arresting—"

"Mom," I said, my voice weak.

"Cuz Martin is threatening to get involved, and I don't want *him* getting in trouble. That's what Vic wants."

Great. More pressure. "Mom, this is crazy."

"You don't understand."

"What?" I screeched. "*I* don't under—?"

"*You* were a child," she shouted. "Think about how your heart broke every time Gregory stepped out on you. Now, imagine that happening and you had two children, two *girls* who were watching you and needing you to be strong. How could Victor leave me, leave *us* so *easily*? He told me that he *agonized* over leaving. Bullshit. Did he send money to help take care of you and Tori? Did he call for birthdays or graduations?"

I shook my head. "No."

"Did he call when Tori disappeared?"

"No."

"It took me forever to leave that apartment," Mom said, "not only because I was waiting for Tori to come back home, but because I was waiting for *him* to come back home, too."

We had finally left the Jungle at the end of my tenth-grade year, moving into a duplex in Leimert Park with big windows, lots of light, no laundry-room bullies, not haunted by ghosts.

Mom hugged herself as she perched on the bed. "I'm asking you to call him not because I'm scared of him. I'm not scared. I'm asking you because . . ." She held my gaze. "Because if you don't, I will go to jail with your father's blood on my hands. Just call him. Please?"

22

MOM'S PLEA—*JUST CALL HIM*—SOUNDED SO EASY. PICK UP THE PHONE, SAY HELLO, and listen. Baking a chocolate soufflé on the moon, blindfolded, was easier. By the time I pulled into Syeeda's driveway, though, I knew:

I'd be Mom's rodeo clown.

Next door, Mr. Mendelbaum, dressed in yellow galoshes, a black suit, and yarmulke, was pushing a trash bin to the sidewalk. Mrs. Mendelbaum, a back-lit shadow in the doorway, pointed from the porch and shouted, "Not there! Over there!"

Syeeda had left on the porch and foyer lights, and the small stained-glass windows at the front of her Spanish-style home glowed. The *Star Wars* theme sounded from my jacket. A text from Sam. *On my way.*

He lived in Echo Park, right outside downtown, and, with the rain, that gave me a little more than an hour to prepare before his arrival.

I hurried into the warm house, rushing past my full packing boxes in the foyer, passing the coffee table and couch crowded with legal pads and pens, tripping over Syeeda's Gucci loafers abandoned near the bathroom, and running down the hallway to disarm the burglar alarm.

After showering, I dabbed more hydrocortisone cream on

my chest rash, then pulled on jeans and a gray cashmere sweater. I didn't have to see myself before saying, "Nope. Too corporate," and stripping again.

Maybe sweats and flip-flops.

"No," I whispered, "too lazy."

What about . . . ? Well . . .

What message did I *want* to send?

I stared at my reflection in the full-length mirror. *What does a thirtysomething divorcée wear that signifies, "I want something to happen, but I'm not sure how much of that happening I want . . . to . . . happen"?*

I hadn't dressed for an at-home dinner since Will Smith was the Fresh Prince and Ice Cube was Amerikkka's Most Wanted, and now . . .

"Screw it." I grabbed clingy black yoga pants and a long-sleeved jersey.

Talk about mixed messages.

I popped an ancient Floetry CD into the stereo, then lit votive candles on the mantel, sideboard, and dining room table. Then, I blew out the candles, turned on the floor lamps, and replaced Floetry with Sting.

In the kitchen, two wineglasses and a bottle of Cabernet Sauvignon sat on the granite island. A note had been taped to the wine label.

You WILL drink this. You WILL relax and slut it up. It's your duty as a patriot. Have fun!—Sy P.S. There are two more bottles in the sideboard.

I poured myself a glass, then grabbed a large pot and skillet from the cabinet.

On the menu: chicken with pesto made from fresh basil that came from Mom's sunroom, haricots vert with sautéed tomatoes, another gift from Mom's garden, and . . .

I looked in the fridge.

Another note from Syeeda had been taped to a pink pastry box.

A pineapple tart. Pineapple. ☺ You're welcome. (Yeah, I know I'm going to Hell. SEXY Hell.)

I didn't know whether to laugh or shriek. Syeeda was touting the benefits of Sam eating pineapple, and yet I couldn't even figure out handshake or hug, a hello kiss on his lips or on his cheeks or no kiss at—

The doorbell rang.

Shit.

I lit three votives, turned off one floor lamp, replaced Sting with John Legend, then ran to the foyer.

Sam stood on the porch with a bouquet of pale purple and white flowers in his hand.

"Samuel!" I shouted.

"Elouise!"

I took the flowers.

He stepped forward and pulled me into his arms, then kissed me lightly on the lips. His embrace felt like a warm, sturdy jacket scented with soap and orange blossoms.

I sighed and relaxed against him. "The flowers are beautiful."

"*You're* beautiful."

I blushed, then said, "It's raining out. Know how I can tell?"

He nuzzled my neck as I flattened against him. "How?"

"Cuz you're getting me wet."

He lifted an eyebrow, then cocked his head. "Oh. Sorry. I thought you were being . . ." He laughed as he slipped off his soaking jacket. He wore a gray T-shirt made from soft, clinging cotton that flattered his pecs, abs, and back muscles. And his boxer-briefs peeked from the waistband of his khaki cargo shorts.

"You look comfy tonight," I said, my skin warming as my eyes skipped around his . . . everything. "You always hide yourself in Brooks Brothers. Seeing that you have these"—I poked his right bicep, then bit my bottom lip—"I like it."

His gaze wandered from my face and down to every curve I had. "I like *this*. No Glock. No vest. Just you." He pulled me back into his arms.

And we kissed, long, deep. Forever.

I stroked his cheek, then led him to the kitchen. "I need help squeezing something."

A moment later, he stood behind me, squeezing cut lime into the pesto with one hand and holding me close in the other.

"This is nice," he said. "Good food . . ."

I reached for the wineglass on the countertop. "A good Cab." I offered him the glass.

He sipped; then I sipped.

"Maybe," he said, "I'll get to enjoy your pie tonight."

I laughed and bumped him away from me. "One home-cooked meal and you get *pie*? You think I'm that easy?"

He only smiled as he poured more wine into the glass. "Just keep drinking."

The doorbell rang, and then whoever it was knocked.

"Jehovah's Witnesses or Mormons?" Sam asked.

"Probably the Mendelbaums," I said, shuffling out of the kitchen, "complaining about our trash cans not being lined up correctly."

I detoured to the stereo again, switching John Legend back to Floetry and "Say Yes."

"Great album," Sam shouted from the kitchen.

I sang to myself as I slow-danced to the foyer. One look out the peephole made me mutter, "Fuckin' A," then yank open the door. "Why the *hell* are you here?"

"*Shalom,* sweetie!" Lena breezed into the foyer, and her stiletto heels *clickety-clacked* against the tile. A steamer-trunk-sized gym bag weighed down her left arm.

"Lena—"

"I wanted to call to let you know that I was stopping by," she said, "but I threw my phone at the valet at Boa—he dinged one of my rims. You know how much one rim costs?"

I glanced back at the kitchen. "Don't care. You're leaving now."

"Umm, no, I'm not." She dropped the gym bag to the floor. "It's mayhem out there, and I'm *exhausted*. Just finished working out—Avarim is *still* amazing, not that I'm supposed to be enjoying his talents since Emil and I are together, but you won't tell Emil that."

Lena had returned to hammer-fisting since she was now dating Emil Dayan, a businessman who had served in the Israeli Defense Forces. To show her commitment to him, she had also downloaded the "Popular Yiddish Terms" app onto her phone, even though Emil's people weren't . . . Yiddish.

And, now, I gawked at her: blue python heels, black leggings, *Purple Rain* tour T-shirt ripped *Flashdance*-style, full makeup, earrings the size of Saturn's rings, and 638 silver bracelets on her wrists. "I'm so confused right now," I said. "Where are you . . . ? What are you . . . ?"

She considered her outfit. "A little *ongapatchka*?"

"A lotta *ongapatchka*," I said. "It's like Claire's and Neiman Marcus had a baby who spat up on you."

She smiled. "Aww, you're so sweet. I'm hungry. Feed me."

"No. Seriously. I don't care if a volcano is erupting downtown. You can't—"

She shushed me, then said, "Why are you listening to Floetry?" She *clickety-clacked* to the kitchen, then shouted, "Oh! Sam! *You're* here."

"Oh! Lena!" he shouted back. "*You're* here."

"Let's get this party started right," she trilled.

"We were doing pretty good without you," Sam said.

"Umm, no. Cuz, first of all, she opened the door. And, second of all, she's dressed like she's going to Youth Church."

Sam laughed, then said, "Should I give her more wine, then?"

I turned down the stereo, then returned to the kitchen. "Stop talking about me."

Sam was pouring Lena a glass of wine from the second bottle.

"Lena," I said, frowning, "you're being rude right now."

She guzzled the wine, then smiled. "I've been drinking." She smiled as she held out the empty glass. "Can't drive. It's illegal."

Sam shrugged, then refilled her glass.

"Emil's out of town next week," Lena said. "Something about some land thing with some warheads or whatever. So, Lou dear, I need to stay busy. I'm down for some Nancy Drewing."

I pulled plates from the cupboard and nearly slammed them onto the countertop.

"I'm gonna put this . . ." Sam grabbed the bowl of pasta and tiptoed out of the kitchen.

Lena hopped up onto the breakfast bar. "You're really pissed that I'm here?"

"It was supposed to be a quiet night," I whispered. "Dinner for two, watching a movie, making out, trying to figure out if I . . . if I . . . Now, though . . ."

Lena poked out her bottom lip. "I'm sorry, sweetie. I'll be more considerate next time."

"There may not *be* a next time."

My phone, now sitting near Lena's thigh, chimed.

Lena grabbed my iPhone. "Stop acting like you resemble Beetlejuice. There will be as many times as you want. Don't worry: I won't stay long." She frowned at the phone's screen, but then the edges of her lips lifted. "Elouise Norton."

"That's my name, don't wear it out."

"You've. Got. *Mail*."

"Yep. Heard it ring." I grabbed the tub of parmesan cheese from the fridge.

The doorbell rang.

Sam shouted, "I'll get it."

Lena's eyes flitted back to the phone. "Who's Dr.Zach@ hotmail and why is he—?"

My heart popped in my chest, and I reached to grab the device from my friend's hands.

But Lena was quicker and sat on it. "Who is Dr. Zach?"

"Ssh!"

We both turned to the doorway: no Sam.

She plucked the phone from beneath her, then used one hand to keep me back. *"Hey, you,"* she read. *"No gossip in the clinic. But how about that coffee?"* She lifted her eyebrows and grinned at me. "You're sneakin' around on Sam *already*?"

"No, I'm not." I snatched the phone from her hands. "You're climbing back into your Range Rover with its jacked-up rim, pulling up the audio version of *War and Peace*, and driving back to Rancho Palos Verde—"

She sucked her teeth. "And here I was, hoping to wear ugly taffeta by New Year's Eve."

"Ugly taffeta? Why?"

"A wedding. Yours. Sam's. Cuz you two are—"

"Lena, I can't even have a night alone with the man without—"

"You don't like him?" Lena's eyebrows crumpled. "Is that why Dr. Zach is texting you?"

I told her about falling in the mud at Bonner Park and being rescued by an attractive stranger. "And that's it," I said. "He keeps e-mailing me."

"Welcome to the twenty-first century. We no longer send sonnets over telegram."

I squinched my nose. "He sent me a picture."

Lena's eyes widened. "Ooh! I wanna see."

I found the selfie he'd taken at the nurse's station.

"He's gorgeous," Lena said. "I wanna see the other one."

I frowned. "Umm . . . Huh?"

She smiled. "Where's the one he took of his dick?"

I blinked at her.

She gaped at me. "Didn't he . . . ?" She sent her fingers flying across my phone's keyboard.

I looked over her shoulder. "What are you doing?"

"Logging into my e-mail," she said, "so I can show you . . . Look."

The largest penis outside of the LA Zoo.

She swiped the screen.

Another penis, this one pinker, not as big.

Swipe.

Another.

Swipe.

Another.

"It's like United Colors of Benetton," I said, gaping at the panoply of penises.

"Now that you're single," Lena said, "you need to be au courant with the dating scene."

My mouth had gone dry. "I don't have to . . . reciprocate, right?"

She laughed. "I don't think Dr. Zach would mind."

I snatched my phone from her grip. "There's nothing sexy going on between this Zach guy and me."

She smirked. "Tell me more about my eyes."

"Nothing sexy is going on," I said, pulling her off the counter.

Lena snorted. "Famous last words."

"For a *whore* with a gallery of genitalia," I said, pushing her out of the kitchen.

Colin was standing with Sam in the living room.

"Why are you here?" I snapped. "Why aren't you with Naughty Nurse Carly?"

"Work." Colin dropped his bag to the couch. "Sorry for interrupting. Hey, Lena."

"Colin," she said, then bit her bottom lip.

She and my partner still flirted even though they both knew nothing would be done about it. They'd had their chance months ago, after her pole-dancing class recital, when they both had said meh.

"We were about to sit down for dinner," Lena now purred, slinking over to Colin. "Let me help you with your . . . *sack*." She took his arm and led him to the table. "Carly—is that the girl Lou calls Trailer Trash Barbie?"

My breath came fast as I glanced at Sam. *He's about to leave. He hates me. He'll find someone else. Anyone else.*

Sam smiled at me. "Hey."

"I'll make it up to you," I said.

He pulled me into his arms, then kissed me. "Hell, yeah, you will." Then, whistling, he ambled over to the dining room table.

Colin sat next to Lena. "If I'm interrupting . . ."

"It's all good," Sam said.

Lena grabbed the bowl of green beans. Colin dumped pasta onto his plate.

What work had barged in to keep him from his date?

But I let him eat as I pushed my food around the plate.

Lena's bracelets jangled every time she brought the fork to her mouth. "Chauncey," she said, "my ex, for those of you who don't know . . ." *Jingle*. "Had the nerve to call me last night." *Jangle*. "He and his husband are trying to adopt a baby." *Jingle*. "He asked if I could serve as a reference." *Jangle*. "Can you believe that?" *Jingle jangle*.

I dropped my fork, exasperated with the jingling bracelets. "Who the hell are you? The Ghost of Christmas Past?"

Lena whooped.

Sam laughed and drained his wineglass.

"Food's good," Colin said to me. To Sam: "Dude, you catch today's games?"

"Ohmigod," Sam said, "what is that coach *doing*?"

And they talked March Madness and their grids, home-brewing, the new Tesla, and, finally, the Clippers. Lena chimed in—as the ex-wife of one of the country's most powerful sports agents, she knew a few things about men and their balls.

"I've had enough," I said, then wiped my mouth with a napkin. "Colin, what work barged in?"

"I was in the neighborhood," Colin said, "since Carly . . . *dances* not far from here."

I cocked an eyebrow. "Crazy Girls?"

He cleared his throat and blushed. "Yeah."

"Trailer Trash Barbie is a *stripper*?" Lena screeched.

Sam, laughing, covered his mouth with his hand.

"*Anyway*," Colin said, "since I was close, I thought I'd update you in person about Chanita Lords's tooth and other . . . things."

"Pardon me?" Lena asked.

I pointed at her. "None of this leaves the room. She had a tooth in her hand."

"It was her second molar," Colin said.

"Any significance?" I asked.

Colin shrugged.

"The second molar," Sam said, "is the last baby tooth a child loses. That happens around twelve, thirteen years old."

I cocked an eyebrow at him.

Sam winked at me. *You like that?*

I bit my lip. *Oh yeah, I like that* a lot.

"The monster extracted it," Colin said, "before she died."

"Can't leave that on voice mail," Lena said, wineglass to her lips.

"No." And, just like that, my body went cold.

"And then there's Raul Moriaga," Colin said. "I called his friend's number."

"And?" I asked.

He shrugged. "It just rings and rings. No voice mail kicks in."

"If we need to," I said, "we'll call his probation officer."

"You make dessert?" Colin asked.

"Not for you," I said. "Anything else?"

"No DNA results on anything have come back," Colin said. "But since this isn't a TV show, that's no surprise."

Lena pushed away from the dinner table. "And now I suddenly want to go home. *Layla tov,* my dears. Sam Seward, would you be a gentleman and walk me to my car, please?"

I narrowed my eyes at Lena. *What are you gonna say to him?*

"I should go, too," Colin said, retrieving his bag from the living room. "Gotta head back to pick her up—"

"Before the wings are gone and all that body glitter starts clumping?" Lena asked.

Colin pointed at her. "Joke's on you. I *never* eat at a strip club." He winked at her, then said to me, "Thanks for dinner."

Sam left the dining room to get his jacket.

Lena stooped near my chair and whispered, "He passed."

I squinted at her. "What?"

She canted her head. "Sam passed my test. Do you really think I'd barge in on you for no reason? I had to test his tolerance and patience for your people. And he passed. Now, get your freak on, girl." She winked at me, then tottered out of the dining room.

I stayed at the table and stared at the puddle of pesto in the bottom of the French porcelain bowl, at green beans drying on plates, at candles burned down to stubs. My mind zigzagged between thoughts of Sam, Lena, and the monster. Work won. Again.

He had pulled out Chanita Lords's tooth and had then placed it in her hand.

Was he—Raul Moriaga, maybe?—telling us that she was no longer a child or . . . ?

The night had certainly turned.

As for Normal Living—guess my visit was over.

23

I AWOKE EARLY FRIDAY MORNING—5:17 GLOWED ON THE NIGHTSTAND'S DIGITAL
clock. Raindrops tapped at the windowpane, and on the
other side of my bed . . . cold sheets. *You shouldn't have sent
him home. You should've guzzled another glass of wine,
pushed work out of your head, and . . . You shouldn't have—*

"Oh, shut up," I muttered, closing my eyes.

I'd call Sam at a decent hour. I'd apologize again for Lena
and Colin. I'd offer him a redo. I'd send him cupcakes.

Truth be told, I wasn't ready for overnights, spooning, or
early-morning fumbling in the dark followed by sunrise head.
I wasn't ready to share my . . . pie. Truth be told.

I turned away from the place Sam should've lain and pulled
the comforter over my head. Thankfully, I was exhausted
enough to doze until the eager sun, fresh from that trip to Fiji
or Antarctica, pushed aside the clouds and brightened the
bedroom with copper-colored light.

A day without rain. Maybe.

As I tugged on my blue wool slacks, my cell phone rang.
Ewoks.

I answered the call. "Good morning, Gregory. I don't have
a lot of—"

"Time to talk," my ex-husband finished, smoky-voiced.
"I've heard that before. I know the drill. But Arianna What's-

Her-Face, our Realtor? I fired her and hired someone else."

"Great," I said, stuffing the tails of my gray shirt into my pants.

"I know you're busy, but this is important. Let's get together."

"Get together with *you* or with the Realtor?"

Greg paused, then said, "Well, with me first. To talk about a few things."

I gritted my teeth, tired of this back-and-forth with him.

"So?" Greg said. "When can we talk?"

I buttoned my pants. "Sunday."

He sighed. "You know, Lou, I—"

"And we're no longer married and I don't have to listen to you complain about me anymore. And now, I'm going to hang—"

"Is it because you're . . . busy?"

"Yes."

"You see *Avengers* yet?"

I shoved my left foot into the right loafer. "I did."

"With Sy and Lena?"

"Nope."

"I'm working on this cool game you're gonna like."

I reversed feet, then tried again. "That's nice."

"It's steam-punk meets—"

"Uh huh, that's nice." I grabbed a suit jacket and a pair of hiking boots from the closet. "Greg, I need to—"

"Who'd you see *Avengers*—?"

"Gotta go. See you Sunday."

Outside, puffy white clouds speckled the clean blue sky. Driving south, I glanced in the rearview mirror: sunlight glinted off the Griffith Park Observatory's golden dome. It was cold—fifty-three degrees—but it was good cold. Face-lift cold.

As I opened the door to the detectives' bureau, the peace

abruptly ended. The March Madness board had been updated—Texas had defeated Arizona State, and Villanova beat Milwaukee—and that was the only nugget of order. Not even eight o'clock yet, and men in cheap suits shouted into telephones, into radios, and at each other. The copy machine shuttled reams of paper around its drum. Metal desk after metal desk held haphazard stacks of folders, rap sheets, BOLOs, and other detritus found in busy bull pens throughout the galaxy.

My desk served as a monument to organized chaos: Sam's flowers, a stack of color-coded folders, bulging accordion files in the credenza, and one sticky note left by Colin slapped onto my computer monitor. *With Luke. Krispy Kreme for surveillance video . . . and donuts!!!*

"Detective Norton?"

A round-faced, round-bodied black man appeared at my desk as though Scotty had just beamed him down from the starship *Enterprise.* He looked clean and neat in his JCPenney dress shirt and blue and silver sales-rack necktie—the costume of a bank teller or customer-service rep at the gas company. His earnest brown eyes flicked here and there, out of sorts with the environment but not wholly uncomfortable with it, either.

"You left a message with my sister yesterday," the man said now.

I squinted at him. "I did?"

He nodded. "About Nita. Or Regina. I'm Maurizio—"

"Oh. Yes. That's right. Maurizio Horsley." I directed him to sit in the empty chair beside my desk. "You and Regina dated."

"I guess so." His legs jittered, and he placed his hands between his knees. "We broke up two months ago."

I grabbed a pen and pad. "Mind telling me why?"

"I caught her forging checks from my bank account."

My pen paused, and I cocked my head. "Really?"

He wiped at the beads of sweat on the bridge of his nose. "I didn't know she was a thief—we didn't live together. I still don't know where she lives. We always met at places."

"And where did you first meet?"

"At the bank where I work. I met her daughter only once. Unfortunately."

"And you say 'unfortunately' because . . . ?"

"Because one time Regina used her to distract me." He shook his head. "Gee was tearing checks out of my checkbook while Nita was showing me pictures she'd taken on her camera."

I lifted my eyebrows. "Wow."

He nodded, and tears filled his eyes like he'd just learned he'd been conned minutes ago.

"You press charges?" I asked.

"She begged me not to. Three strikes."

I studied him—clean nails, trim mustache, nerve pinging near his left temple, fists clenching and unclenching. "How much she take?"

"A little over a grand."

"And you just . . . ? You're a nice guy."

"Her people are . . ." He swallowed. "I don't want any trouble."

"And you think Chanita was in on the con?"

He shrugged.

"You hate them?" I asked.

His eyes dropped to his clenching fists. He sighed, then nodded.

"Do you know that Chanita's dead?"

"Yes."

"Did you have anything to do with her death?"

His eyes widened. "Me? Oh Lord, no! Never. No."

"Would you be willing to give me a DNA sample?"

"Sure. Yes. Please." He opened his mouth and stuck out his tongue.

I chuckled. "Hold on a minute." I glanced around the room—Pepe was hunched over the copier drum, fixing a paper jam.

A minute later, Maurizio Horsley and Pepe disappeared into one of the interview rooms.

Alone again, I turned in my chair. On the whiteboard, Maurizio's name had been written beneath "POI." *No wonder he kept wetting the bed.* I placed a check by his name, then found the Web site for MmmGrace Cupcakes. I ordered a dozen salted caramel, to be delivered to Sam Seward with a note:

You are Magic.

24

CUPCAKES ORDERED. SPIT TAKEN. ONE SUSPECT DOWN, COUNTLESS MORE TO GO.

Lena texted: *Sam! Plz tell me u are basking!! #afternoondelight*

I texted back: *Maybe next time*.

She responded. *What are you waiting for?? #ColonyonMars??*

I chuckled, then let my fingers dance across the phone's keyboard. *Enough time to bask! #afternoondelight*

Colin banged into the office, cell phone to his ear, green and yellow necktie untied. "I had fun, too . . . No, you're . . ." He laughed. "Well, I have work to do, darlin' . . ." He dropped his bag to the floor. "Yep . . . Yep. I'll let you know." He tossed the phone on the desk, then plopped into his chair. "Morning, sunshine. You look happy."

"But you're here," I said, smiling. "Alas, my joy is short-lived."

"Ha," he said, knotting his tie.

"You look nearly recovered."

He swiveled in his chair. "All thanks to my little hottie." He found a picture on his phone and showed me Carly, all done up as a naughty nurse.

I snorted. "She doesn't look a day over sixty."

"She works that pole, though."

"Well, she's been workin' it since the Prohibition."

He flipped me the bird. "So, after gettin' some tender lovin' care from *her,* I'm now the picture of health. Never underestimate the power of a woman."

"One more cliché."

"I'm strong as an ox." He stopped swiveling and pointed at me. "You know? I like Sam. You two are a good match. Like peas and carrots."

I blinked at him. "I hate peas and carrots."

"You'd eat 'em if you used more butter," he said. "And you and Sam? You two got lots of butter."

I rolled my eyes. "So the Krispy Kreme security footage?"

He gave me guns fingers. "Every three days, the manager tapes over shit. So Friday's tape is long gone."

The muscles in my body felt weighted down—this case was pulling me under, threatening to drown me.

"And Luke has the donuts," he said.

"And where's Luke?"

"Stopped at Bang Bang's. Dealing with Chanita's phone and e-mail and all that."

"You left Luke alone with a box of donuts?"

Colin logged on to his computer. "Fat jokes, Elouise?"

"No," I said, "Pepe told me that Luke now has whatever germs *you* had. And Luke never, ever covers his mouth when he sneezes."

Colin winced. "So what's on today's agenda?"

"Back to Bonner Park since there's a break in the weather." I forwarded my desk phone to my cell phone in case Zucca or Brooks called. "Let's get goin' before the rain starts again."

Usually on sunny weekends at Bonner Park, fifteen-year-old Hispanic girls wearing wedding gowns the color of Jolly Rancher candy posed by the Japanese bridge and waterfall. Her sixteen attendants, each wearing more Jolly Rancher candy–colored gowns, and boys wearing zoot suits, all waited

165

to say "cheese" for the professional photographer.

But this rainy weekend, there would be no *quinceaneras* here.

The only people at the lake now were the old codgers. Each man wore a baseball cap—Steelers, Lakers, Raiders, Best Grandpa Ever. No New Orleans Saints. I relied on that hat—nothing else in Vanessa's picture had been as clear and obvious as that hat.

Colin parked in the community center's empty lot. "Wasn't the sun out when we left? Like, ten minutes ago?"

I glanced at the sky—rain clouds the color of S.O.S. pads had hijacked the friendly clouds and the sun.

"Think the park ranger's in today?" Colin asked.

No other car was parked in the lot, and the community center looked dark. The lower portion of Bonner Park was no longer cordoned off by yellow police tape. Wind whistled through the oaks and eucalyptus trees, and the creak of oil dickeys just over the hill carried on the wind.

Colin's teeth chattered as he shoved his hands deep into his jacket's pockets. "Feels like Colorado today. Thought I left that weather behind."

I opened the trunk and grabbed the hiking boots. Colin yanked at the center's door—locked. He peered through the iron grate covering the windows, then knocked on the door. "Maybe he's out stopping bears from stealing pic-a-nic baskets."

I stomped my feet—the boots were warm and dry—then glanced up at the trail that led to the dump site. "Ready?"

"Can't we drive some of the way?"

"We need to see everything—can't do that in a car." I smiled and elbowed him in the abdomen. "Show me your stuff, Mountain High."

Ten minutes into our hike, my cell phone vibrated.

An e-mail from Dr. Zach. *Detective Elouise Norton, I have so much to ask you. What kind of coffee do you like? Books or movies? Rom-com or adventure? Boxers or briefs? I'd like to find all these things out. But when? I'm in clinic all day but call or email me anytime.*

My face flushed. "This guy."

"Sam?" Colin asked.

I slipped my phone back into my pocket. "No. Just this guy I met."

Colin shook his head. "You're a little slut now that you're divorced."

I shoved him. "I'm not a slut. He e-mails, and Lena says that it's normal even though it seems a little . . . stalky."

Colin laughed. "Oh yeah. You *were* dating back when men wrote love letters with *pens*."

"You don't anymore?"

Colin smirked. "Texts, e-mails, Facetime, tweets, it's what you do now, Wilma Flintstone. I get about . . . a hundred texts a day on a *weekday*. When I'm not working?" He whistled. "That's not being a *stalker*. That's bein' handsome and sexy."

I rolled my eyes. "Oh, brother."

"Relax and enjoy the attention. E-mails are normal, got it? Say it with me."

Together, we said, "E-mails are normal," twice.

"Speaking of sluts," he said, "Dakota called me."

"You're the slut in this story then?"

"Uh huh. Anyway . . ." He paused, then exhaled. "She met some guy."

I glanced at him, at his clenched jaw and bobbing Adam's apple. "And you said . . . ?"

He shrugged. "Wished her well. He's an air force captain. I knew him from high school." He shrugged again. "Shorter than me. No neck. Every other word outta his mouth is 'Holy Spirit.'"

I laughed, then said, "You know, I'd pick you over Captain Saved."

He smiled. "Yeah?"

"Yep. If we were in the last days, and you had a gun pointed at my head while carrying a slab of barbecue ribs? Oh hell yeah. It would be me and you, Colin. Me and you."

Colin laughed. "You're a national treasure, Lou."

We walked on, the only noise the clomp of our boots on the dirt trail and the furious chirp of birds in a hurry to find food before the next storm hit. My muscles burned as we continued up the muddy path. Took us almost thirty minutes to reach the top when it would've taken only ten minutes on dry days.

For thirty-seven years old, I was in great shape—back in December, after Christmas, I had returned to Krav Maga, stepping up ab crunches and sidekicks. But today, the hike took my breath away. Add a canvas bag with a hundred pounds of dead weight and throw in rain and mud, and I'd never reach this summit in time to disappear without being seen by someone on the trail.

A white CSI van was parked on the gravel service road closest to Chanita's dump site.

"Guess Zucca had the same idea," Colin said.

Up ahead, yellow tape and the blue tarp stood out against the green. Because the area was still taped off, memorials for Chanita Lords had been left at the trunk of the closest eucalyptus tree. Stuffed animals were drenched from the rain. Battered posters with running, inky messages—WE LOVE YOU! WE MISS YOU! JUSTICE 4 NITA!!—had been nailed to the tree's trunk. Candles no longer burned—their flames had been doused by storm water. Three young women wearing nylon jackets stood nearby taking pictures—crime-scene selfies—as fine drizzle now fell from those steel-wool clouds.

The heavy sky pushed down on me as I walked past the tarp to where the thirteen-year-old had been discarded in the mud.

Zucca and a beauty-shop blonde were placing heavy flashlights into hard cases.

"What's the haps, Z?" I asked

"Looking for It," he said. "Always looking for It." He nodded to the blonde. "You remember Krishna."

Krishna of the ridiculous hair, the cold-sore scar on her upper lip, the imperious blue eyes. The same Krishna who had screwed up a few DNA swabs and specimens by not wearing gloves, and so, in the end, a man who had killed his ex-wife and her dog had gone free because of reasonable doubt. Yes, I remembered Krishna.

And Krishna remembered me. She now gave me the stink-eye since she was still shitting out pieces of leather from my Cole Haan pumps.

Colin didn't speak, either, because he, too, remembered Krishna. Didn't matter if she was allegedly pretty or not, the detective from the Springs had been around me long enough to despise Stupid Ass People Who Let Killers Go Free.

And that is why I now said, "Zucca, walk with me."

He followed me north on the trail.

I stopped at the bluff.

"Lou," he said, "I know—"

"*Really*?" I glared at him, then pointed toward the tarp. "You bring that simple bitch to my scene? To the most important case we'll—"

He held up his hands. "I know."

"No, you *don't*, cuz if you *did*, you'd know that I will effin' go off on her *and* you—"

169

"I promised you that wouldn't happen ever again." His skin was pale and moist with flop sweat. "Today, I watched everything she did, and I'll keep supervising her closely."

"No."

"She has to work on *something*," he said. "I swear: she won't mess up your evidence."

I glared at him for good measure, then stomped back to the scene.

Colin and Krishna were warily eyeing each other.

"So. Anything interesting?" I asked Zucca, the angry quiver still in my voice.

Zucca nodded. "The pupae Brooks collected from the victim during the autopsy were blowflies. Some from here, some not from here. And there were dead spiders in that bag. Again, not all from this park.

"And the grass in the bag she was in," he continued, "didn't come from here. And the dirt contained fertilizer and plant life not from here. And the leaves in the bag don't match the flora in this area, either."

"So we were right," I said. "Another crime scene."

"Another strange discovery," Zucca said. "We found a red View-Master in the bag."

I opened my mouth, then popped it closed.

"You know, the toy?" Zucca said. "There are these 3-D picture discs that you pop in and you look in it to see—"

"I know what a View-Master is," I said. "I'm just confused why she'd have it."

"Did you look and see what the pictures were on the disc?" Colin asked.

"Greece," Krishna said with a shrug. "Mount Olympus, the Colosseum, Parthenon . . ."

My blood ran cold as I took notes with a shaky hand.

"Why did he move her so many times?" Colin wondered.

"Probably to confuse us," Zucca suggested.

"Cover his tracks by making tracks everywhere," I said. "Anything else interesting?"

"Deadly nightshade," Zucca said, retrieving his tools. "Definitely not found in this park."

"So if we find the origin of the deadly nightshade . . . ?" Colin said.

"You'll probably find where she was murdered," Krishna finished.

I turned to my partner. "Up for more walking in the woods?"

25

TEN MINUTES LATER, ZUCCA AND KRISHNA CLANKED DOWN THE SERVICE ROAD
with their boxes and kits. Colin and I, heading in the opposite
direction, stopped at the lone park bench on the bluff.

"Like home up here," Colin said. "Peaceful. Beautiful. My
dad thinks it's all freeways and smog and . . ." He pulled the
digital camera from his pocket and began taking shots. "A
shame someone would screw all of this up."

"Yeah." I gazed down the steep hillside. "He took her
from the bus stop on Friday and left her in another area long
enough to inherit its bugs, dirt, and leaves. When did he
dump her?"

"Early Sunday morning?" Colin wondered. "Higher,
farther back off the trail. Maybe he came back on Wednesday
to check to see if she'd been found yet."

"But why come back at all and take a chance getting
caught? Maybe . . . he's not the monster and was just some
random dude who was on the trail like everyone else."

I sighed. "Stop making sense. It does me no good." I clicked
my teeth as I thought. "And *when* did he do it? The guy in the
hat. The guy with the bat. The guy eating green eggs and
ham, whoever the fuck he is. The park opens at sunrise, a
little after six A.M., and closes at sunset, a little after five
thirty P.M."

172

"A gate blocks the entrance," Colin added. "But someone could easily hop over that."

"An occasional visitor wouldn't know that this bluff exists," I said. "Ten trails, and not all end in wonderfully scenic spots like this."

I pointed to a smaller trail that wound past bottlebrush trees, cactus patches, and very young California poppies and then across the green valley and up to those million-dollar homes. "What if he came that way instead of the bigger trail?"

Colin stared at the smaller trail for a moment, then bowed. "After you."

Together, we half-slid, half-stumbled down the crumbling hillside. Red mud and wet grass rimmed the hems of our slacks.

"You almost forget you're in the middle of the city," I said once we reached flat land. "It must get dark as hell out here."

He pointed to our left, at the huge radio towers equipped with glowing red bulbs. "Just those lights."

We scrambled up a hill and then tottered down into a quiet neighborhood cul-de-sac. A yellow ranch-style house sat on one side of the street. Next to it was a brown ranch with palm trees and a manicured lawn. On the side of the hill we'd just climbed sat a white split-level home with ivy ground cover and, next to that, another split-level house painted salmon. New potholes were forming on Weatherford Drive because of all the rain and because part of the slope Colin and I had just climbed flowed onto the sidewalks.

"You take one side," I said, "and I'll take the other."

Colin ambled toward the yellow house across the street.

I trudged to the nearby split-level and climbed the stairs to the front door.

The white house needed two new coats of paint, modern windows, and a gardener. Despite its shagginess, though, the house enjoyed a great northern view of the basin and an awesome southern view of Bonner Park.

A tanned, honey-blond woman wearing blue surgical scrubs answered the door. She took in my nice blue suit and damp gray shirt, then frowned at my muddy hems and hiking boots."Yes?"

I badged her, then told her that I was working "a case" and that the person of interest may have passed through the neighborhood. "You seen anyone out of place lately?"

She shook her head. "It's very peaceful here. No drama."

"You live alone?" I tried to see past her but only glimpsed the walls of the foyer.

"Actually, I don't live here. This is my boyfriend's house, and he's not home."

"When does he usually get home?"

"Eight, nine o'clock." A pager beeped from her hip.

"You're a doctor?"

"Yes." She pointed to the little black box on her hip. "May I?"

I nodded, then turned to see Colin strolling from the yellow house to the brown house.

"I need to get out of here," she said with a regretful smile.

"What type of medicine do you practice?"

She grabbed her purse from a table I couldn't see. "I'm a surgical resident at Children's." She stepped onto the porch, closing the door behind her. "Should I be concerned? Is this about the dead girl in the park?"

Together, we walked down the stairs. "Yes, it is." I pulled a business card from my coat pocket and offered it to her. "If you hear any neighborhood gossip, give me a call? And could you ask your boyfriend to call me as well? Since he lives in the area, I want to keep him informed."

She took the card and read it. "Certainly, Detective Norton, although, like I said, I don't live here. Only visit a few times a week. And he's always working and rarely home. But if I hear anything, I'll let you know. And I'll make sure he calls."

A moment later, Colin and I headed back down into the valley and toward the chaos of the dark woods. The wind gusted stronger than before, making the radio towers creak and the low grass bend. No one had been at the houses Colin visited, and so he'd left business cards in the front doors.

A hawk's cry drew our gaze skyward. The large bird circled not that high above us.

"Why did he choose this park?" Colin asked.

Eyes on the raptor, I said, "Because he knows it."

The hawk dive-bombed behind the hilltop, then swooped back into the sky. A small creature was now trapped in its talons.

"Why leave her on the trail?" he asked.

Something inside of me tightened into a tiny ball as I watched the raptor with its prize. "Because he wanted us to find her."

26

ONCE AGAIN, THE WEATHER MATCHED OUR MOODS—DAMP, DARK, AND UNCERTAIN. As Colin and I trudged back to the car, neither of us talked. Gusts of wind whirled around us, bearing the smell of dead things. Colin stopped every now and then to take pictures of tree trunks and puddles.

"This sucks," I finally muttered.

Colin said, "Yeah."

"My feet hurt," I said.

"My ovaries hurt," he said.

"My prostate—" My police radio chimed from my hip.

Unknown Caller.

I let the call go to voice mail. A moment later, nerves twitching, I listened to the message.

"Elouise, it's Daddy." Victor Starr's voice—dark like chicory coffee with a hint of arrogant Louisiana. "I know you're still upset with me, but I'm not goin' away. Not until we talk. Say whatever you gotta say to me, just as long as you say *something. Anything.*"

Back in December, I had said plenty.

That afternoon, he had stood on my front stoop, and I had just ended my marriage with Greg after a Hail Mary in the bathroom. Still wearing a towel and nothing else, I had opened the front door, thinking it was my husband who'd plead for one last chance. But a tall man with my eyes and Tori's nose darkened my porch, and before he could open his mouth, the realization that this man was my father had crushed me like burning bricks. He had looked the same as he had when he'd abandoned me on that morning so long ago. Just grayer. Wealthier. Rounder—a middle-aged gut from Porterhouse steaks and creamed spinach.

He had wanted to come in and talk.

I had said, "No."

"Can we talk out here?"

"No."

He had shoved his hands into his coat pockets. "You wanna call your mother?"

"No."

"Don't you wanna know why I left?"

I had glared at him—dragon rage coiled in my belly, claws flexing, preparing to release the fire of ancient hatred. Of *course* I wondered why he left. But that's it. *Wondered*. Even though I possessed technology to search for missing people, I had never typed "Victor Starr" into the search bar. Nor had I asked Mom if sex had been their problem. Like our talk last night, I had sought to avoid that topic just as I'd avoid drinking from a water fountain in Chernobyl.

All of my life, I sought to place blame for his abandonment. Naturally, I had blamed the person closest to me—my mother. That belief softened once my marriage started to necrotize and I realized that my power to control Greg was akin to controlling Halley's Comet.

Until last night, I still wondered if Mom loved Victor Starr. But I had never asked that question, either. I *needed* Mom and Martin together. I *needed* Mom to have a happily ever after.

And so, after my litany of "No, no, no" on that December day with Victor Starr, I had closed the door on him, pulled on clothes, and then curled up on the couch to watch *The Poseidon Adventure* for the three hundredth time. Stubborn, he continued to knock and ring the doorbell.

Even if he'd been chased by bees or zombies or zombie bees, I still wouldn't have opened the door for him. I chose to lay there, mourning Shelley Winters. *There's got to be a morning after.* And there was.

Victor Starr finally stopped knocking and went away.

Although, not really. Because here he was again, leaving messages on my phone, tidal-waving my life, and, worse, upsetting Mom's.

Fucker.

Mom will have her morning after, I decided as my partner and I reached the car. And I would give it to her.

Colin handed me a bottled water and a roll of paper towels. "You okay?"

"Victor Starr called," I said, then guzzled from my water bottle.

His shoulders slumped. "Ah, hell."

"Yeah." I paused, then added, "I hate having this reaction. I should be *happy* that my father calls me, right?"

Colin shrugged.

"Your mom and dad ever gonna come out to visit?"

He forced himself to smile. "You wanna meet my folks already? We haven't even slept together yet."

I smirked. "Your folks would stroke out if you brought me home. What would they do with all their white sheets, cans of gasoline, and wooden crosses?"

"We got a big basement," Colin said with a shrug.

"If they fly out, we can pretend that you're up for a Medal of Valor or something. It would be like an episode of *Three's Company.*"

"What's *Three's Company?*"

"I'm not that damned old, and you're not that damned young."

"Whatever, Lou." He sighed. "Gonna take more than that for him to get over me bein' transferred. At least with your dad, you're the one in control."

At least.

After cleaning my face, hands, and hems with wipes and slipping back into my nice loafers, I sank into the Crown Vic's deep passenger seat. I closed my eyes to force my banging pulse to slow.

Colin interrupted the silence by rattling Tic Tacs and singing a Maroon 5 song.

Nausea washed over me, and I sat up in the seat. "Let's hit Chanita's school and see what we can see."

Colin drove down twisty La Cienega, then turned right onto Parthenon Street. "You gonna call him back?" He reached into the glove compartment and grabbed a bottle of DayQuil.

"I'm gonna vomit," I pawed through the compartment, searching for peppermint candy or a sock to sop up the prehurl spit collecting in my mouth.

Colin reached into his pocket and plucked out the little container of peppermint Tic Tacs.

I accepted the gift and dumped thousands of candies into my mouth.

"He's only gonna keep calling," Colin said.

I crunched and crunched, then shrugged.

We passed the Jungle's neglected apartment buildings, where aluminum foil sometimes doubled as curtains. We passed still-abandoned Santa Barbara Plaza, with its dead and gone businesses shuttered with wooden planks. An evangelical church now leased space in the middle of the depressed complex that had, once upon a time, boomed with fish markets, soul food restaurants, cocktail lounges, and

Crase Liquor Emporium. Every business had suffered from riot-related fires and the urban troika: unemployment, crime, and poverty.

But Victor Starr had escaped this hell, lucky bastard.

"I hate when you're quiet." Colin brought the medicine bottle to his lips and guzzled. "It worries me."

The lump in my throat only allowed me to grunt.

He took another swig. "You okay? For real?"

"Sure," I croaked.

"Lou, you can't solve everything by yourself. Let me help."

"Thank you, Iyanla, but I don't need you to fix my life right now. Try again tomorrow."

He tossed the empty bottle into the backseat. "We talk about all kinds of shit now, right? My sex life. Your lack of a sex life."

"Oy."

"Family, politics—"

"We don't talk politics cuz you're an idiot."

"The point is, we're closer now," he said.

"Yes."

"And we've protected each other from the Crazies. And we control the Crazies so that law-abiding citizens can make a run for it." He tapped the steering wheel. "Guess what I'm saying is . . . I'm here for you, partner."

I nodded. "Thanks, pal."

"And this monster in the Saints cap—we'll catch him. Know why? Cuz we don't let the Crazies win."

I chuckled. "You can rah-rah all you want but law-abiding citizens—even us cops—can't control the Crazies, no matter how hard we try. It's just a matter of time before they eke into the cracks of the kingdom walls. It's just a matter of time before the monster confronts me or confronts you in a dark alley when we're least expecting it."

"So," he said, smiling, "to capture him, all we have to do is search every dark alley."

"What if he makes no distinction between light and dark?"

Colin rolled his eyes. "I hate when you go all Nietzsche on me."

"I'll go back to being quiet, then."

We rode down spruce-lined King Boulevard and slowed as we neared Madison Middle School. The sprawling campus shimmered beneath the darkening skies as though it were Oz. But it wasn't Oz. Far from. I had despised junior high school, the Land of Misfits and Bullies, and I hadn't visited my alma mater since ninth-grade graduation. As I climbed out of the Crown Vic now, the aromas of cheeseburgers and chili mac, rot and mold came to welcome me home.

Tori had been missing during my time at this school, and now, standing here, my hands cramped from remembering the journaling, the crying and the not crying, the numbness . . . I didn't want to be at Madison. And as Colin and I walked those corridors, grief crushed my heart like it had so many years ago.

27

ONLY THE STUDENT LOCKERS THAT LINED THE HALLWAYS HAD REMAINED THE SAME since the 80s. The metal detectors that guarded the entryways certainly didn't exist twenty-five years ago. Students talking on rhinestone-studded Sidekicks—a new thing. Girls showing lots of leg and even more midriff—definitely new. Pregnant girls waddling down the hallways—*wow*. In some ways, they could have been my classmates and me—brown faces bright with youth and pimples. But holy moly guacamole, these girls of the new millennium. Curvier. And the boys? Rowdier. Miniskirts. Plain white T-shirts. Sagging khakis and tattoos? Not possible in ye olden days, where a skirt 0.5 centimeters above the knee got you a trip to the principal's office and a pair of sweatpants to wear until sixth period.

"I'm guessing that locker is Chanita's," Colin said, pointing.

Down the eastern corridor, students had taped to the locker's metal door flowers, notes, and homemade posters that read "We Miss You!"

"Maybe not." I pointed at a locker down the opposite hallway, also festooned with RIP signs. Farther down still, another locker and more posters.

"Damn," Colin muttered, "don't these kids have enough normal shit to worry about?"

"Weird body things, stupid parents, and teenage love affairs?"

He nodded. "But now they gotta deal with their own mortality and mourning dead friends and—?" His face reddened. "Sorry. Forgot that you . . ."

I waved my hand, my attention now directed at the security cameras bolted to the walls at every corridor intersection. In the best of worlds, those cameras were currently working. In *this* world, though, I didn't expect them to.

The administrative office had remained in the same spot, and, since my last year here, not much inside of it had changed. Dingy American flag hanging from the wall. Dusty intercom speaker box covered in cobwebs. More Hispanic mothers than black mothers clutching doctors' forms and birth certificates—that was the only visible change.

We approached the end of the long Formica counter and the tall black woman consulting a ledger with one hand as the other futzed with her long hair twists. She peered at me with a pair of lies in blue contact lenses.

I badged her, then told her that we were investigating the murder of Chanita Lords.

She told me that her name was Alice and that she'd helped Detective Gwen Zapata back on Monday with the missing-child school notification form, which was now a part of Chanita's school record.

The other workers heard our conversation, and the office dropped into silence. Those workers soon called waiting parents to the counter just to hear us talk.

"I noticed security cameras," I said to the clerk. "I'd like to get footage from Friday."

Alice sucked her teeth. "Those cameras been down for almost two weeks now."

I scowled at her, sapped of all patience for people and their wack-ass security systems.

"Budget cuts," she said. "What we supposed to do?"

I pulled the search warrant from the case file. "We'd like to see her locker—*that* still exists, doesn't it?"

Alice nodded.

"And then," I said, "we'd like to pop in on her counselor, Mr. Bishop."

Alice jotted down Bishop's office number on a sticky note. Then, she pecked on a computer keyboard to find Chanita's locker number and combination. "Mr. Bishop also counseled Trina Porter." She looked at us over her shoulder. "Just so you know."

"Thanks for the info," I said, squinting at her.

"Yep. Some of us are plannin' to attend Nita's funeral tomorrow. She was an angel. I hope y'all catch . . . him."

Locker 336. Bottom row. A stone's throw from the girls' restroom. Teddy bears, stuffed unicorns, flowers, and pictures of the smiling and very alive thirteen-year-old Chanita Lords. My pulse thrummed in my ears as we moved the memorials aside. Colin spun the locker's tumbler and pulled up the latch.

Textbooks and notebooks on pink-carpeted shelves. Tiny magnetic mirror inside the door along with pictures of friends and the singer Drake.

I plucked an appointment card from a pen holder.

WOMEN & CHILDREN MEDICAL GROUP:
Your next appointment is: Tuesday, April 1, with Dr. Fletcher.

We pawed through Chanita's things and, again, found nothing strange. Still, we took notebooks, the appointment card, and the pictures of Chanita's friends.

I waited at the school's main entrance as Colin took our meager findings back to the car. No one had stopped us as we wandered the building.

"Stop frowning," Colin said, popping up the stairs. "You're gonna scare the kids." He followed me down the corridors, northbound this time.

"I'm frowning because I haven't spotted one security guard roaming the grounds. Any nut can invade a classroom. Any nut can steal a child."

We walked past closed classroom doors, then stopped at the last office on the first floor. The door was cracked, so I peeked in.

A black man around my age sat on the edge of his desk. He wore a blue dress shirt, no jacket, and no tie. Two girls, both wearing green, black, and white cheerleader uniforms, flanked him. His gaze darted from the girls' chests down to their hips.

Girl 1, hazel-eyed and thick-legged, was touching his arm. She'd have a stripper's body in two years.

Girl 2, dark and pretty, doe-eyed and fake-haired, was laughing as though she'd heard the funniest joke ever. Unfortunately, she looked like she already knew her way around the pole.

Anger spiked in my gut, and I pushed open the door, then knocked on the poor wood like it had kidnapped my sister. "Good morning."

The trio jumped. The girls gasped.

"Payton Bishop?" I asked.

He nodded, then told the girls, "You two should get to class."

"Do we got to?" Hazel Eyes asked.

"Yes, Nikki," he said. "Go."

The counselor's broad, lanky frame suggested that he had played tennis or basketball once upon a time. Graying stubble dusted his chin, and a scar peeked from beneath his bottom lip. A gold band hugged his ring finger.

"Aren't they precious?" Colin said, fake smiling at Bishop. "They grow up so fast nowadays. Really, where does the time go?"

"Who are you?" Bishop asked, arms crossed. "And why are you standing in my office?"

Colin handled the introductions, then handed his card to the counselor.

Bishop went rigid. "Have a seat," he said with forced calm.

Payton Bishop had an Eiffel Tower addiction—there were pictures of the famous monument on every wall. Night at the Tower. Fog at the Tower. Spring at the Tower. Snow globes and wrought-iron sculptures of the Tower sat on every flat surface. Framed postcards and restaurant menus hung on the walls.

The counselor noticed my looking as he moved around to his chair. "Have you been?"

"Not my kind of place," Colin said, dropping into one of the two visitor chairs.

"I went back in 2001," I said, taking the other seat. "Rainy but beautiful."

Bishop smiled at me. "We know each other."

"Oh?" I scanned his desk: a personal calendar, a hardcover journal, and a framed picture of a familiar-looking blonde wearing a pink ski suit.

"We were in most of the same honors classes here. *Payton Bishop*. That doesn't sound a little familiar?"

I would've immediately remembered the names "Myron Englund" or "Billy Stevens." Talk about your unrequited love of boys who didn't know you existed. Still, my mind flipped through my ninth-grade yearbook and . . . *Ah! There he was!* Very skinny. Very short. Eyes as big as a kinkajou's. "You're a Superlative Boy," I said.

"A what?"

"A superlative. 'Most' this. 'Best' that. You were 'Most Shy.'"

"Yep," he said. "Remember Dana Laramie? She won 'Best Figure.' Saw her last week at Target. Weighs close to three hundred pounds, no lie."

"Stuck up," I said, remembering, "after she got that tiny part in *Boyz n the Hood*."

"Yep. I asked her out in high school," Bishop said, smiling, "and she told me that she didn't date boys who drove their mom's—"

"Driver's Ed cars," I said, nodding. "She's 'Ho Number Two' in a movie, and all of a sudden she's Miss Cicely Tyson."

He chuckled and shook his head. "Our honors English teacher, Mrs. Cruz? She died last month. Breast cancer. Remember how—?"

"We should really get to why we're here," Colin interrupted.

"Wow," the counselor said, grinning at me. "You're a detective now?"

"Yep. Let's talk about Chanita and Trina. You counseled both of them."

"Trina for only a year," he said. "Then, Liz Porter put her in the parochial school over on Santa Rosalia."

I nodded. "Chanita's mom, Regina, says you two were always together. She told me that Nita also had a crush on you."

He snorted. "I wouldn't put stock into things Regina says."

"She *is* the girl's mother. She would know who her daughter—"

"No, she wouldn't," the counselor interrupted. "Sorry, but Regina was never around to know who Chanita hung out with or who the girl liked."

He was correct, of course, especially since I personally knew the family terrain. But it just *felt* wrong not to trust a mother in mourning.

"And can I be *totally* honest," he asked, "since we go back?"

I nodded. "Be as candid as you want."

Payton leaned forward. "You know Regina: she ain't about shit. Her sisters and brothers ain't about shit. Miss Alberta found Jesus and wants to make it all right, but the Savior's blood can only repair so much." Payton's eyes didn't leave mine. "Just wanted to remind Detective Norton here of who we're dealing with."

I nodded as I wrote the first line of the Emancipation Proclamation—my new go-to sentence to make people think what they've said was important enough to be written. Everything Payton Bishop had just spouted was true—but it offered nothing new.

I stopped writing and said, "I've been told that Chanita was seen with an adult on the day she disappeared."

He held my gaze. "Who was the adult?"

"Don't know," I said. "But that adult drove a dark SUV."

"What do you drive?" Colin asked.

"A gray Prius."

After a rushed knock on the door, a girl charged into Bishop's office. Rust-colored freckles dusted across her nose and beneath her eyes. She'd be nicknamed "Tiny" or "L'il Tee" in a junior high school clique. She held a cupcake thick with pink frosting, and her smile dimmed seeing Colin and me seated there. She whispered, "Sorry," then leaned past us to drop the treat on Payton Bishop's desk.

The counselor said, "Thank you, Destiny," as she backed out of the office. To us, he said, "As I was saying—"

"So where were you on Friday?" Colin asked.

"Sitting right here." Bishop gave me a quizzical, *What's going on here?* look.

"When did you find out Chanita was missing?" Colin asked.

"Friday evening. Miss Alberta called me. And that night I helped look for her."

"When did you find out that she was dead?" I asked.

Bishop's Adam's apple bobbed. "Yesterday morning. The principal told us."

I glanced at his loafers. Definitely not worn for hiking. But a man with an Eiffel Tower addiction and a blond wife probably owned more than one pair of shoes.

"Wednesday morning," Colin said, "between ten thirty and one thirty, where were you?"

Bishop rubbed his index finger beneath his nose. "Running some errands."

"What type of errands?"

He cleared his throat, then sat back in his chair. "Well . . . School-related things. Going to Staples. Picking up a few supplies. A few other things."

"That it?" I asked.

He narrowed his eyes. "Is that a problem?"

"It wasn't in-service back on Wednesday?"

He frowned. "No. That was earlier this month."

Colin smiled at me. "Shocker: the Meanest One lied to us."

I smiled as I considered the pink cupcake on Bishop's desk. But Colin asked the question. "Were Trina and Chanita into you as much as the girls we've seen this morning?"

"*Into* me?" he said. "You're referring to my *students*?"

"You're right," Colin said. "They *are* your *students*. I forgot. Silly me." He tapped the picture frame. "So is lucky Mrs. Bishop as into you as . . . ?"

Bishop lifted the corners of his mouth, but that smile didn't reach his eyes. "She is, indeed, lucky. And she is, indeed, 'into me.' We've been married for almost three years."

Another knock on the door. Another student—a girl with

long blond braids and a box of donuts. She, too, slipped her offering on his desk. "I got an A on my chemistry test," she said.

Bishop smiled. "Good for you. All things are possible—even an A in chemistry."

She blushed, then backed out of the office that now smelled of sugar and vanilla lotion.

We sat in silence for a moment.

Finally, Colin said, "You're a popular teacher."

Payton shrugged and stared at the pink box.

"It's damn sad about Chanita and Trina," Colin continued. "Two of your students—"

"One is no longer my student—"

"Two of your students have either disappeared or been found dead," Colin said.

Bishop said nothing, but he'd become blinky as though his contact lenses were scratched.

Colin said, "Tragic coincidences."

"Yes," Bishop said.

"You counsel any *boys*?" Colin asked. "No boys have stopped in with bro food like nachos or crullers."

"Most students in our gifted and talented program are girls," Bishop shared. To me, he said, "The school environment has changed drastically since we were students. You may not be aware of it, but the boys—"

"You serious?" I asked, laughing. "I'm very much aware of it. I see it every day, all day. Dead and alive and in between. What do you think I do for a living, *Counselor*?"

Bishop nodded. "Yes, of course. So I'm sure you understand my meaning: there aren't enough of our boys in the GAT program."

"So where were you working before Madison?" Colin asked.

"Lincoln Middle School in Mount Washington."

"Why did you leave?"

Bishop's hand drifted up to his head. "The administration and I didn't see eye to eye. They wanted me to approach each student's education the same way. But everyone learns differently—some by rote, some by application. Not everyone's cut out for college."

"And our alma mater is so enlightened here?" I asked, head cocked.

"Enlightened enough." He sighed. "My problem is this: I'm a truth teller, and so that means I'm always a target."

"Tell me about Chanita," I said.

"She was a sweetheart," he said. "One of my favorites. She had a bright future."

"I've seen some of her pictures," I said. "Very talented."

Bishop slumped in his chair. "I worked hard trying to get her out of here. She had two choices: she could've accepted a full scholarship to Thacher School in Ojai or a partial at Stevenson up in Pebble Beach. I didn't care which she chose; I just wanted her away from these kids and out of Los Angeles."

"Why didn't she take the money and run?" Colin asked.

"She was scared what would happen if she left her mother. Without Nita around, Regina would get into more trouble."

"Chanita confided in you a lot," I said.

Steel returned to the counselor's spine, and he sat back up in his seat. "No, not really—"

"But you knew about her life with her mother."

"I only asked why," he said, shaking his head. "Why, after all the trouble I went through in the application process, why she decided not to attend either school. Chanita and I always talked school and almost always talked photography."

"When was the last time you were with Nita?" I asked. "*Just* you and her?"

Bishop opened his mouth to speak, then closed it.

Colin leaned forward, hand to his ear. "Sorry. Didn't catch that."

Bishop's nostrils flared. "I took her to Starbucks back on Monday."

"To take pictures?" I asked.

"No. To talk. That's when she told me about not going away to school."

I squinted at him. "And that required an off-campus trip?"

Bishop didn't respond—not with a grunt, a head shake, or a blink.

"I'll need your DNA," I said.

He nodded. "I understand."

"You'll come down to the station?" I asked.

"Of course. I have nothing to hide." He exhaled, then folded his hands atop his desk.

"What about the girls who bullied her?" Colin asked. "Treasure . . ."

"ShaQuan and Imunique?" Bishop shook his head. "I got them suspended after they jumped Chanita." He thought for a moment, then shook his head. "It's weird how they just focus on some girls. Chanita didn't call attention to herself— she's a photographer. She *observes*."

"You think the girls had something to do with her murder?" I asked.

Bishop stared at the photo of his wife. As he thought, he twisted the wedding band on his finger. "I don't know who would've wanted to kill Chanita. I only know this: I didn't do it."

28

IT WAS CLOSE TO NOON, AND AN OLDER, TALL, BLACK MAN DRESSED IN A knee-length overcoat and black Kangol cap stood near the entrance to Southwest Division's parking garage. Wet trash, mud, and dead leaves had banked at the curbs. No matter— the man's Stacy Adams shone as though the day had been all sunshine and dragonflies.

Colin slowed the car as he approached the lot. "That him?"

"Yep." My gut bubbled—I wanted to vomit again.

Victor Starr grinned as he spotted me in the driver's seat.

"I see where you get your height," Colin said. "And you have the same smile, and—"

"Shut up, Colin." I grabbed my bag from the backseat, then threw open the door. "If I'm not up in ten minutes, call Sam and tell him I'll need bail."

Out of the car now, I glanced at clouds that sat like cast-iron skillets in the sky. The cold wind stung my face, and my heavy bladder pressed against the lining of my ballistics vest.

Victor Starr took a tentative step toward me. "Lu . . . Elouise."

My gaze roamed to the taco joint across the street, and I found interest in the painted red letters that spelled TORTAS AL CARBON.

"Georgia told me that you . . . that we . . . Thank you. I mean that."

I crossed my arms and glowered at him. *What bullshit are you about to try and feed me?*

"Can we go somewhere and talk?" he asked.

I didn't move from my spot. Instead, I looked at my wristwatch—soon as the big hand hit 2, he'd be standing here alone.

The redwood of a man took another step closer to me. He still smelled of cigarettes, peppermint breath mints, and department-store cologne. "Had a heart attack," he said. "About six months ago now."

I rolled my eyes—*of course.*

"And I realized that I needed to do some things before my time came." He chuckled. "Fortunately for me, my doc says that I got about twenty more years on this earth to do 'em."

I shifted to my other foot as the cords in my neck twanged. *I'm doing this for Mom.*

Nervous, he cleared his throat. "So I live in Vegas now. Me, my wife, June, her son, Curtis. He's about your age, a little older." He waited for my response.

And I *was* responding. My heart boomed in my chest like a cranked-up cannon, and my nostrils flared so much that I could've been caught up by the wind.

"I talk about you all the time," he continued. "June's proud of you, too, and Curtis wants to meet you. He's out of the service now and thinking about becoming a cop."

I clenched my jaw so tight it creaked.

"I've done pretty good for myself," he said with a proud smile. "I own a livery service, with about, oh . . . eight limos, a few town cars, one of those party buses . . ."

He abandoned Mom, Victoria, and me, moved to Las Vegas, found a new woman, landed a new job—no, started a new *business*. Like Mary fucking Tyler Moore, he was gonna make it after all.

And now, he stood before me, the daughter he'd deserted, catching me up on his new life. Church deacon. Driving Floyd Mayweather. Desert-landscaping his house in Summerlin.

"Next time you come to Vegas," he was saying, "I'd love for you to stay with us. Bring friends. Y'all would have an entire wing to yourself. I'll arrange car service, too. No charge."

The grace of God kept me standing and breathing on that grimy sidewalk.

Victor Starr made a sad face. "I heard from my cousin Mary—she still talks to your mom every now and then. Yeah, I heard you're divorced now. Sometimes, it just doesn't work out. But you'll find someone."

A strangled noise gurgled from my throat. If this man had not been my father . . .

"You're not talking," he said, anxious now. "Sorry for just jabbering away."

Hot air burned my upper lip, and suddenly it was no longer dark skies and fifty-three degrees. The world tilted, turned crimson, and was hot as hell. I looked at my watch. *One more minute.*

"Don't you have anything to say?"

I smiled and nodded.

Relieved, Victor Starr also smiled.

Arms still folded, I leaned forward. "Stop harassing my mother," I growled. "If you ignore my warning and contact her again, I *will* file a restraining order against you." I stepped around him and stomped into the humid parking lot. I pulled out my phone with a shaky hand and, after several attempts with fingers that refused to cooperate, successfully texted Mom. *Did as you asked and talked to him.*

Then, I slowly exhaled.

Should I have said more? Asked him why?

"No," I muttered. "You don't get to be a part of me in *any* way."

Except that he *was* a part of me. In *every* way.

Just as I reached the back entrance to the station, my phone vibrated.

Thank you, daughter.

"Anything for you, Mom," I whispered.

Anything for you.

29

A BURNING BUBBLE BOUNCED AROUND MY BELLY. THOUGHT THAT IT WOULD HAVE disappeared after my brief . . . whatever with Victor Starr. But as I rode the elevator up to the homicide bureau, that bubble still floated there like a zeppelin refusing to explode.

Hunched over his desk, Luke sneezed as though the largest pepper flake in the world had attacked his nasal passages. He blew his nose, then muttered, "*Pinche* Colin."

"Told you not to breathe behind him," I said, then beckoned him to come over to me.

He hesitated, then grabbed a few more tissues.

I led him to the alcove near interview room 3.

He leaned on the door, lips tights, mustache quivering. "What's up?"

I pointed at him. "Stop being an asshole."

"He lied to me, Lou," he said. "All this time, he's lied to me."

"He didn't lie—he just didn't tell you his sexual preferences—"

"Which—"

"Don't matter," I said. "When that homeless guy was about to stab you in the gut, did Pepe run away? No. He broke the guy's hand. When you couldn't see cuz you sprayed yourself with pepper spray, did he come up with a better

197

story so you didn't look like an idiot? Who sat with you, at your bedside when—?"

"I never said he ain't loyal," Luke said, eyes burning. "He ain't who I thought he was."

"So he's a coward and stupid and has no business with a badge and gun?"

Luke grunted.

"So, whose unit you transferring to, then?" I asked.

Luke gawked at me.

"L.T. already gave me the okay. You can leave and join some Alpha Male clique with their guns and American flags and twelve-inch heterosexual dicks."

Luke sucked his teeth. "C'mon, Lou."

My eyes burned with tears. "No, *you* c'mon, Luke. You don't wanna be family, fine. You know me: I ain't beggin' you to be where you don't wanna be. Neither is Pepe. You hate someone that much, someone who's had your back since forever, then I can't trust you, and I will not work with you."

Luke sank against the door and his face reddened. "I just . . ." He shook his head and sighed. "Can I think about it?"

I reached for the doorknob. "A day, and then I'm done."

Colin, seated at his desk, dragged his eyes away from his cell phone to look at me. "Everything okay?" He glanced in the direction of the alcove.

"Just disappointed in people right now," I said. "What are you working on?"

"Murder book and Thai." He paused. "And your dad? I see no blood on your shirt, so I'm guessin' he's alive?"

"He is. Pickup Thai?"

"Yep. What do you want?"

"Pad Kra Pow, brown rice." I plopped into my chair as Colin left his. It was now time to focus on somebody else's screwed-up life. And Chanita's glamour shot sat atop her case file.

I logged on to our database and typed "Regina Drummond" into the search bar.

Her mug shot popped on my screen. Soft scowl, hard eyes, hair this way and that as though cops had just yanked her out of bed. Arrested in 1991 for check kiting, but the case was dismissed. Arrested a second time in 2013 for check kiting, put on probation. Arrested last year again for check fraud. Court throws up its hands. Trial set to start in August.

So Treasure and her Mean Girl friends weren't *totally* off about Regina running schemes.

Next search: Versace Lords, Chanita's father, a tattooed humbug with a hare lip and cornrows. Currently doing time in Folsom for a little bit of everything: possession, assault, grand this, grand that. Pretty ambitious considering the slothlike vibe his mug shot gave off.

"Time to play Six Degrees of Separation, LAPD-style," I muttered.

Ten minutes into clicking in and out of arrest records, including that of Regina's hazel-eyed brother Paul, the one I'd loved so long ago, I gritted my teeth and rubbed my achy wrist.

"Looking for deviants in Chanita's life?"

My skin warmed as I continued to nurse my wrist. "I know that voice."

"Yeah?" Sam dropped his black briefcase to the floor and sank into the chair beside my desk. He looked fresh in his blue pinstriped suit and gray tie. He crossed his long legs and placed an elbow on my desk.

"Uh huh," I said. "And why are you here today?"

He frowned and pointed at my arm. "You hurt?"

"I fell back at the park on Wednesday."

He held out his hand. "Let me see."

I glanced around the room.

Colin had left for lunch, and no one was looking our

199

way. So I held out my injured wrist.

Sam brought it to his lips and kissed it. "Twice a day as needed." His gaze landed on the striped roses he'd sent back on Wednesday, and he smiled. "I'm meeting with Detective Jefferson about the dead-tourist case. And I also wanted to thank you in person for the cupcakes. Salted caramel, my favorite."

"I should've let you stay last night."

"Next time?" he asked.

"Next time."

Luke sneezed and sprayed the world with germs.

Sam straightened in his seat. "And you're doing what right now?"

I waved at my computer monitor. "Trying to see who has the capacity to do sick shit like inject a teenage girl with bug repellant."

"And what have you learned?"

"That almost everyone in Chanita's family is deviant with the capacity to do sick shit like needles filled with Raid."

"Yeah?"

"So, incarcerated: two of Regina's brothers, for grand theft auto and second-degree manslaughter. Regina's dad, Tracy Drummond, died in San Quentin five years ago. Armed robbery. Oh, and I found a little prostitution sprinkled among the aunts."

"All that in one family?"

"I won't even go into cousins and nephews." I kicked off my shoes. "That's probably why we're not seeing Al Sharpton and those guys in front of TV cameras right now, holding news conferences, screaming about justice and how I'm not doing my job."

"Sounds like Chanita's people aren't the types the public typically rallies around."

"And that's sad," I said, "because Chanita, from what I've learned, was a great girl. She couldn't help that she had miscreants for family." I peered at him, then said, "They were my neighbors growing up."

He blinked. " 'Neighbors' in the global sense or . . . ?"

"They lived in apartment five. I lived in apartment seven."

"Shit." He frowned. "When you said you were from that area, I didn't think, like . . ."

I squinted at him.

His cheeks colored, and he cleared this throat. "It's just that *a lot* of people, cops, say they're from the rough parts of town, but they're really . . . Any good news?"

"I got to cross off two of Regina's ex-boyfriends." I lifted my hands. "Whoop-whoop."

"You goin' to the funeral tomorrow?"

"Uh huh."

"Think he'll be there?"

Cold prickled my neck. "He'll see her to the end."

"You know what I find interesting?" Sam said. "Chanita's initial disappearance. She's at school, and then . . . she's *not* at school. At that bus stop, and then gone."

"Amazing," I cracked.

"Sarcasm before lunchtime?"

I shrugged. "I find it interesting, but not all that surprising."

"She's been in class all morning," he said. "She goes to lunch, buys her hamburger or whatever. She eats. Twenty minutes later, she doesn't show up to Home Ec, but no one saw her leave the campus. Last place she's seen is the bus stop down the block."

"Boggles the mind," I said, mind far from boggled.

"You go to the school yet?"

"We stopped by this morning."

"Aren't there security cameras?"

"Yes, but they're all aimed at the Bentleys and Ferraris in the parking lot."

Sam rolled his eyes.

"It's a poor school, Mr. Seward. Those cameras are barely hanging on to the wall. I didn't expect the system to work, and, alas, it doesn't work. This ain't Harvard-Westlake."

"You dinging me because I went to Harvard-Westlake?"

I grinned at him and sang, "Different strokes—it takes different strokes."

"Says Miss Scratchin' and Survivin'."

"At first, Regina thought Ontrel Shaw, the boyfriend, was involved," I said. "But then she put all of her chips on Raul Moriaga, the neighborhood perv."

"He in the database?" Sam asked.

I nodded. "Just waiting for the results and trying to confirm his alibi, but that's a joke. A devious, lying bastard actin' like a devious, lying bastard, what else is new?"

"You know I'd love to have DNA," he said. "Juries want that along with a confession and the testimony from an eagle-eyed nun who saw the whole thing going down in real time."

"I'm trying as best I can," I said.

"What else?"

I told him about Chanita's relationship with Payton Bishop. He frowned. "You talk with Bishop yet?"

"Yep."

"Thoughts?"

"He's . . . disturbing." And I told him that Bishop and I had been schoolmates, and about the girl students and their sweet treats, about Bishop's interest in Chanita and their recent off-campus trip.

Sam was squeezing the bridge of his nose by the time I'd finished.

"Is there something . . . ?" I asked.

He plucked at his argyle sock, then let his hand drop to his thigh. "Off the record . . . Well . . . Just keep your old buddy in your sights."

"Okay."

"Ask for DNA, and if he doesn't give it voluntarily, get a warrant and take it from him. It shouldn't be a problem."

I stared at him, then nodded.

"Anything else?" Sam asked.

I pulled out the framed picture of the deadly nightshade bloom from the case file. "When we searched Chanita's room, I saw this."

Sam studied the photograph of the flower. "Am I supposed to hold it out in front of me and the puzzle will be solved or . . . what?"

"Chanita snapped that picture. The berries for this type of flower was with her in that canvas bag. And, oh yeah, every last part of that flower is poisonous. *And* it doesn't bloom until summertime."

"So she took this photo last year?" Sam asked.

I nodded. "If we find out, one, where she was last year and, two, who she was with, maybe we'll find the monster, who may be this guy." I showed him the picture of the man wearing the Saints baseball cap. "Even though I'm not a hundred percent certain he's the monster."

Sam grabbed his briefcase and stood. "Sounds like everything's under control."

"Thank you for the unofficial advice," I said. "Anything for justice, right?"

He cocked his head and peered at me. "No. Anything for *you*."

30

WHY DID SOME GIRLS GET KIDNAPPED AND MURDERED WHILE OTHER GIRLS *DIDN'T*?

As I drove to Syeeda's house, this question stayed with me. Why Chanita? Why Trina? Why Tori and not her friend Golden?

Did Moriaga and Max Crase see something in these girls that only evil men glimpsed?

And why did some of us make it out of the ghetto? I made it, but Regina didn't.

Was it because of the adults in our lives? If so, why did I make it, but Tori didn't?

As I pulled into the driveway, my mind turned to other questions.

Would the monster actually attend Chanita's funeral?

And if he comes, who would I be looking for?

Exhausted, I collapsed on the overstuffed sofa in Syeeda's living room. Raindrops fell, and a wet breeze lifted the silver gauzy curtains that hid the open window. The nerves in my head tightened as though I sat in a crowded Brazilian soccer stadium during the World Cup. I closed my eyes against the light from the lamp on the nightstand—not dark enough—then reached to turn off the lamp. Dark enough now, but the pain only worsened. The healing effect of Sam's kiss had worn off now, and my wrist throbbed as though it was infected with glass and lava.

Call him. Let him kiss the pain away again. And again. And—

I placed a throw pillow over my face and took several deep breaths. Focusing and not focusing, waiting for my banging pulse to slow. In . . . out . . . In . . . *Chanita* . . . Out . . . *Victor Starr* . . . *Shit*. "This is not my beautiful home," I said. "Or my wonderful couch." I grabbed my iPhone from the coffee table and texted Sam. *U around?*

I turned the lamp back on and grabbed the television's remote control. *Click*. Reality show—competitive cake decorating.

My iPhone whistled from the coffee table. A flare shot in my heart.

Sender: Dr.Zach@hotmail.com. *Hello? Anyone there? Wondering about you.*

The flare quickly died. "Brave soul." I ignored the message, popped two Aleve from Syeeda's coffee table stash, and rose to shut the window. Took a twenty-minute shower, then pulled on boxers and an LAPD sweatshirt.

When I returned to the couch with a cup of peppermint tea and thirty Lorna Doone cookies, the red team was making a thirty-foot-tall, NASCAR-themed wedding cake. Sam had responded. *At jail. Would rather be doing nothing with you.*

I texted back. *I'd rather that too*. Out came the laptop from my bag. I sat it next to Chanita's expanding file folder and Trina Porter's missing person report. Once upon a time, I never worked at home. Since the divorce, though, work had been the only thing I did right.

The front door opened, and Syeeda banged into the foyer with an overnight bag slung over her shoulder. "Honey, I'm home."

I tossed her a smile. "Missed you, kitten."

She trudged into the living room and dropped into the armchair. She looked wilted in her silk shirt and jeans. Her bun was more honorary than acting, and stray tendrils of hair frizzed about her head like a corona. "True or false: you banged Sam in the kitchen with a candlestick."

My cheeks flushed. "False. I used a horseshoe."

Syeeda grabbed a Lorna Doone from the pile on the table. "What happened this time?"

"When Lena was telling you my business, did she tell you that she interrupted?"

Syeeda popped the cookie into her mouth. "She left out that part. But she *did* tell me that she warned him that—"

"Oh no."

"If he didn't treat you right, she'd have him bumped off by Emil's weapons homeboys."

"So Sam's gonna stay with me cuz he's scared of being dumped in a vat of concrete?"

Syeeda slumped in the armchair. "That is, if he messes up before *you* mess up."

I snorted, then reached for my cup of tea. "Me? Mess up?"

"Who's Zach?"

I gaped at her. "Lena's mouth—"

"Who is he?"

I sipped from my cup, then said, "I met him at Bonner Park."

"Interested?"

"Nope."

"Why not?"

I shrugged. "He's cute, though. Nice teeth."

"Nice eyes?"

I nodded. "And he's a doctor."

"Your mom would love that."

"He's been e-mailing me."

"So he's interested," Syeeda said. "Another great sign."

"It *would* be foolish to put all my eggs into the Sam basket."

Syeeda smirked. "Your eggs are getting old."

"Thanks, kitten."

She stared at the folder on my lap, then pried off her black riding boots. "Working?"

"Uh huh." I sat the cup of tea back on the coffee table.

"The girl from our neighborhood?"

"Yep. Guess what? I let my father talk at me today."

She reached for another cookie. "Oh boy."

I told her everything: new wife, new life, business owner. I told her that he seemed to know a lot about me, including my divorce from Greg.

Syeeda jammed her lips together, then took a deep breath. "And what did you say?"

"I told him to stay away from Mom and that I'd get a restraining order if he didn't."

"Damn, Lou."

"Then, I went back to my desk to work on the case of *another* black girl living in the Jungle, abandoned by her father, then kidnapped and murdered." I gave her a twisted smile. "Whew. At least Victor Starr made it out, right?"

Syeeda shook her head. "Elouise—"

"I've always envied you," I said. "We practically had the same life. Lived a block apart. Dads both bus drivers. Moms who didn't allow lazy thinking."

She came to sit beside me on the couch.

"Remember when you started your period," I said, "and your mom was out of town for that church retreat?"

"Daddy drove to the grocery store," Syeeda said, smiling, "and bought me the biggest purple box on the shelf."

"And then high school prom."

She laughed. "He sat on the couch with that fake gun when Brian and Tim picked us up."

"Even when you were in college," I said, "he still called you his 'pretty baby' and held your hand when you crossed the street together." Tears burned my eyes. "And that's . . . wow."

Syeeda placed her chin on my shoulder. "Yeah."

"Victor Starr left us, Sy," I said. "He left *me*."

"I know," she whispered. "I know, and I'm sorry."

"You and Kenny and Eva did okay because Frank died after we left Santa Cruz. Victor Starr left when I was a third grader. Tori was in junior high. He had to leave *then*? And leave us with Miss Alberta and her evil brood?"

"Did you ask him?"

"No."

"You need to." Syeeda wrapped her arm around my shoulder. "You don't wanna have any regrets, Lou. Or wonder. Hell, I wish I could talk to my—"

"Your dad didn't leave on his own will."

"I *know* that," Syeeda said. "Still: don't pass up the chance you're given. If that means cursing out Victor Starr until only his silver fillings remain, then do it. Your 'thing' with Sam, or Hot Doc, or with *anyone,* can't blossom until you deal with the past."

Teardrops slipped down my cheek, and I swiped at them. "What does he think is gonna happen between us? That we'll pick up where we left off when I was a kid? I had to fucking . . . *MacGyver* my way out of the Jungle, and he thinks a trip to Toys "R" Us and a scoop of ice cream will just . . . ?" I wandered to the window and peered out at the wet, dark yard.

"He was supposed to take me wolf hunting, Sy. He was supposed to show me how to spot them, how to keep them away, how to kill them." I rested my forehead against the cool windowpane. "If he'd been around, maybe I'd be a lawyer now. Maybe I'd have a better husband, some kids. The cops . . . *Those* sons of bitches taught me how to hunt."

"No, Lou," Syeeda said. "You had survived before the LAPD—"

"And 'surviving' is what we're striving for now?" I turned to face her. "Tori died because she couldn't spot those wolves—she didn't know how to fight Max Crase or Cyrus Darson. And after she disappeared . . . well . . . I made myself into a tiny ball while Mom played possum and pretended we both were dead until the threat passed. I know she did the best she could, but . . . That may be *surviving*, but it ain't *living*."

My stomach ached as I sunk back onto the couch. "If Chanita's father had been around, and more positive than negative, would she still be here? She was a bright kid, you know? And she was . . ." Ice replaced the ache in my gut, and I shivered. "He's looking for a type."

"He?"

"My suspect. Smart girls. Vulnerable girls. Trina Porter and Chanita Lords were both smart. And both were artists. Trina a poet, Chanita a photographer."

"Both were poor," Syeeda added. "Lived with their moms."

"No so-called protector in the home," I said. *Like me. Like my sister.*

"Did you talk to folks at Madison yet?" Syeeda asked.

I grunted as my face warmed—I didn't want Syeeda to know all that I'd learned, who I'd talked to, especially my conversation with Payton Bishop. He had counseled both girls. But I couldn't mention him—Syeeda would grill him, and then she'd write an article. I didn't want that. *Yet.*

SATURDAY, MARCH 22

31

THE LAST FUNERAL I HAD ATTENDED FOR ONE OF MY VICTIMS WAS TWO MONTHS ago, the Tuesday after the King holiday. It had been an exhaustive, four-hour affair with enough singing to fill a hymnbook and hundreds of stories about young Danny Baker, a Dorsey High School running back, a future San Diego Chargers starter with a heart of gold, quick feet, and the looks of a young Jackie Robinson. A good kid, Danny was gunned down fifty feet from his front porch. *What set you from, ese,* they had asked. *I don't bang,* Danny had responded. *I play ball at—BOOM.* Dead. All because he'd gone out to his Altima to retrieve his backpack.

Danny's funeral had sent me down a rabbit hole. Not because the Impala full of Avenues thugs had eluded me—we caught them six hours later at PAWN4CASH with Danny's still-active iPad pinging the Find My iPhone app. The case made me crazy because Miriam and Tony Baker, the boy's parents, had done everything right. Danny didn't hang out. Danny didn't smoke out. School, practice, home, school, practice, home. Still, wolves in Dickies and beaters had found him—at home.

Right after Danny's funeral, I, along with several community servants, had headed to Olive Garden. There, I shared a bottle of Pinot Noir with the handsome, green-eyed assistant district attorney, the one prosecuting the Max Crase case, the one prosecuting the newly jumped-in members of the Avenues and murderers of young Danny Baker.

Despite the drinking and the flirting with Sam Seward that afternoon, my heart ached and my mind lingered on Danny Baker's silver casket, on his weeping mother and his catatonic father. Their dreams, their love, now buried six feet under.

This morning, Colin rode shotgun as I drove down Crenshaw Boulevard to Mount St. John's Cathedral and to the funeral of another child I had not met until God left her for me on a muddy park trail. I would move past the sadness and hopelessness that came with murder and hope that no one noticed my intrusion. At a church as big as Mount St. John's, Colin and I would easily disappear behind the shadows of flowered and feathered hats. We would slip into the back pew, and no one, not even the monster, would know we were there.

The storms had moved on, leaving behind a troop of steel-colored clouds ready to set it off again.

Colin coughed as he knotted his blue necktie. "It can't rain on a child's burial day, right?"

"A kid's dead. Anything can happen." And then I deleted another text message from Victor Starr. So far this morning, he had texted me three times. Each message had been a plea for compassion and patience.

There were now two Mount St. John's—the original, smaller church where Chanita's funeral would take place and, just a few blocks back, the newer, bigger cathedral, which would host Congresswoman Fortier's jazz funeral. After weaving through side streets because of road closures for the bigger service, I finally pulled into the original church's parking lot. A great choice of spots—not many parked cars. Colored People's Time meant that the funeral would start at 10:45 instead of 10:30. But at 10:20, the lot only hosted two Lexus sedans, a black Ford Explorer, several Toyotas, a minivan covered with JESUS IS THE ANSWER bumper stickers, and my Crown Vic. About twenty cars in a parking garage built for a thousand.

Colin coughed into the crook of his elbow, then frowned. "Where *is* everybody? There must've been seven hundred people at Danny's funeral an hour before it started."

I reached for the drugstore bag on the backseat and handed it to him.

He pulled out the new bottle of DayQuil and smiled. "You're so—" He coughed, and his face turned Pepto pink.

"I *am* sweet," I said, "and you're welcome. I need your lungs right now. And all that coughing's gonna scare away the monster." I pulled on my gray wool overcoat as I stared at the near-empty lot. "Maybe the date's wrong on the e-mail."

Colin took a long pull from the bottle as he read the printout. "Date's right, time's right, everything else is wrong, including the spelling of the church."

I'd never seen the outside environs of this property look so abandoned—vendors usually camped about the church's perimeter to hawk gospel CDs, sun hats, sticks of incense, and gift baskets to congregants present for Sunday services, prayer meetings, and concerts.

A powder-blue hearse and a matching late-model family limousine were parked on the street in front of the church. A pudgy motorcycle escort and two male drivers, both wearing shiny black suits, laughed on the sidewalk. The escort shouted, "North Carolina trashed 'em."

Colin and I walked past them and into the courtyard, where a few middle-school-aged girls huddled with their mothers. I remembered one girl who wore large, thick glasses that hid her face—I'd plucked her picture from Chanita's locker door. Alice from Madison's administrative office stood with other office workers. A few grade-school children wearing their Sundays ran around the fountain. The boy skidded and tripped, not practiced in the fine art of horsing around in church shoes.

Organ music—"How Great Thou Art"—drifted from the sanctuary. Fumes of fresh paint and steam-cleaned carpet mingled with the heavy scents of lilies, roses, and other funeral flowers. My spike-heeled boots daggered into lavender pile free of muddy footprints, grape-juice stains, and water spots. An ancient deaconess dressed in white stood at the sanctuary doors. She held programs in her white-gloved hands, and she smelled of peppermint candy and Jergens lotion.

In the sanctuary, sunlight filtered through the red, green, and yellow stained glass and reflected against the stainless-steel crucifix that hung above the altar. A tripod at the altar's base held a large school portrait of Chanita Lords. A closed coffin the color of a seashell's belly sat on the picture's right.

Lots of empty lavender-cushioned pews.

Gwen Zapata sat on one side of the church and talked with a woman with thousands of long braids twisted high into a bun. She saw Colin and me and nodded. Also seated: a round, gray-haired woman dressed in poly blend and pearls. And Mike Summit, the assistant editor in chief at *OurTimes*.

So much for disappearing.

"The woman in braids," I whispered to Colin. "Trina Porter's mom, right?"

Summit quickly left his seat to join my partner and me at the back of the sanctuary. "Detective Norton, aren't you going to introduce me?"

"No," I said, sliding into a rear pew.

"Mike Summit," he said to Colin and offered his hand. "I'm here to bear witness and tell the world that too many of our girls—"

"*Our* girls, Mike?" I asked, eyebrow cocked.

"Just because I'm white doesn't mean that I don't care," he said.

We squinted at him, at his too-tight houndstooth blazer and at the piece of spinach trapped between his teeth. "Why don't you head back to your seat?"

Mike Summit took a step back. "After the service, Detectives, I'll have questions."

"Have a seat, sir," Colin said.

The so-called journalist tromped back to his pew as the woman in braids came to stand before us. A clump of fine moles grew on her left cheek, and her foundation had failed to hide the dark circles beneath her eyes. She held out her thin hand. "I'm Liz Porter."

I introduced Colin and myself.

She nodded. "Detective Zapata told me you're in charge of Chanita's investigation. Do you think . . . ? Is it . . . ?" Her lips quivered, but she swallowed and shoved sorrow aside. "Is this case related to my daughter's disappearance?"

"We can't say anything for certain, Mrs. Porter." The lump in my throat had made it hard to speak.

She dropped her head and sighed.

Colin placed his hand on her shoulder. "But we're coordinating with Detective Zapata. We find something out, we'll let her know, *pronto*."

Liz Porter whispered, "Thank you," without meeting our eyes. She wobbled to her pew.

Before Colin or I could say, "Poor lady," Payton Bishop entered the sanctuary and made his way to the pews occupied by Madison Middle School staff.

The organist changed chords. "Precious Lord, Take My Hand." A somber gospel standard played at most colored funerals and will probably be played at mine.

Up front on the dais, the door to a side room opened, and from it emerged a minister wearing a white and purple robe along with two men in dark suits and a woman in pearls and a flamingo-colored Jackie O–Chanel suit. They sat in the velvet-backed chairs positioned behind the Lucite podium.

"Well?" Colin whispered. "Pick one and let's go."

I whispered back. "Give me a minute. Not a lot to choose from."

At thirty minutes past the announced start time, the pastor stepped to the pulpit and nodded to the deaconess stationed at the doors to the sanctuary. A moment later, the family of Chanita Lords trudged down the church's long center aisle. Three deaconesses, each holding a box of tissues, flanked them.

Regina Drummond wore a simple black dress and flats. She wept as the family male helped her walk. Brother, uncle, or cousin wore black pants and a black shirt, and his tongue kept flicking at the corners of his dry lips. The school-aged girls and boy who had been playing in the courtyard now followed Regina and her escort. Bringing up the rear was Alberta Jackson, with her large soft bosom and no-nonsense hairdo, big purse on one arm and bigger Bible on the other. A Saved and Sanctified Saint who had borne cons of every flavor.

A deaconess directed the family to the front pew, arm's length from that pink coffin.

After a prayer from Elder Kimball, a welcome from Elder Smyth, and the reading of a poem by pearls-wearing church clerk Doris Smyth, the minister stepped to the podium. He hooked his eyeglass stems around his ears. "Jesus says, '*suffer the little children to come unto me, and forbid them*

218

not, for such is the kingdom of God.' "

The organ wheezed to life again. "In the Upper Room."

Colin nudged me and nodded to our right.

The park ranger who had called in about Chanita Lords's being left on that trail high above the city had joined the congregation.

Jimmy Boulard smiled at me and then winked.

My nerves bristled. "*Do not* let him leave this building," I whispered to Colin.

I'd have the chance to speak with Boulard after all, to ask him myself what he saw . . . and to hear what he'd claim he didn't do.

"Chanita has gone on to be with our Father," Pastor Evans said, "and she is happy to know that there are some in this city who have not forgotten her. Some in this city who miss her and mourn her." He spread his arms. "Would anyone like to say something?"

Payton stood from his pew. "I'm Chanita's school counselor. I helped search for her when she first disappeared, and I was hoping that . . . praying that . . . We worked hard trying to find her, you know? And umm . . ." He scratched his temple, took a deep breath, then exhaled. "I just wish I could've done more for her." Then he sat and covered his mouth with his hand.

Alice rolled her eyes.

I needed to have tea with Miss Alice and ask, *Why the side eye?*

Liz Porter pulled herself to stand. She smoothed out the front of her blue pantsuit, closed her eyes, and clutched the back of the pew before her. "I came cuz my baby Trina was snatched back on March seventh."

Hot tears welled in my eyes. I held my breath, remembering how Mom had kept it together until she couldn't anymore.

And on that day she couldn't . . .

Colin took my hand and squeezed. "If you need to leave . . ."

"I'm good." I whispered.

He gave another squeeze before letting go.

"The police ain't found Trina yet," Liz said, "and I thank Detective Zapata over there for not giving up."

Gwen nodded to Liz.

"But I came here today," Liz Porter continued, "cuz I'm hoping that the Lord will have mercy—" And then, she crumpled back into her seat.

Danielle, the middle-school girl with the thick glasses, spoke about her slain friend and her love of photography, Bruno Mars, and trips to museums.

Alberta Jackson spoke: Jesus, photography, Jesus.

Once Alberta sat, Rev. Evans looked to Colin and me. "Would either of you in the back like to say something?"

Just then, Jimmy Boulard rose and shuffled out of the sanctuary.

My neck warmed—we needed to leave. "No. Thank you."

Colin said, "No, thanks."

As Rev. Evans offered a few more words about salvation, redemption, and love, Colin and I darted out of the sanctuary.

No one stood in the vestibule.

"Check the restroom," I told Colin.

Gwen joined us. "Before you leave," she said to me, "I need to tell—"

"Can't right now, Gwen."

I checked the mother's room, the AV chamber, and the kitchen.

No park ranger.

My phone rang, and I glanced at the display: Victor Starr was calling. I hit IGNORE and reunited with Colin in the lobby. "See him?"

"Nope."

The organ wheezed the first bars of "What a Friend We Have in Jesus."

Mike Summit poked his head from behind the doors of the sanctuary.

Before he could ask any questions, I darted out of the church and into the courtyard.

Fragrant blue smoke wafted from the barbecue joint a block north, and the air smelled of beef brisket and pork ribs. Far-off trumpets and trombones blared. A bass drum boomed.

Music?

Colin rushed past me to start searching the outer perimeter of the church.

"Y'all see a man leave just now?" I shouted to the limo driver and motorcycle escort.

"The white boy?" the motorcycle escort asked.

"No," I said. "A light-skinned black guy. Looks like Smokey Robinson."

Both men shook their heads.

Just like that, the park ranger was gone.

All of me went cold and hard.

Mike Summit stood in the breezeway. "What's happening?"

And I went colder and harder.

32

WHERE HAD JIMMY BOULARD GONE THAT QUICKLY?

I pulled the Motorola radio from my bag and called in a BOLO for the park ranger.

"Detective Norton," Mike Summit said.

Ignoring the reporter, I turned my gaze northward, to the sound of those trombones and bass drums. That's when I saw the worst possible thing that could happen at that moment. "You gotta be fucking kidding me," I muttered.

Two motorcycle escorts slowly rolled down Crenshaw with their orange hazard lights blinking. Behind them, a brass band played "Just a Closer Walk with Thee" nice and slow. Six men in tails and top hats flanked the sides of a horse-drawn carriage carrying a copper-colored casket. Behind them, a butter-colored young woman wearing a gold dress and holding a ruffled umbrella strutted, then posed . . . strutted . . . posed. Behind her, a man hoisted a large picture of a fair-skinned black woman—longtime congresswoman Barbara Fortier. Her family, friends, and constituents walked, most holding green, purple, or gold umbrellas, and many of them the same café-au-lait hue as Jimmy Boulard. Cameramen from three television news stations aimed their lenses at the spectacle while a helicopter buzzed overhead for aerial shots.

I gawked at the approaching second line, then muttered

again: "You gotta be fucking kidding me."

Colin ran back to me, gaping at the procession. "What the hell is *that*?"

"Funeral for Congresswoman Fortier."

"With a band and shit?"

"I told you it was a jazz funeral."

"I thought that just meant there was Dizzy Gillespie music instead of hymns."

The strut-pose woman was now strutting and posing yards away from where we stood. And the horse-drawn hearse slowly rolled not far behind her.

"Boulard could be hiding in the crowd," Colin said. "So we're looking for him *and* the guy in the Saints hat? Who may be the same guy?"

I nodded as my heart sank. Every other man wore a Saints baseball cap in honor of their hometown and New Orleans home girl Congresswoman Fortier. "Let's go, then." I took a deep breath, then dove into the moving mass.

There! No—too fat.

There! No—too young.

The horses' hooves clip-clopped.

And the band played on: "Just a closer walk with thee, grant it, Jesus, is my plea."

There . . . No, there . . . No . . . Damn.

After five minutes of weaving in and out for nearly three blocks, and with Angeles Funeral Home now in sight, I worked my way to the sidewalk. Almost every face was partially hidden by hats, umbrellas, and handkerchiefs. People crowding the street. Brass band playing. Mourners singing and shouting. Brass bells tinkling from push-cart ice-cream vendors.

I backtracked to the church, eyes still scanning the dwindling crowd.

"Who are you looking for?" Mike Summit stood before me, pen and pad ready. "What's the big secret? Or shall I say, cover-up?"

I gave him a glare equivalent to thirty beheadings and a caning.

Mike shrank some but didn't retreat. "You know I can go around you." He pulled a steno pad and pen from his back pocket. "I can call my contacts and find out the latest."

I snorted. "Who do you think you are? A *Times* reporter?"

"I *am* a *Times* reporter."

I cocked my head. "You work for the *community* section. And your job is to attend Chanita's funeral, then write about who came, who spoke, how many people showed up and threw themselves on top of the coffin, and what the deaconesses served for lunch. You're not Bob Woodward, Mike Summit, even though you think you are. Sure, you do investigative work. Investigating the best barbecue joint south of Pico. By the way, I disagree with your last breaking news story: Woody's *is not* better than Phillips, and sure as hell not better than Texas Barbecue King."

"You know," he said, "one article and blog post from me can destroy you. One tweet that an abusive cop is leading this investigation, that this abusive cop has a grudge against me for exposing her—"

"Not true."

He sneered. "One tweet stirs up shit. Don't forget: the pen is mightier than the sword."

My stomach cramped from tamping down the urge to laugh at this pitiful little man. He had power for the moment—the power of a five-year-old wielding a spork. I'd let him wave it around until naptime.

Mike grinned. "Do I have your attention now? Don't think I can't go around you."

I chuckled and shook my head. "Honey, I'm the lead detective. When it comes to this case, I am the way, the truth, and the light. There *is* no other way except through me."

Then, radio to my mouth, I called Pepe back at the station and demanded that he contact Jimmy Boulard immediately.

"Is that Chanita's funeral?" Pepe asked.

"Nope," I said, stepping away from Mike Summit. "The congresswoman's."

Someone tapped my shoulder.

I scowled and whirled around. "*What?*"

Gwen Zapata didn't startle. "I know you got something goin' on right now, but you need to know—"

"*What?*"

"Another girl is missing."

The hair on my arms stood straight. "No."

"Marisol Gutierrez, nine years old. Reported missing this morning. But I'm not sure if she's related to this." She nodded at Chanita Lords's mourners now exiting the sanctuary.

Gwen walked back with me to the parking garage, where the motorcycle escort was handing out fluorescent orange stickers with FUNERAL printed in thick black letters. Payton Bishop stood in the courtyard with his arm wrapped around Liz Porter's shoulder. He was whispering in the woman's ear.

"You see that?" Gwen asked.

"Something's loosey-goosey with him," I said.

Colin joined us. "I can't find him, Lou. He could be in Rhode Island by now."

Gwen's cell phone rang, and she turned away to answer it.

"So, are we goin' to the cemetery?" Colin asked as we reached the Crown Vic.

A postcard had been placed beneath the car's windshield-wiper blade.

"Don't know." I plucked away the card. "Depends on Pepe finding Boulard."

Gwen shoved her phone into her coat pocket. "That missing girl I told you about? They found her. She'd gone to the mall with her aunt. So it's all good."

"Wish they all ended like that," I said, glancing at the postcard.

This card was of another oil painting—*A Landscape with Four Nymphs Dancing*, by Giovanni Battista Cipriani—but these four women were playing "Ring Around the Rosie."

"Somebody selling CDs?" Gwen asked.

I turned the postcard over, and my stomach dropped.

No postage stamp. Addressed to me. Same block letters written in the same green ink as the previous "wild rumpus" postcard.

"Like the other one I got," I whispered.

Colin looked over my shoulder at the card. "Is that . . . English?"

R szev gzpvm zmlgsvi. Glnliild hsv droo yv hrc uvvg fmwvi—fmovhh blf hzev svi urihg. R droo xlmgzxg blf. Wlm'g ylgsvi ollprmt uli nv. R zn drgs gsv trioh.

This was no marketing piece.
Who had left this card on my car?
And what game was I now playing?

33

THE SECOND LINE FOR CONGRESSWOMAN FORTIER PASSED, AND THIS SECTION OF Crenshaw Boulevard returned to its regular din of automobiles, buses, and pedestrians. It was ten after one, and the church service for Chanita Lords had ended. Mourners, now piling into their cars for the fifteen-minute drive to Inglewood Cemetery, stared at us detectives camped out in the church parking lot. Payton Bishop, especially, looked flummoxed as he climbed into his Prius. He cast one last glance in our direction, then sped off to bury his student.

I thought I'd also be driving to the burial site, watching every male available lug that pink coffin to its final destination. I thought I'd be embracing Regina and Alberta and assuring them that I would find the monster who had murdered their sweet girl. In reality, I was crouched near the low concrete planter, barely breathing, sweating through my suit, notepad and pen in hand, eyes darting from the letters on my steno pad to the picture of the postcard I'd taken with my cell phone, swapping *v* for *e*, *s* for *h*.

Colin stood over me, holding the evidence bag that contained the original. "Just saw Luke's car pull into the lot. And Zucca just called. He's on another case, so it'll be a while before he gets here. But he can send Krishna now since this card may not be . . . a thing."

"Fine." My eyes darted from *I* to *I* as my hand made each of them *W*.

Gwen had drawn the "Mike Summit" card.

"I'm not going," the reporter told her.

"If you like your nose straight, don't fuck with me," she warned, her small hands on her thick hips.

Mike Summit huffed, then took two steps back.

"More," Gwen growled.

He threw up his hands. "How am I—?"

"More, goddammit!"

He hopped back at least a hundred feet.

"I'm done," I shouted.

Colin crouched beside me.

My hands shook as I read the translated message on the notepad:

> *I have taken another. Tomorrow she will be six feet under—unless you save her first. I will contact you. Don't bother looking for me. I am with the girls.*

This was now a thing.

The monster was here.

He was watching me.

Worse: he was personally delivering mail to my car.

Shit.

"It's like the first card," Colin whispered.

"What first card?" Gwen asked.

Colin explained as I stared at the message.

> *I am with the girls.*

"He doesn't say *when* he's gonna contact you," Gwen pointed out.

228

We had only been inside the church for an hour. Since leaving to search for Jimmy Boulard, discovering the postcard, and translating this message, though, two hours had passed.

My radio chirped—an e-mail from Olympus111 now sat in my mailbox.

"I think this may be . . ." I showed Colin the message. Then, with a numb finger, I tapped the link.

.oot uoy dnA .doog rof enog si ehs erofeb gnol evah t'nod uoY .
uoy dekcip I ekiL .srehto eht dekcip I ekil reh dekcip I .raelc os
prah ,lerual htiw denworc sseddog detnahcne ym si ehS .tser
eht morf tuo sdnatS .detfig si lrig sihT .sevol tseb eht ekam yeht
dna tneitap ton era slrig dlo raey 31 .eutriv a si ecneitaP .enog
ma I won tuB .revo kcolb eno tsuJ .hcruhc eht ta erom dehcraes
dah uoy fi em thguac evah dluoc uoY .evitceteD, gninrom dooG

"Another cipher," I whispered.

"Can't this motherfucker write in English?" Colin spat.

"The Zodiac used to send ciphers," Gwen pointed out.

Luke joined our circle. "What's the haps?"

Gwen explained as I grabbed the pen and pad again. White noise blared in my head as I searched the message for patterns. I looked for frequently used letters—no luck. Three-letter combinations? "This one . . . It doesn't make sense. It's different from the others." My eyes buzzed back and forth, from "detfig" to "sseddog." "Shit, shit, sh—" My gaze fixed on the last word in the message: "dooG."

The next-to-last word: "gninrom."

"Got it," I said.

Mike Summit had inched closer to the yellow tape.

"He wrote it backwards," I whispered. "The words are reversed." I thrust my notepad and pen at my partner. "Write what I'm about say."

Good morning, Detective. You could have caught me if you had searched more at the church. Just one block over. But now I am gone. Patience is a virtue. 13 year old girls are not patient and they make the best loves. This girl is gifted. Stands out from the rest. She is my enchanted goddess crowned with laurel, harp so clear. I picked her like I picked the others. Like I picked you. You don't have long before she is gone for good. And you too.

"One block over?" Gwen said.

"He could be lying," Colin said. "It could be Bishop—he came into the church after us. He could've put the card on the windshield, and he could've sent this message right now."

I squeezed the bridge of my nose. "Gwen, could you pull all missing children reports from the last ten hours? I wanna hit this on all sides."

Gwen said, "Got it," and rushed back to her Crown Vic.

"Maybe," I said, "we can find the girl by comparing the missing child reports against school lists since he seems to target girls in this area."

Colin gaped at me but said nothing.

"I wanna get a signal or triangulate or whatever the hell it is," I told Luke. "And I wanna find out what IP address the message came from."

He nodded. "You'll probably need a court—"

"Handle it, then." I punched in a number on my phone.

Mike Summit was scribbling into his pad.

Neil aka Bang-Bang picked up on the first ring.

I told him that I'd just received a message from a possible suspect and that I wanted any information possible—who had sent it, where it came from—as soon as possible.

Bang-Bang said, "So I have permission to search your in-box?"

"Yeah. Go. Find stuff." I paced the walkway, trying to figure out next steps.

"Detective Norton," Mike Summit called. "A word, please?"

"Just talked to L.T.," Luke said. "He's driving the warrant request to Judge Keener now."

I nodded, barely hearing him. "*She is my enchanted goddess crowned with laurel, harp so clear.* What does that even mean?"

"And what did he mean that he picked *you*?" Colin asked. "And you and the girl being gone for good?"

My stomach cramped, and I stopped pacing to stare at the steno pad. "He's threatening me, isn't he?"

Colin and Luke nodded.

"Detective Norton," Mike Summit called again.

Red-faced, Colin whirled around and shouted, "Say something else, Summit, and I'm taking you in for interfering with an investigation."

Mike Summit gulped and muttered, "Apologies."

Colin, eyes still bugged, turned back to me.

"We'll have to do this the hard way." I told him my plan.

He blinked at me, then said, "Seriously?"

My phone rang.

"I got something." It was Bang-Bang. "The e-mail was sent from a cell phone belonging to Regina Drummond's account." He then recited Chanita's phone number.

"Shit," I said, "can you—?"

"Find which tower it used?" Bang-Bang asked. "I'll call you back."

Luke ended his own phone call. "Captain knows this is becoming political, so he made some calls, and some poor joker in the school superintendent's office is e-mailing over a list of all middle schools in the area with gifted and talented programs."

"But how will we get lists of all the *girls* in the GAT program?" Colin asked. "It's the weekend. Schools are closed."

I gritted my teeth. Another barrier. "Someone in the superintendent's office needs to come in and pull the lists. Maybe this girl was absent yesterday."

"Or maybe he took her this morning," Luke said.

Colin made a show of checking his wristwatch. "Ticktock, Lou."

I shrugged off my jacket and dropped it on the planter. "We need those lists. If that means the mayor of Los Angeles and every cop in this city has to call every effin' household in 90008, so be it. I'm finding this girl."

34

SHE IS MY ENCHANTED GODDESS CROWNED WITH LAUREL, HARP SO CLEAR.

I studied the picture of the new postcard. *What am I missing?* I glanced south down Crenshaw and saw swirling red and blue lights and bright head beams on an approaching radio car. Behind the car were tangerine-colored light bars of the CSI van.

I typed "nymphs" into Google's search bar: *female divinity . . . animate nature . . . not immortal . . . bound to places . . . classifications . . . the Muses.* Then, I searched "Olympus": *Tallest peak in Greece . . . home of the mythical Olympians . . .*

Colin's radio blipped. "Yeah?"

"I got Boulard," Pepe said, "and I'm bringing him over to you guys right now."

I returned to the Muses article. "The Muses," I read aloud, "were the personification of knowledge and the—"

"Got here as soon as I could." Krishna sat down her metal toolbox and pulled a spiral binder from her duffel bag.

I handed her the paper bag containing the new postcard. "He put it on my windshield, beneath the blade."

She pulled out a chain-of-custody form, told me where to sign, then took the card.

Pepe's silver Impala screeched into the parking lot. A man sat in the backseat.

"You wait for the names," I told Colin, "and I'll talk to this guy."

Colin nodded and looked at his watch again. "It's almost two o'clock."

Blood rushed to my head. "I know, partner."

Every passing second meant less chance of finding the girl . . . unless the monster was now seated and cuffed in the back of Pepe's Impala.

"Take him out," I told Pepe. "Let him feel freedom. Stand at the perimeter with Luke and Gwen. I'll cap his ass, though, if he thinks I'm just a girl with a gun."

Jimmy Boulard and I leaned against the lot's retaining wall. He had changed out of his suit and now wore his green ranger uniform.

"Is this necessary?" he asked, eyeing the armed detectives.

I shrugged. "Depends. I've called you several times now. You haven't called me back."

He studied the treads of his dusty hiking boots. "What number did you call?"

With my eyes also on those boots, I recited the number.

"My son's place. I don't live there anymore." He reached into the pocket of his chinos.

Gwen, Pepe, and Luke raised their guns.

Boulard froze. "Just want a smoke." He gulped, then asked, "May I?"

I nodded, then said, "Couldn't wait to get out of that suit, huh?"

Grit covered his khaki shirt and the golden hair on his forearms. No dirt, though, could diminish the tattoo of the bald eagle perched upon the USN banner. He shook a cigarette from the pack of Camels and stuck it between his cracked, thin lips. "Had to go back to work. I'm leading a walk with some Girl Scouts up in the park today. So I'd appreciate it if we sped this little discussion along."

"Fine," I said. "How did you know Chanita Lords?"

"I don't."

"Why'd you come, then?"

He shook his head, then picked tobacco from his tongue. "I was one of the unlucky folks who found her. Just seemed like the right thing to do." He sighed. "And my granddaughter mentioned that she knew Chanita."

"Yeah? What's your granddaughter's name?"

"Can't tell you that," he said. "Don't want you asking her questions without me or her daddy present. She's having a hard time as it is. She tried comin' today, but I didn't see her in the sanctuary."

"She in the seventh grade?"

He took a drag from his cigarette. "You're not talking to her without her daddy or me."

"Very nice of you to come to a girl's funeral," I said, my gut twisting into a knot. "A girl you didn't even know."

"That against the law?"

I crossed my arms, and my right hand brushed against the shoulder holster's soft leather. "Of course not. Chanita seemed like a good girl. Very talented."

"Guess the bar is low for 'good' nowadays." He took a final drag from his cigarette, then dropped the butt to the ground.

"So she *wasn't* good?" I asked, staring at Jimmy Boulard DNA, now on the asphalt.

"From what I've heard, she engaged in behaviors that *good* girls shun."

"Like what kind of behavior?"

"Like sexual behavior."

"Thought you didn't know her."

"I don't." He smirked. "I got ears, though, and I'm not dumb. You ain't gotta do much to know what these girls are up to nowadays. The whaddya call it? Sexting. The naked pictures."

I hid a yawn behind my hand.

"Oh, you bored?"

I shrugged. "Your misinformed outrage over Chanita's morality, or lack thereof, makes me sleepy, and frankly it pisses me off. Because who the fuck do you think *you* are?"

"You asked me a question," he growled. "Don't be pissed cuz you don't like my answer. Hell, none of this surprises me. I just hate that them girls on the trail pulled me into this mess."

"Yeah," I said. "When they found you, you were clearing brush on that rainy afternoon."

He nodded, either missing or ignoring my sarcasm.

"So is that a usual practice?" I asked. "Clearing brush during a storm?"

He offered a smile that showed stained, crooked teeth. "Well, you yuppies like your trails clear. I always get complaints about bushes being on the pathway. Imagine that. *Vegetation*. In the *wilderness*. Next, you folks will be demanding a Trader Joe's by the volleyball court."

"And a vegan cupcake place where I can bring my Weimaraner after yoga."

His smile died. "And here I was, planning to tell you all that I know."

"And here I was, planning to let you go home today."

He chuckled.

I chuckled but didn't mean it. "So, who do you think killed Chanita?"

"The amigo who moved into the neighborhood last summer."

I cocked my head.

"We live across the street," he explained, "and the

236

neighbors are all whisperin' back and forth. And, yeah, he lives in Nita's building. Name's Raul Moriaga." The park ranger glanced at a passing group of tight-jeaned teenage girls walking along Crenshaw Boulevard. The girls ignored us—Jimmy Boulard and I were both too old to be noticed. "He's been in jail before," Boulard said.

"Who told you that?"

"Ain't nobody need to tell me shit. I got a computer and I got the Internet." He squinted at me. "Things have changed since you moved out, Detective."

My skin flushed. "You know I lived in the Jungle."

"Like I said, neighbors are whisperin', I got a computer, and I got the Internet."

I crossed my arms—sweat had dampened my silk shirt.

He chuckled, then said, "I heard that Moriaga used to watch her walk by all the time, that he'd make kissing sounds at her. She'd never be interested in a loser like that."

"Ontrel Shaw ain't Sidney Poitier," I pointed out, "and she was interested in *him*."

Jimmy Boulard toed the cigarette butt. "Ontrel Shaw ain't nothing but a thug. Girls think he's exciting. Tough guy, my ass. Ontrel so big and bad, how he let Nita wind up dead?"

"Can you do me a favor?" I took out a small steno pad and pen from my back pocket and handed it to him. "Can you write down your name and new address since you no longer live with your son? Also, your phone number and any e-mail addresses, in print, all caps. Better to understand. Please?"

He blinked at me, took the pad and pen, and started to write using his left hand.

I watched him print, certain and then uncertain that he had written the nymph postcards.

He scrutinized what he wrote, then handed me the results. "So this Raul Moriaga. Why do you think—?"

"Not just me."

"Why do you and the neighbors think he's the one?"

"Assault," he said. "Molestation. Rape. And for no reason. Just senseless."

My limbs numbed. "Is there ever a *good* reason to rape, molest, or assault someone?"

Jimmy Boulard blinked at me, visibly agitated by my question. "You know what I mean. They come to our neighborhoods and they mess with our girls, and you cops know these cats are snooping around, but you hassle regular folks like me. I'm glad I only got sons. Don't ever have to worry about them being helpless, being weak. And I brought them up to stay away from gals like Chanita." He snorted, then threw me a sideways glance. "*Is there ever a good reason.*"

He squinted at the girls who had just passed us. "I saw the oddest thing yesterday. I'm at the bookstore, just flipping through some magazines, and I look up cuz I smell all this perfume in the air. These two females walk past me. Look like the ones down there." He nodded in the girls' direction—they were now talking to two guys in a tricked-out Nissan Armada.

"Lotta makeup. Lotta jewelry. One was wearing these pants with the word 'Juicy' on the ass. They walked past me and right into the children's section. And they're talking to each other in these little girl voices, and I'm thinking, *What the hell?* Are they girls or are they women? Looking at them, you'd think they were twenty years old. What mother buys her twelve-year-old girl pants with 'Juicy' on the ass? They're sitting there, reading *Where's Waldo* and Harry Potter, wearing whore's makeup and them pants. What's a man supposed to do in that situation?"

My breathing quickened, and I pushed out, "Be a man?"

Boulard continued to stare in the distance. "They think

they're adults. But if you treat 'em like adults . . ." He looked back at me, his eyes dark and haunted. "You got monsters out there, Detective. You ever become a mother—and I can tell that you ain't—do all that you can to keep your daughter away from those monsters."

He clucked his tongue. "That Raul Moriaga? He lives in another world. Yeah, you a detective and all, but trust me: that's a world you don't know nothing about."

"Gee, thanks, Dad." I placed my hands on my hips. "So: I need your DNA."

He blinked at me. "Why?"

I laughed. "You obviously don't watch a lot of TV cop shows. There was someone else's body fluid on Chanita. I wanna check to see if that mystery fluid belongs to you."

He eyed me and chewed the inside of his cheek. "You think *I* killed Nita?"

I fake gasped. "That thought never occurred to me."

He blinked.

"Is that a 'yes' or a 'no'?"

"How long will it take?" His eyes ping-ponged between me and Crenshaw Boulevard.

"I got the Q-tip if you got the spit."

"I didn't kill her."

"You wanna know how many times I've heard those exact words? Probably just as many times as you get complaints about bushes on the trail. One more thing: can you show me the bottoms of your boots?"

"Why?"

"Because I asked nicely. Next time won't be so nice."

He hesitated, then lifted his right boot.

I used my phone to take pictures of his soles. Then, I radioed Colin and asked that he bring Krishna over with her DNA collection kit.

A moment later, Colin and I stood yards away, watching the CSI tech run a long cotton swab along the inside of Jimmy Boulard's cheek. Krishna had also plucked the cigarette the ranger had just smoked and abandoned on the asphalt—you could never have too much spit.

"Krishna didn't pull much off the car," Colin said. "What about this guy?"

I shrugged. "I can't read him. I sniff evil but not which kind. And standing there with him . . . He's a little over six feet, and pretty muscular for an old guy."

"Strong enough to carry a dead girl to that trail?"

I shrugged. "Compared to our other suspects, he knows the park best."

"He smart enough to send ciphers?"

"Possibly. He has a navy tat."

"Can we hold him?"

"Not yet, but we can watch him." I held up my tiny notepad. "And we'll see if the writing here matches the writing on the cards."

My radio blipped. "Lou!"

Colin and I both straightened as though Lieutenant Rodriguez stood before us.

"I'm five minutes out," our boss announced, "and I got a list."

35

THE FRONDS ON THE PALM TREES THAT LINED CRENSHAW WERE RUSTLING, AND seagulls circled overhead as clouds gained bulk and lost light. The sun fought to stay relevant, and I prayed that God would, for once, tilt the playing field in our favor.

Pepe and Lieutenant Rodriguez used the hood of Gwen's black Crown Vic to study the list of girls in the gifted and talented program at John Muir Middle School. Colin and I, at the car's trunk, studied the list from Madison. We were all comparing the lists of absent girls at Madison against Gwen's list of missing children since Thursday.

"Ten girls didn't go to school yesterday." Colin had taken off his tie and had balled it into his jacket pocket.

"Read me the names," I told him.

"Gracilyn Platt. Wakeisha Simmons. Teona Lewis . . ."

My eyes scanned the entries. "Those names aren't on my list."

She is my enchanted goddess crowned with . . .

I grabbed my phone and typed into the search bar "Greek muse laurel hair harp." Hits. Lots of hits. "Gwen!" I shouted.

"Yeah?" She was hunkered in the car's backseat with lists of her own.

"He calls the girl his 'enchanted goddess' and mentions 'laurel' and 'harp' and . . . I think he's referring to Terpsichore, the Muse of dance. Any of these girls—?"

"Allayna Mitchell," she blurted. "She's fourteen and she's a dancer over at—"

"You knew about her and didn't tell us?" I snapped.

"She's not one of mine," Gwen explained. "The call came in after I clocked out."

"Who caught it?"

"Darby Dean."

I shook my head. "Who?"

"She just landed in Missing Persons," Gwen said. "I don't like her cuz she keeps shit to herself like she's fuckin' Batgirl."

"Found her." Colin yanked out the report for Allayna Celine Mitchell, completed by her mother Vaughn Hutchens. We huddled around him. "Reported missing around three thirty this morning. She lives on Nicolet."

"In the Jungle," Lieutenant Rodriguez said.

Allayna was starting to fit the profile: middle-school-aged black girl who lived in the ghetto. Was she also Payton Bishop's student?

"Call Dean," I told Gwen.

A moment later, a woman with a child's voice was complaining about being pulled out of bed. "I just closed my eyes after working, like, all fucking night. Everything's in the report."

"No," Gwen said, "it's *not* all in the—"

"Are you trying to, like, throw me under the bus?" Dean whined. "That's so not—"

"Hey," I interrupted, "I don't know you, and I give zero fucks about your sleep. So I'm gonna need you to shut up and listen to what I'm asking you, all right?"

And then, I repeated the question Gwen had just asked her.

"She was supposed to, like, come home from dance class," Dean said, "but she didn't."

"What type of kid is she?" I asked.

"Her mother said some kids saw her as, like, stuck-up, but she was just shy. Vaughn showed me a video of one of her performances, and, oh my gosh, on stage, she, like, stopped being, like, this poor girl from the hood. It was, like, like . . . she'd been transported to, like, another place. Like she was under some weird spell."

Enchanted goddess . . .

I flipped the pages of Allayna Mitchell's report to view the picture her mother had given Darby Dean: a caramel-skinned girl with large, cocoa-brown eyes and cheekbones sharper than whetstones. She was tall for fourteen and almost too thin to be healthy. She carried her head high—"dancer" eked from her pores even in this photograph taken in bad lighting.

"Maybe she came home," Lieutenant Rodriguez said.

Gwen punched in a phone number.

I nibbled my lower lip. *Please be there. Please be there.*

No answer.

Gwen's face darkened. "I'll try her cell."

No answer.

Gwen shook her head. "I'll try Vaughn."

"No. Let's just head over to the apartment," I said, already moving to my car. "Oh." I stopped in my step.

Krishna was still looking for any traces of the monster on my Crown Vic.

A moment later, I was riding shotgun in my boss's unmarked Taurus. The cabin smelled of cigarettes and spicy cologne. School pictures of his twin girls, Annabelle and Maribel, lived in the visor.

"This day's been absolutely bat-shit bizarre," Colin said from the backseat.

Lieutenant Rodriguez swerved between cars with his sirens screaming as we told him about the funeral, Jimmy Boulard, and the second line.

My radio chimed with an e-mail. From Olympus333. The prior e-mail had come from Olympus111—he'd already switched addresses.

I read the message, and all feeling left my face. "Pull over," I said, my voice flat.

Lieutenant Rodriguez started to ask why, but my complexion must've said it all. He screeched into a grocery store parking lot.

Gwen's car swerved to stop beside us.

"He just sent another message," I said.

Could Jimmy Boulard or even Payton Bishop had sent this so quickly?

eman yb reh wonk lliw uoY

?snaem taht tahw wonk uoy oD .reverof esum lufituaeb ym eb

lliw ehs ,setunim net ni ereh ton era uoy fI .kraP rennoB ta myg

elgnuj eht ta gnitiaw eb lliw eW .ah ah aH .emit dedeen I dnA

.dnuora yalp ot detnaw tsuj I .ereht ton si ehS .elgnuJ eht ot

evird ton oD .esiuolE raeD

Gwen and Pepe crowded my window. "What's wrong?" she shouted.

"What's it say?" Colin asked.

My eyes skipped around the paragraph.

"We need to—"

"Why are we—?"

My rapid breathing and all the talking kept me from focusing.

"Shut up," Lieutenant Rodriguez shouted. "Everybody just . . ."

I closed my eyes, waited until my pulse slowed, then took a deep breath. "Pen ready?"

Colin said, "Yeah. Go."

I skipped to the last word: raeD. "It's backwards again."

Dear Elouise. Do not drive to the Jungle. She is not there. I just wanted to play around. And I needed time. Ha ha ha. We will be waiting at the jungle gym at Bonner Park. If you are not here in ten minutes, she will be my beautiful muse forever. Do you know what that means?

You will know her by name.

36

DON'T LET THIS BE ALLAYNA MITCHELL. DON'T LET IT BE ANYONE. LET THIS BE a *hoax. Just a big joke. Kids screwing around with us. Please, God.*

At La Cienega Boulevard, Lieutenant Rodriguez turned left and raced up the three-lane highway. Colin called in every available badge from here to Mars. And I held my breath as I e-mailed the monster.

> Please think about what you're doing. What do you need me to do to stop? What's your name? What should I call you?

After sending three pleading messages like this, I received a response.

> SENDER UNAVAILABLE.

"I *won't* believe it," Colin said.

"Won't believe what?" I asked.

"That he'd dump a body in the middle of the day with people around."

"It's cold and wet," I pointed out. "The trails are still muddy, and the sun—" I looked at my watch: ten minutes to four and three minutes left until the deadline. "The sun will be setting soon. There won't be many people around."

Radio cars had already blocked the entrance to Bonner Park, and the parking lot was bright with countless red and blue swirling lights. A few civilian cars still remained in their spots with their owners quarantined by patrol cops, while unmarked Crown Vics and Impalas parked this way and that. Uniformed officers and detectives, including Luke, stood in clumps, waiting for us to arrive. The noise from police radios competed with the thunderous roar of an approaching police helicopter. No news crews. Yet.

Lieutenant Rodriguez pulled into a space created just for him, and I jumped out of the car before the engine cut off. Colin followed me as I ran to the playground, praying one last time—*please, no*—although I knew my request may not be answered, not today. But that was faith—believing until the end even as all signs pointed toward darkness.

Pepe met us at the edge of the sandbox. "No one's here."

I looked at my watch: our deadline had passed two minutes ago.

"He said they'd be at Bonner Park, right?" Colin asked.

"How many jungle gyms are there?" I asked.

"Three down here," Pepe said. "Two up top."

"We'll need to search each," I said.

"I brought this." Luke, map in hand, rushed over to a nearby picnic table. He spread out the park map, and we all huddled around it. He circled each play area with red pen.

"Okay, listen up, people," Lieutenant Rodriguez shouted above the noise. "Gomez, you'll stay down here and supervise interviewing any wits. Martin and Hinds, you'll go to the playground up top . . ."

As he handed out assignments, my gaze wandered to the playground's twelve-foot-high tube slide just a few feet from where we stood. A piece of pink paper fluttered on the green slide's upper platform—it had been taped to a metal safety bar, near the entry. The wind was now tearing at that pink paper, and at any moment it would fly away.

Eyes glued to that piece of paper, I left the huddle and crept toward the slide.

"Lou," Lieutenant Rodriguez barked.

I stepped into the sandbox, which was damp from the rain and littered with squashed juice boxes and empty Cheetos bags.

"Lou!"

I stood at the bottom of the slide's steps.

The wind had loosened the tape's hold even more, and the paper lifted higher, slapping both sides now of the green plastic tube.

I placed my right foot on the first step. Then, I placed my left foot on the second step.

The paper was almost free from the tape's grip.

I climbed the next step . . .

Then, the next . . .

Holding my breath, I reached the second-to-last step. The pink paper broke free from the tape as my hand shot out and grabbed it. Words had been written in thick green ink.

"Lou, what the hell are you doing?" Lieutenant Rodriguez and the search team had tromped over to the base of the slide.

I climbed back down to the sandbox and held out the pink paper.

My boss didn't take it. Instead, his eyes scanned the words. "Son of a *bitch*."

"What does it say?" Colin asked.

White noise filled my head, and I stepped back from them. "My prints are on it."

Colin shook his head. "It's a substitution one again."

Wrw R hzb qfmtov tbn? R nvzm ollp-lfg klrmg. Gsv ervd

uli olevih. Hrc nrmfgvh rm svzevm. Sz sz sz.

"Figure it out," Lieutenant Rodriguez shouted.

I blinked at him.

"*Now,* Detective!"

I snapped out of the spell and stared at the substitution cipher.

Pepe offered me a pen and pad.

I sat on the slide's lip, my eyes ping-ponging around the message for "E" and "THE."

Colin crouched in front of me, and whispered, "Faster."

The "R" had to be an "I."

"GSV" was "The."

"Lou," Lieutenant Rodriguez growled.

I ignored him.

"Ollp-lfg" . . . That spelled . . . "*look-out*"?

My throat burned with bile. I swallowed hard, sending acid back to my stomach.

"Svzevm" had to be—

"Lou!" Lieutenant Rodriguez barked.

"*Heaven,*" I blurted. "It says, 'Did I say jungle gym? I mean lookout point. The view for lovers. Six minutes in heaven. Ha ha ha.'"

37

COLIN PALED, AND HIS MOUTH MOVED WITHOUT MAKING A SOUND.

"Which lookout?" Pepe asked.

"There are seven trails in this park," Luke said. "Only trails three and five have lookouts."

"He's talking about where he left Chanita," I said. "Trail five."

"We'll split into two groups," Lieutenant Rodriguez shouted. "Gomez, stay here and block the entrance—there's only one way in and one way out of this park by car. Grab a few uniforms and interview everybody you can." He pointed to Gwen. "Zapata, you help him out."

My group would take trail 5.

"Be prepared," Lieutenant Rodriguez warned. "That son of a bitch may still be here."

After chucking my funeral boots and borrowing someone's two-sizes-too-big work boots, I hurried northeast with Colin and two other cops up to trail 5.

The trails were still muddy from the storms. Dump trucks and earthmovers hadn't left their spots since yesterday, and more red mud had slid against the tires. The heavy machinery would need their own tractors to dig them out.

In a matter of seconds, the back of my shirt was drenched with sweat.

"Six minutes in heaven," Colin said. "Isn't that the game where one kid picks two other kids to go into a dark closet and kiss for . . ."

"Seven," I said. "Seven minutes in heaven, not six. Not that the one-minute discrepancy matters. Unless it does."

The helicopter raced across the sky above us and then circled.

"He's playing games with you," Colin said.

"Children's games," I said. "The ciphers, the kids' book, hide-and-seek . . ."

We walked up the steepening trail. My feet rubbed and slipped in the large boots.

"If he beats *you*, then he's king of the world." When I didn't respond, he continued. "Can we say 'serial' now? The circumstances are too coincidental. The girls' ages, the school they attended, this park."

I held out my arm and stopped walking.

Colin also stopped in his step.

The blue tarp was gone. The stuffed animals, posters, and candles left to honor Chanita remained. And no duffel bag had been dumped on the trail.

Colin sighed with relief. "So maybe he's fucking with us. Again."

My gaze skittered from the trail to the bluff, and my right hand rested on my holstered Glock. "We're not at the lookout point yet."

We walked, passing the site where we'd found Chanita Lords. My heart boomed with every step I took, and, as we neared the bluff, I slipped my gun out of its holster. The creak of leather behind me told me that others on my team were doing the same.

We came to the bluff. A large green canvas bag sat on the lonely gray park bench perched at the bluff's lip.

My stomach dropped.

Colin groaned.

The others fanned out across the bluff as Colin and I moved closer to the bench. The closer our approach, the clearer the sound of . . .

Tinkling music.

I cocked my head.

Colin pointed to the canvas bag.

I took a step closer . . .

A white music box appliquéd with pink ballet slippers and flowers sat atop the canvas bag. The lid was up, and a tiny ballerina *en pointe* slowly pirouetted to Tchaikovsky's "Swan Theme." A few blowflies crept over the canvas bag, but only a few.

Colin's arms remained extended, with his Beretta pointed at the bag.

I holstered the Glock, then used my phone's camera to take pictures of the music box and the canvas bag, of the windswept bluff and the lonely park bench. And then, it was time.

I pulled on latex gloves, then slowly dragged the bag's thick zipper.

There she was. One hand frozen into a claw, the other in a tight, brown fist . . . Skin purple and green . . . Pink T-shirt . . . Glossy leaves and black berries. No bugs except for those few flies.

Colin toggled his radio and in a small, weak voice, he said, "Found her."

Whistles sounded. Radios crackled. Men shouted. The helicopter roared in our direction. All came to where we stood. And then, there was quiet down here on the ground.

Luke crossed himself.

Pepe did the same.

Colin covered his mouth with his hand.

Lieutenant Rodriguez muttered, "Damn it," then lifted the

radio to his mouth. "We're gonna need the coroner . . ."

I tore my eyes away from the girl. My mind was mush—in ten minutes, I wouldn't be able to recall any detail except for . . . her. *Get it together, Lou.* "Let's take pictures of everything," I croaked, "since we can't touch her until the ME comes."

The music from the box stopped.

I jerked. "He's here."

"*Who's here?*" Colin asked.

I pointed to the music box with a steady finger. "He had to wind that up to play."

Lieutenant Rodriguez squinted at me, then his eyes widened.

"A music box only plays for a few minutes," I explained to Colin. "He can't be far."

Lieutenant Rodriguez whirled away from me, whistling and shouting for more bodies to find the monster.

Colin led the group to strip-search the hillside, looking again for a clue, any clue.

And I stayed with the girl.

Do the work.

I pulled a pencil and small pad from my jacket pocket and sketched the hillside, the girl, trees and shrubs, and her proximity to trail 5. Then, I stared at those hills covered with wild sage and chaparral. Far in the distance, the Hollywood sign twinkled on another LA hillside. My eyelids fluttered, and my knees threatened to lose all strength. A part of me did collapse in the dirt, paralyzed as the smell of death overwhelmed me and forced its way into my nostrils, my skin, my clothes. But the other part of me—the tiny part that always survived—gripped her pen so tight that it creaked.

My phone vibrated—a text from Victor Starr. *Just give me a chance. I'm not a bad person. I'm trying to do better. Please.* An exhausted whimper slipped from my lips.

Lieutenant Rodriguez touched my shoulder. "You okay?"

I stared dumbly at him, unable to respond.

"We'll catch him, Lou. Good call on the music box."

He said something else, but his voice was drowned out by the noise of car tires crunching up the gravel and dirt trails. Over the next hour, the once-quiet park swarmed again with cops, Zucca and his bunny-suited forensic techs, and, finally, Brooks and his small team. Patrol units had strung yellow tape across every bush and shrub. And Brooks's team had erected another large blue tarp over the bench.

Colin found me, notebook crunched in my hands, gazing down at La Brea Avenue. "Didn't find much. More shoe prints, so they're making casts." He sighed. "Zucca's beat."

I turned to him. "Aren't we all?"

Colin's sweaty face was covered with leaves and dirt.

I plucked a crumpled leaf from his damp hair.

"Lou!" Brooks was calling me from the tarp.

We joined the ME.

"Ready?" Brooks asked.

I pulled up Allayna's picture on my phone, then ducked beneath the tarp with my team. I stared at the picture, then stared at the teen on the bench.

One of these girls is not like the other.

There's something awesome and terrifying about the soul. It makes your plain brown eyes mischievous. Makes your smirk a smile. And once the soul returns to Whoever gave it, you become a template, an Almost-You, a Madame Tussauds replica, but not for long, because then biology changes you into less than that. And that was this girl on the bench. Almost-Her.

"She's wearing one of those name necklaces," Brooks said, pointing at the girl's neck.

"What does it say?" I asked.

Brooks straightened the charm of gold cursive letters. "Laynie."

You'll know her by name.

"Well?" Lieutenant Rodriguez asked me.

"We'll need her mother to confirm," I said.

"But what do *you* say?" Brooks asked me.

"It's Allayna Mitchell."

"He left her with a music box," Colin said.

"Just as he left Chanita with a View-Master," I said.

Camera for the photographer. Music box for the ballerina.

"He wants them to be entertained," I said. "Entertained as they transition."

"Transition where?" Lieutenant Rodriguez asked.

I closed my eyes. "Into their new lives as Muses, as nymphs. As his."

38

OUR SEARCH HAD TURNED UP SIX MEN—THREE OVER THE AGE OF SIXTY, ONE WITH an amputated left arm, one off-duty sheriff's deputy with a solid alibi, and one who barely weighed 120 pounds and stood an inch over five feet. No one saw anyone lugging a green canvas bag.

And now the sun had abandoned Los Angeles and silver fog raced over us like ghosts.

News choppers hovered at the far edges of the park, giving the LAPD helicopter plenty of space to circle and hover. Flashlight beams danced all around the urban forest in search of the man who had slain another girl. What were the reporters up in the sky and down below saying to the public? What were *we* saying to the public? And was Allayna Mitchell's mother watching?

I needed to notify Vaughn Hutchens. My stomach twisted—I dreaded having to tell another woman that we, the LAPD, had failed. *Don't wanna do that. Not at all.* So I filled out more reports, took more pictures, did everything I could to delay having that awful conversation.

But I could no longer busy myself with the details of death.

Syeeda texted me. *Just saw news on TV. Who is she? Should I send someone?*

I didn't respond—couldn't. Not now.

"I'll go downtown with Allayna," Colin said, following Brooks to the coroner's van.

As Lieutenant Rodriguez drove me back to Mount St. John's Church, we talked on automatic about the nonsense that murder police talk about: the evils of men, the Dodgers, the Lakers, the best chili burgers in LA, the evils of men again.

Krishna had finished processing my Crown Vic hours ago, and it still sat in the church parking lot, waiting to head to my next dragon windmill.

"You goin' over to the mom's?" Lieutenant Rodriguez asked as I opened the trunk of my car. "It's dinnertime. Fucked up to tell her at dinnertime."

"Is there ever a good time?" I took off the too-big boots and grabbed the flats I kept handy for times like this.

"Good luck," he said. "See you back at the station."

Before I pulled out of the parking lot, my phone rang.

"Hey, Mom," I said, "can't talk right now, I'm—"

And that's when I spotted it, on the hood of the Crown Vic. A marble figurine.

"I know," Mom was saying. "I just wanted to tell you that Victor hasn't called all day."

Face numb, I ducked back out of the car and gaped at the statuette. *What the—?*

Mom said something, and I said, "Uh huh." I held the phone out and snapped a picture.

A goddess—she wore a laurel wreath and her harp rested on a pedestal. *Terpsichore.*

Who put this here? The same person who put Melpomene on my car? The same person who had been playing games with me since Wednesday?

I threw an anxious glance around the abandoned parking lot.

"Okay," Mom said, "I'll let you get back to work. Love you, kiddo."

Heart pounding, my thoughts staggered from one thought—Allayna Mitchell—to another more menacing thought—Muses. Because those pieces meant something. But what?

At King Boulevard, I turned right and headed west to the Jungle. My police radio chimed, this time with a forwarded e-mail from Dr. Zach.

Haven't heard from you—hoping to have seen you again by now. Here I am, in case you've forgotten me. In the attached picture, he wore blue scrubs. A stethoscope hung around his neck. He had crossed his muscular arms.

I frowned. "Bad time for this, Zach."

But what did he know? Women liked men in scrubs. Even *I* liked men in scrubs. But not en route to a death notification.

Allayna and her mother, Vaughn, lived on Nicolet Avenue, two blocks northwest of Chanita and Regina. I parked a block away from her apartment complex, then trudged past alleyways that reeked of urine, trash, and dead animals. Spent bullet casings and used condoms gathered in the muck near the storm drains. A filthy, one-eyed teddy bear sat on an abandoned couch like a patient in a doctor's office.

Rage, fatigue, and sadness pressed down on my shoulders, crushing my vertebrae against each other and slowing my already-ponderous gait.

It was seven minutes to eight o'clock, and black and brown boys in their early teens rolled scooters and skateboards on sidewalks and in the middle of the street. Some lived in the surrounding Necco-wafer-colored apartment complexes, like the gritty yellow building wearing a large orange banner advertising rental prices that started at $449.

I saw all of this just passing through. Didn't wonder what

I'd see if I poked around in Poverty's medicine cabinet—because I knew.

My old neighborhood.

Home sweet hell.

While Regina Drummond had a park and a hillside to break up her street's bleakness, Vaughn Hutchens only had other depressed, concrete-slabbed apartments as her view. Her building—a mint-colored, two-level complex named Baldwin Gardens—hid behind black iron security gates that sat open and secured nothing. Rusted grocery carts and torn laundry baskets littered the common area. The scent of fried meat and onions, burnt toast, and laundry dryer sheets wafted in the air.

The Mean Girls sat in patio chairs next to a swimming pool filled with concrete. Each girl clutched a large bag of Flamin' Hot Cheetos and a liter bottle of orange Crush soda.

Seeing these sullen, mouthy children again made the hairs on my skin stand.

The cursive print on ShaQuan's tight pink tank top spelled BITCH. "What's up, Detective Elouise?"

Treasure and Imunique, also wearing tank tops, turned in my direction.

"What are you guys doing here?" I asked.

They held up their hands. "Don't shoot," ShaQuan said with a twisted smile.

"Ha, not funny," I said.

"I live here," Treasure said, fingering one of her thousands of braids. "In apartment six. Is that a problem?"

I ignored the burning in my stomach. "Nope. I came to talk to Allayna Mitchell's mother. Y'all know Allayna, right?"

"Uh huh," Imunique said. "Where Detective Cutie Pie at?"

I squinted at her. "Who?"

"She crushin' on Captain America," ShaQuan said, grinning.

Imunique kicked ShaQuan's calf. "You trippin'."

"Detective Taggert is . . ." *Standing over Allayna Mitchell's corpse right now.* "Busy with other things." "Uni," Treasure said to her friend, "maybe you can move to Culver City and become a cop and get a cute white-boy partner."

Imunique lifted her hands and said, "Whoop-whoop."

"Vaughn just got home," Treasure said.

Imunique rolled her eyes. "She been out looking for her precious angel."

ShaQuan sucked her teeth. "We get threatened every day, but ain't no cops tryin' to protect *us*. Y'all just wait 'til somebody pull the trigger and blood gets spilled. Even then, y'all just step over the blood and go to Denny's and shit."

"Fuck Allayna," Imunique spat.

Treasure glared at her friend.

"Yeah, I said it," the chubby girl boasted.

"Treasure," I said, "what's wrong?"

She shrugged, then swiped her wet eyes. "I just . . . I feel bad for Vaughn."

ShaQuan noticed Treasure's tears and sucked her teeth again. "Here we go."

Imunique kicked Treasure's tennis shoe. "You need to stop actin' like you care. You know you can't stand Ghetto Barbie."

Treasure muttered, "Yeah," then picked at a scab on her tattooed wrist.

"Any ideas on this one?" I asked. "Mexican gang-banging child molesters or . . . ?"

Eyes to the concrete, each girl shook her head.

"She probably ran away again," Treasure said. "Or killed herself for real this time."

My blood chilled. "Allayna's run away before? *And* she's attempted suicide?"

Treasure nodded.

ShaQuan giggled. "Maybe it worked this time."

A door opened, and the voice of a *telenovela* actress echoed through the courtyard.

"Really wit' that?" Imunique growled.

ShaQuan twisted in the direction of the sound, and shouted, "Y'all need to turn that Mess-i-can shit down. This ain't no Ti-a-ja-wana."

"And, no, I don't want no damn Chiclets," Imunique added.

The door slammed close.

"I'm guessing you don't like Allayna," I said.

"You guessed right," ShaQuan said.

"She stuck-up," Imunique said. "Always kissin' up to the teachers. *Miss Hendricks,*" Imunique trilled in falsetto, *"do you need me to make copies? Mr. Bishop, want me to staple?"*

"She always carryin' her dance bag around," Treasure added. "She never put it in her locker even when she don't need it cuz she want the whole world to know."

"She think she all that cuz she dance," ShaQuan said. "Who *can't* dance?"

"Act like she Queen Bey," Treasure said. "She ain't all that, but everybody treat her like she da bomb."

"*I* can dance," Imunique bragged.

"Twerkin' ain't ballet," Treasure pointed out.

"*Ballet,*" Imunique spat. "That's some stupid white people shit."

"Black dance companies *do* exist," I countered. "Alvin Ailey in New York. Debbie Allen's Academy, not far from here—"

"*Who?*" Imunique snarled. "I ain't heard of no Ailey-Allen-who-give-a-fuck."

"They ain't had to suspend us," Treasure lamented. "She wasn't even that hurt."

"Excuse me?" I said.

"She a fuckin' mental case," ShaQuan said, her finger making the "crazy person" circle at her temple. "Who the hell steal pills from the store to kill theyselves? And the cops let her go."

"If it woulda been *us*," Imunique said, "we'd be at juvie right now."

"*Again*," Treasure said, smiling.

"Ha ha," Imunique said.

"But Laynie *special*," ShaQuan said, "cuz she can *dance*."

"You jumped her, too?" I asked.

No one spoke.

"Allayna's mom press charges?"

ShaQuan groaned. "I don't even care no more. I don't care if she ran away or got kidnapped or ODed on fuckin' Tylenol. I'm sick of always getting suspended."

I sighed. "Did Vaughn press—?"

"She got restrainin' orders," Treasure said, matter-of-factly. "Like we wanna be all close to her precious angel."

"And how we supposed to stay away from her if she live by Treasure?" ShaQuan asked. "We supposed to hang out somewhere else? Why can't *they* move away since *they* so perfect? Since they think they better than us?"

"She tried to hang with us this one time," Imunique recalled. "She thought she could trick us, but we knew she was only around so she could hook up with Tre's brother."

"Justin," Treasure said, nodding. "Justin and his stuck-up girls get on my *nerves*."

Like synchronized swimmers, the trio emptied their Cheetos bags into their mouths. ShaQuan chugged from her soda bottle, then belched. Treasure and Imunique giggled and offered uncommitted "uhhs."

"All y'all cops keep talkin' to Vaughn," ShaQuan said, "but ain't nobody talked to us or asked us what *we* thought, how *we* feel. Y'all forget we people, too."

"So what *are* your thoughts?" I asked. "How *do* you feel? Seriously."

"Why you care?" Imunique asked.

"Cuz Jesus wants me to," I said, eyes narrowed. "And I haven't forgotten that you're people. That's why I'm still here. Cuz bad shit shouldn't happen to you, ShaQuan, or to you, Treasure, or even you, Imunique. Or to Allayna and Chanita, but it did, and it ain't right."

"Where you been, then?" Treasure countered. "You ain't come around here when Laynie first went missing."

Cuz I only come around when people are dead. "I'm here now," I said. "When was the last time you saw Allayna?"

"Monday night," ShaQuan and Imunique said as Treasure said, "Thursday."

I cocked my head and peered at the trio. "Please, girls?"

Treasure dropped her gaze.

"What time on Thursday, Treasure?" I asked.

"After school," she whispered.

"Where?"

"Near Fat Burger."

"The one on Marlton?" I asked.

She nodded.

The dance school was also in that shopping complex, located across the street from the abandoned Santa Barbara Plaza. Did Allayna attend that school? If she did, had she gone to class on Thursday?

"What was she wearing?" I asked.

Treasure shrugged. "Clothes."

"You speak to her?"

"We said hi," ShaQuan said with a twisted smile. "We was gonna walk her home."

"How nice of you," I said. "And did you walk her home?"

263

Treasure shook her head. "She got a ride."

"From?" I whispered, nerves prickling beneath my skin.

"Whoever drove that dark SUV," Treasure said.

"Notice a license plate this time?"

"Nope," ShaQuan said. "Didn't want to."

I ignored her and focused on Treasure. "Treasure, did you notice . . . ?"

She took a while but finally nodded, then shrugged, then shook her head.

"When was the last time she and Justin hung out?" I asked.

"They was kickin' it at my house on Sunday night," Treasure said. "They was on the couch, watching DVDs and stuff. Kissin' and goin' on, but she wanted to stop."

ShaQuan sneered. "She always wanna stop. *I* think she tryna get him in trouble. I—"

A police helicopter thundered above and away from us, and soon the circling with the searchlight began. The girls glared at the bird in the sky, then hoisted their middle fingers. Sirens wailed closer . . . closer . . . That bright white light shone closer . . . closer . . .

"Ain't Chanita's funeral tomorrow?" Imunique asked.

"It was today," I said.

ShaQuan giggled. "Oops."

"They ain't had to stick her in no gym bag," Treasure said. "That's some wack shit."

ShaQuan and Imunique snickered again, but agreed that sticking Chanita Lords in a gym bag was, indeed, some wack shit.

With tears in my eyes, I shook my head, awed and disgusted by these young women. "You guys really think this is funny? I know you didn't like Chanita, and obviously you don't like Allayna, either, but *damn*. Are y'all really who the world thinks you are? Who the world thinks *I* am? Angry black women who don't give one fuck about anything? Are you really nasty little bitches through and through? Seriously: do you want to go to hell?"

Shamed, the girls stared at the concrete, and, for that brief moment, they looked like children again.

"Anything else you can tell me?" I asked.

"Anything else you can tell *us*?" Imunique spat. "Like, why you ask us stupid-ass questions all the time?"

"She just wanna find out why Allayna gone, dum-dum," Treasure explained.

"She ain't gone." ShaQuan dropped her empty Cheetos bag to the ground. "She *hiding*."

I rolled my eyes. "Is she hiding with Chanita for the insurance money?"

ShaQuan did the head-neck swivel. "She *hiding* cuz that's how she wants it."

"Maybe if *I* disappeared," Imunique said, "maybe people will pay *me* some attention."

"My foster mother would probably be happy if *I* disappeared," ShaQuan said, smiling, even though her eyes held sadness. "But I ain't lettin' that bitch be happy." She forced herself to laugh. Sounded as empty as that cheese-curls bag now drifting across the pool of concrete.

Treasure shrugged, and her eyes hardened. "Maybe if Laynie didn't try be all that, not try to be so damn special, she'd still be walkin' around and carrying that damn dance bag." She blinked, then gaped at me.

"What?" I asked.

"I just remembered . . ." She swallowed hard, then said, "2BT."

"And what is 2BT?" I asked.

She smiled and crossed her arms.

"Don't fuck with me, little girl," I growled. "What is 2BT?"

Her smile dimmed, and she sat upright in the patio chair. "It's all I remember. The license plate from the truck that took Laynie started with 2BT."

39

2BT.

An incredible lead from an unlikely source.

"You shittin' me?" Lieutenant Rodriguez said.

I stood near the quiet mail room in Vaughn Hutchens's apartment building. The wind had picked up even more, and now a small funnel of supermarket circulars, lint, and cigarette butts swirled between the laundry room and the entry gates.

"No, sir," I said. "She swore to me that she remembers. That's enough for a BOLO."

Even though the Department of Motor Vehicles didn't capture color, the agency could still run 2BT through their computers and generate a list of SUVs with that plate sequence.

And now I breathed a sigh of relief so deep that I lost a pound. *Moving forward.* Partial plate or not, though, I still had to do the hardest task: tell a mother that her daughter was dead.

In the open front door to apartment 2, two men in sweaty T-shirts and cargo shorts distributed MISSING and HAVE YOU SEEN? flyers between two postal bins. Muddy shoes and tired faces, they'd probably been searching for Allayna all day.

The guy wearing the Red Sox cap saw me walking toward them. "You a cop, ain't you?"

His cornrowed partner scowled at me and shook his head in disgust. "Somebody gon' help us look? We was out all day, and ain't one cop show up."

"Where'd you look?" I asked. That pound I'd just lost landed back in my gut.

"Ballona Wetlands," Red Sox said. "Laynie like goin' there, so we figured . . ."

Ballona Wetlands was four miles away, in Playa Vista, near my former Shangri-La condo. Close to the Jungle but as far away as the Shire.

"Go on in," Red Sox said. "Vaughn's here."

A tan sofa, a lopsided entertainment system, and cardboard boxes filled with gewgaws and whatnots remained in the otherwise-empty living room. Squares of carpet that had sat beneath pieces of furniture looked brighter and flatter than areas that had been exposed to smoke, food, and foot traffic.

Although most of the furniture had been removed and tchotchkes had been packed into boxes, framed pictures still hung on the walls. Allayna and Vaughn sharing cotton candy at the county fair . . . Toddler Allayna wearing a tutu as Vaughn, wearing a pantsuit and a prideful smile, stood behind her . . . Allayna and Vaughn driving mini-Indy cars at the slick track.

"Hello?" I cried out. "Ms. Hutchens?"

"Hold on!" a woman shouted from the rear of the apartment.

There were more photos hanging, but none taken with mother and daughter together. Allayna holding a bouquet of roses after an event . . . Vaughn wearing an ARCO hard hat and standing with a white man who also wore an ARCO hard hat . . .

Vaughn Hutchens strode into the living room with a pink lampshade in one hand and a bottle of drinking water in the other. Her butterscotch face looked worn and gaunt. She had gathered her long hair into two coiled buns on the sides of her head, Princess Leia–style. "Who are you?"

I held out my hand. "Detective Elouise Norton. I'm here about your daughter, Allayna."

Vaughn narrowed her eyes—she was trying to figure out if I was a good cop or a bad cop. Not knowing that I was the worst cop, she accepted my handshake, then motioned to the boxes scattered around the living room. "Excuse all this. Can't stand this city no more. Laynie can't handle it no more, either. When she gets back home, we're moving to New Mexico."

"Why New Mexico?" I asked.

"Lots of colors and lots of nothing. None of the past."

We perched on the couch. I pulled out my binder, quickly turning past pages of Allayna's death scene.

Vaughn pulled a box of Parliaments and a purple lighter from her jeans pocket. "No one is listening. No one is helping. It's just me, most of the time. Frustrated. Alone. The news shows on TV talk about white girls who disappear. Their mommas get to tell the entire world stories about their babies, but have reporters come here and asked me anything?"

"Have you been watching the news today?" I asked, heart in my throat.

"Nope. Didn't want to hear about Chanita's funeral."

No news cameras wanted to hear about it, either—none, except Mike Summit, had shown up, choosing instead to cover the funeral of Congresswoman Fortier.

"What would you want the world to know about Allayna?" I asked.

Vaughn took a drag from the cigarette, then blew smoke into the air. "The truth."

"Which is?"

"There's a rumor that Allayna was fooling around before

she went missing. She wasn't that kind of girl. I didn't even let her go to the movies with boys. People figured she had a lot of boyfriends cuz she was pretty. But she wasn't into all that. People are also sayin' that she was mentally unstable and suicidal."

"But she wasn't any one of those things?"

Anger lit Vaughn's eyes. "What if she was? Is it her fault that she's missing? Anyway . . ." She cocked her head. "You're not from Missing Persons, are you?"

I shook my head. "I'm a homicide detective."

She stared at me, the grim reaper's press agent, and light filled her eyes. Finally, she gasped, then mewed like a kitten. Her eyes crossed before she closed them.

And then, I told her that we had found a girl, dead, that afternoon. I showed her that picture in my binder.

She nodded and whispered, "Yes."

The cigarette burned between her fingers.

We sat very, very still for several minutes.

"We . . ." Vaughn stared at the cigarette. "We used to do everything together. And then . . . We didn't understand each other anymore." Fat tears slipped down her gaunt cheeks, and she cried without making a sound.

I watched her and waited.

"Dancing," Vaughn whispered. "Listening to her iPod. Writing poems. That's what she loved the most."

"That evening before you reported her missing—"

"She had dance at Miss Debbie's," Vaughn recalled, "from three thirty to four thirty. I told all this to Detective Dean."

"How did she usually get home?"

"She walked. Marlton to Santa Rosalia to Nicolet."

"Where did she go to school?"

"Madison, over on—"

"I know it. I went there, too."

She squinted at me, then puffed her cigarette.

"And the last time you talked to Allayna?"

"Thursday at lunchtime," Vaughn said. "I'm working a new shift, so I don't get to see her much. So I checked in with her. Told her that I put her costume in the cleaner's."

"And you called 911 when?"

Vaughn flicked ashes into the water bottle. "At three thirty Friday morning, when I got home. She wasn't here, and she hadn't slept in her bed."

"Did you keep calling your daughter even after we got involved?"

She nodded. "And I left messages on her voice mail."

"Her father?"

"Ain't around." She tapped ashes into the bottle. "He's never been around."

"Boyfriends?"

"I don't have time for boyfriends."

"Who was her school counselor?"

"Payton Bishop."

My scalp crawled, and I cleared my throat before asking, "How was that?"

"He's very supportive," she said. "Very kind. A little nosy. Extremely sanctimonious. He thinks I'm holding my daughter back. He thinks he's smarter than me."

"Did he and Allayna spend a lot of time together?"

"Like out of school?" Vaughn shook her head. "He calls *me* all the time. Tells me to take Laynie to this performance and to fill out this form or that form. It's like he doesn't trust me to handle my daughter's future. Like I'm neglectful and selfish and working the graveyard shift cuz I *enjoy* working the graveyard shift."

I swallowed, worried that my next question would cause the cigarette now hanging from Vaughn's lips to either flip

.o my lap or be put out in my eye. "I've talked to a few . . .
.udents about Allayna, and they seem—"

"You talkin' about the girls who beat her up? Them evil little bitches out there?" Vaughn pointed toward the courtyard. She shook out another cigarette before smashing the one still stuck between her lips. "You know what? The last time they beat Laynie up, they recorded it. Then they put it up on YouTube."

My eyes widened. *"What?"*

She yanked her phone from her back pocket, tapped the YouTube app, then handed me the phone.

I tapped the video link for "nov12Laynie."

Over a thousand views.

A camera phone had captured ShaQuan and Imunique kicking Allayna Mitchell, now curled into a tight ball on the asphalt. The person recording—sounded like Treasure's laugh—was cheering on her friends. ShaQuan grabbed Allayna's hair bun and yanked her head out from the protective ball. Bloody cuts covered the dancer's already-swollen face.

What the *hell*?

Kids got jumped back in the day, but never this vicious or this . . . celebrated. And the beat-downs were never caught on tape.

The recording left me breathless, and a headache was forming behind my eyes. As a cop, I'd seen many jacked-up things throughout my career—and this video was now in the top ten.

"I showed the video to them bastards at the school," Vaughn said, taking back her phone. "And they didn't do not one thing. The principal said cuz it didn't happen on school grounds."

"And the police?"

"Laynie was too scared to talk, so it wasn't worth getting the police involved."

"The girls said you took out a restraining order."

"I lied to them," Vaughn said. "I typed up some bogus

272

letter just so they'd stay away from my daughter."

"But you saw that she'd been assaulted," I said. "And so . . . Allayna returned to *Madison*? The same school the girls who beat her *also* attended?"

"Oh. So it's *my* fault?" She scowled and pointed again to the courtyard. "Them little heifers, they're the ones responsible for all this."

And I told her that those little heifers saw Allayna climb into a dark SUV. "Do you know any adults who may own a dark SUV?"

"Nuh uh."

"You know anyone who may have interacted with Allayna without your knowledge?"

"No." With a shaky hand, Vaughn stuck the cigarette into her mouth.

"I've been told that Allayna's attempted suicide in the past," I whispered.

She shook her head as her eyes filled with tears. "More drama than what it deserves." She sighed. "Laynie took some Tylenol PM. You can't die taking Tylenol PM."

My face warmed as I pushed back anger. "But she wanted to harm herself."

Vaughn shrugged.

"Was she seeing a therapist or talking to a pastor or someone about her feelings?"

Vaughn stared at the burning end of the cigarette. "I didn't see a need for that. She was healthy. She was fourteen." A teardrop rolled down her cheek, and the cigarette bobbed in her fingers. "Every girl is crazy at fourteen."

"I also heard that she's run away—"

"Oh my *lord*." Vaughn shoved the cigarette into the water bottle.

"When she left those times—?"

"It was only once," Vaughn snapped.

"When she left that *one time*," I said, "who did she run to?"

"I don't know, but she came home and—" She glared at me with wet eyes. "I know what you're thinking. If I can move *now*, why didn't I move us two months ago? It's cuz I ain't got it like that. You think I'd be living here if I did? And New Mexico just happened cuz of a job opportunity, and I didn't think . . . I was taught not to run away. I wanted Laynie . . . I thought this was one of those life lessons. I didn't want her to be a coward, okay? I didn't want her always *needing* me to solve her problems, okay?"

I nodded since she needed me to nod.

She rose from the couch on weak legs and stumbled over to the kitchen counter. She rummaged through her Coach purse and pulled out a piece of folded pink paper. "I didn't give this to Detective Dean cuz I didn't think . . ." She stared at the square. "Did Laynie do it herself?"

"We're conducting the autopsy at this moment," I said.

Vaughn returned to the couch to hand me the paper.

I unfolded the square: pink Sharpie ink, and the round letters of a fourteen-year-old girl with good penmanship.

Vaughn, it's your fault that I'm writing this. It's your fault that I'm dying slowly every day. It's your fault that I'm dead now. I hope you get your promotion. I hope you get that office with a window. I hope you get everything that you dreamed of and always put before me.

Allayna, Your Dead Daughter

My hands shook—Allayna hadn't put herself into that canvas bag and left herself on that bench. Still, this note told me something else—she wanted, no, *needed* to be rescued.

Vaughn shook out another cigarette from the dwindling pack.

"Did you know she felt this way?" I asked.

"No."

"You think Allayna knew the person responsible for her death?"

Without hesitation, Vaughn said, "Yes. She didn't go off with strangers."

"What about the two men out there?"

"Warren and Kwame?" She shook her head. "They're like my brothers."

"I'll need to talk to them. And Justin. What do you think about him?"

"Laynie and Justin were back and forth. I love him; I hate him."

"Do you think he could've hurt her?"

Vaughn stared at her knees. "I don't know anything anymore."

"Did he help in the search?"

"His mom wouldn't let him. She's very protective."

"This is *Treasure's* mother?"

Vaughn smirked. "Right?"

"And you said Allayna had her own cell phone?"

"Yes. A Droid Mini. And like I said before, I kept calling and calling. And like I told Detective Dean yesterday, there isn't a family locater app for that phone."

"Have you noticed any strange numbers on the bill?"

Vaughn shrugged, probably numb now.

"Will you give me permission to pull your phone records? Maybe we'll be able to identify the cell towers that were close or—"

She nodded, then signed the waiver I slid before her. The name I read there could've said "Vaughn Hutchens" or "Genghis Khan."

Thinking about the state in which we'd found Chanita's

body, I asked Vaughn, "Has she broken any bones lately? From dance or . . . wherever?"

"Back in November, after getting jumped," Vaughn said. "No injuries since then."

"And have all her baby teeth fallen out?"

She shook her head. "Took her to the dentist during Christmas vacation. She still had some back ones that needed to go."

"Did she keep a diary or journal? Something that captured her inner thoughts?"

Vaughn trudged back to the kitchen, then returned with a box filled with pink binders and journals. She dropped the box at my feet. "Some stuff's in here."

I thanked her, then said, "Mind if I look around her room?"

She zombie-walked down the hallway, just as Chanita's mom had, just as Monique Darson's mother had, just as every mother had once I told them the news.

Allayna's bedroom walls were covered with posters and pictures of dancers—from Debbie Allen and Mikhail Baryshnikov to Savion Glover and Josephine Baker. Her desk held countless music boxes of every size—no empty space for the box we'd found on the park bench. A student planner sat in between stacks of magazines and DVDs. Three pairs of toe shoes dangled from the desk shelf.

I flipped though the planner: Allayna had a precalculus test on Monday, a paper on Catherine the Great due Wednesday, and a doctor's appointment at four o' clock on Thursday.

When I returned to the living room, Vaughn plucked an eight-by-ten photograph from a photo album's sticky page. She studied the picture for a moment, then held it out to me. "Use this."

It was a black-and-white photo of Allayna wearing a dark leotard and sitting in a sea of polka-dot tulle. "Will you offer a reward like you're doing for the other girl?" Vaughn whispered.

I took her sweaty, weak hands in my sweaty, strong ones and squeezed. "Yes. But more than that: I'll do my best to catch him. I won't stop until I do."

40

DENIAL: VAUGHN HUTCHENS WAS NOW BEING CRUELLY PUNISHED FOR LIVING IN IT for so long. Even when faced with the truth—Allayna needed her more than ARCO needed her—Vaughn still refused to believe and adapt.

And despite my skill in getting time-hardened thugs and baby-faced murderers to confess, and despite my sorority-girl-sista-friend-shoop-shoop credibility, I still couldn't convince Vaughn Hutchens to accept that all had not been right in her home for months, maybe even years, before Allayna's death.

So, at almost nine thirty, I told her that I'd call her soon, hopefully with more news. The box of Allayna's notebooks in my arms, I left the grieving mom with Warren and Kwame. Shoulders tense, I hurried across the empty courtyard, out the gate, and down the block to my car. I dropped the box into the trunk, then started back to the apartment complex.

The thunder from the roving helicopter and its bright searchlight kept the street clear and kept me from having to explain my existence to a different kind of neighborhood watch. On the way back to Baldwin Gardens, I called Pepe and told him that Vaughn had signed the waiver to allow us to pull Allayna's phone records. "And maybe 2BT will show up soon."

"About that," Pepe said. "DMV computers are down."

Because *of course* they were.

"And," Pepe said, "no prints except yours on those little statue things."

Because *of course* there weren't.

Behind the closed door of apartment 6 came the televised roar of sports fans.

I knocked.

Inside, a woman shouted, "Turn dat down. You deaf?"

The television's volume dropped.

The door opened, and a draft washed over me—curry and onions. A tiny, dark-skinned woman wearing silver-rimmed glasses and teddy-bear-printed scrubs stood before me. She rolled her eyes. "You here 'bout Laynie?" She had an accent, Trinidad or Antigua.

"Yes. And you are . . . ?"

"Oria Abraham, Justin's mother."

"Treasure's mother, too?"

She gave a curt nod. "Who you wan' talk to now?"

"Justin, please."

She frowned, then turned her head. "Come, now."

The television muted, the leather couch squeaked, and a tabletop lamp clicked on, filling the room with soft yellow light.

I spotted Jesus and Mary candles and small icons of various saints on shelves alongside pictures of a tall kid holding a basketball, taken with and without the bundle of sass standing in front of me. There were no pictures of a teenage girl.

That tall kid came to tower behind his mother. He wore a white CROSSROADS basketball jersey and clutched a gallon of red Gatorade. At six foot five, he was strong enough to carry a girl, especially a dancer like Allayna, up a trail.

"Hi, Justin," I said. "I'm Detective Norton and—"

Over on the other side of the courtyard, at Allayna's

apartment, a man wailed. His cries were soon joined by the cries of a woman, and then another woman's screams of, "No, God, no." Doors started opening, with people poking their heads out, murmuring, whispering, and shouting.

Oria Abraham stared at neighbors creeping toward Vaughn's apartment. Then, she gaped at her son.

"May I come inside?" I asked.

Justin's breathing came fast, as though he had been running up and down a basketball court. "Oh no," he said, backing away with tears bright in his eyes. "Oh no, no, no."

"Dat girl on de news," Oria Abraham said, "was dat Laynie?"

"Yes, it *was* Allayna Mitchell," I said. "Justin, I'm gonna need you to sit before you pass out."

Justin sank into the armchair and groaned.

I sat on the couch.

Oria Abraham stood behind her son, arms crossed.

And UConn continued to beat Villanova.

"How old are you, Justin?" I asked.

"Sixteen."

Shit. A minor. Oria had to stay.

"You dated Allayna, correct?" I asked.

"Kind of." A tear rolled down the bridge of his nose. "We broke up, and then we got back together again."

I pointed to his jersey. "You go to Crossroads?"

"Yes, ma'am."

"On scholarship," Oria Abraham added.

As though I couldn't figure out that a kid who lived *here* couldn't afford tuition to a school that cost almost thirty thousand dollars a year.

"And we don' wan' no trouble," Oria warned me. "No *commesse,* understand?"

"That's up to Justin," I said, then added, "and Treasure.

Justin: why did you and Laynie break up?"

"Cuz Tre's friends made life hard on us."

"Friends, meaning ShaQuan and Imunique?"

"Yes, sir, I mean, ma'am."

"Are you aware," I said to Oria Abraham, "that your daughter and her friends assaulted Allayna Mitchell back in November?"

The woman was shaking her head even as I spoke. "Treasure didn't assault her—she recorded da fight."

Awed, I could only gawk at her. "Fine. Treasure didn't *touch* Allayna," I said, "but she certainly rejoiced in the poor girl getting beaten. I *heard* Treasure laughing. I could play the video for you if you'd like."

Oria Abraham's mouth snapped closed, and she glared at me.

I turned back to Justin. "So you broke up with Allayna because . . . ?"

Justin kneaded his hands. "I thought it would be easier if we just—"

"Treasure's just wit' dem badjohns," his mother interrupted, "because . . . protection. She and Laynie were *padnas,* real close like."

Needles prickled up and down my left arm—this woman was killing me. "Please, Miss Abraham—"

"It's *Mrs.*," she spat. "I'm no babymomma. My husband, he died of a heart attack." She crossed herself.

"My apologies, then." To Justin: "So Treasure's friends broke you apart?"

"That wasn't the only reason. Allayna . . ." He dropped his head, and his wide shoulders slumped. "She had some . . . issues." He looked up at me, and now tears rolled down his cheeks.

"What kind of issues?" I asked.

"She was vexing him," Oria Abraham said. "All da time. She—"

"Mrs. Abraham," I said in my CAPS LOCK voice.

"She had mental issues," Justin said. "Always depressed. Always wanting me to run away with her. I felt bad for her cuz she mostly lived by herself. Her mom worked late and . . ." He dried his face with his jersey. "So I stayed around mostly cuz I was scared she was gonna hurt herself again or run away for real this time."

"Justin tall for his age," Oria Abraham said, "but he still just a fella. He shouldna worry 'bout t'ings like dat."

"A personal question, Justin," I said, leaning forward. "Were you and Laynie sexually active? There may be . . . DNA on her, and we'll need to know whose DNA it is, understand?"

Oria Abraham's simmering anger heated the room.

But Justin didn't flinch. "We weren't, Detective Norton. I have my basketball career to think of first—I don't want a baby messin' that up." *And my mom would kill me,* his wide eyes said.

"Did you know Chanita Lords?" I asked.

His eyebrows furrowed. "Who?"

"What about Trina Porter?"

He tapped his mother's elbow. "That's the missing girl. I see her mom on the news all the time. She came to speak at Mass. Remember, Ma?"

Oria Abraham didn't nod, nor did she shake her head.

"When did you see Allayna last?" I asked the kid.

"On Monday, after I got home from practice. She showed me her solo out there in the courtyard and . . ." He smiled, then bit his lower lip. "She's . . . incredible. She's so happy when she's dancing."

"And where were you on Thursday afternoon, say, around three thirty?"

"I was playing ball. A game against Brentwood."

"Did you help search for Allayna yesterday or today?" I asked.

He dropped his head. "Nuh uh."

"Why not?"

Oria Abraham lifted her chin, then placed her hands on Justin's shoulders. "I wouldn'a let him. He too young for all dat. School and basketball, dat's what he should worry 'bout."

"One last thing," I said. "I'd like a DNA sample to compare—"

"No." The woman shook her head. "Nuh uh."

Justin twisted to look up at his mother. "Ma—"

"Boy," she said, "don't be screwin' up your face—"

"I don't mind, Ma. I didn't do—"

"I want a court order," she told me.

"Ma," Justin shouted, "I—"

"Mrs. Abraham," I said, "I'd only need—"

"*Court. Order.*"

Justin opened his mouth and leaned toward me, ready to offer as much spit as possible.

Oria puckered her lips but said nothing.

I closed my binder and stood from the couch. "Your mother has that right, Justin." To Oria, I said, "I'll get a court order—for Justin *and* Treasure. Just to make sure your daughter wasn't recording again when Allayna took her final breath."

41

AFTER LEAVING ORIA AND JUSTIN ABRAHAM, AFTER LISTENING TO THE ANGRY CRIES
and heartbroken wails coming from Vaughn Hutchens's
apartment, I needed joy, positivity . . . I needed Sam.

But he wasn't answering his office phone or his cell phone.
So I texted him: *You around? Need to talk. Long hard day.*

Heavy-hearted, I trudged back to the Crown Vic and
threw a glance at the sky—no helicopter. Just a bright white
moon and a star. When had been the last time I'd glimpsed
a star?

With one hand clutching the steering wheel and the other
clutching my phone in anticipation of Sam's response, I drove
east to the dance school.

Allayna had walked Marlton and Santa Rosalia to get
home. Two worlds coexisted here—the ordered one at the
Baldwin Hills Mall, protected by thick black gates and
security guards, and the wild one, Santa Barbara Plaza,
abandoned, overrun, and run-down with weeds, trash, and
crumbled concrete. A graveyard.

Treasure had claimed to see Allayna climb into the dark
SUV near the corner of Marlton and Santa Rosalia.

I pulled to the curb and saw nothing remarkable—a
homeless man sleeping on a bus stop bench that advertised
Sylvester Stallone's latest *Expendables* flick, a YMCA and

Trina Porter's school, Holy Grace Christian Academy on the south side of the street. The dance academy sat to the east, and the disintegrating plaza sat behind me.

I glanced at my phone.

No word from Sam, so I tried one more number he'd given me.

His landline at his Echo Park townhouse rang twice before someone said, "Hello?" A woman's voice.

I froze.

"Hello?"

I cleared my throat. "Hi. Is Sam there?" *Maybe I called the wrong number. Maybe—*

"He's out walking the dog. May I take a message?"

"Please tell him that Detective Norton called."

"Oh, hey, Lou," she said, "it's Rishma."

My gut twisted. *Rishma.* Ex-wife. Sri Lankan. Very pretty. Senior VP at some engineering firm in Century City.

"I'll tell him you called. Will he need to step in other people's blood or is this just a nice and clean case update?"

"It's . . ." I had been blinded by her voice and could no longer see the YMCA or the school or anything at all. "Just . . . He can call when he has a moment."

"Okay," she chirped.

I disconnected before she could say anything else. I sat there, fighting the cold shakes, trying to breathe but unable to take more than a sip of air.

Alone. I was alone. Again.

So be it.

I busted a U-turn on Marlton, then called Syeeda. "You may see me tonight or not."

"You're exhausted, Lou," she said. "You're always indefinite when you're exhausted."

I laughed. "You may be right. Or not."

"But what can you tell me before you return to the Bat Cave?" Syeeda asked.

I chewed my bottom lip, flipping through my mind's index cards for shareable bits. "Allayna was spotted getting into a dark SUV."

"Really? Did the witness get the plate number?"

"Maybe."

"When will 'maybe' become 'hell yeah'?"

"Soon," I said. "Don't want him ditching the car cuz he read about it in the paper. I'm pleased yet a little amazed that I didn't see Mike at Bonner Park."

"He said you all threatened him."

"Not enough, in my opinion."

"People in the neighborhood are pointing at Raul Moriaga."

"I can neither deny nor confirm that," I said.

"He's a registered sex offender," she pointed out.

"Indeed."

"And?"

"And we're comparing DNA as we speak," I said.

"You'll let me know before you let anyone else know?"

"You're my first love, Scoop."

"Speaking of love," she said. "Sam?"

I loosened my grip around the steering wheel. "I can neither deny nor confirm."

"Ruh roh?"

"No idea. None. Nada." I sighed. "I gotta go."

The Starbucks on Crenshaw Boulevard was packed with beautiful black folks—they lounged at tables and divans while drinking upside-down caramel macchiatos and mocha lattes. Rihanna bleated from the speakers, "umbrella-ella-ella" competing with the hiss of steamers, the roar of grinders, and cell-phone chatter. As I waited for my turkey and sun-dried tomato panini and passion-fruit iced tea, I snagged a small table out on the patio. I tried not to think of anything—Chanita, Allayna, Sam, 2BT . . . Sam.

A hand touched my shoulder.

I jerked and grabbed the hand, preparing to break it.

"*Whoa!*" a man said.

I released his hand, then offered an apologetic smile. "Sorry."

Zach Fletcher grinned down at me and shook his head. "I need that hand." He looked the same as he had at Bonner Park back on Wednesday—soft brown eyes and great teeth set against an olive complexion. He wore those blue scrubs he'd worn in his earlier e-mail to me and clean, black Nikes. The strap of his battered leather messenger bag crisscrossed his broad chest. He held a bicycle helmet beneath his arm. "What are *you* doing here?"

"Taking a break from the madness," I said. "What are *you* doing here?"

"Just finished clinic hours," he explained. "We're a block away, in the complex with the cobbler place out front."

"The cobbler lady knows me by name," I said. "Blackberry. I always—"

My iPhone played the *Star Wars* theme, and Sam's picture lit up the screen.

With a trembling finger, I tapped IGNORE CALL.

Zach pointed at the empty chair across from me. "Is someone sitting . . . ?"

"No," I said. "Please. Sit." The barista waved at me, and I stood.

Zach sat the helmet on the ground next to my bag. "Oh no. You're leaving?"

I pointed at the counter. "Just going to fetch my dinner. I'll be back."

A minute later, Zach eyed my sandwich and tea. "You deserve better than *that*."

I plopped into my chair. "I'll imagine it's a rib eye and a glass of Merlot."

"Last time we saw each other, you were wet and covered in mud." He canted his head and smiled. "Today, all clean and dry, you're even more beautiful. A wonderful trick or do you wake up that way?"

My cheeks warmed, and I gaped at my sandwich as though a centipede wheeled a unicycle across the bread.

Zach threw back his head and laughed. "Sorry. Didn't mean to embarrass you, but I calls it as I sees it."

I cocked an eyebrow. "I know for a fact that I look like the last beat-up, dented can of dog food left on the supermarket shelf. I, too, calls it as I sees it."

My phone vibrated, then vibrated again.

Sam was now texting me.

"I'm on my fifth cup of the day," Zach said, tapping the top of his reusable mug. "Can't wake up. Guess it's the weather."

I picked at my sandwich. "We should be hibernating like the other mammals."

He smiled—he really did have nice eyes. And nice teeth. Nice . . . lots of things.

"You *must* have something better to do on a Saturday night than hanging out with a cop," I said, trying to smile.

"First of all," he said, "just a cop? Whatever. And second, is that your way of asking if I have a girlfriend? I don't have a girlfriend, to answer your inferred question."

"Ah." My phone vibrated again.

Zach was watching me.

"What?" I asked.

"Ignoring someone?"

"Yes." Then I smiled. "You from LA?"

"Changing the subject, then. Okay. Yes, I'm from LA. I grew up all over this beautiful, wretched county. And state. And country." He chuckled to himself, then shrugged. "My dad was in construction, and he dragged us where the work was. We were never there long enough to make good friends. *But!*" He held up a finger. "I can pack a suitcase in under five minutes."

I bit into my sandwich but didn't taste a thing. "You said 'us.'"

"I have an older sister." He sipped from his mug. "*Had* an older sister. She died in high school—we were pretty close. With always having to move, we only had each other as friends most of the time. We did everything together until she . . ." He stared at my sandwich.

I knew that pause, that averted glance. "I'm sorry."

He scratched his jaw. "She got caught up in the wrong crowd. Got in a car with a bunch of guys one night after a kegger. Ended up naked, beaten, and dead on the side of the road, right out of Henderson, Nevada. Payback for her being . . . her."

"They catch the guys who did it?"

"Only one guy. And, no, they did not. Then it was just Dad and me."

"What about your mother?" I asked.

He considered me with dead eyes. "She ditched us long before that. Ran away with some trucker the day after my fifth birthday."

"Damn."

"Yeah."

"We have a lot in common," I said, futzing with the straw in my tea.

He grunted. "Your mom ran away with a trucker, too?"

I said, "Ha," then, "No. My bus-driver dad ran away to

Vegas when I was eight. And my sister was murdered when she was seventeen."

He leaned forward, elbows on the table. "Seems we've both lost a lot."

I slumped in my chair, body tired from losing parts of me and using spit and gumption to keep the rest from falling apart.

He tapped my hand. "Let's not worry about a long time ago. Hell, I'm over my mother, over my sister, over everything. To be honest, I wouldn't be where I am today if I'd had the mom, the dad, a dog named Bingo, and a little red wagon. What's the saying? 'Adversity causes some men to break and others to break records'?" He shrugged and held up his cup. "I'm in a good place. A great place."

I placed my chin in my hand. "And what is that good-great place?"

"I'm a successful physician seated in a coffee shop with a beautiful and intelligent woman who can wrestle a two-hundred-pound man while wearing heels."

I gave him dueling gun fingers. "Two-hundred-*fifty* pound man."

He lifted his cup higher. "Here's to fucked-up long-time-agos and happily-ever-afters."

I hoisted my iced tea.

Here, here.

And Sam's picture lit my screen again.

"Moment of disclosure," he said. "I googled you."

I frowned.

He held up his hands. "Just to make sure you weren't one of those . . . crazy cops."

I grimaced and folded my arms. "Yeah?"

He smiled. "It's a necessity nowadays, running background checks. Dating ain't what it used to be, back when we were kids." He held out his hand. "We good?" That smile again.

My heart pounded as I shook his hand. "Guess I'm not a crazy cop, then?"

"Nope," he said, "but you should probably update your LinkedIn profile."

I laughed.

"So," Zach said, "since you're sitting here, chillaxin' with me, I'm guessing you've caught whoever killed that girl in the park."

"Unfortunately, I haven't. I'm just taking a quick break before diving back in. I haven't eaten since breakfast."

He winced, then waggled his finger and tsked-tsked me.

"I know, I know."

"How's it going, if I may ask?"

I gave him the "approved for public consumption" update on Chanita Lords. I told him about Chanita's funeral and about her being bullied. I complained about inattentive or overloaded parents who force their kids to grow up alone in a world full of monsters.

Zach bit his lip and stared glumly at the street beyond the window.

"Sorry for being such a downer," I said, "but you asked."

"Death doesn't bother me," he said with a shrug. "Hell, I used to be an EMT back in medical school. I saw death in its most naked state, and you wouldn't believe . . ." He cocked his head and chuckled. "You're a homicide detective—I guess you'd believe it."

I said, "Ha, yeah."

"So are there any suspects?"

"Can't say."

He cocked an eyebrow. "Is that a yes?"

"It's a 'can't say.'"

"But from what you said earlier, sounds like the two cases are connected."

"Hunh." I found interest in my now-cold sandwich.

"When my sister Leanne died," he said, "people blamed her for her being killed. They said she was 'too sexy.'" He rolled his eyes. "And I, a young boy, grew up hearing that, and so I also blamed her for dying, even though a little part of me knew . . . All this murder business. Doesn't it scare you?"

"That's why I drink," I said, lifting my cup of iced tea. "Usually something much stronger than this. And, yes, it *is* scary sometimes, but I like the challenge. I like righting wrongs. I like . . . being an avenger. Truth, justice, and the American way."

"We're all put here to do something." He looked pointedly at my iPhone. "What do the men in your life think about your mission?"

"My ex-husband . . . That's not him calling. Anyway, me being an avenger was just one of our problems."

"And the one blowing up your phone? Is he begging you to put down the gun and take up guitar or glassblowing?"

I dabbed at crumbs with my middle finger. "He and I may have been . . . premature. He, too, has a new ex, and he may still . . ." My pulse jumped. Just to admit that Sam could still love . . . My heart rested whenever we were together. And with my job, my heart was always pounding. So it was lovely to feel it beat at a normal pace. Now, though . . .

Zach touched my hand. "You're sad."

"Bad habit of mine."

My iPhone *caw-cawed*—Colin's picture, no smile, all business, filled the screen. "I have to get this."

"Brooks just finished up," my partner announced.

"Let me call you right back," I told him.

"Gotta go?" Zach asked.

"Yep."

He led me through the crowd to reach the exit. Out in the

parking lot, the growl of traffic bounced off concrete and the thick, dark sky. The scent of frying meat wafted from the Wienerschnitzel—a better option than the coffee-shop panini.

"I needed that," I said, leaning against the Crown Vic's door. "Thank you."

"If you ever need to talk and commiserate and just . . . *be*, then . . ." He pointed at his chest. "I'm the guy for you."

I laughed. "I'll keep your application on file. You okay biking in this part of town at this time of night?"

He smiled. "Proud owner of a ghetto pass since 2004. I treat seventy percent of the population here, so I'm good."

"Well, thanks again."

Zach stepped back, then said, "I want to see you again, Elouise. But right now you don't have to figure out if *you* want that."

I said nothing and glanced at the moon, now aglow behind clouds.

"Don't worry. When it's time, we'll see each other again. Maybe we'll *both* be in a good-great place."

I shrugged. "Maybe."

He turned on his heel and strode toward the bike rack outside the coffee shop.

And I stood there, unsure of what had just happened.

A dream. This is all a dream.

And then my phone vibrated.

A text from Colin.

Shit, Lou. The monster used bug poison again.

42

IT WAS PAST TEN O'CLOCK ON A SATURDAY NIGHT, AND I DIDN'T EXPECT TO SEE HIM hunched over my desk. Sam, dressed in a blue warm-up suit, stood as I weaved past the cuffed and the victimized, the badged and the lawbreakers. He stood, hands on his hips, towering over me. "It's not what you're thinking."

As I waved him out of the way, my heart pounded because it always pounded when he was near. "I don't have time, Sam, unless you're here to talk about a case."

"Lou—"

"And how *is* your wife these days?" I dropped my bag near the wastebasket. "She sounds happy. Guess all is well in the House of Seward?"

He held up his hands. "Can we talk without the—?"

"No," I spat. "I've done the 'she was just answering my phone and I don't know why she's here' bullshit or have you forgotten? I did it before and it diminished me and—"

"But it's not what you—" He stopped. "Yes, You've heard *that* before, too. But she's not my wife anymore, all right? We are divorced. We are not together. It was over between us even before the divorce."

I pulled the case file from the bag.

"She dropped Roscoe at the house," he explained. "He's sick and she can't take care of him and . . . Nothing's going on, Lou. I swear that's the truth."

I started toward the conference room.

He grabbed my hand. "Lou, don't—"

I glared at him and then at his hand on mine.

He let go. "Please don't walk away. Tell me what you want."

I squinted at him. "I want someone who doesn't have to ask me that."

He didn't blink. "I can do that, and whatever else you need."

I gaped at him, then said, "I can't. Not now. Girls are literally dying around me."

He dropped back into my chair. "Then I'll wait."

I stared at him a moment more. "Sam. Go. Please. I'll call—"

"No, you won't. You'll find sixty more things to do, and I'll look up and it's Christmas and I'm still waiting to hear from you."

I jammed my lips together—he knew me. "I'll call you. Promise."

Flushed, he paused, then said, "Okay." Because he knew that I'd never break a promise. Not even if keeping that promise destroyed me.

As I finally took my seat at the conference table, Colin glanced at his wristwatch. "I called you at—"

"Shut up, Taggert." I reached for a paper plate, two slices of pizza, and a can of Diet Coke, then sat between Neil and Pepe. I nodded to Gwen, who was shoving ketchup-smothered french fries into her mouth.

"Can we get started now?" Lieutenant Rodriguez asked as he picked cheese from his pizza slice and dropped it on a tired napkin.

I slumped in the chair and stared at walls covered with a

295

giant area map of 90008, at the pictures of the girls' homes, trail 5, the park bench, and boot imprints.

Brooks clicked on the projector, and we were greeted by a picture of Allayna Mitchell on a stainless steel table. "The victim was fourteen. African American, eighty-seven pounds . . ."

After twenty seconds of listening to his update, I wanted Brooks to skip the parts I already knew: Allayna's age, weight, height—all of that. But he didn't skip those parts. "Methodical" was hardwired into his DNA, and he planned to go through every slide.

Colin could barely control his giggling at my irritation as Brooks's monotonous voice droned on and on.

"Did the same guy kill her or not?" I interrupted.

Brooks glared at me.

I glared back. "I know I'm being an asshole, but it's late, and I'm tired, and you're tired, and we've lost time, and I need to know some shit sooner rather than later, all right?"

"No fingerprints left behind," Brooks said with a sigh. "Allayna Mitchell was also holding a tooth in her hand. The second molar, just like Chanita Lords."

"Extracted before she died?" I asked.

He nodded.

"I asked her mother about any recently lost teeth," I shared, "and she told me that Allayna still had her back ones."

Brooks and Zucca scribbled this into their notepads.

"Second molar," Brooks said. "One of the last teeth a child loses . . ."

I tapped my pen on the notepad. "He's making a statement—maybe he's prematurely pushing them from childhood to womanhood. The tooth—and I may be reaching here—may be their fare to the next world. The world of nymphs."

"The coin the dead pay the ferryman to cross the river

296

Styx," Neil said. "A do-good action, picking up the tab, so to speak, but with a tooth instead."

"Was this guy a Greek major in college?" Colin asked. "He's really into this shit."

I nodded, adding that to my profile of the monster.

Brooks continued. "When we found her, she'd only been dead for about twenty-four hours. Her small intestine was empty—she'd eaten her last meal about eight hours before she died." He clicked to a slide that showed dark patches of skin all around Allayna's body. "Differing lividity," he explained, using a laser pointer to show us the dark patches on her back and sides. "Again, just like Chanita Lords."

"Where is he killing them?" Pepe asked.

"In or around the same place," Zucca said. "The same kind of leaves and berries. Deadly nightshade."

"And again," Brooks said, "not much bug activity."

"Why does he do that?" Gwen asked. "The insect repellant?"

"Maybe he wants to be seen as doing something good," Lieutenant Rodriguez offered.

Colin nodded. "Girls hate bugs."

"Or," I said, "maybe he just wanted to hide the smell of decomp, which the bug spray would help to do. Which makes it hard to determine time of death. But there wouldn't be extreme decomp since her mother only reported her missing early this morning."

"So how did she die?" Lieutenant Rodriguez asked Brooks.

"High levels of atropine from the plant." Brooks clicked to a picture of Allayna's face. "Sunken eyes and pupils dilated so much her eyes look black." Another picture. "Pale liver with lots of petechiae." Another slide. "Mushy, soft brain, which tore easily. Petechiae in the corpus callosum." Last picture. "Petechiae on the anterior of the heart." He rubbed his eyes. "High amounts of acid and bile in her stomach. She had an ulcer the size of a walnut."

"An ulcer at *fourteen*?" Colin asked.

Brooks nodded. "She was also so thin she had stopped menstruating."

The pictures, and the pizza's greasy cheese and pepperoni, had made me nauseated, and I dabbed at my clammy skin with a napkin.

"Other elements similar to Chanita's case," Brooks said, "are the broken left foot and puncture marks on her thighs. Unlike Chanita, though, Allayna was losing her hair. Throw in the ulcer, and I'm thinking she was under a lot of stress."

"Vaughn insisted that Allayna was healthy," I said. "Nothing to see here folks; move along. Her daughter planning to kill herself certainly wasn't something to freak out about, either."

"She was *suicidal*?" Gwen asked, wide-eyed. "Detective Dean didn't mention that."

I pulled Allayna's note from the file, then read it aloud.

Gwen whispered, "Wow. Poor kid."

"Gomez," Lieutenant Rodriguez said, "any update on the 2BT license plate?"

"DMV computers are back up, so I got this." Luke held up a long printout speckled with yellow ink. "Going through it now and highlighting every plate that starts with 2BT. About seven so far. I'll send out a few radio cars when I get a complete list."

"What about Chanita's phone?" I asked.

Luke shook his head. "The only calls made and received . . ." He scanned a page of the printout. "Are to and from her mother and grandmother. She didn't have a text or data package. No recent e-mails."

"You talk to her friends?" Colin asked.

"Yep," Pepe said. "Nothing there—she took pictures, she was on the newspaper, she talked about Ontrel. That's it." He slid over a thin manila folder. "The friends' witness statements."

"This deadly nightshade," I said, turning to Zucca. "Which parts are poisonous?"

"All parts," he said, "but the roots and berries are the most toxic. And roots, of course, grow year-round."

"Surgeons use atropine," Brooks added, "to regulate the patient's heartbeat. And believe it or not, when mixed with other agents in small amounts, it's pretty useful. It's used to treat Parkinson's, whooping cough, arthritis, hemorrhoids . . ."

"Talk about a pain in the ass," Luke said, then laughed at his own joke.

"Any mythology attached to deadly nightshade?" Lieutenant Rodriguez asked.

Brooks nodded. "Atropine is derived from the genus *atropos,* which is the name of one of the three Fates."

"Let me guess," I said. "The one who chooses how you die and then whips out her scissors and cuts your string?"

Brooks pointed at me. "You win a brand-new Chrysler LeBaron."

I smiled. "And I'd like to thank World Book Encyclopedia for keeping me company throughout my youth." I tore away a piece of pizza crust, but the alley-ooping in my stomach kept me from eating it. "But you don't have to buy chemical-grade if you're growing the plant in your backyard, right? Or it can be a potted plant. Kept inside."

"Possibly," Zucca said. "It doesn't get taller than four feet."

"We can go back to that neighborhood near the park again," Colin suggested, "and do a thorough door-to-door. Checking backyards . . ."

"But we don't know if he's there or somewhere in Topanga, twenty miles away," Pepe pointed out.

"*Ese,* it's just an idea," Luke said.

Spots of red colored Pepe's cheeks. "*Ese,* it's just reality. And say we go into people's yards, but he actually has it in his basement?"

Luke sucked his teeth. "You scared of—?"

"Hey," Lieutenant Rodriguez said. "Knock it off."

"The music box," I said.

"No prints except for hers," Zucca said. "And there's nothing remarkable about that box. One of my techs found them on every major retail Web site."

"What about . . . ?" I pointed to the tacked pictures of the shoe bottoms. "Any matches?"

"Nope," Zucca said, flipping through reports. "But it comes from a man's right Timberland boot, size twelve. And before you ask, yes, Jimmy Boulard is a size twelve."

"So it's possible that he made the print?" Lieutenant Rodriguez asked.

"Yes," Zucca said.

"Anything special about the canvas bag he put them in?" Gwen asked.

Zucca shook his head. "Any army-surplus store has them."

I turned to Neil. "Bang-Bang, let's go back to the phones."

He shook his head. "The last messages from Olympus used the tower right in the park, which isn't surprising since he left her there. Other than that, no calls. No pings. Nothing. I'm guessing he took the batteries out of the phones."

"DNA back yet from Ontrel Shaw, Jimmy Boulard, or Raul Moriaga?" I asked, going through my list.

"Still waiting," Zucca said. "But I can say this with certainty: the guy's a nonsecretor."

Colin screwed up his face. "Umm . . ."

"A . . . what?" Gwen asked.

With a small smile, Zucca said, "I'm guessing that only Doc

300

Brooks knows what that means. Okay. So. In every person's—"

"Twitter version, please," I said, rubbing my temples.

"Olympus's spit doesn't have a certain protein in it that lets us determine if it matches the bodily fluids we found on Chanita. He doesn't *secrete* that telltale molecule." Zucca looked at me. "How's that?"

I gave him the A-OK sign.

"Is that a rare thing?" Lieutenant Rodriguez asked.

"Yep," Zucca said. "Which, again, makes it a good thing."

I tapped my pen against the pad. "So we'll know Ontrel, Jimmy, or Raul *didn't* do it if their DNA samples show that they *are* secretors."

"Correct," Zucca said.

"And Payton Bishop still hasn't come in yet to give DNA?" I asked.

Pepe said, "Nope."

"What about the kid?" Colin asked.

"Justin Abraham?" I said. "His momma wants a court order first. So could you . . . ?"

Colin said, "Yep," then jotted in his notepad.

"Luke," I said, "you talk to anybody from Eighteenth Street?"

He nodded. "One of my cousin's girlfriend's cousin's uncle is a shot caller, and *he* said it ain't none of them, especially when I told him about the bug-repellent injection. He said they don't fuck wit' no dead bodies. A few knew *of* Chanita cuz of who her people are and the boy she was hanging with, but as far as Jaime know, ain't no order been given to kidnap and kill certain types of girls from the Jungle."

"How does Allayna's suicide note affect the case?" Lieutenant Rodriguez asked.

"Don't know if it does," I said. "But it could add to our profile—a girl needing to be rescued. A monster offering her what her family couldn't."

301

"Protection," Colin said.

"The two postcards he left," I said, back to my list.

"Written by the same right-handed person," Zucca said, "with the same green marker."

"Jimmy Boulard is left-handed," I said. "And his writing sample is wildly different than the postcards."

"The park ranger's not looking like Olympus," Pepe said.

"And no prints on the card except yours, Lou," Zucca said, "and on one of them, from someone here named Ruthie Lerner."

"Luke's girlfriend," Colin said with a smirk. "She's the secretary in charge of the mail."

"L.T.," I said, "can we pull video from the day that first postcard was dropped off?"

My boss nodded. "I'll get on it after this."

"How do you know he dropped it off?" Gwen asked me.

"No stamp," I said, shrugging. "Anything else, folks?"

"This fucker likes puzzles," Luke said.

"Boulard is a navy man," Pepe said. "He could've written it. He could be ambidextrous."

"Don't have to be trained anymore," Neil said. "There are computer scripts online that will write a cipher for you." He tapped on his tablet. "Read me a few lines from one of those messages he sent."

I recited parts from the "six minutes in heaven" e-mail as Neil typed.

"Look." He turned the tablet around—the easy-to-understand words had become a substitution cipher, *E* for *M* and on and on.

"He gets off on confusing people who he thinks are smart," Colin said, pointing at me.

"He wants control," I said, "and he's forcing me to play on his field. Forcing us to investigate these murders the way

302

he wants them to be investigated."

"He wrote the 'ha ha ha' message in enough time to leave it at the park before you all arrived," Zucca said.

Brooks nodded. "A do-gooder. If you aren't already, you may want to check out suspects in those professions: other police officers, teachers, firemen, ministers, doctors . . ."

"Seriously?" Luke said. "A cop?"

"Harold Shipman was a doctor," I pointed out. "Kenneth Bianchi, one of the Hillside Stranglers, was a security guard. Michael Swango, another doctor."

"What about the obsession with nymphs?" Pepe said.

I flipped through my notes. "I did some looking and learned that a subset of nymphs are classified as Muses. Arts."

"And both girls were in the arts," Colin said. "Ballet and photography—"

"And Trina wrote poems," Gwen added.

Neil tapped on his tablet, then read from it. "Poetry, history, song, tragedy, hymns, dance, comedy, and . . . astronomy?"

"The e-mails he sent were . . ." I paused. "Sent from Olympus. A place. Not a person. The figurines he left— Muses. He saves these girls, changes them."

Colin snorted. "Let's back up. Goddesses don't *die*. That's the point of being goddesses."

"Nymphs are not immortal," I pointed out. "They don't die of old age or disease like us, but they *can* die."

"And according to this, human females can be turned *into* nymphs," Neil added.

I turned back to older notes. "There are nine Muses."

"So is he planning to kill nine girls?" Colin asked.

"Who says he hasn't already?" Lieutenant Rodriguez said.

"Because I'm still here," I said.

"He threatened her, remember?" Colin said. "And Lou is the ultra-Muse. The one who got herself out."

I turned to Neil. "Who's one of the bigger gods? A do-gooder, like Brooks said."

Neil tapped his tablet. "Pan is both good and bad . . . Apollo, god of light and sun, truth and prophecy, brother of the . . . Muses."

"Bishop mentioned that he was a truth teller," Colin said. "That's why he was transferred to Madison from his old place."

"So what?" Pepe asked. "We monitor every girl in every arts program at Madison?"

I sat still, eyes on the center of the table and the gnat buzzing over the open pizza box.

No one spoke. All puffy, bloodshot eyes landed on me.

"Lou?" Lieutenant Rodriguez's voice cut through the quiet like a cement truck.

I tugged my earlobe, then said, "If that's what we need to do, then that's what we'll do."

SUNDAY, MARCH 23

43

AT ALMOST ONE IN THE MORNING, IN MOIST AIR THAT SMELLED OF WOOD SHAVINGS and rosemary, I turtled up the flagstone walkway to Syeeda's front door. Every muscle ached, and my mind . . . I had too many Internet browsing tabs open, and all of them had timed out. I had wanted to drive to Sam's, but I was in no condition to discuss bullshit and suss lies. I'd keep my promise to him on another day—a day that included sleep and a proper meal.

Syeeda sat on the living room couch, laptop bright, a late-night rerun of *Twilight Zone* muted. "I didn't think I'd see you." An open bottle of Cab and a near-empty wineglass sat on the coffee table next to a big bag of Doritos.

"Why are you still up?" I asked, dropping my bag to the foyer floor. "Writing?"

"Something like that, yeah." She poured wine into the glass and slid it toward the armchair. "Working on something Mike turned in."

"The article about Chanita Lords?" I reached for the tortilla chips.

"Uh huh." She closed the laptop and forced herself to smile.

I cocked an eyebrow. "You know Mike Summit writes like a lobotomized helper monkey with one eye and no thumbs." I shoved three chips into my mouth and crunched.

Syeeda rubbed her face. "It'll be fine."

"Sure it will. It better be, or I'm gonna find a new paper to not leak to."

"Promises, promises." She brightened some. "Hey, if I need to get more info—"

"Nope."

"Or to confirm—"

"Nuh uh."

"But—"

"Good night, Sy." I picked up the glass and guzzled the wine. Shoved three more Doritos into my mouth, then left the writer to her work.

In my temporary bedroom, I placed my Glock on the nightstand, stripped out of my clothes, then took a long, hot bath. I fell asleep as the foam and bubbles broke apart. Somehow I dried off, slipped into a T-shirt, climbed into bed, and fell asleep.

But a flock of screeching wild parrots made me open my eyes.

I glanced at the digital clock beside the Glock.

5:48 A.M.

I burrowed deeper into the pillows, then pulled the comforter up to my neck.

How long could I keep doing this job—finding dead girls in parks, finding dead cheerleaders in condos, finding dead wives in their own bedrooms—until I finally burned out?

How did Lieutenant Rodriguez and other longtime murder police do it? If I'd had the time, I'd guzzle a box of wine a day; but there was never enough time and never enough boxes of wine to completely numb myself anyway.

Why wasn't I one of those psychotic cops always looking for a fight, always at the corner bar at end of watch, always marrying, then divorcing some floozy, broad, or stripper?

Rumor had it that looking at the world through whiskey glasses lessened the evils of this world. With a gut full of single-malt Scotch, boogeyman transformed into babies wearing bad hats, and the mighty devil shrank into a harmless fly buzzing in your ear.

Why the *hell* was I still sober?

I pulled my knees to my chest.

The heater clicked on, and a draft of warm air drifted to the bed. The light in the room changed from copper to gold as I lay there. Sober.

I sat up and stretched, and my bones creaked and clicked as I climbed out of bed and stepped over to the window. I stared out at the dewy backyard still draped in shadows beneath the clear sky.

No rain.

I grabbed my phone and gun from the nightstand and found a one-sided text-message string from Victor Starr. I didn't read any of it but held my breath as I tapped out one sentence.

If you want to know what I think, meet later today. Your hotel.

Seconds later, he replied. *Yes. Thank you. Airport Radisson.*

I shuffled to the foyer and to my bag. The aroma of fresh-brewed coffee greeted me. I plopped right there on the tile floor and reviewed notes and sketches from both girls' cases.

Trail 5 . . . Canvas bag . . . leaves and berries . . . View-Master . . . 13 y.o. . . . music box . . .

Nothing new stood out.

I pulled from Chanita's file that photograph of the deadly plant and used my phone's magnifying app to peer at it enlarged. Inch by inch, I looked . . . searched . . . "What's . . . ?" In the far left side of the picture was a thin slice of . . . a tiny, tiny . . . a vertical . . . rope and a connected black . . . My eyes jumped from the flower to the rope and black thing, flowers . . . rope . . . black thing . . .

Some of those tabs in my brain closed and the circles stopped circling and I *saw*.

A moment later, now dressed in jeans and a black sweater, I poured myself a travel mug of coffee and left a note for Syeeda on the coffeepot.

Thanks for letting me stay here. It means so much to me.
Love you,
L.

44

THE FRONDS OF PALM TREES LINING KING BOULEVARD RUSTLED AS HEAVY CLOUDS the color of battleships gathered over the ghettoes of Southern California. It had been so wonderful to see the sun, if only for an hour. Seagulls gathered at every other intersection over bags of leftover fast food, their gold beaks scattering hamburger buns and shredded lettuce across the asphalt. Despite the approaching storm, despite my line of work, my breath came easy—like I'd just returned from Cabo after a long week of rum-filled, sexy nights.

I called Colin. "Anything happen while I slept for five hours?"

"Five hours?" he said. "Who you think you are? The queen? And, yes, two things came in. Number one: Ontrel Shaw's DNA doesn't match."

"I kinda expected you to say that. Number two?"

"Neither does Jimmy Boulard's."

That easy breathing hitched in my chest. "I kinda *didn't* expect you to say that."

He chuckled. "So that leaves . . . ?"

I squeezed my eyes shut. "Payton Bishop, who needs to give DNA, and Justin Abraham, Allayna's ex, who didn't do it, and I know that like I know that you're picking Tic Tacs and bacon from your back teeth at this very moment."

He paused, then said, "How did you . . . ?"

"And Raul Moriaga is still on the list," I continued.

"He's in the system," Colin said. "Why aren't his results back yet?"

"I'm almost there," I said, pulling into the station parking lot.

The detective's bull pen was strangely quiet. None of my team sat at their desks or wandered the corridors. Sounds of cheering came from the break room.

"Oh hell no!" Pepe shouted.

"He shoots like a girl," Gwen added.

Fifteen pairs of eyes were watching the Stanford versus Kansas game.

Colin slumped on the raggedy futon near the watercooler. He saw me standing in the doorway and waved. "What's up, Lou?"

Shoulders tense, I strode back to the bull pen with Luke, Pepe, and Colin following me.

"You bring breakfast?" Colin asked.

"Not my turn." I grabbed Chanita Lords's growing case file from my desk and plodded to Lieutenant Rodriguez's office with the trio still behind me. Soon, we all crowded around the big man's desk.

I pulled our Chanita Lords's photograph of deadly nightshade. "Chanita took a picture of what killed her."

Lieutenant Rodriguez shrugged. "And?"

"What is *this*?" I pointed to the rope segment at the edge of the picture.

Each man squinted at the rope.

Colin smiled and nodded. "That's a swing."

Everyone else said, "Huh?"

"A rope swing," Colin said. "You guys never had one in your backyard?"

"You know where I lived," I said, eyebrow cocked.

"I lived in apartments," Pepe said. "No backyard."

Both Luke and Lieutenant Rodriguez nodded.

Colin blushed, then grinned. "Didn't any of you go to summer camp in the woods?"

We blinked at him. Summer . . . *camp*?

Colin gaped at us. "You tie rope around the limb of a big, strong tree, like an oak. Get a plank of wood, bore a hole at each end, pull the rope through, knot it, and you have a swing. Some folks use a tire—that's what this looks like."

"I've seen swings like that on TV," Luke said, nodding.

I pointed at Lieutenant Rodriguez. "See? That's why diversity in the workplace is so important." I considered that rope and section of tire. "So we're looking at a backyard again. A backyard with a strong tree and a tire swing."

"Like I said yesterday," Colin said.

"And *where* is this backyard?" Pepe asked.

Lieutenant Rodriguez shrugged. "Can't tell from the picture."

"Like *I* said yesterday," Pepe pointed out.

"And who's certain it's a yard?" I asked. "Taggert just said he played on them at camp."

The room dropped into silence.

Lieutenant Rodriguez sat back in his chair and folded his hands across his belly. "Anything else?"

"Can you find out what's the holdup on Raul Moriaga's DNA?" I asked.

"So he's still a possible suspect?" Lieutenant Rodriguez asked.

"*Possible* but not *definite*," I said. "We haven't been able to eliminate him, nor have we been able to confirm his alibi. He could be telling the truth or . . . not. We just don't—"

"That's *Lou's* opinion, sir," Colin interrupted. "*I* think we have enough for an arrest warrant. If he's registered, then I'm guessing that he's probably on probation. Let's grab him before he flees the state. Disappears into Mexico."

"Grab him for what?" I snapped.

Colin shrugged. "Littering. Loitering. Some other bullshit misdemeanor."

I shook my head. "We need to be careful."

"Evading arrest," Colin said. "He's done it before—twice, right? He gave us a bogus number for the friend in San Diego he claims he was with the day Chanita went missing, or is lying to police officers something we should say 'fuck it' to? The mud on his shoes looks just like the mud in the park, and dumb-ass even admits that he talked to Chanita." Colin rolled his eyes. "L.T., are we supposed to sit and wait because Lou's scared of startin' a race war?"

"First of all, I'm not scared of *shit*," I said, anger starting its familiar dirt-devil swirl in the center of my gut. "Second of all: *starting* a race war? One's already under way, Colorado. You just don't know what the hell you're looking at. And, lastly, I don't want to collar Moriaga yet cuz we haven't even connected him to Allayna Mitchell's murder."

"*Yet*," Luke added.

I squinted at him. "Don't make me knock that cup of Kool-Aid from your hand."

"You know what an arrest like this could do for us?" Luke asked, peering at each of us with a gleam in his eye.

"The black community would *love* us for getting this guy off the street." Colin pointed to Lieutenant Rodriguez. "The mayor, your *boss*, would love us for closing this case."

"And if Raul Moriaga is innocent?" I asked, bristling.

"I would never-ever use the word 'innocent' when we're talking about some *gonorrhea* who's raped a hundred girls," Luke said.

"Is Lou showing sympathy to a child molester?" Colin asked, his eyebrows high. "A pedarast? A *rapist*?"

My cheeks burned. "No. Hell no. It's just . . . I want us to be careful."

Colin clucked his tongue, then cocked his chin. "John Wayne said, 'Courage is being scared to death but saddling up anyway.'"

"And John Wayne Gacy said, 'You can kiss my ass.'"

"Lou." Lieutenant Rodriguez gave a curt shake of his head.

"Do any of you think for one minute that Raul Moriaga sent those ciphers?" I asked. "That he's into mythology and nymphs and shit?"

"You sayin' Mexicans can't be that smart?" Luke asked, squinting at me.

"That's what it sounds like to me," Colin said, shaking his head.

I gaped at them. "Seriously? You're calling *me* racist?"

"If the white sheet fits," Luke said, then smiled.

"Shut up, Gomez," Lieutenant Rodriguez snapped.

"Okay," I said to our boss. "You tell me what to do then. Wait and be close to certain about Moriaga? Or arrest him and fuck up my case just so everybody can go back to see if Stanford will beat Kansas?"

Colin groaned. "You're being a—"

"Say the word," I growled. "I dare you."

"Lou," Lieutenant Rodriguez said, "maybe Taggert is right."

That dirt devil became an F1 tornado: still dangerous, but no one would die. Yet. "Taggert right about investigating a crime like this? In a *city* like this? With color at play? *Really*, L.T.?"

Lieutenant Rodriguez rubbed his jaw. "One more day, all right?" He grabbed the handset from his phone. "Lemme see what's the holdup on the DNA."

I shot Colin a glare and stomped out of the office.

"I'm just doin' my job," Colin shouted after me.

Before he'd come to Los Angeles, Colin Taggert would have never traipsed into Raul Moriaga's apartment, would have never visited with Chanita's family, would have sped past Ontrel Shaw and those Mean Bitches in the Jungle. He had dodged doing shit like this—finding out what people were hiding, being suspicious of everything and everyone, and having the courage to deal with threats and conflict . . .

Still.

Why *did* Moriaga give us a bad number?

Where *did* that mud come from?

That aquarium. All those girls.

Maybe . . .

45

AN HOUR LATER, I ENDED MY CALL WITH THE OFFICER MANNING THE FRONT DESK
and tossed a ball of crumpled paper at Colin's bent head. "We
have a visitor downstairs. Could you be a dear and get her?"

"Sure, but . . ." He paused, then swallowed. "Just wanna
say, you know, about all that in L.T.'s office . . . Didn't mean
to, you know . . ." He cleared his throat, then blushed.

I blinked at him, feeling my cheeks warm. "I . . . know
you . . . work hard and . . . I . . ."

He squinted at me. "You're apologizing . . . to *me*?"

"Umm . . . Just . . ." I cocked an eyebrow. "Attaboy. Now
please retrieve our guests."

He hesitated, then pushed the triggers of Allayna Mitchell's
murder book and the three rings *tcheted*. "Who is it?"

I rubbed the bridge of my nose. "I think it's one of the sexy
cheerleaders we met in Payton Bishop's office. And forgive me
for saying 'sexy,' but that's who she'd be in the movie version
of this twisted case."

He shrugged into his brown corduroy blazer. "Why is she
here?"

"Maybe she knows the owner of that dark SUV."

That's what I hoped as Colin and I sat in interview room 1
across from hazel-eyed Nicole Brewer, one of the flirty
Madison Middle School cheerleaders that had been draped

over Payton Bishop's desk on the day we visited. No tiny cheer uniform today. Instead, she wore a gold sweater dress still a little too snug for a middle-school-aged girl. Her mother, Brandi Washington, sat beside her with a purse-sized Bible on her lap. Brandi was also hazel-eyed and Sexy-Saved in her leopard print wrap dress. The mother and daughter held hands, four knees bouncing, matching eyes darting from the wall to the cans of Sprite on the table.

"Miss Alice said we could trust you," Brandi said.

Colin squinted. "Who?"

"She works in the office at school," Brandi explained. "She wear them blue contact lenses. Anyway, we been tryin' to figure this thing out on our own, but . . ."

Nicole cleared her throat, then flapped her hand at her face. "I can't even sleep no more."

"Nikki been in therapy," Brandi explained, "and she takin' Paxil now."

The girl clutched her hands to her chest. "I could get in a lot of trouble and . . ."

Brandi patted her daughter's shoulders. "Nikki, now what I tell you about that?" She smiled. "Nikki was baptized at service this morning. That's one reason we here talkin' to y'all."

I smiled. "Congratulations. That's a very important step in life. Very meaningful. And sometimes it requires us to do the right thing, even when it's . . . scary."

Nicole blinked. "Can I be synonymous?"

I cocked my head. "So that no one knows who you are?"

"Uh huh."

"You're a minor," I said. "So your identity will be protected for the moment."

"*For the moment?*" Brandi sniped. "So he'll know?"

"I really can't say right now, Ms. Washington. That's up to

the lawyers who will prosecute the case." *If there is a case.* "And who is 'he'?"

"You gotta protect me," Nicole shouted, "cuz I already stole something and . . . and . . . I can't take it back." She erupted into a sob and wept into her hands.

"And I don't want him coming after her," Brandi said, "cuz then *I'm* gonna have to take care of it, you feel me?"

Who is "him," I wanted to shout. I wanted to shake Brandi Washington hard so that every information-stuffed flea and tick dropped off of her and onto my notepad.

Colin scooted closer to Nicole and touched her shoulder. "We'll do our best to keep you anonymous. I'll see to it personally." He avoided my pointed look cuz what the *hell,* we couldn't guarantee *shit.*

The cheerleader reached into her Michael Kors purse and pulled out a black hardbound journal with gold-edged pages. "It's Mr. Bishop's. I took it from his car on Friday, when he drove me home after the game."

"He was actin' *inappropriate,*" Brandi said. "They was sitting in the car—"

"But his woman called," Nicole explained, "so he wasn't payin' me no attention. The journal was sitting there in the backseat next to my book bag. So when he parked and started talkin' to her, I got out, opened the back door, and took it cuz I knew what was in it."

My stomach burned, and that fire spread up toward my chest and neck. "What did he do to you in the car, Nicole?"

She closed her eyes. "He kissed me good-bye, but not like . . . not innocent-like, where you kiss the other person's cheek. He used his . . . his . . ." She bit her quivering lip.

Colin's face had reddened until it had reached the end of the spectrum at purple.

"Did you know Allayna or Chanita?" I asked.

319

Nicole took a deep breath, then nodded. "He'd kick me or my girls out his office if one of them showed up." She picked at her gold nail polish. "I didn't like them too much. Guess I was jealous or something."

"He ever tell you to keep your . . ." Colin cleared his throat. "Special friendship secret?"

Nicole nodded again.

"And what if you decided *not* to keep it secret?" I asked.

Nicole met my eyes with her tear-filled ones. "He said . . . that everybody would know I'm a whore and that I'd go to jail—just like he would. That no one would want to be around me cuz no one likes girls who been to prison. And that the older girls in jail rape the younger ones and that I'd never get another boyfriend cuz he'd know."

I glanced at my partner.

The vein in the middle of Colin's forehead was now banging against his golden skin. Jaw clenched, he took deep breaths to control his anger.

Brandi pulled her daughter into her arms but kept hard eyes on us. "I always thought he was too involved with my daughter. And I *really* got suspicious, cuz she was startin' to change. Acting all weird."

"Weird, like . . . ?" Colin asked.

"Whenever we went out," Brandi said, "she'd wanna eat sushi, and I'm like, 'We don't eat no damn sushi. Who gave you sushi?'"

"Mr. Bishop took me and some other girls to sushi after school," Nicole explained. "Or he'd bring some and we'd eat it in his office at lunchtime."

"This journal." I pointed at the book but did not touch it.

"I stole it cuz . . ." Nicole caught her breath. "He ain't right. This book ain't . . ." She shivered with the heebie-jeebies. "I don't wanna go to jail."

"She ain't done nothing to go to jail for," Brandi said. "*He* the adult. *He* know better."

"Your mom's right, Nicole," I said. "You don't have to worry, all right?" Then, I asked Colin to take Brandi's and Nicole's fingerprints.

Both mom and daughter shouted, "Why?"

Colin held up his hands. "Just as comparison—both of you touched the journal, right?"

The duo nodded.

"We need to compare your prints against his."

A small part of me was buying champagne and confetti. Was I now holding evidence that proved Payton Bishop killed Chanita Lords, Allayna Mitchell, and possibly Trina Porter?

Don't get excited. Keep calm.

I used a paper towel to pick up the journal, then hustled back to my desk with the book. I snapped on latex gloves, then held my breath as I flipped to the small, neat print on the first page.

Those notepads. Whiteboard markers, blank CDs

"Just a list." I turned the page.

Lesson Plan for 9/21–9/26. Schedule Career Day
Individual sessions, last name c

I flipped forward and stopped at an inserted school picture of a teen girl with long, flat-ironed hair and a bright smile. She was cute, a little wonky-eyed, curvy, skin the color of peanut butter. I plucked the picture from the crease and read the writing on the back.

To my favarite conciler. Love, Peaches.

"Just a student," I whispered. And with that spelling, a non-GAT student.

Onward.

Another picture, this one double-exposure. The girl wasn't as cute as Peaches—she wore heavy makeup to hide pimples, which only made the pimples look worse. Her fuchsia lips were lined black.

You are the finest man HERE. XOXX, Chrishonda.

"Just a student with a crush," I whispered.

Seven more pictures, all girls, each addressed to Payton Bishop. *Did boys give school pictures to their male teachers?*

Onward.

More lesson plans . . . More lists of school supplies . . . A five-by-seven snapshot on photo paper.

Oof! The air left me as though I'd been sucker punched in the gut.

Peaches, the girl with the long hair and bright smile, lay naked on a pink comforter in a pink bedroom. Hearts, stars, and pink-inked words had been written on the back of the photograph along with, *"U know U want this."*

Maybe she . . . Maybe he . . .

My mind worked to explain away the snapshot, but my thoughts sputtered and stopped, a lawnmower out of gas. Was there an *innocent* reason for an adult to possess a picture like this?

Maybe she . . . Maybe he . . .

I wanted to tear up this picture and flush it down the toilet. Then buy a new toilet.

My hands shook as I slipped the picture back into its place. Didn't want to, but I had to turn the page and see how this ended.

JOY)AIRS.
OD=psamm
Bl'cicfo
MA[glove
Dh=kovyl

"Passwords?"

In the last pages, a slip of paper had been folded into a tiny square, then tucked into the journal's crease.

I unfolded it: www.littlelola.com.

I closed the journal with a *pop*. Enough. No pictures or mentions of Allayna Mitchell or Chanita Lords. *Hell, that could be in another journal.* I stared at my desk, at Sam's dying roses, at the picture of Syeeda, Lena, and I posing with a sombreroed donkey in Tijuana fifteen summers ago. A stone the size of Orlando sat in my gut.

Payton Bishop would be looking for this book.

He'd kill to have it back.

Back in interview room 1, every pair of eyes turned to me, hopeful and bright.

"Okay," I said. "So this journal is not . . . good."

Brandi whispered, "Thank you, Jesus."

Colin's eyebrow cocked. *That bad?*

I nodded. *Worse.*

"When was the last time you saw your friend Chrishonda?" I asked Nicole.

"This morning, at service."

"And Peaches?"

"She's my niece," Brandi said. "I talked to her momma, my sister, last night."

"Does your sister know about . . . ?"

"Nuh uh," Brandi said. "I'm not sayin' nothing to *nobody* until you say it's okay. Alice only know cuz Nikki on them

323

pills and gotta go to the office to take 'em."

"Miss Alice asked me what was makin' me so anxious," Nicole explained, her knees jiggling. "And it just . . . poured out of me."

I smiled at the girl. "So Nicole. When is the next big school event?"

"Tonight," she said. "We play Orville Wright."

I squinted as the idea gelled in my mind. "What if—?"

"I'll do it," the girl blurted.

I chuckled. "I haven't even—"

"But you *will* ask me to do something," Nicole said, nodding, "and I'll do it."

46

COLIN DIDN'T WANT TO HOLD PAYTON BISHOP'S JOURNAL EVEN THOUGH IT HAD been stuffed into a plastic bag. It now sat on his lap like a soiled adult diaper.

Drizzle from the platinum-colored clouds above spotted the windshield, and pedestrians already hoisted a rainbow of open umbrellas. Heart in my throat, I raced east on King Boulevard, shoving the Crown Vic between buses and cars, all Sunday drivers at twenty-five miles per hour.

"Put on some gloves," I told my partner, "open the bag, and look for yourself. You shouldn't take my word for it."

Sam texted me back. *Yes I'm here. Can we talk about last night now?*

Colin glared at the journal. "I'm homicide, not . . . *this* shit."

"You're a cop," I snapped. "Don't know about training in the *Springs,* Detective Delicate Orchid, but I had to look at child porn, taste cocaine, and get blasted in the face with pepper spray, among other fucked-up things. Geez, Colin, make life nice and easy for once. Please?"

Colin opened the journal, still in the bag, to the picture of Peaches. "Aw, hell, Lou." He closed the book. "So are we gonna arrest this Chester?"

At the sports arena, I made a left onto Figueroa. Five miles ahead, the city's skyscrapers peeked from behind the veils of marine layer and rain clouds. "I'd like to make an informed decision first."

The tall white building of the district attorney's office looked dingy and lopsided beneath those stark gray clouds. Sam's office was located on the fourth floor, and the only light came from the open window looking out to Temple Avenue. He sat at his desk in jeans and a gray T-shirt, and my breath caught seeing him there. He smiled when he saw me, but that smile strained as he saw Colin trundling behind me.

"So this visit is business," he said as he moved manila folders from the chairs to the credenza. "Your text didn't say."

"Cuz I wanted to make sure you'd stay here," I said.

He grunted, then moved back behind his desk. "So what's up?"

"This." I placed the bag with Payton Bishop's journal in it on Sam's desk. Then, Colin and I plopped into the guest chairs.

Framed pictures sat on Sam's desk: his parents, his sister Phoebe, President Obama, his Jack Russell terrier, Roscoe. The note card I sent along with those sea-salt-caramel cupcakes now lived on the edge of his computer monitor.

"Remember when you told me to focus . . . somewhere?" I said.

Sam hesitated before saying, "Umhmm."

I bit my lip, then stared at the journal.

Colin, eyes also on the journal, tossed a pair of latex gloves onto the desk.

Sam squinted at us, then picked up his coffee mug. He sipped slowly, then tugged on the gloves, pulled the book out of the bag, and flipped through the first pages. "Lesson plans, lists. And you got this *where*?"

"A student kinda stole it and gave it to us this morning," Colin said.

Sam placed the book back on the desk. "Ah." He clicked his nails against the coffee mug.

"Is it admissible in court?" I asked.

"Did you ask her to kinda steal it?" Sam asked, eyebrow cocked.

Both Colin and I shook our heads.

"Then, it *may* be admissible. No guarantee, though."

"You should keep browsing, then," I said.

Sam scratched his jaw. Then, he did as I asked, pausing at every school portrait he found, reading the salutation, freezing once he reached that five-by-seven bedroom shot. His jaw clenched, and his lips thinned into a grim line. "Does he know that you have this?"

I whispered, "No."

He reached the page with the crossed-out words and the questionable URL. His eyebrows lifted and he grunted.

"So?" I held myself rigid, threatening to break in half if he said something I didn't want to hear.

"Are you now one hundred percent he's the one?" Sam asked. "Or even eighty percent?"

I shook my head. "Although this helps." And then I told him about the postcards and figurines, and Bishop's self-regard as an enlightened truth teller inspiring gifted girls.

"He's supposed to come in and give DNA," Colin added, "but he hasn't yet."

Sam rubbed his mouth, then turned to type into his computer.

Colin and I glanced at each other and shrugged.

Sam kept typing, stopping to read every now and then before typing again. Finally, he pushed away from the computer. "Three years ago, Payton Bishop was dismissed from his prior position as vice principal at a middle school over in Mount Washington. Improper conduct with one of the students."

"*What?*" I yelped.

Sam held up a hand. "In some ways, the charge was hard to prove. He pled to a misdemeanor—soliciting a minor for lewd conduct. He got a demotion and a transfer."

"A *demotion?*" Colin screeched.

"With the understanding that if another student came forward, we'd go nuclear on him."

Awed, I shook my head. "What the *hell,* Sam? Did you all need to catch him in the *act?*"

"A lot was unclear," he said. "And in a case like this, the plea made sense. It was his first offense, combined with murky details and an unreliable witness."

I sighed. "Unreliable because . . . ?"

"Because he married her as soon as she turned eighteen, which means she'd never testify against him. So we had nothing."

"Okay," I said. "You all slapped his hand, which meant . . ."

"He wasn't required to submit DNA," Sam said.

Colin scowled at him. "Are you *kidding* me?"

Sam shrugged. "You don't like it, but it's the law."

"And the fox," Colin said, "gets to stay in the henhouse."

"So what do you want to do?" Sam asked.

I told him my plan and watched his face for any tells.

But there was no flushing. No twitching nerves. No clenched jaw. Sam was a poker-faced pro. Except for his eyes, which were now the color of stormy seas.

"Well?" I asked.

He sat back in his seat. "Defense could argue entrapment. Or his wife could back out of it after having second thoughts."

"She's young enough to be pissed off, though," I said. "She thought *she* was the only one, and now she finds out that he's messing around with other girls and possibly killed two?"

Sam squinted at me. "And if he catches on that she's working with us?"

"Then . . ." I shrugged.

Sam sighed, then clicked his teeth together. "If you wanna grab him for *this*"—he pointed to the journal—"you can. But then hold your breath and hope that his attorney loses the motion to have his client's little book of sick tossed out because of how it came into your possession. And unless you get hard evidence—hell, even circumstantial evidence—of him killing Chanita and Allayna, he's only looking at a year or so for the picture. Your call."

47

COLIN AND I HAD BARELY STEPPED INTO THE SQUAD ROOM WHEN AN ASHEN-FACED Pepe came to stand at my desk. "Lou, L.T. wants to see you."

"Okay." I ignored his stricken look, especially since Pepe and Luke had been fighting all week and since I was finally in a good mood and a great place for solving this case. I sat at my desk, logged onto my e-mail account to search for Hayley Bishop's phone number.

Pepe cleared his throat. "He wants to see you *now*."

My buoyant heart fell to my feet. Mind whirling—*What happened? Who died?*—I hurried to my boss's office.

Even though the air conditioner worked, the air in Lieutenant Rodriguéz's office felt thick and charged. Arms crossed, the big man stood at windows that offered a view of a palm-tree trunk and bricks from the bail-bonds joint across the street. The twenty-six-inch television on the credenza glowed—a news story had been paused, and the red chyron at the bottom of the screen said "BREAKING NEWS." The close-up shot of blond reporter Olivia McAllen kept viewers at home from seeing where she was now reporting.

I cleared my throat. "Pepe said you wanted to—"

"Read that." He pointed to a sheet of paper left on the guest chair.

DNA Analysis . . . Raul Moriaga . . . DNA profile from #R12-3 (Lords) is not consistent with the DNA from #M39-7 (Moriaga) . . .

I dared to smile. "So I was right: Raul Moriaga *didn't* do it."

His glower deepened. "Read the newspaper on my desk."

I only spotted *OurTimes,* which, I guessed, qualified as the newspaper.

"The article beneath the fold," Lieutenant Rodriguez added.

The article had included the glamour shot of Chanita and a recital picture of Allayna.

Potential Suspect Named in Kidnapping-Murders
By Mike Summit

Raul Moriaga has been identified as a potential suspect in the kidnappings and murders of Chanita Lords, 13, and Allayna Mitchell, 14, crimes that have shocked the small suburb of Los Angeles known as Baldwin Village.

Lead Los Angeles Police Department homicide detective Elouise Norton would not offer comments about the two cases, but believes that the two girls' murders are connected. Law officials were recently seen leaving Moriaga's apartment with several bags of evidence. An unnamed source not authorized to speak about the case said that Moriaga's shoes may match the shoe print left at the crime scene, and that he has been spotted multiple times with minor girls in the neighborhood. In a strange coincidence, the suspect lives in the same apartment complex as one of the young victims.

A search through public records shows Moriaga's multiple arrests and convictions for child-related sex crimes including rape and oral copulation. Moriaga, a native of Chihuahua, Mexico, has legally resided in the United States since 1975.

According to the Legislative Analyst's Office, in 2013, Latinos comprised almost 41 percent of California's jail population, a group that makes up more than half of the State. Statistics from the Bureau of Justice report that sex offenders are about four times more likely than non–sex offenders to be arrested for another sex crime after their discharge from prison—5.3 percent of sex offenders versus 1.3 percent of non–sex offenders. Of released sex offenders who allegedly commit another sex crime, 40 percent perpetrated the new offense within a year or less from their prison discharge.

OurTimes writer Syeeda McKay contributed to this report.

"No. No, no, no." My face had numbed, and my heart pounded as though a giant tried to burst through its back door—not only from seeing my name in an article that I had specifically said "no comment" to but also from reading my off-the-record mention to Syeeda about Moriaga living in Chanita's apartment complex and from reading that someone (Mike Summit?) had watched Colin and me leave Moriaga's apartment with bags of his shoes, and *especially* from reading inflammatory remarks and insinuations about Latinos and sex crimes. And who the hell was this unnamed source who'd seen Moriaga with girls?

This has to be a dream. Any minute now, Lena will say to me, "Wake up, Lou. You fell and hit your head. You're okay now."

Lieutenant Rodriguez snatched the newspaper from my hands. "What the *fuck*? Raul Moriaga isn't a *suspect*. Or have you already forgotten that you stood right where you're standing now and busted Taggert's ass about it? You all but cleared Moriaga an hour ago!"

"No, sir. I haven't forgotten. But I didn't—" I swallowed my excuse. The article had my name right there at the beginning of the second paragraph. "I was asked a question and—"

"You shoulda said, 'No fucking comment, motherfucker, now fuck off,'" he yelled. "Are you that desperate to be a Hollywood Cop? To see your name in lights?"

"No, sir." Tears burned the back of my throat.

"Your *friend*," he shouted, pointing at me. "*She* did this. She got *you* to say shit off the record, and *you* fell for it. And I know it's her because you don't say *shit* to anybody else *but* her. She's your fuckin' Achilles' heel, Detective."

"Lieutenant Rodriguez—" I blinked and blinked and panic made me cold and sweaty. "I'm sorry—that sounds lame, I know that, but in all honesty: I had *nothing* to do with this story. Anyone with an Internet connection could find out Moriaga—"

"Bullshit."

Then, anger burst in my belly. "I'm not falling on my sword for this. I didn't tell them *any* of this. I *never* mentioned shoe prints. I'm *not* the unnamed source. I didn't leak—"

"Look at this shit." He grabbed the television's remote control from his desktop. "I paused it just so you know I'm not some church-lady Henny Penny sayin' the sky's fallin'."

The camera zoomed out—Olivia McAllen stood in front of apartment security gates.

I knew those gates.

It was obvious that Olivia McAllen didn't frequent the Jungle—fear glistened in her wide, blue eyes. Apartment residents and bystanders lingered in the reporter's shot. Mugging for the camera, waving, hopping up and down, seeking any attention from the world—even a news story about two dead black girls was akin to appearing on *American Idol*.

The reporter shouted over the ruckus behind her. "New developments in the brutal kidnappings and murders of two teen girls from Baldwin Village. Police have identified a suspect known to law enforcement as a past sex offender. Raul Moriaga, a twenty-eight-year-old day laborer, has been in and out of prison for several felonies, including"—she glanced at her notepad and shook her head—"rape, assault, molestation . . . The list goes on and on. Police believe that Moriaga *may* be a person of interest in these two cases that have shocked and saddened this tight-knit community."

The frame jumped to earlier tape of Raul Moriaga climbing out of his shiny black Camaro. Wifebeater, tattooed arms bared to the world, the wispy porn mustache, that long scar that ran from his nose to his jaw . . .

Of course *he did it. Look at him. Look at that blue teardrop tattoo beneath his eye.*

Moriaga tried to move past the reporters to enter his apartment. Unsuccessful, he shoved the camera away from his face. "Just leave me alone," he said. "I ain't done nothing to those girls. Just leave me alone."

Lieutenant Rodriguez turned off the television but kept his eyes on the dark screen. "Well?" he asked. "You got somethin' else to say?"

I could barely speak—a cabbage-sized lump sat in my throat. "I have nothing to add, sir."

He glared at me and chuckled without humor. "Be a cop or

be a girlfriend. You can't be both. Especially with—" He pointed to the newspaper, then waited for me to nod.

I did not nod.

"Get the hell out of here." Then he threw the remote control at the television and turned back to the window with no view.

I stomped down the hallway, reaching the detective's bull pen. Pepe, Colin, and Luke gaped at me as my stomp weakened into a stagger. But I didn't stop moving.

The fluorescent bulbs in the women's bathroom were too white-hot, too bright and dazzling to be anything except the sun. I stumbled into the last stall as tiny bursts of pain exploded in my head. My eyes watered with tears thick with glass shards. My knees gave, and I dropped to the tile and gripped the sides of the toilet. I leaned forward until my forehead touched the cool seat. My mouth filled with warm spit, and my belly shimmied—

I vomited.

Bacon, toast, coffee—all of it spewed out of my mouth and formed a brackish island in the middle of toilet water. I shuddered, then heaved again. Then again. And then . . . nothing.

Done for the moment, I stared at the places my hands should've been, but only saw porcelain. My body hurt—those internal explosions had torn away chunks of flesh.

I'm disappearing. That's why my body hurts like this. That's why I can't see me. I'm having an out-of-body experience fully conscious.

Then, more shuddering. More vomiting. Burning eyes. Finally, my muscles relaxed. Spent, I sat back against the cold metal door. I shut my eyes, counted backwards from 100 . . . 96 . . . 92 . . . My pulse slowed, and the shivering eased . . .

90 . . . 89 . . .

Don't remember reaching 85.

48

I WAS STILL COLLAPSED ON THE BATHROOM FLOOR WHEN MY JEANS VIBRATED AND pulled me from that place cops go when they're tired and frustrated. All around me, metal doors banged opened and locks clicked. Toilets flushed. Water ran in sinks. Rubber soles squeaked on the tile floors. My jeans vibrated again—my phone was ringing.

I stood without swaying. No pain. Clear vision. Normal heart rate. Sweaty, but that had come from sleeping (or whatevering) in a public toilet while wearing a cashmere sweater.

How long have I been down here?

Had the argument between Lieutenant Rodriguez and me been real? Had I dreamed it?

I padded to the sink. Washed my hands. Splashed my face with water and dried off with a paper towel. Then, I plucked my cell phone from my jeans pocket.

Two texts. One from Lieutenant Rodriguez. *Yes, I'm still pissed—you have one more time to fuck up, then I'm giving the case to Glickman and Bose. And then shit will go in your file.*

My stomach alley-ooped. Not a dream.

The second text came from Zucca. *The mud on Moriaga's boots does not match dirt from park. But! The boot print from Lords scene matches boot print from A.Mitchel.Size12 Timberland. Rpt later.*

I pushed back my shoulders and strode to the locker room. Off went the jeans and sweater. I showered, brushed my teeth, brushed my teeth again. Tugged on black track pants and a soft LAPD T-shirt. I pulled my hair into a ponytail, then brushed my teeth a third time.

As I tromped back into the detectives' bull pen, my colleagues stopped talking. All eyes, even the two cuffed thugs on the bench, landed on me as I retreated east to my desk.

A porcelain vase of lavender roses sat near my computer keyboard.

"Lou?" Colin whispered.

With a shaky hand, I plucked the card from the bouquet and read:

> *HOPE YOU LAND IN A PLACE WHERE*
> *SOMEONE LOVES YOU BEST OF ALL. Z.*

"Lou?"

"Time to work." I shoved the card into my pants pocket.

Colin rolled over to my desk. "You okay, partner?"

It took every facial muscle I had to fake a smile. "Awesome."

He frowned. "I hate when you fake it."

"That may change everything, dude." I pointed to the journal, still in its evidence baggie.

"Except that Chanita, Allayna, and Trina aren't mentioned," Colin pointed out. "I looked through it again." He leaned close to me. "What did L.T. say to you? What happened?"

"He yelled. I yelled. The sun rose, and soon the sun will set." I logged onto Madison Middle School's Web site: smiling kids, a wise-looking teacher instructing from a hi-tech whiteboard. Football players in a huddle. Every one of them were targets— and as the gatekeeper, I was failing to keep them all safe. I clicked on the school's calendar. "So there's a basketball game

337

that starts at six o'clock tonight. Got any plans?"

Colin pointed at the bouquet. "No, but you do. Sam's got that ill-na-na."

I rolled my eyes. "First, boys can't have ill-na-nas, you dope. Stay off Urban Dictionary. Second . . ." I stared at the perfect velvety buds. "Those aren't from Sam."

Before Colin could respond, my desk phone rang.

Fifteen minutes later, my partner and I found ourselves back in the Jungle and standing in front of Chanita Lords's apartment building.

Usually when slick yellow tape was stretched from one fixed point to another, a crowd of looky-loos pressed against it. *Usually* by the time lighter serum has ringed the darker blood, potential witnesses have filled their hoisted camera phones with fifty pictures capturing the sneaker beneath the death tarp or the leg twisted beneath the body.

But there was none of this today. Not even the ghetto Greek chorus loitered nearby. Four patrol cops and two detectives stared at the dead guy hidden beneath a blue tarp in the middle of the street.

Colin and I ducked beneath the yellow tape.

Thomas Jefferson, tall, black, and skinny, was scribbling in a pad and pointing his flashlight at sections of the asphalt.

I glanced around the scene. *Red cup, red cup, empty Alizé bottle.*

"Hey, Jeff," I said.

Jefferson regarded my track pants and sneakers. "Casual Friday on a Sunday?"

"Got blood on my sequins and mink stole this morning."

"Just that you're always suited and booted."

"Yeah. Circumstances. May I . . . ?" I nodded to the victim on the wet asphalt.

"Certainly."

The two other dicks stepped back as Colin lifted the sheet.

Raul Moriaga's thin face was now swollen and pulpy. His bloody wifebeater had been ripped apart. He lay in a mingled puddle of storm water and the crimson stuff that had given him life. He wore a single black Paul Rodriguez Nike.

Colin muttered, "Shit."

I stared at Moriaga's weasel face—his half-mast eyes saw nothing.

"Guess his cousin will be gettin' those fish again," Colin said.

"You were looking at him, right?" Jefferson asked.

"Yeah." Then I told him about Chanita Lords, Moriaga's possible involvement, and his relevant past.

"So folks found out about his connection to Chanita through the news?" Jefferson asked.

I shrugged. "But Chanita's mother has always suspected him. You may wanna talk to her and to Ontrel Shaw, the girl's boyfriend."

"Shaw's Jungle Bloods, ain't he?" Jefferson asked.

"Yep, so tread carefully," I said.

"So what happened here?" Colin asked, nodding to the dead man on the asphalt.

Jefferson scratched his eyebrow. "A group of unidentified black males told Moriaga that he needed to confess to killing the girls. He refused, so they beat him. Finally, he said that he did it, probably hoping that they'd stop. But his confession only made it worse. Someone pulled out a knife and stabbed him ten times." Jefferson clicked on the flashlight and showed us eight slits along Moriaga's back, his left bicep, and left wrist. "He bled out before the ambulance arrived."

I grunted, uncertain how to feel about a predator permanently booted from society.

"One of the wits who saw nothing," Jefferson was saying,

"told me that he deserved it. She said that the neighborhood had enough problems without somebody stealing and raping and killing children. She said somebody needed to do something since the cops weren't."

"And the guys who beat him?" Colin asked.

Jefferson smirked. "What guys? No one saw a thing. Moriaga got jumped by ghosts."

49

THE COFFEE GRINDER CHEWED WHOLE BEANS, MASKING THE FUNK OF MILDEW AND traitor in Syeeda's office. My college friend, sweatshirt sleeves rolled to her elbows and hair gathered in a loose bun, hummed as she filled her coffee maker. The weekend news played on the flat-screen television bolted to the north wall. The weekend edition of *OurTimes* sat on her desk. Syeeda tried to smile. "What do you want me to say?" She poured creamer into a mug, then licked her sticky index finger.

"Oh . . ." I shrugged. "Nothing special. Just, 'Sorry, Lou for writing a—' "

"I didn't write it."

"Your reporter *did*," I snapped. "And you let him put my name in it." I didn't want to have this conversation—every part of me thrashed on the inside, bucking against the onslaught of words my brain had prepared during the drive over from the Jungle.

Syeeda flicked her hand, then grabbed two sugar packets from a tray. "Your name's been in hundreds of articles. And this isn't the first time Rodriguez has reamed you for no good reason." She sighed as the second mug filled with hot coffee. "You're right—I was supposed to write it, not Mike. You're right—it was shitty writing, and even after I bled all over it, it was *still* shitty writing. But he called my boss, Lou, and complained, so I had to let him do it. And I had to let some stuff go in, like the stats." She tore open the sugar packets.

I glared past her and out the dirty window to rundown Crenshaw with its wig shops, smoke shops, and Wienerschnitzel that sometimes included bullets with its chili dogs. "You obviously don't respect what I do. You obviously don't care that a man is dead because—"

"Dude, I'm sorry, all right?" Syeeda handed me one of the mugs. "I'm sorry that I didn't get permission from you to—"

"Don't be passive-aggressive."

"Folks read a story that told them nothing new," she argued, sticking the stirrer into her mouth. "Everybody knew that Moriaga was a sex offender—"

"And yet he somehow, miraculously, continued to *breathe* until you printed a story—"

"Oh, Elouise." She rolled her eyes. "I got a tip, okay? An unnamed source who told me that he'd been watching Moriaga, that he'd seen him more than once scoping out Chanita and other kids in the neighborhood. He actually sent me a picture of Moriaga talking to a twelve-year-old girl at the park two days ago. And so I made the call."

"Who's this source?" I asked.

"You know I can't name my source."

"*Who*?" I demanded.

She shook her head.

"I don't believe you."

"What did you want me to do? *Not* report it? I have a picture of this guy being a goddamned predator, and yet I decided *not* to print the picture, even though my boss was saying that I should. Yes, you're doing your job. But I'm doing my job, too. Calling attention to this *sick shit* and to a neighborhood predator that you all wouldn't take off the street. He's dead? You're welcome. Now he'll never rape another kid forever and ever."

A knock on the door.

Syeeda shouted, "Yeah?"

Mike Summit popped his head in. "Should I be on this conversation since I wrote—?"

"No!" boomed from both Syeeda's and my mouth.

Mike Summit blushed and closed the door with a quiet *click*.

Syeeda hugged her elbows. "Lou—"

"No." I stood and sat the coffee mug on her desk.

She sucked her teeth. "Don't be like this."

I grabbed my bag from the floor. "Be like what?"

"Stay. Chat." She pulled off her sweatshirt—beneath it, she wore a FRANKIE SAYS RELAX T-shirt. "So what's up with you and Sam?"

I cocked my head. "You do realize that I'm working, right? You do realize that my ass is grass in about six hours and that I'm here to ask you to refrain from printing any more bullshit and racist, unsubstantiated conjecture. I'm looking for a *monster,* Syeeda. One who chews up little girls, spits them out, and leaves them in the park for me to find. And guess what? No matter who he was, Moriaga didn't kill those girls. It's not his DNA on Chanita. He's dead and *you* helped make that possible." "We wrote a story based on the information we had at the time," she said.

"But you didn't have all of the information—"

"Cuz you didn't give me enough," she shouted. "And you're not the only person in the world who knows shit. The people who live there—"

"If you'd just given me more time—"

"In this business, we don't get a lot of that. And Moriaga was setting up another girl—"

I shook my head. "But he didn't kill Chanita. He didn't kill Allayna. And now my colleagues will be hunting black boys

343

who thought they were avenging something."

"I'm sorry, okay? I understand what you're saying and that wasn't our intent." She leaned against the credenza and continued to chew on that straw. "So Mike said there was some excitement at Chanita's funeral yesterday before Allayna Mitchell—"

"No comment," I growled.

"Off the record, then."

I shook my head.

She gaped at me.

I gave another head shake, then ante-upped with a frown. "Who sent you the picture of Moriaga and the girl?"

She called my frown with a frown of her own. "Hell no."

"You and I need to take a break, then."

"Seriously?" she asked, tossing the stirrer into the waste can.

"I give you information. You give me nothing back." My stomach twisted into hot knots. "Is that all I am to you? Another *source*?"

"You're accusing me of *using* you? Now you're questioning our *friendship*?"

Am I? I nodded.

Tears glistened in her eyes. "I've *always* been there for you, even when it has nothing to do with my job." She threw up her hands. "Fine, I admit it: I give zero fucks about Moriaga being dead."

"Wow," I whispered.

"I'm wearing white, too, Elouise," she said. "I want justice for all, too, and if *you're* not gonna protect—"

I pointed at her. "You shall *not* compare my job to yours, cuz I'm looking at you right now, at your cute little torso all freed up and shit, wearing quirky T-shirts that say 'relax.' Wanna guess what I'm wearing under my—?"

"I know, all right?" she shouted.

I strode toward the door.

"You're leaving?"

"Looks like it."

"Is Rodriguez making you choose between the boys in blue and your girls in pink and green? Girls who've cried with you and been there for you since childhood?" The heat of her anger rolled toward me like solar flares.

But her hotness had only made me icy. I opened the door and squinted at her. "You chose between me and your job when your boss told you to give the story to that fucker out there."

"So you *are* choosing, then. You don't care—"

"About who? You? Black people? Now I'm not *down* enough cuz *you* fucked me over?"

Syeeda crossed her arms and canted her head.

I squinted at her. "And when was the last time *you* visited the Jungle?"

She opened her mouth to respond. No words. She reached for the coffee mug and brought it to her lips. But she didn't drink.

I nodded, then said, "Thanks, pal."

50

IT WAS FIFTEEN PAST THREE, AND LENA AND I SAT AT AN OUTSIDE PATIO TABLE beneath one of Airport Radisson's heating lamps. Every five minutes, jets just a few feet aboveground roared over us, rattling our drink glasses and the tray of chips and spinach dip. Lena's orange Birkin bag and my battered messenger bag sat in the chair Syeeda would have occupied. At the bar inside, men of many colors all glowed TV-mosaic purples, whites, and reds. Every face was glued to flat-screen televisions and to college kids hustling up and down a basketball court.

Lena pushed her phone in my direction.

"I'm not calling," I said. "I have nothing to say to her right now. She basically called me a sellout."

Lena gave me a raspberry.

I had three hours to myself before meeting Colin back at the station. And I had chosen to use that time to close circles and trim dead-ends in my personal life. Call it a psychological "control burn" of overgrown trees and brush that kept me stooped and weak.

Lena shivered. "Oh my *lord,* it's so effin' cold." She wore silver short-shorts and an artfully ripped Hello Kitty sweatshirt.

"Maybe you should wear clothes in the winter," I said, eyebrow arched.

"Maybe I should cut out my gallbladder with a rusty melon

baller first. And it's spring now, so—" She gave me another raspberry. Then she picked up the phone and waggled it.

I sipped my tonic water. "Stop it or I'm gonna throw your new phone into the pool."

"Ugh. I hate when you two put me in the middle. And I'm glad I don't have to worry about 'keepin' it real.' I was always surrounded by Oreos."

"You're the Oreo queen."

"Didn't even know a Crip until I dated what's his face. The hot one with the tats and the cornrows. That summer was like, education abroad or . . . ecotourism."

I glanced at my watch.

"Almost time?" she asked.

I nibbled on the lime wedge. "Uh huh."

"So have you and Sam . . . canoodled yet?" she asked. "Or is he now in the discard pile like his predecessors?"

"We had an argument last night. His ex-wife answered his phone. He claims that nothing's happening. I don't feel like believing him right now. We're . . . too soon anyway."

She plucked a green olive from her dirty martini. "You never get past two weeks cuz everything's too soon. Is that Dr. Zach guy the next sucker on the sampler platter?"

My face flushed. "No."

"You went out with him."

"Not true." I reached for another tortilla chip. "We happened to be at the same place at the same time. I may be a blue-collared cop, but iced tea and a soggy panini will never count as a date in my eyes."

"And the flowers he sent?"

I shrugged, then ate the tortilla chip.

"Why are you having such a difficult time with this?" She leaned forward and whispered, "Is it because he's not black?"

My head fell back and I stared at the sky. "Oh my—"

"You have to get over that," Lena said. "Open your mind. And then . . . open your legs."

I looked at her. "His color, *whatever* the hell he is, does not bother me. And I'm not ready to open my legs for anyone right now." I paused, then added, "I don't think."

Lena was staring at me. "Sam and his ex—"

"Worries me. I don't think she's over him, which . . . When she answered his phone . . . I just . . . They were married fifteen years, so I get it. I won't come first in his life, so why try?"

"You don't know that," Lena argued.

"I *do* know that. I've never come first in *anyone's* life. Not even my mother's because Tori was always there even when she wasn't. Sam will get bored or lonely or *something* cuz it's *always* something.

"And what kind of future is that, Lee? Always waiting for the shoe to drop because it *will* drop. It *always* drops. Say Sam and I or whoever he is have a family, and I achieve Normal. I'll be home with the kids, and one day, out of the blue, I find myself praying that he shows up for the piano recital this time, knowing that he won't. And then I have to explain to the kids that Daddy has to work late. Or break the news that Daddy won't ever come home again."

"Lou, he's not—"

"My father?" I chuckled. "My ex? *Your* ex? I'm tired of seeing the backs of men."

"My dad didn't leave," she pointed out. "Neither did Sy's. Many men stay. You just got unlucky." She offered a sympathetic smile, then drained her martini glass. "Stop being the skeptic all the time. Sounds *exhausting*. Think *good* things sometimes. Ignore evil at least three hours a day."

"That's a long time," I said, slumping in my chair.

"I watched you at dinner the other night," Lena said, "when Colin and I barged in on you and Sam—"

My phone chattered with the Ewoks ringtone.

"What does *Gregory* want?" Lena said, lip curled.

"We were supposed to meet today to talk about house stuff."

"You believe that?"

I smirked. "Of course not."

She stared at me without speaking.

I avoided her eyes and took the olive skewer out of her martini glass. "As you were saying about dinner?"

"You're . . . lighter with Sam," she said. "You shine brighter with him. So different than when you were with *him*." She pointed at my phone.

I sighed. "Serves me right for putting all my eggs in one bastard."

"Stop channeling Dorothy Parker, all right? Zach. Sam. Any man other than Gregory. It's okay to play the field. Just be happy doing it."

"And then I, too, will have thirty dick pics in my Gmail?"

"You'll never have more than me, *ma chère*. You're too scared of hell and Jesus and your mother."

I threw my head back and laughed.

"Seriously," she said, "in your best optimism, what do you want from Sam? Speak it into the universe."

I let my head fall back again, and I stared at the smooth belly of the Virgin Air jetliner passing over us. "I want the assurance that he'll always be there for me." I straightened in my chair to look at my friend. "Now, what's supposed to happen? When will the universe respond?"

She shrugged. "No clue."

"You're useless."

"Call Syeeda now."

"No."

"I talked to the professor today," she said, not missing a

beat. "He wants me to fly back to New York for his retirement party."

I popped an olive into my mouth. "Will there be mimes and *foie gras* and Josephine Bakers wearing banana skirts and James Baldwin impersonators reading passages from 'Blues for Mister Charlie'?"

She giggled. "Is it some reverse-oedipal daddy thing that I want a man like him?"

"A man who adores you, who is amused by you, a man who is willing to spoil you all the days of your life?" I shook my head. "Nah."

She glanced at the clock on her phone. "The time has come, *ma chère*."

I slowly inhaled, then exhaled. "I don't wanna do this. Why am I doing this? Too much free time. And nature abhors a vacuum."

Lena grabbed her bag from the chair. "I'm glad you called me—I worry that you're gonna stroke out sometimes. All stress and no canoodling makes Lou a dull girl."

"Fine."

"Don't call Greg."

"Why not?"

"He's your Kryptonite."

"Okay."

"Call Sam instead."

"Why?"

"Cuz he's . . ."

"The rays of the sun?" I asked, smiling.

Lena blinked at me, ignorant of the source of Superman's superpowers. "I was gonna say, 'cuz he's fine as hell and deserves your consideration.' But sun rays are also a good answer. Really, Elouise. Be more receptive—people come into your life for a reason."

"Yes. Thank you. So, with everything going on between me and Sy right now," I said, "can I live at the beach with you for the moment?"

Lena lifted an eyebrow. "If I say no, where will you stay?"

I canted my head. "If I say, 'over at the Dark Side,' what will *you* say?"

"Fine," she huffed. "I'll do anything to keep you from Greg. *Oh!*" She dug in her bag and pulled out a packet of watermelon Pop Rocks. "Use these next time you and Sam are together."

I stared at the packet. "Really?"

She winked at me. "I know you're the Altoids type, but switch up. Remember: don't sprinkle them *inside*. We don't want you in the ER."

I said, "Umm . . . Okay."

We walked arm in arm to the lobby.

"You're gonna be okay," Lena said. "I promise."

"Yep. And now go put some clothes on."

She grinned. "Only if you take some off."

We hugged again before she *clickety-clacked* back to her Range Rover.

51

MISTY RAIN NOW FELL FROM LILAC-COLORED CLOUDS. A HELICOPTER BUZZED A few blocks east, and then sirens wailed—like thunder and lightning, those two.

After taking several breaths, I returned to a lobby that resembled every Radisson hotel lobby in the world. Generic prints of sailboats and wine bottles, fake and real potted plants, and brass fixtures. Businessmen wore their neckties loose, their cocktail glasses high, and their gazes tight on the basketball game or on the cocktail waitress's freckled cleavage.

Victor Starr sat at a small table near the elevator bank. He had trimmed his gray hair since I'd seen him on Friday. His wool coat lay across his lap, and a Kangol cap hung on his knee. He was staring at the bouquet of white Peruvian lilies near his beer mug.

My heart pounded as I stood before him. "Hello."

He gazed up at me and tried to smile. "Appreciate you seeing me before I flew back home." He handed me the lilies. "These are for you."

Didn't want to, but I took the bouquet.

"I also got you a little something . . ." He reached into his coat pocket and pulled out a small jewelry box. "This is for you, too."

I stared at the royal-blue case, refusing to take it.

He sighed, then opened the top: a diamond-encrusted pony with sapphire eyes sat on a small white pillow. "When you were about five or six, you used to always say, 'Daddy, buy me a pony. Please, Daddy, just a little one.'" He puffed out his chest and grinned. "Took me some time, but . . . Here's your little pony."

I rolled my eyes and stomped out of the bar to the poolside lounge. No one sat in the padded chaises beneath the cabanas, but a black cat perched at the pool's lip.

Victor Starr had followed me. He had pulled on his coat and put on his hat and still clutched the jewelry box. "Lulu, just let me—"

I stopped in my step and whirled around to face him. "Do you know that Tori was kidnapped and murdered and then buried in the basement of that liquor store on Santa Rosalia and that we finally found her *bones* back in June?"

His eyes darkened, and his facial muscles twitched. Finally, he took a breath and nodded.

"Why did you leave?"

His Adam's apple bobbed. "Because on that day, on that Sunday, I was mad and I was weak, and when I got into the car to get the paper, I drove and . . . I just kept driving, and when I stopped, I was so . . . far away. So far away. By then, it was late—hours had gone by, and I was too scared, too tired, to drive back. And I knew that you and your mom and your sister would be okay. And you were." He smiled. "You made it, Lulu. You were always my strong girl."

"*Your* strong girl?" I pointed at him. "You have *nothing* and *everything* to do with me being so-called *strong*."

He blinked and searched for words to say. "I-I wasn't good enough—"

"For *who*?"

"For all of you," he shouted. "You think I wanted us living there, barely getting by?"

"You were supposed to do three things." I held up three fingers. "Provide, nurture, and guide. And 'provide' didn't mean diamonds, Maseratis, and prime rib and shit. That didn't mean a big house up on the hill. It didn't mean vacations in Tahiti. We ate every night. You took me to see ponies in Griffith Park. You taught me how to ride a bike." I shook my head and crossed my arms. "You left us because that wasn't enough for *you*. *You* wanted to leave. *You* broke us."

He stared into the pool water. "No. Your mother was strong. I knew she could do it without me. She told me all the time that she could do it without me."

I chuckled without humor. "Oh, so it's *her* fault?"

"She did it, though. She raised you and look at how good—"

"Are you fucking *kidding* me?" I gawked at him. "Tori is *dead*. We are less one person today, or does that type of math not exist in the land in which you live? I'd like to go to that place, where being dead and being left behind and being scarred is doing good."

He squared his shoulders. "Are we gonna have a civil discussion or not?"

"*Not.*" I took a step closer to him, frown chiseled so deep in me that my toes were bleeding. "You didn't have to drive back that night for my mother." I jabbed my finger at his chest. "*You* should've drove back that night for *me*. You should've come back for *Tori*."

Tears shone in his eyes, and his chin quivered.

"Were you okay being without us, Victor?" I held up a trembling hand. "Don't answer that—I know the answer. Cuz other than your weight loss from your recent health woes, you look great. You have a livery and a big house in Vegas. So why are you here?"

"Your mother and I," he said, "we had a deep, deep love. And even though I'm with someone, I'll always love Georgia.

And I know that she'll always love me."

The world brightened—I'd see the face of Jesus soon if we kept going in this direction.

He pulled his wallet from his back pocket and flipped it to a picture.

It was a faded shot of Victoria and me, ages nine and five, sitting on a porch swing. We wore sundresses and ate oranges. "I look at this picture every day," Victor Starr said. "And I'm here because I want us to be a family again. I want you to meet my wife and my stepson and—"

"*You* want?" I cocked my head. "I'm not interested in what *you* want. I'm not interested in meeting *your* family. I have a mother and I have a sister whose ashes are now drifting over Kansas. I have friends and a lover and coworkers and people who need me, people who want to be with me and have never left my side. I don't need *you* anymore cuz I've done the hard part.

"That means I don't wanna see your fancy house or your fancy cars or your wife's fancy purses or stand in your air-conditioned living room or eat your prime rib from Wagyu cows. I don't want to experience anything you deprived *my* family of when you abandoned us." Spent, I inhaled cool air, then slowly let it out.

"Is that it, then?" he whispered, his gaze on that picture of girls who no longer existed.

Well, is it? I thought a moment, then dropped the bouquet of lilies on the closest table. I turned on my heel and left him there at the pool with that black cat.

Yeah. That was it.

As I stomped back to the parking lot, my phone rang.

"You gotta stop her," the woman caller shouted.

I stopped in my step. "Who is—?"

"Brandi, Nicole's mother. You gotta stop her."

355

"From what?"

"She's trying to catch Mr. Bishop herself," Brandi said. "I think she's gonna try and tape him, tape them . . ." She let a sob escape and cried, "Oh Lord, my baby."

Cold clutched my heart as I ran to my car. "Where is she now?"

"I got the phone locater on," she said. "She's at the school."

52

NIKKI'S NOT ANSWERING," I SAID, PHONE TO MY EAR.

Colin eased the Crown Vic past Madison Middle School. Pepe, in a Taurus station wagon, had parked across the street from the main entrance. Luke's Impala was parked at the entrance to the teacher's parking lot. Radio cars slowly patrolled the neighborhood.

Students now dribbled out of the front gates. By the slump in their shoulders and shouts of "Fuck Wright," I could tell that Madison had lost the game. The girls traveled in packs, with most of them wearing short skirts or tight skinny jeans. The boys wore baggy chinos and oversize white T-shirts.

No rain, but the storm gathering in my stomach intensified the longer we sat here.

Brandi Washington had remained at the station with Lieutenant Rodriguez.

I keyed the mic on the car radio. "Luke, did she get in over there?"

"Nope. But the rabbit's exiting over by you."

Where was Nicole?

"I'll call in a BOLO." After finding Payton Bishop's car registration for his Prius and for his wife's Mini Cooper, I grabbed the radio and issued a "be on the lookout" for both cars.

My phone rang.

"I'm looking at the app," Brandi Washington said, "and the little dot is moving."

"To where?" I asked.

"Like . . . on La Cienega."

Colin turned left onto King Boulevard.

Soon, we sped past the Baldwin Hills mall.

"She's still on La Cienega," Brandi said.

"Think they're going to the park?" Colin whispered.

I nodded, then called Lieutenant Rodriguez to arrange backup to join us.

"They're in the park," Brandi shouted. "The dot ain't moving no more."

We headed to Bonner Park.

Colin switched off the Ford's headlights and rolled past the park's entry. Pepe and a black Yukon filled with Gino Walston and his Violent Criminal Apprehension Team followed us. Luke and a radio car blocked the entrance with pylons.

No one sat near the lake. No cars were parked in any of the lots. No lights shone in the community center. A pair of raccoons scuttled on the side of the road with leftover sandwiches in their mouths.

"He's gone up farther," Colin whispered.

We crept up the narrow road, passing parked tractors and pickup trucks.

Colin finally pulled over to the slight curb and parked. Shoulders tense, he slipped his Sig from its holster, then climbed out of the car. Glock in hand, I pushed open the passenger-side door. I tapped my torso—no give, all Kevlar.

Oil rigs, like dinosaurs in the dark, creaked as their heads swung up . . . down . . . The stink of sulfur mixed with skunk, both caught in the wet nighttime air. And big men dressed in black LAPD combat gear hoisted big guns— manmade and God-given—ready to rumble.

Gino Walston winked at me. "You cool?" A small camera had been bolted to his helmet.

I curtsied. "I'm cool."

"*We* cool?"

"Of course. Always." After *Captain America,* our heavy petting in the back of his Expedition had resulted in . . . absolutely nothing. He had called me for a second date, but I . . . didn't see the need.

Pepe, Colin, and I followed the VCAT up the hill. Less than a mile away lay the trail where we'd found Chanita Lords.

Parked beneath a radio tower, the Prius glowed red. No one sat in the cabin.

"It matches," Colin said, pointing to the car's rear license plate.

I crept west, toward the grassy lawn, where visitors usually flew kites and tossed Frisbees. Gino led a group to the north end of the lawn.

I heard them before I saw them.

"It's safe," a man said. "We've all been baptized. Trust me: the feeling won't last long."

A girl giggled.

Nikki, I mouthed to Colin.

We moved closer to the line of eucalyptus trees.

"You've changed me," the man claimed. "No, you have. My life is more exciting because of you. I don't choose just *any* girl. I have to see that special *something* in her."

We passed through the line of trees.

Payton Bishop and Nicole Brewer lay on a serape with a pack of Corona longnecks and a bag of cheese curls between them.

I turned to Gino and pointed to his helmet camera.

He nodded and gave a thumbs-up.

We all lifted our guns.

Bishop leaned over and kissed Nicole.

Strike 1.

And in this game, all you needed was one strike.

Nicole pulled back and giggled.

Right then, I wanted to squeeze the trigger and destroy this effin' pervert-predator.

Bishop moved closer, then eased his hand beneath her pleated skirt.

She pushed his hand away, then giggled again.

He clenched her wrist. "Since when are you bashful?"

"And since when you in a hurry?" Nicole's gaze darted around the landscape—and stopped once she spotted me.

Payton Bishop craned his head to see what had captured her attention.

Shit.

The counselor gasped.

"Police," I shouted. "Don't move."

Bishop scrambled off the blanket. He grabbed Nicole's hand and pulled her to her feet.

She fought him with each step. Finally, he pushed her, then darted across the lawn and into the grove of eucalyptus trees.

I ran after him. Legs burning, I didn't stop even as my sneakers skidded across the grass.

Bishop also tried to sprint but failed horribly because of slippery leaves and holes the size of pumpkins. Instead, he ran in spurts.

I scurried after him. In the darkness, between spruce trees, fallen branches, and thick roots, ankles twisting from stepping on pinecones and rocks.

Bishop's right foot skidded, but he regained control.

A helicopter thundered over the canopy, then circled back. A cone of white light from the bird above shone before us and lit upright trees, fallen trees, and peat moss. Branches and leaves snapped and crunched all around me—no help in the dark.

Were we heading north? Or were we heading east?

Every tree, every stump looked the same.

Shit, shit, shit.

Up ahead, I spotted a clearing between the trees. *Lights! Houses!*

We were getting closer to the bluff and to the valley that separated the park from those hillside homes.

The helicopter's light found Bishop's back.

The counselor's arms went up and out, and he sailed through the air for a moment, then landed with an *oomph* on the ground.

In seconds, I closed the distance between us and stopped a few steps away with my Glock out before me and aimed at the space below his left shoulder blade. "Don't fucking move!"

Bishop froze with his face in the dirt.

Yes! Yes!

"Don't shoot," he shouted.

And then, all of me calmed. I caught my breath, then yanked my radio off my hip. Gun still aimed at his heart, I keyed the mic. "This is Norton. Got him. Over."

53

Y'ALL GOT *MY PHONE?* THE FIRST WORDS OUT OF NICOLE BREWER'S MOUTH AFTER rescuing her from that cheese-curls-littered blanket in the park.

After assuring her that her iPhone made it out okay, after swearing that I'd get it back to her after downloading the recording, I hugged the brave girl and left her with her mother.

Colin sat at his computer. "Sounds a little muffled but . . ." He clicked PLAY, and Bishop's voice crackled from the computer's speakers. "Couldn't wait to see you . . . Got your favorite Smirnoff apple things . . . Man, you are fine as hell . . . These aren't from CVS. Got 'em at that erotica shop on Sepulveda . . ."

"We got him," I said, high-fiving my partner. "His ass is grass."

"We gonna mention this?" he asked.

"Nope," I said, smiling wide. "Let's keep it in our pocket. He may need a nice surprise."

The temperature in interview room 3 was kept a brisk sixty-one degrees. The room's hard metal chairs made your tailbone ache. The bare white walls closed in on you after ten minutes of sitting and staring at nothing except bare white wall and the one-way mirror. Soon, the Slump took over your spine and shoulders. Soon, your forehead was just three inches from hitting the cold metal table. You shivered. Your teeth chattered. Your ass ached. Interviewees started talking to us just to feel warm and comfy again, even if that meant warm and comfy in a jail cell. Interview room 3 worked.

But it didn't work on Payton Bishop, who, after an hour of being left alone in that room, sat upright in one of those metal chairs. Hands clasped before him, he looked as though he were waiting for the accountant to tell him that he'd be getting a refund after all. Even in his stiffness, he kept glancing at the walls, swiping his sweaty face against the shoulders of his dirty green polo shirt, then rubbing the angry welts on his wrists left by my handcuffs.

Colin and I stood on the other side of that one-way mirror. The part of me that Snoopy-danced had now slumped in a corner. I winced as I rotated my left wrist—injured back on Wednesday, better on Saturday, aching like hell again today.

"You should get that checked out," Colin said with a chuckle.

I smiled at him. "I'll go on Monday." I grabbed a manila folder from the tabletop that was filled with pictures of missing children. "Let the wild rumpus begin."

Colin and I strolled into the frigid room.

I glanced at my watch—going on eleven o'clock.

Colin sat knee to knee with Payton Bishop. "Nice seeing you again, sir. So, first, there's this." He slipped a form near Bishop's hands that explained his rights. "Of course, we're hoping that you just tell us your side of the story."

Bishop smiled. "What time is it? And why are you treating me like a criminal?"

Seated across from him, I wanted to vomit and then shove his face in it. "Tell us what we're misunderstanding. Because that's obviously what this is, right? A misunderstanding?"

Payton Bishop stared at his clasped hands.

"Also," I said, "you can *voluntarily* give me the DNA that I asked for days ago. I emphasize 'voluntarily' cuz now that you've fucked up the deal you made with the DA, guess whose spit I can take without saying, 'May I?' or 'Please?'" I pointed at him, then cocked my head. "Giving me spit may not help you with the necking session in the woods, but it *may* eliminate you as the number one suspect in the murders of Chanita Lords and Allayna Mitchell."

Bishop continued to stare at his hands.

Colin winked at me. "Let him think about it."

"Okeydokey." I leaned back in the chair, crossed my legs, and stared at our guest.

White-hot rage crackled just beneath my skin. My left eye twitched, and heat from my nostrils burned my upper lip.

Five minutes passed in silence.

Then Colin started popping his pen against his teeth—a habit that drove me loony but right now came in handy.

Bishop winced and closed his eyes.

We sat in the quiet for another minute.

I swallowed my anger and opened the manila folder. "Margaret Thatcher said, 'I am extraordinarily patient, provided I get my own way in the end.' Guess who's gonna get her way in the end?"

Payton Bishop smirked. "Nine wise men said that I have the right to remain silent because anything I say can be used against me in a court of law."

"Yeah, they did. And you were Mirandized back at the park." I dropped a picture in front of him. "You know this girl?"

The counselor gazed at the photograph. Flat eyes. Tight jaw.

I replaced that picture with another. "What about this girl?"

Payton Bishop looked at the photograph. No reaction.

I presented six more pictures.

Each time, the counselor's expression remained blank.

I considered two more pictures in the folder, then selected the double-exposure picture of Peaches, the girl in his journal. "What about her?"

Payton Bishop sank in his chair and pretended to be bored.

I plucked the picture of naked Peaches in the pink room from the folder. Seeing this photograph again made my hands shake. "She look familiar now?"

He flushed, then tried to find something interesting to look at on the ceiling.

"Detective Norton," Colin said, "maybe you're going about this the wrong way. You're making certain assumptions."

"I am, indeed." I fake smiled at Bishop again. "I apologize. I'm only human." I sifted through the remaining pictures in the folder and found another. "So . . ." I slid the shot before the counselor. "You know this *boy*?"

Bishop pushed away from the table. "What the fuck are you suggesting?"

I held up my hands in mock protest. "Stop bein' an old lady about it, all right? I'm just accommodating any preferences you may have."

Payton Bishop settled back into his chair. "I'm not gay."

"You're into girls, then," Colin confirmed.

"This is ridiculous," Bishop shouted. "I cannot believe . . . Why have you arrested me?"

I cocked my head. "You know why we arrested you."

"How long you been dating children?" Colin asked.

"They're not *children*," Bishop spat.

Colin and I exchanged amused looks.

"Okay," I said. "*Fine*. How long have you been dating *females* who are under the age of consent, which, in the state of California, is *eighteen*? That better, *Professor*?"

Payton Bishop didn't speak, but the bulging vein banging in the middle of his forehead was calling me every m-f, four-letter, *c* word in the English language.

"Okay, not professor," I said. "Should I call you Apollo?"

"I have no idea what you're talking about."

"Allayna and Chanita," I said. "What happened there?"

"Nothing happened there."

"Why did Trina leave Madison?"

He drummed his fingers on the tabletop.

"Counseling went too far and they threaten you?" I asked. "They say they were gonna tell your secret?"

"I have no secrets," the counselor boasted.

"Your wife know about the sushi dates with your students?" Colin asked. "Or about the donuts and cupcakes they bring you? Cuz if she doesn't know, then that's called a secret."

I snapped my fingers. "Oh, wait. Wasn't your *wife* your *student,* like, only yesterday?"

Colin gasped and clutched his imaginary pearls. "Get the fuck outta here." He grinned and pointed at Bishop. "It's like that Van Halen song, 'Hot for the Teacher,' but reversed."

"How did she feel about your demotion?" I asked. "Was she all, 'That husband of mine, up to his old tricks again. And will he pick up his damned socks already?' "

Payton Bishop smirked. "Mock me all you want. My wife and I started dating only after she became eighteen years old. *Legal* in the state of California. As far as my career goes, I am one of the most accomplished educators in this city. Two times awarded—"

I waved my hand. "Yeah, and you were certainly teaching Nicole Brewer at the park tonight. Talk about going above and beyond. Where shall I mail your trophy? And do you spell 'Payton' J-E-S-U-S?"

He shot me a glare. "You really are a bitch."

I grinned. "Guess who's gonna be somebody's bitch next week this time?"

"Tell us about Nicole Brewer," Colin said.

Bishop gave a one-shouldered shrug. "There's nothing to tell."

"You've fucked her up good," Colin said. "Poor girl's in therapy. Taking handfuls of antianxiety meds. Kept it all in. But then she accepted Jesus as her personal savior, and she told us everything."

Bishop rolled his eyes. "What's my bail price?"

"Don't know," Colin said. "That will take some time to figure out. Hell, you may not even get bail since you're a flight risk."

"I'm not a flight risk," he said.

"You was sure 'flighting' in the park a few hours ago. Which means *more* jail time." I glanced at his brown suede boots. "You're pretty quick for wearing those things."

Colin also looked, then cocked an eyebrow. "Could you lift one up so I can see the sole?"

"Do I have to?"

"He's asking nicely," I said. "He can always confiscate them and give you complimentary, jail-style flip-flops to wear."

Bishop paused, then lifted the left boot.

Swirls. Whorls. Timberland logo.

Yes! All I needed now was DNA.

Colin used his camera phone to take pictures of the boot's tread. "Back to Nicole," he said as he shot. "She could be wrong, you know. You work in these schools. A lot of these girls have no dads, no positive male role models around. So they mistake a man's genuine concern as sexual interest. That's very possible, don't you think?"

Payton Bishop swiped his hand across his sweaty brow. "Yes, that is possible."

"Do you think that's *probable* in your situation?" Colin asked. "That some of your female students aren't familiar with nonsexual, mentorlike relationships?"

Payton Bishop relaxed some and offered Colin a grateful look. "I think that's what it is. Yes. They don't understand." Then, he turned to me. "You *must* remember what it was like to not have a father around."

"I do," I said. "And, yes, you know, I had to learn that my male teachers weren't interested in me in that way. I get it." Then I scowled. "But I'm not stupid, either. Fathers don't put their hands up young girls' skirts."

"I didn't mean . . . ," the counselor said. "These girls are so bright. I thought they'd know that I . . . that . . . They have so much potential. But there's no one else in their lives who are committed to helping them."

"You're just doing your job, right?" I said, bile burning my throat. "Exposing them to better things. More promising paths in life. 'Each one, teach one.' "

He clapped twice, then pointed at me. "*Exactly.*" He pointed to the picture of Peaches. "I complimented her *once*. Told her that she had pretty eyes, and all of a sudden she's sending me pictures, bringing me cupcakes . . ."

"So help me understand, then," I said, crossing my arms. "We searched your car at the park, and I found condoms. You and your wife use rubbers? Also, those pictures I showed you earlier? I found them, along with passwords to child porn sites, in your journal. This is all just my casual looking. What will I find when I poke around in the dark corners? Girls tied up in the basement of your house? That seems to be in vogue right now, tying up females and keeping them captive in guest rooms and basements and whatnot. So help me understand all this."

Payton Bishop shrugged. "Don't know what to tell you."

With a trembling finger, I pointed at the picture of Peaches. "You reacted when I slipped her picture in front of you."

"I didn't react."

"Tell me about her," I demanded, my voice tight.

The counselor's knees bounced and he folded his arms.

I leaned forward and growled, "I'm gonna serve a warrant to search your house. And your office. And your phone."

Payton Bishop's lips quivered, and he closed his eyes.

I sighed. "Nicole says—"

"She came on to *me*," Bishop said. "Nicole—" He dropped his head and closed his eyes.

A knock on the door, and Pepe stuck his head in the room. "A moment, please?"

I squinted at him. *Now?*

Pepe nodded. *Uh huh.*

We met him in the hallway. "They found another girl," he said, then quickly added, "She's alive. She's at Freeman Hospital in the Marina. She's in pretty bad shape. Conscious and then not conscious."

"Who is she?" I asked, my heart pounding wildly in my chest.

"Right now, she's Jane Doe. African American. Thirteen or fourteen years old. She may or may not be connected. Broken bones, cuts, bruises . . . It's a miracle she survived."

"Who found her?" Colin asked.

"A woman in a minivan saw her wandering La Brea, right below Bonner Park."

"When?" I asked.

Pepe swallowed. "Tonight, while we were there."

"She may not be related," Colin offered. "She may be just . . . some . . ."

"We really need her to come out of it, don't we?" Pepe said.

369

This case was like sculpting water.

Colin and I returned to the box, trembling with a mix of fear and anticipation. *Who is she? Is she a Muse? Is she—?*

Colin noticed my averted eyes, then kick-started the interview with Payton Bishop. "We should be transferring you to Men's Central soon since we have enough to hold you."

Bishop paled. "Men's Central? Hold me? For what?"

"Statutory rape," I said, barely containing my glee. "Soliciting a minor. Possession of child pornography. Resisting arrest. Being a fucking asshole. Quick question. You into botany?"

"What?" the counselor said as tears now slipped down his cheeks.

"Botany. You know, *plants*?"

He blinked at me, not understanding the question's relevance.

"We found a few berries in the trunk of your car." A lie but a good lie. "Purple, shiny. Glossy, green leaves. You visit any places with lots of leaves and berries?"

Payton Bishop wiped his face with the heels of his hands. "I sometimes drove Chanita to Bonner Park."

"I see."

My inner-Snoopy was dancing again.

"Just to take pictures," he explained. "Nothing else."

"Uh huh."

"You own a house up there?" Colin asked.

That made Payton Bishop laugh. "On my salary?"

"Do you *rent* a house up there?" I asked.

The counselor swallowed, then said, "Yes."

Yahtzee!

"You like puzzles?" Colin asked.

Bishop's brow furrowed. "What do you mean? Like crosswords and . . . ?"

"Yeah," Colin said. "Puzzles."

Payton Bishop blinked again, uncertain of the right answer. "No, I don't like puzzles."

I rolled my eyes, not believing him.

Two uniforms entered the room.

"Wait!" Payton Bishop stood from his chair. "Nothing . . . *illicit* happened between Chanita and me. She was too . . . *fractured*. I didn't kill her. Don't send me to Men's Central."

"And Allayna?" I asked.

Payton Bishop's mouth opened and closed. "I . . . I'm done talking. I want my lawyer."

And that was fine with me—for the moment. I would have a man who had preyed on the most vulnerable girls behind bars. And he fit the profile of the monster—a self-appointed protector of smart, young women, a god who lived (rented, owned, who cared?) on a hill high above the park. His Olympus.

A Jane Doe survivor and Nicole Brewer's recording: two Christmas miracles three months late or nine months early. I'd take it.

After booking the counselor, I dashed out of the building, heart racing, lips moving in silent prayer, pleading with God to let Jane Doe awaken long enough to name Payton Bishop as the monster.

MONDAY, MARCH 24

54

MINUTES AFTER MIDNIGHT, I RODE SHOTGUN AS COLIN HURLED US WEST ON THE 90 freeway. The high-rise apartments of Marina del Rey twinkled in the dark, and the residents of those million-dollar spaces slept, screwed, or watched late-night sailors slip into the harbor. Their double-paned windows muffled the wails of ambulance sirens at the nearby hospital where Jane Doe recovered after being found barely alive near Bonner Park.

An e-mail from Olympus456 made the Motorola radio in my lap chime.

> Dearest Melpomene, you denied her my great gift. The rumpus will end soon. There are many worlds left. Many worlds with good things to eat.

"No ciphers," Colin said. "And he called you—"

"I know." *Melpomene, the Muse of tragedy.* I read the message as worry churned my gut.

"Sounds like he's disappearing soon," Colin said.

"This isn't Payton Bishop," I whispered.

"Maybe it is," Colin said. "Maybe the e-mail just took a long time . . ."

Tears burned my eyes, and I took a deep, exhausted breath. "Maybe, but I don't think so." My mind turned over phrases written in the message. *Wild rumpus . . . Worlds . . . Good things to eat.* I tapped my phone's screen.

"What are you looking for now?" Colin asked.

"The text of *Where the Wild Things Are.*" I selected the video of the children's story being read by Christopher Walken.

Colin glanced at me. "Why are you—?"

"Sh!" I closed my eyes as the famous actor recited words that had peppered many of the monster's messages to me. At the 2:15 mark, my eyes popped open.

. . . someone loved him best of all.

Every hair on my body stood. "Oh *shit*!"

The Motorola beeped—the dispatcher told me I had a call come over the switchboard.

My pulse banged in my aching wrist as I waited to be connected.

"Is this Detective Norton?" The woman sounded scratchy, as though she had been chain-smoking the cheapest packs of cigarettes between bouts of crying.

"Yes, it is. Who—?"

"This is Liz Porter. We met at—"

Wide eyes on Colin, I said, "You're Trina's mother." I fumbled for a pen and notepad.

"I know it's early, or late or whatever," she said, "and I know you have so much to do, but I really need you to talk to my daughter."

I opened my mouth but couldn't speak.

"That girl they found on La Brea?" Liz said. "That's my baby. Trina's alive."

55

THICK SILVER FOG ROLLED OFF THE PACIFIC OCEAN AND TRANSFORMED MARINA DEL Rey into a faded memory. The orange tip of Mike Summit's cigarette glowed as he stood near the sliding doors marked EMERGENCY. Other news cameras and reporters also hunkered around Freeman Hospital, but Summit was the only one I wanted to strangle. But being this close to the hospital, the doctors would certainly revive him with shocks to the heart and a giant clamp to extract my foot from his throat. Ignoring the stabby anger within, I raced past Mike instead of assaulting him.

Four uniformed cops and Gwen Zapata, a gnome in her oversize gray trench coat, stood outside Trina Porter's hospital room. "Her left foot is broken," Gwen told us. "Looks like it's been broken for weeks now."

"Needle puncture marks?" I asked.

"No marks."

"Tooth?" Colin asked.

"Still there. She's totally dehydrated, though. Like she hasn't had water for days."

"They do blood tests?" I asked.

"Still out," Gwen said. "And Pacific sent over a team to scrape her fingernails, do some swabs, rape kit—all of that."

"She awake?" Colin asked.

Gwen nodded. "Pumped up with meds, though."

"But she doesn't fit the pattern," Colin said to me. "She's been missing for almost three weeks now. Why'd he keep her alive?"

Before I could answer, Liz Porter stepped out of the room. Her bloodshot eyes filled with tears even as she smiled at me. "You came." She pulled me into a hug.

As we stood there, I prayed that this painfully thin woman would have a happier ending than Regina and Vaughn. "Will she talk to me?" I asked.

"She's scared of . . ." Liz Porter glanced at Colin, and then she blushed. "She just wants me around, but I told her that we have to trust somebody so that we can catch him. She kept beggin' me to take her to the police station or to take her home but—" A sob burst from Liz's chest. She forced herself to breathe, to gain control. Succeeding but still shaky, she continued her story. "She's broken up really bad, inside and out. I told her we had to come to the hospital. Detective Zapata—" She nodded in Gwen's direction. "Detective Zapata told me that she was gonna call you, but we'd been here for over two hours now, and she hadn't called you, so I did."

Gwen shrugged. "*Technically,* Liz—"

"I know," the woman interrupted, "Trina isn't dead, thank God, but you all need our help. And, Detective Norton, I couldn't trust that you'd get any information Trina had in time."

"Did she tell you how she escaped?" Colin asked.

"She said something about a little room in the ground," Liz said, shaking her head. "Dirt floor, bugs . . . She told me that he forgot to lock the door, and she climbed out and just ran."

"I'd like to tape our conversation," I said. "Do we have your permission?"

Liz Porter eyed Colin. "But she can't know that *he's* there.

Right now, she's scared of men. And, to be honest, so am I."

I turned to Colin. *Deal or no deal?*

He nodded. *Deal.*

The room's heavy salmon-colored curtains had been pulled, and the only light came from the fluorescent tube above the girl's bed. A small vase of white roses sat on the roll-away table, and a single "Get Well" Mylar balloon bobbed near the television set.

Colin slipped behind a rolling screen as I approached the girl's bedside.

Trina Porter's face was bruised and swollen. Her left foot and arm had been wrapped in casts, and tubes snaked from the IV stand to her free arm.

She's alive. Why is she alive?

My hands shook as I tapped RECORD on my iPhone.

Liz Porter, on the other side of the bed, touched Trina's hand. "Sweetie, Mommy's here."

The girl's eyes fluttered like the broken wings of a dying butterfly.

"Hi, my love," Liz whispered.

"Mommy," the girl croaked, "I wanna go home. I want Bunny. I miss her."

"Not yet, baby. And Bunny misses you, too. She can't wait for you to walk her when you're better."

Watching this simple interaction between mother and daughter almost made my knees buckle. *Could I talk to this brave girl?* In my line of work, I never talked to brave girls who had fought *and* survived.

"Sweetie," Liz said, "Detective Norton is here. She wants to ask you a few questions, okay? She's a very nice lady, and she's gonna catch whoever did this to you."

Trina's eyes lolled in my direction. The monitor that recorded her heart rate showed bumps in her pulse. She licked her split bottom lip but had no spit. "I don't wanna go back."

"I'm here to help, Trina," I said, my eyes on those squiggly lines. "You have nothing to fear." I waited as her pulse slowed. "Your doctor says that you haven't had water in a long time."

She winced, then whispered, "No."

"Did the person who took you away give you anything to drink?"

She swallowed. "He gave me, like tea. One time . . . and . . . I wasn't me so I didn't . . . drink anymore." She licked her lips again.

"Can you describe him?" I asked. "What does he look like?"

She peered at the ceiling.

"Was he a black man?"

"No."

"Was he white?"

"I . . . don't . . ."

"Hispanic?"

"He's . . . something . . . not black."

"Is he fat?"

"No."

"Tall?"

"Tall. Not skinny. He's . . . medium."

"Where did he pick you up?"

"On the corner."

"Near . . . ?"

She stared in the distance. "Phillips."

"The barbecue place?"

"Yeah."

She got in the car. Chanita got in the car. Allayna got in the car. Who would be trustworthy enough for a girl to willingly . . . ?

"When you first got in the car with him," I said, "did you ride for a long time?"

"Not that long."

"Do you remember what you saw as you drove?"

"Hills," the girl said. "When I ran . . . near the park, I could see . . . red lights. And . . . it . . . forest. Hills." The lines on the monitor were also becoming hills.

My own heart pounded hard—I didn't have much longer before the drugs took her. "Did you know him before he took you?"

"Uh huh."

"You trusted him?"

"Uh huh."

"Was he your teacher?"

"No."

"Is he a counselor?"

"No."

"Someone you—?"

"I don't wanna be here," she said, voice cracking, pulse spiking.

"This place will help you get better," I said. "These people—"

"He told me . . . He'll kill me if I say anything."

I shook my head. "There are a million police officers at this hospital, Trina, and they are all here to protect you. Someone who doesn't belong here will not be getting near you."

"But he belongs here." A plump tear rolled down her bruised cheek.

My heart lurched—I knew. "What do you mean, Trina? How does he belong here?"

Trina was trembling, and the hills on the monitor peaked, one after the other.

Any minute now, a doctor or a nurse would come in and shut me down.

"I know this is hard, sweetheart," I whispered, "and I know

you've been through so much, and I know that you're scared, but he can't hurt you anymore. We will find him. And with your help, we will put him in jail, and he will never get out. And he will never hurt another girl, okay? But for that to happen, for him to be punished, you have to tell me everything."

The door opened, and the scent of gardenias rode on the draft.

Liz whispered, "Dr. Akira's here."

"Trina," I said, "you have to tell me: who is he?"

"He works here," she whispered. "He's a doctor." Then, she closed her eyes, and the peaks lost their sharpness.

Colin waited with Dr. Barbara Akira, the head of pediatrics, outside Trina's room. Dr. Akira, a short, stout Japanese woman with a burgundy shag, wore a diamond ring the size of Uranus. "Anything we can do to help," she said, now looking up at me, "just ask."

"How many pediatricians have privileges here?" I asked.

"Forty-two." She reached into her smock pocket and pulled out a beeping pager and gave it a glance. "Sorry. Yes. Forty-two."

"How many are men?" I asked.

"Almost half."

"We can't have male doctors or nurses caring for her," I said.

"I'll tend to Trina myself," Dr. Akira offered.

"We'll need to protect her," I said to Colin. "Around the clock. She's *never* alone."

Moments later, I sat at Dr. Akira's desk, scrolling through pictures of male pediatricians practicing at Freeman Hospital.

Blond, blue eyes, broken nose.

Persian, balding, fat face.

Graying goatee, thin as a shaft of wheat . . .

None were the tall, medium-built man described by Trina or the women at Bonner Park.

I scrolled past three more pictures, and then I saw him. Not black, not skinny. Friendly smile, warm eyes. He was the one who'd done this. The one who had done this and was now preparing to return to the place where his Muses awaited. Before this moment, I'd only known him by his first name.

Zach.

56

AFTER TAKING A STATEMENT FROM LIZ PORTER, AFTER INTERVIEWING FIVE MALE pediatricians in Dr. Akira's office, after tying Pepe and Luke to chairs outside Trina Porter's hospital room, I snatched the keys to the Crown Vic from Colin's hand and raced back to the Jungle.

Teddy bears and candles had been left at Raul Moriaga's front door—memorials for the man killed by ghosts. Some teddy bears had been slashed, and white stuffing now drifted around the courtyard. Most candles had been knocked over—and one upright candle held a small turd instead of a wick.

Regina Drummond hugged me before I could even say, "Hello." This morning, her eyes glistened with joy instead of sadness. She had ditched the kimono for jeans and a T-shirt. She had recently visited a salon—her hair smelled of flat-ironed oil sheen. She looked fine, on the mend—but so did a wound wearing a fresh scab. One stupid move, and she'd be weeping again.

"That reporter from *OurTimes* called me," she said, wiggling her nose. "He feels . . . skeevy, though."

I laughed. "No comment, but I'd trust your gut."

"They moved my court date," she said. "Maybe they'll have some mercy on me. Ain't no punishment worse than . . ." Her nostrils flared—the scab was threatening to rip off.

Early-morning sunlight filled a living room that testified to an active existence. The apartment smelled of toast and bacon, and a plate of it sat on the couch next to an open *Essence* magazine. The television, broadcasting an episode of *Maury,* showed the titular host and a young black woman named Visa, there now to identify all the men who could've fathered her two-year-old daughter, Pleasuria.

"Where's your mother?" I asked.

"At my auntie's in Lancaster." Regina sat beside me on the couch. "After what happened yesterday with Raul—"

"He didn't do it."

She blinked at me, then her eyebrows crumpled. "What you mean?"

"His DNA doesn't match what was found on Chanita."

Her face hardened.

"Did you know that folks were gonna go after Raul?" I asked.

"Nuh uh."

Right then, I believed in Santa Claus more than I believed Regina Drummond.

"So the man who killed my daughter . . . ?"

"Is very, *very* close to being caught."

She sighed, then aimed the remote control at the TV. With one click, Maury and Visa disappeared. "But he ain't been caught yet?" That scar would be off any minute now.

"I just have a few quick questions, and I tried calling—"

"Phone got cut off," she said with a shrug. "Had other things to worry about. Bills? Please. I'm having a hard enough time comin' up with the cash to pay for Nita's headstone."

I eyed her a moment: was she being truthful or was she up to her grifting ways? "Before I leave, give me the mortuary's number. Me and my partner, we'll handle it, okay?"

A smile brightened her face, and her eyes shone with tears

again. Too moved to speak, she simply bobbed her head.

No matter what Regina Drummond did for a living—kiting, grifting, fraud—her comeuppance shouldn't have been the murder of her daughter. And that daughter certainly didn't deserve death and no headstone as payment for her mother's sins.

"What did Chanita do last summer?" Pen poised to write, I waited for Regina to say "camp" or "summer school" or . . . anything.

Instead, she shrugged. "I was . . . away most of the summer. I know she hung out at the park a lot, taking pictures. She sent me some. Just like the picture I gave you, the one with them purple flowers. I'm thinking she was with Mr. Bishop or somebody."

I scribbled in my notepad. "Did Chanita have a regular pediatrician? You know, for physicals, shots . . . ?"

"I take her to a clinic over on Crenshaw," she said. "Women & Children Medical Group. It's in the shopping area right across the street from the funeral home. The cobbler place is next door. There's a camera store there, too."

"What's the doctor's name?"

"Umm . . . Doctor . . ." She reached beneath the coffee table and grabbed the accordion file there. She thumbed through papers and receipts. "I don't remember his first name, but his last name is Fletcher."

I wrote the name as though my pen had been dipped in molasses. "Is he an older man? A young guy? Black? White?"

She shook her head. "Not a black guy. White or maybe Latino but not Mexican. Anyway, he's around your age. Cute. Very sweet. He'd give us samples when I couldn't afford the entire prescription. Sometimes, he didn't even charge for the visit cuz he just wanted Nita to be well. He's doing God's work."

I hustled back to the car.

God's work.

Phone to ear, I made a call.

Vaughn Hutchens's hello sounded ragged and thick.

"Sorry," I said, "I know it's early."

"I'm up," she said. "Talking to Donald about the arrangements for Laynie's service."

"Donald?"

She paused, then said, "Laynie's father."

Something inside me twisted and burned. Because *now* he was back?

"I saw the story on that dead Mexican," she said. "Is it true? Did he do it?"

I told her about Moriaga's innocence . . . in this case.

She sighed, then asked, "And the new girl who escaped?"

"She gave us some information, which is why I'm now calling you. Did Laynie see a regular doctor?"

"Laynie was at the doctor's office all the time," Vaughn said. "Sometimes, she'd go on her own since my hours were strange. She went to Mercy Medical Group, down the hill on Santa Rosalia. Across from where those new condos are."

"Crase Parc and Promenade?"

"Uh huh."

"Do you remember her doctor's name?"

"Dr. Fletcher."

I thanked Vaughn, then ended the call. My T-shirt stuck to me—I had sweated enough for three women. And now ice was forming where I had sweated. I shivered as my mind played images of meeting Zach in the park, of his text messages to me, talking in the Starbucks parking lot, my hand in his . . .

No. Too much.

My mind scratched it all, then twisted those memories into balls of paper. I called Colin. "Both girls went to the same doctor," I blurted as soon as he answered. Then, I told him about my conversations with Regina and Vaughn. "Both girls saw the same doctor but at different clinics. His name is Zach Fletcher."

"I'm looking at the list to confirm," Colin said.

I held my breath as he flipped through the pages.

The page turning stopped. "Yep. He's on the list."

"I know him."

Colin didn't speak at first, but then said, "Come again?"

And I told Colin that Zach Fletcher had been courting me or gaming me ever since Wednesday. That on Saturday night, over coffee, he'd told me that he worked at the clinic near the cobbler place. That the message written on the card Zach Fletcher had sent with the flowers yesterday had also referred to *Where the Wild Things Are.*

> *Hope you land in a place where someone loves you best of all.*

"Shit, Lou," Colin whispered.

"The girls went with him because they trusted him," I said. "And they trusted him—"

"Because he was their doctor."

And I trusted him because he was a doctor.

I groaned, then rubbed my face with my free hand. My stomach and head hurt—my brain was kicking both and calling me "stupid" and "blind" in between kicks.

"So what's the plan?" my partner asked.

"Let's find out where he lives," I said. "Get his license plate number from the DMV and put out a BOLO. I'll drive to one of the medical offices—send a car over to cover me."

"Yep," Colin said. "And keep your radio on."

I turned the key in the ignition. "See you on the other side, partner."

57

CRENSHAW BOULEVARD WAS PEPPERED WITH EARLY-MORNING COMMUTERS, AND a line had formed in Krispy Kreme's drive-through. No clouds—the storms had passed, leaving a perfect sky the color of a robin's egg. At the shopping plaza across from the funeral home, I made a right onto the small side street, then parked.

I called Colin. "Where y'all at?"

"Driving to the house," he said. "And it's right on the side of the park, Lou. We stopped there when we walked over on Friday—you talked to his girlfriend. White girl, blond . . ."

I closed my eyes and saw the golden-haired pediatric surgeon in my mind.

"Lemme call you back," Colin said. "L.T.'s blowin' me up."

I climbed out of the car and made my way through a dark alcove that reeked of urine and spilled beer. Tucked in the corner was a medical office situated between an ancient tax-prep place and a shuttered scrapbook store. I peered into the windows of the clinic.

Lights off. A treasure box on the carpet near the reception desk was filled with goodies for kids to take after their shots and pokes. Magic wands . . . toy cars . . . a gold sheriff's badge . . . a photo frame . . . a ballerina music box . . . a book of children's poems . . .

I tugged at the door.

Locked.

"We're closed today," the man behind me said.

All feeling left my face.

Zach Fletcher pointed a Beretta at the back of my skull, then moved so close to me that I smelled mint on his breath.

I saw his reflection in the clinic's grimy window. His puppy-dog eyes were still friendly, and his perfect teeth still gleamed. He wore jeans and a blue long-sleeved shirt, as though he were stopping at Home Depot for lightbulbs and grass seed.

"Let's take a drive," he said. "Don't have much time—got a girl waiting for me."

The cop part of me told me to chance it, to pull the mini-Glock from my ankle holster and to see what happened next. But he had a girl waiting—*what girl?* And where was she?

My Motorola crackled—was Colin listening?

With his gun still aimed at my head, Zach directed me to the run-down parking lot behind the clinic. "We're walking to the black RAV4."

No one else was in the lot, and so we reached the small SUV with a license plate starting with 2BT undisturbed.

"I'm not getting in," I said. "Never get in the car with a kidnapper."

"Even if he has another girl in a special secret place?"

"What's her name?"

"She's very much alive," he said, still behind me. "A little slow from her cup of special tea. C'mon, Elouise. I have a wonderful surprise for you in the car."

My breath came quick. "And if I go, you'll let her go?"

"Yes."

"Alive?"

"Yes."

As soon as I get her, I'll shoot him and end this.

"You're driving," he said. "Open the door."

I hesitated. "Maybe you should—"

He whispered in my ear, "Every minute we stand here, she's closer to death."

A moment later, he was seated in the back passenger seat. The gun now nuzzled the base of my skull.

I clicked on my seat belt, then pushed the Toyota's ignition button.

"Look back here and down to your right for your special surprise."

I obeyed and—"Oh my God." Icicles jammed my heart.

A girl, her mouth covered with gray electrical tape and her hands bound with twine, huddled down in the back passenger step well. She was in her early teens. Her mocha complexion was gritty from dried tears and snot, and her brown eyes were slits, swollen from crying.

"Now, you will back out of this space," he calmly instructed. "You will smile, and people who see us will think we're being silly lovers on a Monday morning. Since you're so interested in what I do when I'm not writing prescriptions and performing Pap smears on thirteen-year-old mothers, we will take a hike on one of those trails, where I go on and on about the flora and fauna. Sound good?"

"Zach," I said, barely breathing, "let her go. I'll still keep my end of the bargain."

He nudged me with the gun again. "I'm at the beginning of your spinal cord. You will want to focus if you wish to walk or breathe or think on your own. One can't live without a brain. I know this. I'm a doctor." He paused, then held up a water bottle filled with brown liquid. "Or I can give her this now." Zach glanced down at the girl. "You thirsty, Taylor?"

The girl whimpered and nodded.

Zach started to unscrew the bottle top.

"Don't," I shouted. "Okay? I'll . . ." I gripped the steering wheel tighter, the leather moist beneath my clammy palms. I pulled out of the lot and made a left onto Crenshaw Boulevard.

"Did you like the ciphers?" He sank behind my headrest, and the cool barrel remained at the base of my skull. "It was a joy to watch you move about the board, not knowing that I was in total control."

A warm drop of sweat trickled down my side. I pressed the gas pedal, and the Toyota's engine responded.

He wrapped his arm around my neck, surprising me with his speed and strength. "Choose your adventure, Detective," he whispered, then squeezed until I understood.

"Where are we going?" I whispered.

In the rearview mirror, his eyes met mine. "To the place where the wild things are."

58

I WOVE WEST ON STOCKER BOULEVARD. RAMBLING HOMES SAT HIGH ON THE HILLS. Morning joggers walked up steep sidewalks and along the hillside trails. The rains had turned the land muddy—in a week, though, poppies and wild mustard would poke through the saturated earth.

Would I get to see another LA spring?

"Daydreaming?" the monster asked.

"We're going to Bonner Park," I said, my body clammy-cold.

"Yes."

The girl—Taylor—moaned until her moans became cries.

He shushed her and whispered, "It's okay; it's okay."

My phone, stowed in my bag with my police radio, kept playing the *Star Wars* theme.

"Why are you doing this?" I whispered.

"I have to. Turn right."

I accelerated onto La Cienega Boulevard.

"You're a *doctor*," I said.

"Do you think I've killed every patient I treated?" He snorted. "I'm not a monster. Taylor here I met at the library. She's writing an article on Pluto for Astrology Club. Guess some scientists don't consider Pluto a planet anymore. Taylor was gonna prove them wrong. Such a smart, brave girl."

"The girls you take," I said, "they're—"

"Exceptional?" he finished. "Yes. Chanita, Allayna, Tawanna, and Bethany. I don't hate them. I like them. I *love* them. I wish I didn't, because then I wouldn't have thought about them all the time. I would've looked somewhere else. But they stand out. And they, like the Muses of old, resent those who don't see how special, how wonderfully supreme they are. And as their big brother, it is my duty to solve everyone's problem."

Apollo—the god of healing. Son of Zeus. Olympus, where the gods . . . *Shit*. I knew this.

"When I read about your sister and where you came from?" He clapped once, then sighed. "I had to have you. You're my Moby Dick. But, unlike Ahab, I caught you and survived."

I didn't speak.

He poked my skull with the Beretta. "Kill. Heal. Kill. Heal. That's what I do. Sometimes, in the end, they're the same thing." He chuckled, then sighed. "You've killed."

"No," I whispered, a lump in my throat.

He cocked his head. "It's okay—you're uncomfortable in your role. You hold the knife but refuse to use it. But, see, I'm not scared. I fix it. Balance it all. I rescue the sick. Reward the gifted. Balance the bad with good."

I glared at the road ahead, at the city sparkling before me. The first day of sunshine in weeks, and here I was, on my way to someone's death. Mine.

"I know what you're thinking," he said. "Dahmer. Right? Am I right? I'm not crazy. Shouldn't compare me to him."

A fat tear tumbled down my cheek. "Why did you keep Trina alive for so long?"

"My poet needed to compose an elegy before we all returned home. She came up with something but . . ." He shrugged. "I've read her prior poems—she could do better than what she wrote about all of this. So I gave her time to get over her . . . writer's block."

I cocked my head. "You've read her other . . . ?"

"Why are you so surprised?" he asked. "We talk a lot. They tell me so much. Share so much. No one ever listens to them. They seek me out all the time. Chanita and Allayna? They both came in after they'd been jumped. And Trina . . . Well, see, her daddy died over in Afghanistan, and we talked about that.

"And I wondered, What have they done to deserve living in the ghetto, around people who don't care, who don't *see*? Hopeless. A waste. I made it better for them. And now they will be remembered.

"I wanted Trina's poem to capture all of this, but . . . well . . ." His voice sounded wet and shaky.

Was he crying?

"I talk with them as they lay dying," he continued. "I find great comfort in that. They do, too. They find great comfort in my being there beside them. That I won't use a gun or a knife or . . . Tea is calming. Civilized. See how I'm talking to you right now? And in the coffee shop . . . You can't say that I'm not a great listener." He glanced down at Taylor. "Don't worry. We're almost there."

Almost where? "You said you'd let her go," I whispered.

"And I will."

"You'll let her go in *this* world?"

He smiled. "Ha. Yes." He caught my gaze in the rearview mirror. "I thought more people would've come to Chanita's funeral. Maybe Allayna's service—"

"You were there, at Mount Saint John's."

He smirked. "I told you I was. Even spoke to the escort and limo driver."

My grip weakened around the steering wheel. *So close. He had been so close.*

"In Pakistan last year," he said, "more than nine hundred females were murdered. Honor killings. On the other side of the world, almost six hundred aboriginal women and girls in *Canada* were either missing or were murdered over the last ten years. Maybe more."

"Why are you telling me this?" I asked.

We reached the entrance to Bonner Park. No one sat in the kiosk.

He nudged the gun. "Keep driving. As I was saying: almost two hundred million girls are missing in the world, and you're going balls-out and using all your superpowers to avenge *eight*?"

Bile burned in my throat. *Eight? He's killed* eight? *There are nine Muses. Who's next? Taylor? Me?*

He sighed. "This really makes no sense, Elouise. You're upset with me, but you give that son of a whore Moriaga all the freedom in the world to do as he wants."

My eyes met his in the rearview mirror. "Moriaga?"

"The pervert that you cops have let rape and disfigure how many girls now? But have you even thanked me yet?"

"Thank you? For what?"

He cocked his chin. "I reported him to your friend's little newspaper when he cornered that girl at the park. Even took a picture of him to prove that he hasn't changed. That he still continued to be a threat to the community. That it was only a matter of time before he raped another one."

Sweat prickled my underarms, and my vision started to fade. "You're no different from Moriaga. You both lurk in the shadows—"

The Beretta jammed into my neck. "I've *never* forced myself on a *child*. Never. They *wanted* to be with me. If we'd had more time, you'd want to be with me, too. Not once did I force them. *Not once*. Take it back. Take. It. Back."

Tears burned my eyes. "You don't hear yourself. You don't see how—"

"Is that pity? Are you *pitying* me?" He sighed again as I slowly drove up the narrow road. "So peaceful and beautiful here—I can see this park from my house, you know."

Bursts of sunlight cut through the trees. Bobcat excavators and tractors for clearing poststorm brush sat on the side of the road like sleeping heavy-metal dinosaurs.

"Pull over here," he said, "but don't stop the car."

I tapped the brake: *25 miles per hour . . . 15 . . . 10 . . .*

He leaned over and opened the back right passenger door.

I glanced back. "What are you—?"

He remained in the backseat as he pushed Taylor out of the car. "Bye, sweetie." He closed the door, lifted the Beretta, and aimed it at my right temple. "Shall we?"

Taylor had found her feet and was now running back down the hill.

I watched the girl's reflection in the rearview mirror until the tears in my eyes blurred my vision. *I'm the ninth Muse.*

"Let's go," the monster said. "We don't have a lot of time."

I swallowed the lump in my throat, then eased the RAV4 past the muddy tractors.

"Those storms created a few landslides," he said. "I couldn't get up here as much as I needed. Guess they're cleaning up now. Our tax dollars at work. Oh, what wondrous prizes they'll find."

A tear slipped down my cheek. Syeeda: we hadn't made up. Sam: we hadn't talked about us. Mom: I hadn't told her about my talk with Victor Starr. Greg: the real estate agent. *Shit.* I hadn't resolved so many things in my life, and now . . .

Would they miss me? Yes, they would. But then they'd move on. Mom had lost a daughter, lost a husband. The worst of the worst she'd survived . . . and she had still moved on.

A sob pushed against my chest, but I tamped it down. Still, it burned and bubbled there, gaining mass and heat.

"Why are you upset?" Zach Fletcher asked. "I kept my promise. And now you're a hero. Maybe you'll get a Purple Heart after the dust clears. A six-gun salute or whatever it's called. A junior high school named after you."

He placed his mouth against my ear, and his breath warmed my neck. "I was planning to leave you alone, especially after our coffee date on Saturday, even though you're it for me. The Muse that avenges the deaths of all God's children. A true goddess." He slowly exhaled. "But you tried to stop me from doing the thing I love the most."

I tapped the gas pedal just . . . so . . . then considered his reflection in the rearview mirror. "You can stop this."

He grinned and met my eyes in the mirror. "But I don't want to. Not anymore. I like it here. In the dark. And I'm not sure there's a cure for my . . . habit."

The Motorola radio pinched my sweaty side, and I prayed that the line had remained open, that Colin could hear this conversation, that—

"There will always be dead girls, Detective Elouise Norton," Zach Fletcher said. "There will always be lost girls. Good and bad. Rich and poor. Smart and . . . You can't save all of them."

My stomach twisted. "I know that."

"I'm leaving Los Angeles. Finding a new spring, new Muses. They're everywhere. Maybe I'll go to the suburbs. Maybe—"

Swerving came out of nowhere—part of a hillside had tumbled onto the narrow road.

"Shit." He hung on to the back of the driver's headrest.

I came out of the curve and avoided veering off the road and down the steep hillside.

He jammed the gun at my neck. "Do it again."

Less than a mile ahead, I spotted another herd of machinery and orange pickup trucks. "Why this park?" I asked. "Eight in one park—that's a lot."

He chuckled. "You mean nine. And I'm not worried. You're tall, but you won't take up much space."

I pressed the gas pedal.

The RAV4 accelerated.

"Slow down, Elouise," he warned. "You'll crash and die. Do you want to meet your end on a park road and not in a beautiful glen that's been chosen just for you?"

Lightness came over me. "Streets of gold. Pearly gates. A *crown*?" I met his gaze in the rearview mirror. "I'm ready to be where someone loves me best of all. Are you?"

He lifted the gun. "Lou—"

"Checkmate, you sick son of a—" I stomped the gas pedal, and the Toyota's motor roared. I jerked the wheel to the left. At sixty miles per hour, I raced toward the orange pickup that sat on the side of the road.

Zach Fletcher screamed, "Stop!"

I couldn't stop. I wouldn't stop.

Metal smashed against metal.

Glass exploded all around the cabin.

I smelled baby powder . . . rubber . . .

And then I saw . . . blackness.

59

WHITE LIGHT PULLED ME FROM DARKNESS.

Light in one pupil.

Light in the other pupil.

Darkness again.

The chatter of walkie-talkies . . . bursts of static . . .

I opened my eyes as far as they could open.

Blue sky. A hawk flying in circles, riding the current, free . . .

My breathing . . . tight, quick . . . I blinked.

My face felt crunchy, loose like gravel. I swallowed. Metallic, goopy thickness. Crunchiness in my mouth.

I saw . . . the totaled SUV . . . air bag still inflated . . . blood . . .

Crumpled orange pickup truck . . . hood crushed like an accordion.

A man's . . . legs . . . arm . . . blood.

Your name?

"What?" I croaked.

"What is your name?" a deep voice asked.

I closed my eyes, then opened them again.

Now, I stood near trail 5 and the park bench on the bluff.

Chanita Lords crouched before me with her camera capturing the cloudless blue sky.

Allayna Mitchell, bag slung over her shoulder, pirouetted in the field of golden poppies.

All around me, girls that I didn't know, girls of every shape and shade sat in clumps, smiling, laughing. All free. They were so beautiful.

I don't remember everything after that collision on the park road. The ride to the hospital. Doctors. X-rays or plaster slopped over my broken left wrist. Don't remember any of that.

Colin held my hand in a room somewhere—I remember that. Luke with his hand on Pepe's shoulder—I remember that, and I remember smiling.

Colin told me that Taylor LaSalle, the girl in the Toyota, had survived, that he and Pepe had found the hidden space in the large backyard where Zach Fletcher had kept the girls. He told me the blond girlfriend had no clue girls had been kidnapped and stowed in that underground septic tank. No clue that the bushes near the back fence, the ones with the beautiful purple flowers, were poisonous deadly nightshade. And he told me that the other predator, Payton Bishop, had plea-bargained for a reduced sentence.

I remember . . . pills. Sips of water. Sips of soup. Sleep. Mom. Sitting in a living room—not my living room in Playa Vista. Not Syeeda's living room. Brittle. Numb. Shadows lengthening on the hardwood floor. The sound of waves. Lena's house. Ocean. Sam. Pills.

Sam stood in the doorway of the bedroom. Mouth a thin line. Eyes dark. Arms crossed, fingers gripping his elbows.

I blinked.

Open french doors. The scent of salt and sea. Lena and Syeeda.

Sam lay beside me. Arms open. Arms around me.

The television screen. Richard Dreyfuss. UFOs. My mother sitting at the end of the bed. Soup. Pills. Greg standing in the corner of the bedroom. Zach Fletcher beside me in bed, then standing over me.

Fully awake but unable to move. Crying.

"Is he dead?" I asked Lena one of those times she rescued me from a nightmare.

"Yeah."

"He was here," I whispered.

"No, sweetie," she said. "You stopped him. Rest now."

The light dimmed, then brightened. Strange aches bloomed in the middle of my head.

I swallowed, and it hurt to swallow. "Am I here?"

"You're here," Sam answered. "I'm here, too." And then he kissed me.

I remember his kiss and feeling his heartbeat on his lips. How I slept without bad dreams.

"You're here," he said.

And then he held me until the bedroom fell into shadow.

ACKNOWLEDGMENTS

SO MANY PEOPLE HAD A HAND IN BRINGING THIS BOOK TO LIFE. FIRST, THERE'S you—your dedication to this series and offering advice, well-wishes, chances to read, chances to sign are so meaningful to me. For that thing you did? Thanks so very much. David, Maya, Mom, Dad, Terry, Gretchen, Jason, Jill, and Kristin. I want to thank you by name because your extraordinary support of my silly dream to be a world-famous author should be documented in the Library of Congress... and googleable.

ABOUT THE AUTHOR

RACHEL HOWZELL HALL IS A WRITER/ASSISTANT DEVELOPMENT DIRECTOR AT CITY of Hope, a national leader in cancer research and treatment. She is the author of *A Quiet Storm*, which recieved a starred review from *Library Journal* and was chosen as a "Rory's Book Club" selection, the must-read book list for fictional television character Rory Gilmore of *The Gilmore Girls*. In 2014, Titan published the first novel in the Detective Elouise Norton series, the critically acclaimed *Land of Shadows*, which received a starred review in *Publishers Weekly*, was included on the *Los Angeles Times*' "143 Books to Read This Summer" and the *Telegraph*'s "Top Ten Crime Books for Summer." Rachel was also a featured writer on NPR Crime in the City. She lives with her husband and daughter in Los Angeles, the land of exceptional drought.

SKIES OF ASH
A DETECTIVE ELOUISE NORTON NOVEL
RACHEL HOWZELL HALL

Los Angeles homicide detective Elouise "Lou" Norton and her partner Colin Taggert arrive at the scene of a tragic house fire, summoned by a 9-1-1 call from a terrified Juliet Chatman, who perished in the blaze along with her two children, Cody and Chloe. Left behind is grieving husband and father Christopher Chatman, hospitalized after firefighters forcefully restrained him from entering the inferno. Chatman is inconsolable, devastated that he couldn't save his beloved family.

Unless, of course, he's the one who killed them. Or was the fire sparked by a serial arsonist known as The Burning Man? Searching for justice through the ashes of a picture-perfect family—the Chatmans and her own—Lou doesn't know if she will catch an arsonist or be burned in the process.

"Fast, funny, heartbreaking and wise… Elouise Norton is the best new character you'll meet this year, and Rachel Howzell Hall is the best pure storyteller you'll read this year."
Lee Child, *New York Times* bestselling author

"Lou Norton is a black female cop worthy of following in Philip Marlowe's footsteps down the mean streets of LA."
Telegraph

TITANBOOKS.COM

LAND OF SHADOWS

A DETECTIVE ELOUISE NORTON NOVEL
RACHEL HOWZELL HALL

Along the ever-changing border of gentrifying Los Angeles, a seventeen-year-old girl is found hanged at a construction site. Homicide detective Elouise "Lou" Norton's new partner Colin Taggert, fresh from the comparatively bucolic Colorado Springs police department, assumes it's a teenage suicide. Lou isn't buying the easy explanation. For one thing, the condo site is owned by Napoleon Crase, a self-made millionaire... and the man who may have murdered Lou's missing sister thirty years ago. As Lou investigates the death of Monique Darson, she uncovers undeniable links between the two cases.

Lou is convinced that when she solves Monique's case she will finally bring her lost sister home. But as she gets closer to the truth, she also gets closer to a violent killer. After all this time, can he be brought to justice... before Lou becomes his next victim?

"Readers have met with gimlet-eyed gumshoes, dead-eyed tough guys and doe-eyed femme fatales. But they've never met anybody quite like Hall."

The Times

"A racially explosive Los Angeles provides the backdrop for this exceptional crime novel."

Publishers Weekly (starred review)

THE DEVIL YOU KNOW

ELISABETH DE MARIAFFI

The year is 1993. Rookie crime beat reporter Evie Jones is haunted by the unsolved murder of her best friend Lianne Gagnon in 1982, back when both girls were eleven. The suspected killer, a repeat offender named Robert Cameron, was never apprehended. Now twenty-two and living alone for the first time, Evie is obsessively drawn to researching the real story of who killed Lianne. She leans on childhood friend David Patton for help – but why does every trail seem to lead back to David's own father, Graham? As she gets closer and closer to the truth, Evie becomes convinced that the killer is still at large – and that he's coming back for her.

"De Mariaffi delivers the requisite heart-in-mouth moments of pure paranoia, but she balances these thrills with shrewd character studies and the odd nugget of wisdom."
New York Times

"[F]or those who love a good whodunit with an unpredictable ending... totally riveting novel."
New York Journal of Books

"[De Mariaffi] expertly builds suspense throughout this character-driven debut novel. As it nears its climax, readers will dread turning the pages for fear of what comes next."
Library Journal

DUST AND DESIRE

A JOEL SORRELL NOVEL
CONRAD WILLIAMS

The Four-Year-Old, an extraordinary killer, has arrived in London, hell-bent on destruction... PI Joel Sorrell is approached by the mysterious Kara Geenan, who is desperate to find her missing brother. Joel takes on the case but almost immediately, an attempt his made on his life. The body count increases. And then Kara vanishes too... as those close to Joel are sucked into his nightmare, he realizes he must track down the killer if he is to halt a grisly masterplan – even if it means sacrificing his own life.

"A gritty and compelling story of the damned and the damaged; crackling with dark energy and razor-sharp dialogue. Conrad Williams is an exciting new voice in crime fiction, and Joel Sorrell is a character you will want to see plenty more of."
Mark Billingham

SONATA OF THE DEAD

A JOEL SORRELL NOVEL
CONRAD WILLIAMS

It's four months on from the events of Dust and Desire... Joel
Sorrell has recovered from the injuries he sustained in his fight
with The Four-Year-Old. A body has been found, sealed into
the dead space behind a false wall in a flat in Muswell Hill.
Beheaded and surrounded by bloodstained pages of
typewritten text, it is the third such murder committed by a
killer known as The Hack. And it may be linked to his
daughter's disappearance.

PRAISE FOR THE AUTHOR

"Williams is so good at what he does that he probably shouldn't
be allowed to do it anymore, for the sake of everyone's sanity."
Publishers Weekly **(starred review)**

"Conrad Williams writes dark and powerful prose balancing
the poetic and elegant with needle-sharp incision."
Guardian

AVAILABLE JULY 2016

For more fantastic fiction, author events, competitions, limited editions and more

VISIT OUR WEBSITE
titanbooks.com

LIKE US ON FACEBOOK
facebook.com/titanbooks

FOLLOW US ON TWITTER
@TitanBooks

EMAIL US
readerfeedback@titanemail.com